Immortal by Morning

Abril blinked in confusion. She had already forgotten his question and was, instead, thinking about the fact that, if he moved one inch closer, their bodies would be brushing against each other. She almost wanted to lean forward that one inch herself.

"Abril?" he whispered.

"Yes?" She was staring at his chest now. He looked like a marble sculpture, and she found her hand rising to flatten itself on his chest to be sure he was flesh and blood.

Abril thought she heard a small groan slip from Delacort at her touch, but she wasn't certain because she was busy struggling to suppress the moan she herself wanted to release at the rush of sensation that ran through her own body at that simple act. The man was beautiful.

LYNSAY SANDS

Immortal by MORNING

AN ARGENEAU NOVEL

AVON

An Imprint of HarperCollinsPublishers

IMMORTAL BY MORNING. Copyright © 2025 by Lynsay Sands. All rights reserved. Printed in the United States of America. No part of this book may be used or reproduced in any manner whatsoever without written permission except in the case of brief quotations embodied in critical articles and reviews. For information, address HarperCollins Publishers, 195 Broadway, New York, NY 10007.In Europe, HarperCollins Publishers, Macken House, 39/40 Mayor Street Upper, Dublin 1, D01 C9W8, Ireland.

hc.com

First Avon Books mass market printing: July 2025
First Avon Books hardcover printing: July 2025

Print Edition ISBN: 978-0-06-329215-4
Digital Edition ISBN: 978-0-06-329216-1

Cover design by Amy Halperin
Cover art by Tony Mauro
Cover images © iStock/Getty Images; © Dreamstime.com

Avon, Avon & logo, and Avon Books & logo are registered trademarks of HarperCollins Publishers in the United States of America and other countries.

HarperCollins is a registered trademark of HarperCollins Publishers in the United States of America and other countries.

FIRST EDITION

25 26 27 28 29 BVGM 10 9 8 7 6 5 4 3 2 1

Immortal by
MORNING

One

Abril was just returning from walking her boss's dog around the block when her phone began to ring. Stopping halfway up the long driveway, she pulled her cell phone out of her pocket and glanced at the display. The words *Boss Lady* were on the screen.

Starting to walk again, she answered with, "Hey, Boss Lady."

"Oh God, do you still have that as my display name?" Gina Spaldine asked with exasperation rather than greet her.

"Sure do," Abril said on a laugh. "It *is* fitting after all."

When the only response was a dubious grunt, Abril changed the subject and asked, "How's the trip going?"

"Great!" Gina said with sudden enthusiasm. "Italy is gorgeous! If I could speak the language, I'd move here."

"You said the very same thing about Spain, France, Puerto Rico, and Rio de Janeiro," Abril reminded her with amusement as she reached the top of the driveway and stopped in front of the garage doors.

"And I meant it every time," Gina told her. "These spa resorts are amazing. I swear they build them in the most glorious spot in each country."

"They probably do," Abril agreed, her gaze dropping to Lilith as the large yellow Labrador retriever tried to move away, tugging on the leash. Pulling the Lab back, she quickly bent to turn on the collar for the wireless fence that kept the dog safely in the yard. She then gave her an affectionate pet before undoing the leash to let her run loose.

Straightening again, Abril glanced around the three-acre parklike setting that was Gina's yard and commented, "But I think your house is in a pretty gorgeous spot too."

"It is," Gina admitted, her tone saying she was pleased with the new home she'd purchased. "That's why I bought it. Speaking of which, how is construction going?"

"Uh . . . good." Abril glanced toward both the great gaping hole in the ground along the side of the house, and the big yellow vehicle that sat silent and unmoving next to it.

"Good?" Gina questioned, stress entering her voice. "You didn't sound too confident when you said that, Abs. What's wrong?"

Abril grimaced at the question. She'd rather been hoping to keep this problem from Gina, but should have known better. She was terrible at hiding anything. "It's nothing really," she assured her quickly. "It's just that—Well, you know they finished the master bedroom, en suite bathroom and kitchen renos yesterday and planned to start digging the foundation for the addition this morning?"

"Yes. They were pretty close to finishing inside when I left for the airport the day before yesterday." There was a frown in Gina's voice. "What happened? Did they hit the gas line while digging the foundation or something?"

"No, no. Nothing like that," Abril assured her.

"Well, then what is it?"

"The digger thing . . . excavator?" she guessed before rushing on, "It crapped out on them about mid-morning. They had to stop for the day and wait for someone to come look at it. They're hoping that will be first thing tomorrow morning."

"Tomorrow morning? They couldn't get someone in today or bring in another excavator to continue on?" Gina sounded annoyed now, and Abril wasn't surprised. Her boss was not the most patient of women. It had taken forever to get these renovations started, and now that they were underway, every delay that came up—and Abril was sure there would be many—was just going to piss off Gina.

"I guess not," Abril said finally, her voice soothing. "But we had a pretty good rain just before lunchtime and they would have had to stop anyway. And Jared assured me that he was positive their guy would be able to get here first thing in the morning to fix the excavator. He also promised they'd work Saturday to make up for the lost time."

A long silence stretched along the phone line and then Gina muttered, "Right. Okay. Well, these things happen I guess."

Abril murmured an agreement, her gaze shifting

to Lilith as the Lab leaned into the six-foot round in-ground pond to drink out of it. Unsure if drinking the pond water was safe, Abril was just about to call her away when Gina spoke again, distracting her.

"So, have you had any visits from nosey neighbors yet? Or complaints about the noise?"

"Complaints no. Nosey neighbors yes," Abril admitted, and then added, "At least I'm guessing nosey since I didn't get to talk to them myself. That neighbor from the house one over to the left and across the street, Kim I think her name is?"

"Yes. Kim," Gina agreed.

"Well, she and another woman came by just before lunch and were talking to some of the workers. I didn't notice right away though, and by the time I did, and then got Lilith's leash on and took her outside, Kim and her friend were already halfway up your very long driveway, leaving."

Very long was an understatement when it came to describing Gina's driveway. Her house had been built on the back of a pie-shaped three-acre property. The driveway was a good two hundred feet long. Maybe more, Abril thought and then added, "I was about to call out and walk down to talk to them and make sure they didn't have any complaints about noise, but before I could Jared stopped me to tell me about the excavator thingie breaking down."

"But construction will definitely be starting up again tomorrow, right?" Gina asked, obviously more concerned about the renos getting done in a timely manner than in what her neighbors thought.

"As long as they're able to get it going again, yes," Abril said cautiously, thinking it was better to prepare her for the worst-case scenario. After all, no one knew what the problem was. What if they needed to order a part and wait for it to be delivered before they could make repairs?

"Well, if they can't fix it or find a replacement excavator by tomorrow, tell Jared to get to work on pulling out the indoor garden in the meantime. I know the carpet hasn't arrived yet, but they can still dig out the plants and dirt, fill it in with the gravel, and pour and spread the concrete to be ready for when the carpet does get there," Gina said firmly. "I really want all the inside stuff done before I get back. It'll eliminate the bother of the construction crew tramping in and out of the house and distracting us while we're working."

"That would be nice," Abril said slowly, and then grimaced and told her, "Except Jared explained that the carpet isn't the only reason they didn't move on to the indoor garden before starting outside. He said it was more economical to bring in the gravel and concrete for both the indoor garden and the foundation at the same time. He plans on having a couple of men dig out the indoor garden right before the gravel comes for filling the foundation, and the same with the concrete. They'll pour it outside and inside from the same deliveries. He said that way there also wouldn't be a great gaping hole in the living room floor for days or weeks for someone to fall into."

Abril had no trouble hearing Gina's mutter of irritation before the woman said, "Well, that makes sense, I guess. I just can't wait to be rid of that indoor garden. I hate the plants in it."

Abril smiled crookedly, relieved her boss wasn't throwing a fit at the news she'd just imparted. Her relief had her teasing, "You mean you hate watering those plants on weekends when I can't make it in."

"That too," Gina acknowledged. "But I hate the plants as well. Honestly, I don't know what the Bransons were thinking. I mean, could they possibly have found uglier ones? Between that nasty, spindly palm tree or yucca thing that looks like a bent and emaciated old man, and those overgrown cornstalks—"

"They aren't cornstalks," Abril interrupted with amusement, but admitted, "They do kind of look like them though. Fifteen-foot cornstalks. And, yes, they are ugly." After a brief pause, she teased, "But you didn't even mention the Naked-man orchids. Won't you be happy to be rid of those?"

"Oh, well, those aren't so bad," Gina said. "In fact, I find them kind of cathartic."

"Cathartic?" Abril echoed with surprise.

"Yeah. Anytime I think of William and his taking off like he did, I go down and pinch the little pecker off one of the Naked-man orchids."

"Oh gawd, Gina!" Abril cried on a disbelieving laugh. "You don't!"

"I do. Well, at least, I did," she assured her. "And I'll miss doing it. In fact . . ." She paused and then said thoughtfully, "Maybe rather than get rid of the garden altogether, I should just have them pull out everything but the Naked-man orchids and plant different, more attractive trees and bushes around them."

Abril grimaced at the words. Gina had vacillated for months between changing plants or digging up the garden and either replacing it with flooring or adding a water feature in its place. Her indecisiveness had nearly driven Abril and the contractor crazy. It had been a relief when her boss had settled on removing the garden and making the living room larger.

Much larger, Abril thought. The indoor garden was twelve feet by twelve feet, with a three-foot walkway alongside it. Once the garden was gone, the living room would be thirty-five feet by fifteen feet. That was much larger than she felt any living room needed to be, but had no desire for Gina to keep that damned garden. Mostly because she would be stuck continuing to water and tend it and Abril had also hated watering the ugly plants. She wasn't eager to water different ones now, so warned, "Whatever you like, but as I already told you, my coming over on the weekends to water the garden was a favor I won't keep up after this. So if you choose to keep the indoor garden, you'll have to tend to it yourself, or hire someone to do it for you."

Much to her relief, Gina breathed out unhappily and said, "I suppose it's better to stick with the plan and get rid of it altogether then. I mean the indoor garden is the main reason I bought the house, but I can't remember to water it myself, and don't want strangers coming and going on the weekends, so if you won't water it for me . . ."

A long pause followed. Abril knew her boss was hoping that guilt would move her to fill that silence with an offer to continue the weekend waterings, but that wasn't happening. She'd already done that for Gina for over six months now and it had been a pain in the ass. An unpaid pain in the ass too, she thought with irritation. She hadn't minded at first because it was only supposed to be for a month or so before the renos started. Unfortunately, the start date for that had got pushed back, and then got pushed back again, and then again. Six months later they had finally started, but she was thoroughly over it.

House and dog sitting for Gina during the last of the renos, which her boss had escaped by flying off to warmer climes, was the last of the favors she would do, and she was only doing that because she was being paid well for it. But after this she was only working normal hours. There would be no more coming in on weekends to water the plants and oh-while-you're-here-can-you walk Lilith/run out and grab me groceries/pick up my dry cleaning, or anything else. Abril liked her boss, but that liking would only stretch so far.

"Right, so the original plan of removing it stands," Gina said when Abril remained silent. Not letting her respond, her boss added, "I guess I should get off the phone. We're going to do a little shopping before dinner."

"Okay. Have fun," Abril said.

"Will do," Gina assured her. "You have my number if there are any more problems. Call if you need me, Abby."

"I'm sure everything will go fine."

"Famous last words," Gina said with a laugh.

"Yeah, I'll knock on wood," Abril told her grimly.

"You do that. And call me if they find bodies or buried treasure in the indoor garden when they dig it up."

"Bodies?" Abril asked with a disbelieving laugh.

"Yeah. Well, I'm still trying to figure out where William went. Months of dating and he just disappeared into thin air. Maybe he fell into the garden and the ground swallowed him up."

Abril hesitated, unsure what to say. She knew Gina

had fallen hard and quickly for William. And he'd seemed to be just as enamored. After months of dating, and another month of practically living at the house, the man had gone out for milk and never returned. His sudden disappearing act had hit Gina hard. It was why she'd arranged this trip with a couple of girlfriends, to get away, relax, and get over William. It seemed that the getting over him part wasn't working out so well. Not yet anyway.

"It's a joke, Abs," Gina said quietly, drawing Abril from her thoughts. "William can go hang for all I care."

"He wasn't good enough for you," Abril blurted. "I mean he was cute and fit, but the guy was dumb as a stump."

"Yeah," Gina murmured wearily. "Anyway, I should get going. Make sure you send those contracts to Rutherford. I've already started to work on ideas for those ads he wants and am eager to discuss them with him, but won't do so until he signs on the dotted line."

"Already gone," Abril assured her. "I sent them by courier last night. I'll let you know as soon as he signs and sends them back."

"Thanks. You're a star," Gina said, some energy returning to her voice now that the subject was changed.

"That's why you pay me the big bucks," Abril teased.

"Yeah. Remind me to give you a raise when I get back."

"Yeah, yeah. Go have fun," Abby responded on a chuckle.

"I plan to," Gina assured her, and then added, "Ciao."

"Ciao," Abril said with a smile and had started to

pull the phone away from her ear when Gina suddenly cried out, "Oh, wait! I almost forgot what I was calling for in the first place."

Eyebrows rising, Abril paused and said, "Yes?"

"I was calling to check on Lilith."

"Ah." Abril smiled, not at all surprised to hear that Gina was concerned about her baby. The woman doted on her pup like most people did on their children.

"Is she okay? Is she eating well? Is she missing me?" Gina asked and Abril didn't miss the note of hope in her voice.

"Yes, of course she's missing you," she said, glancing around now for the dog in question. "She starts barking and jumps up to run to the door every time she hears a vehicle in the driveway, only to drag her butt back and flop down onto her bed when it isn't you but a courier, or the construction guys."

"Aww," Gina said, a smile in her voice. "Well, give her a cuddle from me and tell her Mommy loves her."

"Will do," Abril said absently, turning to peer around the empty front yard of the three-acre property when she didn't spot the Lab by the pond or anywhere else to the side of the hole and excavator.

"Have a good day. Talk to you tomorrow."

"Mm-hmm," Abril murmured and slid the phone into her pocket when the dial tone sounded telling her that Gina had hung up.

Fretting over whether she really had turned on the collar for the wireless fence as she'd meant to do, or had somehow done it wrong leaving Lilith free to run off, Abril started toward the back of the house. She intended to check there for her before panicking and widening her search to the neighborhood.

Rather than going all the way around the huge excavator, Abril took the lazy route, walking between it and the hole. The path got narrow where the vehicle sat, and she reached for the large bucket to hold on to it as she made her way past, but her hand never made contact with the cool metal. Before it could, the ground she was walking on suddenly gave way beneath her.

Fortunately, they hadn't got far in digging out the foundation before the machine had broken down that morning. The hole was about ten feet long and twenty feet wide, but only three or four feet deep. This was a good thing, Abril decided when she came to a halt at the bottom of the pit. While the sudden fall was a shock and knocked the breath out of her, she wasn't hurt as far as she could tell.

Abril took a moment to regain her breath, and then blinked her eyes open when a bark preceded a wet tongue scraping across her cheek. She'd found Lilith. Abril put out a hand to the eager dog to keep her from licking her again.

"Thank you. I'm okay, sweetie," she murmured, petting the animal with one hand while urging her away with the other. "Let me get up."

Whether Lilith understood her words was debatable, but at least the Lab gave up trying to lick her to death. Turning away, the dog trotted to the far side of the partially excavated area that was closest to the house. Breathing out a sigh of relief, Abril struggled to her feet on the soft, uneven ground and tried to brush off the dirt now covering her coat and jeans. Unfortunately, while the rain earlier had been brief, it had still managed to drop a lot of water. It had turned the dirt to mud that was not brushing off. Instead, it was smearing on her beige wool coat and faded blue jeans.

Cursing, Abril gave up trying to remove the muck and glanced around for Lilith. She relaxed when she saw that the dog was busily digging in the dirt close to the wall.

"Helping the construction crew, Lilith?" Abril asked, looking around to try to find the best way to get out of the hole without bringing more dirt down on herself. Where she'd fallen seemed like the best place to get out. The rest of the sides to the hole were pretty straight up and down and closer to five feet than the three or four she'd first thought. Where the ground had given way, however, the side was now sloped. It was also made up of soft, loose dirt. She could get out that way, but suspected she'd have to basically crawl to do it.

Grimacing at the thought, Abril glanced to where the Lab was still digging. Slapping the side of her leg, she called, "Lilith, come!"

Lilith did not come. She didn't even glance around at the call. Abril scowled at the dog's lack of obedience. The pup was usually pretty good about listening and happy to follow her about, but right now she was ignoring her completely and continuing to dig almost feverishly, something she had apparently been doing for some time. Her golden fur was drenched in dark earth; on her paws, lower legs, and face. There were even a couple of splotches of it on her back.

Muttering under her breath about having to bathe disobedient pups, Abril slid her now cold hands into the pockets of her coat to keep them warm, and headed over to collect the dog.

The construction had been planned to start last fall, the end of September to be exact. The renos hadn't started until the end of March. Now it was the last week of April when the days fluctuated between warmish and cold and back. Today was really cold, but not cold enough to freeze the muddy earth she was presently squelching through.

"Lilith! Stop and get over here!" Abril ordered more firmly, retrieving the leash from her pocket when she felt it in there. When her latest command had no more effect than her others, Abril's muttering changed to complaining about unruly puppies who didn't listen and made their humans traipse through nasty mud that was ruining their shoes. That carried her across the remaining distance to Lilith.

"Bad puppy," Abril growled as she bent to latch the leash to her collar. She'd tried to put a firm note into her voice, but it obviously didn't fool the dog into thinking she was no longer the pushover she usually was for the furball. When Abril straightened and tried to tug the Lab away, Lilith resisted.

"For heaven's sake, Lilith!" Abril said with exasperation, and yanked on the leash. "Come on. Let's go inside. It's cold out here." Not above bribery at this point, she tacked on, "I'll give you a treat. Two treats even if—Holy shit," Abril breathed when Lilith suddenly stopped her digging to move closer to her, apparently ready to give up in exchange for the promised treats. Now it was Abril who wasn't leaving. She simply stood there, gaping with disbelief for several minutes.

It was the cold assaulting her feet as they sank into the mud far enough to allow the frigid slush to cover and seep into her shoes that finally drew her from her shock. Breath leaving her on a gasp, Abril snatched the phone out of her pocket with a suddenly shaky hand. She punched in 911 as she backed toward the edge of the hole, pulling Lilith with her.

The moment her call was answered and the operator asked what her emergency was, Abril cleared her throat and said, "There's a body in my boss's garden."

"Ma'am, did you say there's a body in your boss's garden?" the operator asked sounding shocked.

Abril couldn't blame her. This was a small town on the outskirts of London in Ontario, Canada. Things like this just didn't happen here.

But apparently, they do after all, her mind pointed out as she stared at the skull now half-exposed in the dirt. Letting her breath out on a resigned gust of air, she said, "I'm afraid so. Or a skeleton, I guess. At least the dog dug up a skull. Can you send someone out, please?"

Two

"Get in, Crispin. We have to go!" Alexander Roberts barked when Crispin opened the passenger door of their assigned vehicle.

Eyebrows rising at his partner's impatient greeting, Crispinus Delacort slid into the car and pulled the door closed. They'd only separated moments earlier when Roberts had left him to finish a conversation he'd been having with another detective and gone to get the car. His partner had been fine and much more relaxed then. Now he was practically vibrating with excitement. "What's the rush?"

"We have a case," Roberts announced as he hit the gas sending the car shooting forward.

Guessing his partner had got the call on the car radio as he'd driven around to pick him up, Crispin quickly did up his seatbelt and asked, "So, what is it this time? A cat up a tree, a kid playing truant, or someone caught shoplifting?"

"None of those," Roberts answered him. "Murder."

"Really?" Crispin asked with surprise. As a homicide detective he supposed he shouldn't really be surprised they'd got called to a murder. But they'd only had eight of them in London over the last year. Half of those had needed little to no detective work done since the perpetrators had called in the deaths and confessed at the same time. That had left four murders that had actually needed solving. It hadn't made for a lot of work for him and Roberts. Unfortunately, that meant they'd spent the better part of their time helping out with piddling cases like chasing down truant teens. "Are we sure it's murder?"

"Must be," Roberts said as he headed out of the parking lot, tires squealing. "A body in a garden."

"What?" Crispin gaped as Roberts turned on both the lights and siren.

"You heard right," Roberts assured him, his expression a combination of grim tension and a strange almost glee. "A body buried in a garden. Most people choose a cemetery for the last resting place . . . if it isn't murder."

Crispin understood the glee thoroughly. While it might appear unseemly to most people to have that reaction to a body being found, it was what he and Roberts had been trained for and were paid to take care of. It was nice to actually use their training and earn their pay for a change.

"Where is the garden in question?" Crispin asked.

"Out of the city, just past Byron," Roberts said.

The news made Crispin stiffen. His voice was careful when he asked, "How far past Byron?"

"Still in our jurisdiction," Roberts reassured him.

Crispin nodded, relaxing a bit in his seat. It would

have been just their luck to get a case like this only to arrive and find themselves muscled out by the Ontario Provincial Police because the case was out of the city's environs. It appeared that would not be the case, however.

Despite speeding with lights and siren blaring, it took more than twenty minutes to reach their destination. Crispin knew they were getting close when Roberts killed both the siren and lights. Sitting up in his seat then, he glanced around with curiosity. They were passing farms and fields, and then they turned onto another road, a crescent, Crispin saw as he read the street name.

"Wow," Roberts breathed suddenly, drawing his attention away from the street sign.

Crispin glanced to his partner, and then followed his gaze to the road ahead. It was a truly breathtaking view; dark green grass and large old trees, mostly cedar, spruce, and white pines on both sides of the street. It was like they were driving through a park. He didn't even notice the houses at first, not until he turned his head to look for them. They were all set back on what appeared to be two or three acres of parkland each, and every one was a different design of large majestic home. Not one was unattractive. It was a vast difference from the cookie-cutter houses on tiny postage-stamp bits of land that had been being built for the last twenty years or so. Which meant these homes were probably twenty-five or thirty years old, he supposed, but not one looked like it was. They were all well maintained.

The house they wanted turned out to be the largest on the road, with the largest property, and sat smack dab in the middle of the curved crescent.

"Wow," Roberts repeated, as he steered them slowly up the driveway. "So, this is how the other half lives."

Crispin peered at him with disbelief. "Your house is twice the size of this one, and sits on forty acres."

"Yeah, but I'm 373 years old," Roberts pointed out.

"So?" he asked with amusement. Roberts said it as if his nearly four centuries was long-lived. But he was just a babe to Crispin who had been on the earth for nearly three millennia.

"So, I've had a lot more time to make the money to buy the land and build my house," Roberts pointed out.

Crispin nodded. Being immortal, or a vampire as most mortals would call them, had its advantages. Having the time to build up personal wealth was just one of them.

"The owner of this house is a mortal," Roberts went on. "How the hell were they able to afford this? For that matter, how the hell have all the mortals on this street been able to afford these homes?"

Crispin shrugged and peered toward the house again. "Hard work maybe. Or inheritance and hard work," he added as his gaze landed on the man, woman, and dog standing in front of the house. The man was a patrolman in uniform, one he knew, Officer Tim Peters. He was a smart guy with aspirations of becoming a detective himself someday. He'd been on hand at more than a few of the murders they'd investigated over the last several years.

His gaze moved on to the woman and dog; a pretty, petite blonde who couldn't be more than thirty years old, and a yellow Labrador retriever on a leash. The woman was young to have the kind of success that would land her in the largest house on the largest property on this crescent.

Roberts seemed to agree and as he parked next to the patrol car, he commented, "I'm thinking inheritance or a lottery win, most like."

Once out of the vehicle and moving toward the pair, Crispin noted that the pretty blonde was presently looking somewhat stressed. Not surprising, he supposed. Finding a body in your garden had to be something of a shock, but that wasn't all that was stressing her, he realized when she greeted them.

"Thank God, you didn't come in a police car. It's bad enough having one police car here. As it is, Gina will have fits about that and the gossip it will no doubt cause in the neighborhood. But a second one would definitely be an issue."

Crispin exchanged a glance with Roberts at her words. It was true they had an unmarked car. However, the neighborhood would soon be crawling with cops and technicians, all of them arriving in police vehicles bearing the London Police logo.

Fortunately, Peters saved them from having to admit as much when he said, "Ma'am, these are detectives Roberts and Delacort. Sirs, this is Miss Abril Newman. She's house-sitting for the homeowner, a Ms. Gina"—he flipped back a few pages in the small notepad he held and finished—"Ms. Gina Spaldine. She's presently vacationing in Italy."

Crispin nodded at the woman, "Miss Newman."

After Roberts also greeted her, Crispin glanced to Peters and raised his eyebrows. "So, what do we have here? The report was a body in the garden?"

"Ah, yes. Actually, it's not a garden anymore. It apparently was at one time, and part of it still was prior to this, but they were digging it up for the foundation of a planned addition," Peters explained, leading them to stand in front of a large hole along the right side of the house. It was about twenty feet wide, nine or ten feet long, and about five feet deep. "Apparently the excavator broke down, the men left and Lilith"—he paused to explain—"the Labrador retriever. She dug up the skull. It's really a skeleton, not a body."

Crispin and Roberts followed his pointing finger to the disturbed area five feet below the sliding doors where a human skull was half uncovered.

"I'm just going to take Lilith for a bit of a walk around the yard while you catch them up. If that's okay, Officer Peters?" Abril Newman asked and Crispin glanced around to see that she was standing back and struggling to hold onto the Lab as it fought to follow them to the hole.

"Of course. Go ahead," Peters said, and then glanced quickly to Crispin and Roberts in question as he realized that he was no longer in charge of the scene now that the two detectives had arrived.

"That's fine," Crispin assured him.

Relaxing, Peters told the woman, "We'll shout when the detectives are ready to talk to you."

Offering a quick smile and nod, Abril Newman headed for the open yard beyond the excavator, having to use a lot of strength and effort to drag the Lab with her. The animal seemed desperate to return to the bones she'd uncovered.

"The dog dug up the skull?" Roberts asked. "Not the construction crew?"

"Yes, sir," Peters affirmed. "Not just the skull either. She got loose while Miss Newman was talking to me and started to dig up what I think are parts of a second body in the opposite corner over there. A pair of hands."

Eyebrows rising, Crispin managed to pull his attention from Abril Newman's curvy behind to peer at the officer with sharp interest, but it was Roberts who asked, "There's more than one set of remains?"

Peters hesitated, and then said, "Well, it's either a second skeleton or it belongs to the skull and the body was chopped up and spread around the area."

Crispin immediately jumped lightly down into the hole to get a better look at the revealed skull, fully expecting Roberts to follow. Instead, the man said, "I'll be right back."

Surprised, Crispin watched his partner rush back to their car. It wasn't until he opened the trunk and reached in to grab the hand broom and dustpan kept there that Crispin understood what he was doing. Roberts had bought the hand broom to clean up any messes in the vehicle after another detective had apparently eaten donuts in the car and left a dusting of white powder everywhere. After a brief look through the trunk for anything else of use, Roberts closed it.

Knowing his partner would join him momentarily, Crispin squatted next to the skull to get a closer look. The forehead down to the jaw was on view, the eye sockets and nose hole were filled with the dark, almost black earth surrounding it, but everything else was pretty dirt free, almost like the skull had been washed.

"Miss Newman suspects the Lab was licking the skull before she found her and saw what she was up to," Peters said suddenly from where he still stood at the edge of the hole, looking down at him. "Apparently, the Lab likes to eat dirt for some reason."

Crispin grunted and then glanced to Roberts as he dropped into the hole and squatted beside him.

"Let us see if it is just the skull or not," Roberts muttered. Given that the earth was so damp, he bypassed the hand broom for the dustpan and began to cautiously sweep away the top layer of dirt, starting just below the jaw. He was careful only to scrape a light layer away, then another and another. After that, he switched to using his hand to brush the dirt aside until he uncovered bone. The cervical vertebrae of the neck, Crispin recognized, and picked up the broom to brush away the now light dusting of dirt left on the neck bones as Roberts continued his own efforts farther down and in a much wider sweep.

"I think this is the clavicle," Roberts said suddenly.

Crispin stopped what he was doing to examine the results of his partner's efforts. Roberts had cleared away enough dirt to reveal the rotting remains of part of a shirt and what appeared to be a clavicle showing where the collar was open.

"Yes," he agreed. "Obviously the head was not removed from the body. Although I suppose they still could have cut off the hands."

Roberts frowned. "I would like to keep going to find out, but we are going to catch hell for disturbing the scene as it is."

"We could claim the dog did this," Crispin said with amusement. "Or put the dirt back."

Knowing he was joking, Roberts didn't comment as he straightened.

Crispin stood then as well and asked Peters, "You said the dog uncovered more bones?"

"Over there." Peters pointed to the corner ten feet away along the wall.

Nodding, Crispin crossed to that area with Roberts. They both paused to peer at the bones in the dirt. Hands. One was on show from the distal phalanges at the tips of the fingers, past the wrist bones to the ends of the ulna and radius of the forearm. The other only had the finger bones and some of the metacarpals on display. One of the distal phalanges had been moved a little away from the others, but that had probably happened from the dog digging.

"So, if the hands were cut off there are still at least two bodies, but more likely it is three at this point," Roberts commented finally.

"Three?" Peters asked with confusion. "I mean, if those hands don't belong to the skull, that's only two bodies."

"I am guessing you did not get a good look at the hands?" Crispin asked.

"I . . . well, no. The dog was determined to go back to her digging, and Miss Newman was having trouble controlling her. It took both of us to get her away from the bones," he explained. "Then we waited in front of the house for you to arrive."

Crispin wasn't at all surprised at that news. He'd suspected it had been something along those lines, because anyone who had gotten a good look at the bones on display would have realized—

"They are both right hands," his partner told Peters. "Two right hands here belonging to two different bodies, and if the first skeleton still has its hands attached, that means three bodies."

"Damn," Peters breathed with wonder. "That means this was a multiple murder. These may even be the victims of a serial killer."

Three

Abril was beginning to get more than a little annoyed. She was freezing her butt off out here while the men stood around talking. She knew Officer Peters had to give them his report, but how long could that take? It wasn't like she'd had a lot to tell him that he would have to pass on.

The house wasn't hers. She was house-sitting and the dog had dug up the bones after the digging had ended abruptly when the excavator had crapped out. There! She'd said it all in two sentences. Well, she supposed she'd left out a couple of bits, but seriously! She was cold! Her jeans were soaked from the mud she'd fallen into, leaving her legs feeling like two blocks of ice, and while the mud on her hands had dried and started to flake off, her fingers were actually beginning to feel hot and tingly. Wasn't that a sign of frostbite or something?

"Miss Newman?"

Abril swung around with relief at that call, and urged Lilith to move back toward the men when the taller, good-looking one waved her over. She grimaced inwardly at the thought. Really, both men were good-looking. One was dark haired, and well-built with dark eyes, a strong jaw, and full lips. The other also had dark hair, but was a couple of inches taller, a couple inches wider, and had the most beautiful silver-blue eyes Abril had ever seen. He also had longish stubble on his face. She had always preferred the tall, dark, and handsome type, but usually preferred clean-shaven too. However, that stubble was really attractive on this man . . . She found him sexy as hell.

And that was probably a really inappropriate thought to have at a murder scene, she acknowledged, her gaze sliding to the open hole. She had no idea what had happened to the people Lilith had uncovered, but it seemed pretty obvious they hadn't died of natural causes. Otherwise, they'd have been buried in a cemetery rather than in what used to be a garden along the side of the house.

She peered around what she could see of the street as she crossed the yard. Considering the distance between the houses, and the trees and bushes filling the yards, she suspected it wouldn't have been hard to bury the bodies without being seen. Especially since there were no streetlights on the crescent and it was black as pitch at night.

"We have some questions for you, Miss Newman. But we can go inside to ask them if you like. You are obviously cold. You are shivering," the shorter detective, Roberts, said as she reached the men coming out of the hole.

"Inside would be good," Abril agreed, grateful at the thought of soon being warm again.

"Peters, keep an eye on the site until forensics gets here. Make sure no animals or anything else disturb the bones," Detective Delacort ordered and Abril couldn't help noticing that he had a really deep, sexy voice even before he added, "Once the team does get here, come inside. We might need your help with canvassing the crescent."

"Yes, sir," Peters said solemnly.

Abril actually felt bad for the guy. He'd been out here quite a while with her already while he'd taken down the information and then had waited for the detectives. He was obviously feeling the cold. His fingers, ears, and nose were all red from it.

"I'll make coffee and bring you one," she offered. "How do you take it?"

Peters hesitated, and then shook his head. "That's okay, miss. I wouldn't want to put you to any trouble."

"It's no trouble," she assured him. "How do you take it?"

"One cream, and one sugar," he said finally and offered her a grateful smile.

Abril nodded. As she turned to lead Lilith to the front door, she heard Roberts say, "Pull your car up closer to the excavated area and you can wait in it with the heat on, Peters."

"Yes, sir," Peters said smartly.

Abril glanced over her shoulder, intending to give the detective an approving smile for thinking of the officer's comfort, but her view was blocked by a wall of man. Detective Delacort was directly behind her. Blinking, she raised her gaze to his face, realizing only then that he was more than tall, he was extremely tall. He must be a good six two to her five five. How had she not noticed that before now?

"Watch your step." Detective Delacort's concerned voice was deep and silken. When she was slow to turn her attention forward, he caught her wrist, drawing her to a halt.

Abril flushed at the physical response she had to his touch and finally looked around to avoid his gaze and saw that she'd been about to walk into the half wall that ran alongside the steps to the landing of the front double doors.

"Oh. Thanks," she breathed, as confused by her reaction to him as she was embarrassed by her own clumsiness. When he released her wrist, she took a shaky breath and quickly walked around the short wall to mount the steps.

When Lilith began to tug then, obviously not interested in going inside and abandoning the treasures she'd dug up, Abril said, "Treat."

That was the magic word. Lilith stopped digging her feet in and yanking her head around. Instead, she was suddenly up at the door, waiting for Abril to catch up.

"She is food driven," Detective Delacort commented.

"Oh, yeah, definitely food driven," Abril agreed, managing a wry smile. "Masked bandits could break in and kill all of us and she'd let them do it and even wag her tail while they did if they threw her a couple of treats. She is not a very good guard dog."

Delacort chuckled, his warm breath brushing her ear. That and the deep, rich sound of his amusement actually sent a shiver through Abril's body. It was because of the cold, she assured herself. That was a shiver of cold, not excitement. Dear God, the man was gorgeous and sexy as hell and—*You are obviously delirious from the cold*, she told herself firmly. *There is a dead body or three in the garden. This is no time for flirting, or even noticing the man is attractive. Get inside, get these wet clothes off, make coffee, and answer their questions like the smart executive assistant you are.*

"Shall I get the door for you?"

Abril blinked at the question, and then realized she was standing in front of the double doors, her fingers merely lightly clasping the door handle. Before she could shake herself out of her stupor, Delacort suddenly reached past her to do as he'd offered. His fingers glided against hers as he grasped the handle and opened the door.

Abril closed her eyes as his chest pressed against her back and she was half encompassed by his arm and body. The chaos that set off inside her wasn't just embarrassing, it was downright alarming. She'd never reacted like this to anyone, ever in her life. What was he? Some kind of warlock or something with a love spell, or more accurately a lust spell that was turning her into a bitch in heat? Hell, if she had a tail like Lilith, it would be wagging right now. She was actually surprised her tongue wasn't hanging out.

Abril was tempted to lean back into the man, but before she could, she was dragged forward as Lilith suddenly lunged through the open door.

Eyebrows high on his forehead, Crispin gaped after Abril as she stumble-jogged through the entry and out of sight to the right, pulled along behind the Lab. He then turned to Roberts when his partner chuckled.

"Are you laughing?" he asked with disbelief. Roberts rarely laughed. The man was usually the inscrutable stare type of guy, but he was definitely laughing now.

"Oh, yes. I am laughing," Roberts assured him. "Between her thinking if she had a tail, it would be wagging, and your fascination with where that tail would be on her, I just cannot help it."

"I am not fascinated with her ass," Crispin growled with irritation, telling himself it was true. He'd merely been peering at her behind because he was . . . well, behind her.

Roberts released another chuckle. "Sure. So if she had been facing you, you would have been eyeing her other goods?"

"No, I would not. I—Wait." He narrowed his gaze on his partner. "Are you reading my thoughts? You are," he accused when Roberts merely shrugged. "How the hell are you reading my thoughts? I am older than you."

"I do not know, my friend," Roberts said, slapping him on the shoulder and moving past him to enter the house. "You are a detective. Sort it out. How could I possibly be able to hear your thoughts? When are older immortals vulnerable to being read by immortals younger than themselves?"

Crispin opened his mouth, closed it, and then his eyes widened incredulously. "No," he said, denying the thought that immediately came to mind. Then, re-alizing that he was just standing there on the stoop alone, he stepped inside and pushed the door closed behind him.

Pausing, he peered around what he could see of the house. He was standing in a large foyer with a set of closed double doors directly ahead across an expanse of white marble. The closet? He suspected so, then glanced to the left where the marble gave way to a cream-colored carpeted walkway beside a large indoor garden full of tropical trees and plants. Crispin was impressed until he noted the plants themselves. They really weren't very attractive, but then to each their own, he supposed and glanced past the garden to the living room beyond. Finding that empty, he turned to look to the right, peering through an open doorway. He had just recognized that it was a very large kitchen when he heard Abril Newman's voice.

She was saying something about "good girl" and "treats" he noted and gave up his position by the door to enter the long, rather spectacular kitchen. It had to be forty feet long and at least sixteen wide, with a long island running down the middle between the cupboards and counters on either side. Everything was white except for the countertops, which were made up of a silver-streaked black granite. The floor was some exotic hardwood he'd never seen before. It was gor-geous though, the strips of wood a variety of reddish brown tones with distinctive black striping.

"It's tigerwood."

Crispin jerked his head up at that announcement from Abril, unsure what she was talking about until she added, "The floor. It's tigerwood."

For one moment he was terrified that she too could read his mind and then Roberts said soothingly, "You were staring at the floor."

"Oh. Yes," Crispin said, relaxing a little. "I have never seen it before. I have never seen hardwood in a kitchen before either though, so . . ." He shrugged.

"Yeah, that's Gina," Abril said with a faint smile as she turned to what appeared to be a coffee bar area. There was a tea kettle, a Keurig with a milk frother, and a normal coffee machine all side by side. It was the coffee machine she was working with, scooping grounds into the filter to make a pot of the dark brew. "She tends to do things a little different than everyone else."

Finished with the tin, she put it away and switched on the coffee machine. But as she turned to join them, she slipped on something and started to fall back.

Panic punching at him hard, Crispin shot forward to catch her, one hand sliding under the back of her head to prevent it hitting the countertop, the other catching her arm to stop her fall. In the next moment, she was on her feet again and he was peering down at her with concern. "Are you all right?"

Abril peered up at him with obvious confusion for a moment, and then her gaze dropped to his lips and stayed there. Her expression began to change. It softened, her mouth opening slightly, her tongue slipping out to run along her lips. But it was the increase in her heart rate, and the scent of arousal suddenly coming off her that really caught his attention. It stirred a responding arousal in himself and Crispin tightened his hold on her and started to draw her to him, intending to kiss her.

"Shall I give Lilith the promised treat?" Roberts asked, interrupting the moment. "Where do you keep them, Miss Newman?"

Confusion crossed Abril's face and she gave her head a shake, then began to pull away from Crispin to turn to look at Roberts. "The treats?"

"Yes. You promised Lilith one as soon as you made the coffee," he reminded her, but Roberts's gaze was on Crispin.

"Oh, yes," she murmured, moving farther away from Crispin and leaving him feeling bereft. After centuries of having a complete lack of interest in sex, he wanted to pull her back and claim her mouth, uncaring that Roberts was there. He wanted to pull her against his body and—Christ! She was his life mate, he realized with dismay. The thought had occurred to him out on the stoop, but he'd denied it to himself then, unwilling to even give thought to the possibility. But there was no denying it now. Sex was something an immortal lost interest in after a century or so of life. Only finding a life mate could reawaken such desires. For Crispin it had been more than two and a half millennia since he'd felt such urges, but they were definitely awakening now. That could only mean that Abril was his life mate. Or a possible life mate, he supposed, since she could refuse him if she chose.

"Finally sorted it out," Roberts said with open amusement.

"I'm sorry?" Abril paused in the act of taking the lid off a white tin container with a dog bone painted on it, and glanced toward his partner with confusion.

"Oh. I was talking to Delacort, not you." Roberts gave her a smile, and then offered, "If you tell me where I can find a mop and bucket, I will clean up the floor for you so you do not slip again. Next time you might hurt yourself."

Abril peered down at the floor. Seeing the frown that crossed her face, Crispin glanced down as well to see that there was mud all over it. There were several tracks; paw prints from the pup, and footprints from him, Roberts, and Abril, as well as chunks of dirt that had obviously dropped off Abril's clothes or the dog's fur. She wasn't surprised, both she and Lilith looked like they'd rolled in it.

"Maybe you should go change," Crispin suggested solemnly.

"Yes. I should probably—Oh, Lilith no!" she cried suddenly, and rushed past him after the dog as she headed for the doorway to the rest of the house. While the Lab didn't stop, she did slow enough for Abril to get close enough to step on the leash still attached and dragging behind the Lab. That did make the dog stop.

Bending, Abril snatched up the leash handle and straightened, then hesitated, her gaze going from the dog to the doorway and then around the room almost helplessly.

Crispin had no idea what she was thinking or looking for; he couldn't read her mind. He did try, but was unsurprised to come up against a blank wall. This seemed like further verification that she was a possible life mate for him. While immortals could read mortals and any immortal younger than themselves, they couldn't read the mind of their life mate.

"I will hold on to Lilith while you go clean up and change," Roberts offered, crossing the room to take the leash from her.

"Oh, no, I—" When her protest ended abruptly and she simply handed over the leash and turned to walk out of the kitchen, Crispin knew his partner had taken control of Abril and given her a mental push to do as he suggested. That irritated the hell out of him.

"It is rude to take control of the mind of someone else's life mate," he pointed out grimly.

"I think so too," Roberts agreed. "But sometimes it just makes things easier." Ignoring his scowl, he handed Crispin Lilith's leash and walked down to a door at the end of the kitchen. Opening it, he disappeared through it.

Crispin had started to follow him when Roberts reappeared with a mop, bucket, and two miscellaneous bottles of some kind of liquid under his arm. The room was obviously some kind of broom closet.

"Pantry," Roberts announced, correcting his guess. After setting the bucket in the sink, he removed the two bottles from under his arm to examine the labels before holding one out toward him. "Go wash Lilith."

"What?" Crispin asked with confusion, and then glanced at the label on the bottle when Roberts gave it a waggle. It was dog shampoo.

"Go bathe Lilith." Roberts spoke slowly, as if he thought Crispin didn't understand the order.

"I understood your words, Alex," he said irritably. "But why on earth would I do that?"

"Because if you do not, then I am going to wash the floor and Lilith is going to muddy it all over again, and Abril will have to wash the floor when we leave, as well as give Lilith a bath."

"Fine." Crispin snatched the bottle from him and

started to turn away, only to realize he had no idea where he was supposed to bathe the dog.

"There is a guest bathroom down that hall," Roberts said, pointing to the hallway about fifteen feet from the sliding glass door.

When Crispin showed surprise, Roberts shrugged. "Before she left the room, Miss Newman was thinking that she would have to bathe the dog. She was thinking she would do it in the guest bathroom up the hall to avoid the dog going across the cream-colored carpet in the rest of the house."

"Oh." Crispin started toward the hallway, tugging lightly on the chain so that Lilith would follow.

Four

Abril's breath came out in gusty relief as she skidded into her bedroom and quickly closed the door behind her. The last couple of minutes had been somewhat harrowing. She'd left the kitchen, only to freeze as she got halfway across the marble floor of the entry and her gaze fell on the pale carpet beyond. She'd peered down at the black mud covering her clothes, and back to the cream-colored carpet unsure what to do.

Biting her lip, she'd considered the situation briefly, peered nervously back toward the kitchen, and then had done the only thing she could. Taking off her coat, she'd laid it down with the cleaner inner lining to the marble floor, then she'd quickly stripped off her jeans, taking her shoes with them. Dropping them on her coat, she'd then rolled the whole mess into a ball, snatched it up and run through the living room to the guest bedroom she was occupying while house-sitting.

Now she leaned back against the closed door and

sighed her relief at reaching the safety of the bedroom without being spotted running around in her underwear. Wouldn't that have been embarrassing?

More than just embarrassing, she thought pushing herself away from the door and crossing her room to the attached bathroom. It would have been mortifying, humiliating even, Abril decided as she dumped her dirty coat, jeans, and shoes into the clothes hamper in the bathroom.

She turned toward the sink then, and stopped dead when she saw her reflection in the mirror. While her legs were bare and mostly clean, there were still streaks of mud that had leaked through the heavy denim to mark her skin. The rest of her, however, was much worse. Her coat had been open and her white blouse was stained dark brown down the center. Her hands and face were streaked with it as well. When she turned her head, she could see that her hair at the back was one big clump of mud from her fall into the hole next to the house.

Abril groaned to herself as she considered that she'd stood around looking like this during her entire encounter with Officer Peters, and detectives Roberts and Delacort.

"Great first impression, girl," she muttered to her reflection and then grimaced as she looked herself over again. A quick washup in the sink was not going to do the trick. She definitely needed a shower. That thought in mind, she quickly turned on the shower, and then stripped off her shirt, bra, and panties. All three had been muddied to one degree or another, the muck having oozed determinedly through her outer clothes to taint them.

Not wanting to dirty her robe, Abril wrapped one of the large bath towels around herself, grabbed the hamper and made a quick trip to the laundry room to get her wash started. With that done, she rushed back to her room, eager to step under the rushing water and wash away the mud drying on her body.

The shower took a little longer than Abril had expected thanks to her hair being so muddy, but she was as quick as she could be about it. Once done, she dried off, and dressed. Abril didn't bother with makeup or fiddling with her hair. She'd already left the detectives alone much longer than intended, so she simply ran a brush through the wet strands, made a face at herself in the bathroom mirror, and then headed out of her room.

A glance at the clock as she entered the kitchen told her there should only be half an hour left of the washing cycle before she could switch her laundry to the dryer. That was something she wanted to do the moment she could since she had only one coat here and needed it to take Lilith out for potty breaks. Worried about getting distracted and forgetting to do it, she said, "Alexa, set the timer for twenty-eight minutes."

Abril waited for Alexa to announce that the timer was set, and then turned her attention to the detectives. Both men were seated at the island. Roberts was drinking from what appeared to be a glass of water, while Delacort was holding a coffee mug in hand. Lilith was on the floor between the two men.

The scene was almost cozy, Abril thought as she moved to the coffee machine. Casting an apologetic smile over her shoulder to the two men, she grabbed a mug out of the cupboard and then began to pour herself a coffee as she said, "Sorry I took so long. I tried to be quick, but"—she shrugged—"best laid plans and all that."

"It is fine," Roberts assured her easily. "I noticed the mud in your hair and expected it to take a bit of time for you to get it out. We just did what we could to help out and keep busy while we waited."

Abril was a little confused by the words, unsure what they could've done to help. Before she could ponder it too much, Lilith nudged her nose into her hand, distracting her. Startled at the fact that the dog had got up and come to her side without her noticing, Abril automatically gave the dog an affectionate pet. Feeling her damp fur, though, she looked at Lilith properly and noted that the yellow Lab was no longer mud covered. In fact, she was sparkling clean.

"Oh my gosh you gave Lilith a bath," Abril gasped. Glancing at the men, she grinned and asked, "Did you take her outside and hose her down?"

Detective Roberts looked amused at the question. Detective Delacort, on the other hand, sat up a little straighter, his mouth thinning. He was obviously insulted at the very suggestion, which made her frown. She hadn't meant to offend him. She just couldn't think of any other way they would've done it. They didn't know the house.

"Delacort gave her a bath in the guest bathroom down the hall while I washed the kitchen floor," Roberts explained.

"Oh! Well, thank you, Detective." She was smiling at the taller man when the rest of what Roberts had said suddenly caught her attention. *Delacort gave her a bath in the guest bathroom down the hall while I washed the kitchen floor.*

Abril straightened from petting Lilith and peered around at the hardwood floor. The tigerwood too was sparkling clean with not a trace of the mud that had been tracked around it earlier. In fact, she hadn't seen it this clean since Gina's housekeeper had quit two weeks ago. Unfortunately, Gina was hard on staff and was constantly losing and having to replace them. Well, actually, Abril was the one stuck with the chore of replacing staff, and she'd been looking for a replacement cook/housekeeper these last two weeks without luck so far. She needed someone who could handle Gina and wouldn't quit after a week. Abril would rather not have to replace another housekeeper a month from now.

"Both Lilith and the floor look lovely. Thank you, gentlemen," she said now. "Your help is greatly appreciated. Especially since it wasn't your responsibility, and must have been done out of pure kindness," Abril finished solemnly, and almost laughed when both men appeared to squirm a bit, obviously unused to, or at least uncomfortable, with her praise. Roberts just looked a bit discomfited as he waved away her thanks, but Delacort actually blushed. Abril thought that was positively adorable, but knew better than to comment on it, or tease him as she really wanted to do.

Picking up her coffee, she carried it over to claim the chair at the end of the island. "Okay. I know you have questions for me. I guess we better get to it."

Both men nodded, but it was Roberts who started. "Peters told us that you are house-sitting for your boss, a Miss Gina Spaldine, who has only owned the house for—" He paused to check what she suspected were his notes on the small tablet he'd pulled out, and then said, "She bought the house last summer, so eight months?"

"Almost nine," Abril corrected. "Gina bought the house from the Bransons at the beginning of August. It's now the end of April, so pretty much nine months ago."

"Right," Roberts tapped something into his tablet, and then asked, "Do you know anything about the Bransons?"

"Well, let's see," Abril murmured thoughtfully, and considered what she knew about the previous owners of the house. The Bransons had been kind enough to offer a tour and an explanation of how everything worked, things like when the septic tank had last been emptied and would need it again. When the filters for the furnace and water treatment should be changed, etcetera. Gina had left all of that up to Abril to sort out, so she'd spent some time with the couple, and they'd been friendly and chatty.

"The Bransons are a family of five—the parents, two sons, and a daughter," she began. "The children were all grown up and gone so they were downsizing." She paused, searching her mind, and then added, "They'd lived here for twenty years and there was only one owner before that who had built the house and lived here for four or five years before selling to them. I don't know their name, but the story Mrs. Branson told me is that the husband was the contractor, it was their dream house, but . . ." Abril shook her head. "She wasn't sure after all that time, but it was something along the lines of there was some kind of accident, the wife was paralyzed and used a wheelchair and the house just wasn't set up for that, or she couldn't stand living where there were so many memories of her life before the accident. Or both." Abril shrugged.

Roberts nodded. "Is there anything else you can tell us about the previous owners?"

"The Bransons?" she asked, unsure if he meant them or the couple before them.

"Yes. The Bransons," Roberts confirmed. "Do you know their first names? Or where they moved to?"

"You're thinking the bodies in the garden were put there by the Bransons?" she asked with dismay.

"That idea troubles you?" Detective Delacort asked gently.

Abril shifted in her seat and then shrugged help-lessly. "I mean I don't really know these people, but they were very nice to me. They didn't seem like crazy serial type killers to me."

Knowing that what she thought didn't really mat-ter, she stood abruptly and headed for the hallway to the guest bedrooms on this side of the house. She and Gina were temporarily using them as offices until the addition was finished. "I'll go check the purchasing contracts. That should have their first names on it."

She paused at the mouth of the hall to turn back and add, "Although, it seems to me they said they'd purchased a new house in Port somewhere or other." She frowned, trying to recall which town it was. There were a lot of lakeside towns an hour or so on either side of London named Port something or other; Port Bruce, Port Burwell, Port Stanley, Port Glasgow, Port Franks . . . Unfortunately, she couldn't recall at that moment which one they'd mentioned moving to.

Shrugging the concern away, she added, "I remember

that they owned a store in the city, a craft shop or something. I can't remember what it was called, although Mr. Branson told me the name at the time." Abril grimaced apologetically. "Unfortunately, I had no idea then that it might be important so didn't commit it to memory."

"Of course not," Detective Delacort said reassuringly.

She smiled at him with gratitude, and then turned into the hall again, saying, "I'll get those contracts."

Abril was a very organized person. It was what made her good at her job. She had a place for everything and kept everything in its place, so she was able to find things quickly when needed. Gina was less so, and apparently had gotten into the files at some point and mucked them up. Abril had filed away the purchasing contracts in a special file that she now couldn't find. It took several minutes for her to track it down, minutes during which she became more and more irritated and silently cursed her boss.

She knew that was silly. In the end, the files were actually Gina's, not hers, and her boss had every right to do what she wished with them. Unfortunately, though, it made her life more difficult when Gina ran roughshod through the filing cabinet. Something she'd done repeatedly since Abril had started to work for her.

Finally finding the contract in question, she pulled it out, slammed the drawer closed, and hurried out of her temporary office.

Five

"I found them!" Abril announced as she hurried into the kitchen, only to slow to a halt as she saw that Delacort was the only one still there.

"Forensics arrived," he explained when she peered from him to the empty seat where his partner had been. "Roberts went out to greet them and explain the situation."

"Oh." Nodding, Abril continued forward. She set the papers she'd fetched on the island before him, then reclaimed her seat. "That's the contract for the purchase of the house. Their names are Fred and Wilma."

Detective Delacort's eyebrows rose, but he pulled the pages closer to glance over them. After a moment, he said, "You are not kidding, Fred and Wilma are their names."

"Yeah, I was a little surprised too, at the time." She smiled faintly. "I mean, I don't want to be rude, but the only time I've ever heard of someone being named

Wilma before this was as a kid watching *The Flint-stones*. And his name being Fred? For real?" she asked with a grin.

"*The Flintstones*?" Detective Delacort echoed.

"It was a cartoon," she explained when he peered at her with obvious bewilderment. "Wilma was Fred Flint-stone's wife."

"Ah." Delacort smiled faintly. "I fear I have never seen the cartoon, and it has been much longer than the twenty years or so that it must've been since you were a child since I have heard the name Wilma."

Abril's eyebrows rose at the comment. He didn't appear to be that much older than her. By her guess, the man couldn't be more than maybe thirty years old, and that was a bit of a stretch really. He looked closer to twenty-five, but she suspected he had to be closer to thirty to be a detective. Of course, she could be wrong about that. Maybe it was ageist to think that homicide detectives would be older. Shrugging that concern away, she asked, "Will you be able to find them? The Bransons?"

He nodded as he perused the contract. "Now that we have their names, we should not have any problem finding them. If worse comes to worst, we can always contact their Realtor on this sale to see where they bought and moved to after here. The Realtor for this sale probably handled the purchase of their next home as well," he pointed out.

Abril nodded agreement, and then bit her lip briefly before saying, "You don't really think the Bransons are responsible for—I mean, maybe it was the family who lived here before the Bransons. Or maybe the house was built on an ancient burial site or something."

"It is possible the family before the Bransons are responsible for the skeletons Lilith found," he allowed and then said gently, "But the bones are not part of an ancient burial site. Roberts and I uncovered more of the bones attached to the skull and some material was revealed. Part of a faded blue denim shirt."

"Definitely not ancient then," Abril murmured.

"No," he agreed. "But the forensics crew will do their bit. Hopefully, they will be able to date the skeletons by the clothing they are wearing. If not, maybe we will get lucky and they will find something else with the bodies to tell us if it was the Bransons or who they bought the house from who is responsible for their deaths."

"Like ID," she suggested. "Learning who they are and when they went missing would help with that. But I'm sure the Bransons aren't responsible."

Delacort closed his notepad and smiled at her sympathetically. "You liked them."

Abril shrugged. "I never met the kids, but the parents were good people. They even emailed me after Gina moved in to make sure we found everything all right and didn't have any questions."

"Emailed you or Gina?"

"Me," she answered, and explained, "I'm always the contact for Gina. I was the contact with her lawyer and real estate agent too."

"Is that because your boss is difficult to get along with?" Delacort asked with interest.

"I wouldn't say that," Abril said carefully, not because it wasn't true, but because Gina was her boss. She wasn't going to insult her boss. In fact, she was always very careful to never paint Gina in a poor

light, no matter how irritated she got with her sometimes petulant, tyrannical behavior. Well, usually,
she thought with a pinch of guilt. Unfortunately, in a
moment of camaraderie with Officer Peters as they'd
waited by the skeletons . . . Well, it had been freezing
cold, and they'd been chatting to pass the time and she
may have mentioned that Gina had a problem holding on to employees, otherwise she'd have someone to
take the dog inside for them.

Abril was not going to say that again. Heck, she was
more than a little shocked that she'd even said it the
once. The cold must have been affecting her so that
her brain had not been functioning properly.

"Peters said you did," Delacort told her gently.

Abril cursed under her breath and then smiled with
chagrin. "Okay, I may have told him that she has a
little trouble keeping employees, but, really, she's a
good person. She's very creative, very talented, very
intelligent, and she can be charming. Unfortunately,
she's always very busy and has a dearth of patience,
which can make her abrasive at times when dealing
with certain issues."

"Very diplomatically stated," he told her with
amusement and then changed the subject. "So, you are
staying here for how long?"

"Until Gina comes back," she said simply.

"Which is when?"

When Abril hesitated, he asked, "You *do* have an
end date for her vacation, do you not?"

Abril blinked at his turn of phrase. He had a very
old-fashioned way of speaking. So did his partner.
Neither of them had yet used a single contraction. She
found that curious, but didn't comment on it and sim-

ply said, "She has a return ticket for two and a half weeks from now."

"But?" he queried, gaze narrowing on her.

Abril rolled her eyes. She was very aware that her expressions pretty much gave everything away in life. She'd never be a good poker player, or make her way as a con artist. Giving it up, she said, "But that's not a guarantee that she'll be back two and a half weeks from now."

Delacort's eyebrows inched up his forehead a bit. "She does not stick to her plans?"

"It's more like her plans are a sort of loose guideline," Abril corrected. "She *will* set a date and time for things to happen. However, if something pops up to interfere with those plans, she's open to changing them."

"Riiigghht," Delacort drew out the word, and then asked, "You do not have a problem with being expected to stay here indefinitely and at her whim?"

Abril smiled faintly at his expression. He was looking almost offended on her behalf. He wasn't the first one to have that reaction. But he was the first one to have it so soon after meeting her and before they'd become friends. On the other hand, she supposed she didn't normally tell people things like that right off the bat either. Shrugging those thoughts aside, she let her smile widen. "I mean what's there to have a problem with? There's a pool here, a hot tub, a games room, an exercise room . . . I mean, it's kind of like an exotic luxury hotel."

"Only without the staff to look after you." His tone was dry.

"Which means I don't have to tip anyone," she pointed out lightly.

He smiled reluctantly, and then asked, "You do have your own home, though?"

"Oh, right. You probably need my address for your report, don't you?" she said with realization. "I have a little studio apartment in the city." She rattled off the address and then grinned at the expression that covered his face. It was somewhere between horror and dismay. Her apartment was actually only a half a block away from the police station, an area that was possibly the worst part of the city. That was rather ironic to her mind. She would've thought that the police station being so close would mean it was an area where people behaved and crime was low. Unfortunately, it was just the opposite. The area was mostly populated with halfway houses and drug dens, with a few apartments and a lot of older houses offering rentals. It really was a bad area. She'd encountered strung-out junkies, passed-out drunks, and countless used needles on her way to her car in the mornings, and worse while making her way inside at night. But her studio apartment was newly renovated, lovely, and cheap because it was hard to get tenants there.

Seeing the struggle Delacort was having with the fact that she lived in such a dumpy area, Abril explained, "I used to have a penthouse in a better part of town, but with the hours I worked, sometimes I didn't even get home. I would just sack out on the couch in my office and get up the next day to continue working. In the end, I was paying a lot of money for a place that I only got to sleep in at the best of times, and sometimes not even that when I have to travel with Gina to deal with customers and clients."

"Do you have to travel a lot for work?"

"I probably spend a third of the year traveling for work," she guessed, and knew it was a conservative estimate, it was probably more than forty percent of the time. "Anyway, it seemed a waste to pay so much for a place I rarely got to enjoy, so I ended up getting rid of the penthouse and just getting the little studio apartment to sleep in for now. It saves me a heck of a lot of money, which I've just been socking away in the bank and investing."

Smiling faintly, she told him, "I could probably buy a house right now if I wanted. It would just be a waste of money because I'd rarely be there."

"You're very practical," he commented solemnly.

"That's me. The incredibly practical chick," Abril said lightly, and then her tone becoming more serious she said, "I'm very detail oriented. It makes for a good executive assistant, but also makes me boring."

"I do not see you as anywhere near boring," Delacort countered at once.

Abril was pretty sure her eyebrows flew right up off her face at that point. She managed to pull them back down and act as if she wasn't terribly flattered as she assured him, "Well, you'd be the first person to say so."

"I find that hard to believe."

"You're just saying that because I've got multiple skeletons in my garden. Well, my boss's garden anyway," she corrected herself.

"You do not think it is one body chopped up and spread around?" he asked with interest.

"Well, I suppose it could be, but most people don't have two right hands," she pointed out.

A smile of approval grew on his face. "You noticed

the two right hands. Well done. Peters did not notice that and he is an officer."

Abril shrugged. "Detail oriented, remember?"

"Yes, you certainly are."

They peered at each other in silence for a moment until Detective Delacort suddenly cleared his throat and straightened in his seat. Pulling out a notepad, he flipped it open to a blank page and asked, "Can you give me a full name please Abril?"

"Abril Anne Newman," she answered easily.

He made a note and then asked, "Can I have your phone number?"

When Abril's eyes widened slightly in surprise, he quickly added, "For the report."

"Oh, of course," she said flushing with embarrassment and wanting to smack herself in the forehead for thinking he might actually want her number for some personal reason. As nice and flattering as that would have been, she'd never been a femme fatale that men fell all over. Clearing her throat she quickly rattled off her phone number and watched him write it down, then glanced out the sliding doors when movement caught her eye. The excavated hole was directly outside the doors and somebody was climbing out of it using a ladder.

Curious, Abril stood and moved to the doors at the end of the kitchen. Her excitement turned to concern once she could see down into the busy beehive that the partially excavated area had become.

There were a lot of people in the large hole, all wearing special gear that covered them from head to toe in white so that the only thing showing was their faces and those were half obscured by masks. Seeing the white coveralls with hoods they wore over their heads and outerwear, the white boot covers over their shoes and boots, and the gloves on their hands, Abril felt guilt slide through her. She hadn't had any protective covering at all to prevent contaminating the scene.

Worse yet, Lilith had been all over the area. But then Officer Peters and the two detectives had been without protective gear as well, she recalled and would have relaxed a bit, but now that that worry was eased, others were crowding in to take its place. Like, there were a lot of people bustling around outside now. A lot. Too many to be able to guess how many. She actually had to count quickly under her breath. Apparently, not quietly enough she realized when Detective Delacort asked, his voice distracted, "Hmm?"

"Oh, nothing. I was just counting the people working out there. There seem to be a lot of them," she added a little worriedly and glanced toward the parking area in front of the house. The sliding door overlooked the side yard. She couldn't see much of the driveway, just the front ends of one, two, three—

Giving up her position by the door overlooking the hole, she moved to one of the large front windows to get the full picture of the driveway and parking area. Her face blanched with horror as she took in the many vehicles, both cars and vans, and all of them bearing the label *London Police*.

"Gina's going to kill me," she breathed with dismay.

The rustle of clothing announced Detective Delacort's approach as he joined her at the window. The heat of his body told her he'd arrived and stood directly behind her. As did his breath against her ear as he said, "She cannot blame you for this. You did not bury the bodies in the garden."

Abril let her breath out slowly, resisting the sudden ridiculous urge to lean back against his chest. Instead, she straightened slightly, and shook her head. "No. I didn't bury the bodies there. But by now the whole neighborhood must be aware of the foofaraw taking place in her yard and that's what she'll blame me for."

"What could she possibly expect you to do? You cannot prevent us from doing our job. That would be illegal."

"True," she murmured, but knew that made little difference. Gina would be upset, not at her necessarily, but she would definitely be upset that her beautiful new home had bodies buried around it. Not to mention that the police were now filling her driveway and parking on the street in front of her house as they dug up those bodies and investigated. Sadly, Abril was the only one Gina could vent to about it. And would. Unfortunately, that would take the shape of yelling and screaming at Abril unhappily and it would feel like she was getting hell.

"Wait," she said suddenly, as her gaze slid over a man carrying several large black zippered bags toward the excavated area. "He must be carrying at least a half dozen body bags."

"Yes," Delacort agreed, sounding a little mystified at what her point might be.

"But—" Sidling out from between him and the window, Abril crossed back to the sliding doors to look down into the excavated area again. Yes. As she'd thought she'd noted when she'd first looked, the people in the hole were still working, still uncovering bones in at least three different spots in the hole.

"Dear God. How many skeletons are down there?" she breathed with dismay.

Delacort joined her at the door and peered out at the working members of the forensics team.

"More than three apparently," he said quietly and then placed a hand on her upper back when she slumped where she stood. Frowning, he asked with concern. "Are you okay?"

"Yes, I just . . ." Her voice died off as his hand began to move, gently massaging her tense muscles. It felt so good. Seriously. Her tension was melting under his talented fingers, her body leaning into the pressure as he kneaded her shoulders with first just the one hand and then with both as he stepped behind her. His hands moved down to her trapezius muscles and Abril heard herself moan as he worked her. Then he let his hands move to her sides to grasp her by the waist.

For one minute, she was afraid he was going to set her away from him and stop what he was doing, but then his hands began to move again. The kneading became more of a caressing though, and she raised her hands, one clasping the window frame, the other pressing flat to the glass as his fingers slid up her sides until the tips of them trailed over the sides of her breasts before gliding back down to her waist again.

While Abril's muscles had relaxed under his touch, everything else seemed to be tightening. Her nipples were becoming hard little buds, her toes were curling on the hardwood, and her thighs were pressing tight together in response to the tingling and pooling that had started between them under the influence of what he was doing . . . and in anticipation of more.

Much to her disappointment, though, there was no more. His hands suddenly stopped massaging and caressing. Instead, he simply held her, his hands resting lightly at her waist, his breath stirring her hair, his body hard against her back and butt.

Abril's eyes had drifted half closed, but blinked open now with realization. She'd leaned back so far into his touch that she was resting against his chest and other parts, in effect, requiring him to spoon her or let her fall.

"Coffee." The word came out on a breathless squeak as she forced herself to straighten away from him. She quickly slid out from between him and the door and took a step away. "I promised Officer Peters coffee."

"Roberts took him a cup when he went out," Delacort told her, his voice deep and so goddamned sexy that it garnered the same response as if he'd caressed her again.

Swallowing, she licked her lips and made herself meet his gaze. "I'm sorry. I shouldn't have—" Abril paused abruptly because . . . what could she say? *I shouldn't have enjoyed your touch so much I leaned into you and got all turned on?* She couldn't say that. So, what could she say to end the sudden awkwardness she was feeling?

Lilith caught her attention by shifting to her feet and staring at her, tongue hanging out and tail wagging. Inspired, Abril said, "I should take Lilith out to do her business."

She didn't wait for a response from him, but hurried over to Lilith and then hesitated. She would have to keep the Lab on a leash until the forensics team had finished working in the excavated area, and she wasn't sure where the leash she'd had on Lilith earlier was. It didn't matter, she decided. Gina had at least half a dozen extra leashes. Thinking she'd worry about where the other one went later, Abril hurried to the coat closet beside the sliding doors to grab one, then walked back to Lilith to snap it onto her collar.

She led the Lab out of the kitchen to the entry, and was reaching for the door when Delacort caught her arm to stop her. Turning in surprise, she peered at him in question.

"Shoes," he said simply.

Abril glanced down to see that not only did she not have shoes on, but she was missing socks as well. Embarrassed by her own stupidity, she muttered under her breath and tugged Lilith with her as she hurried to the large coat closet across from the entrance. She'd brought a pair of dress shoes for work, and runners for after work. The presently mud-covered shoes in the laundry room were her work shoes. She would be using her running shoes.

"Do not forget a coat."

Abril straightened abruptly in alarm.

"What is it?" Delacort asked, spotting her reaction to his words, but Abril didn't bother to respond, she was rushing away from him through the living room to the hall, dragging Lilith with her. Not that she really had to drag her, the pup was more than pleased with this new game and happily ran along beside her as Abril raced up the hall to the laundry room.

The good news was, the washer was done. The bad news? Laundry Fairies hadn't put her coat into the dryer for her and shifted her muddy jeans and other clothes from the floor into the washer . . . and her coat was now clean, but wet, she saw when she pulled it out of the washer and held it up. She was turning it to be sure there were no traces of mud left that would necessitate another run through the washer when Lilith decided she'd had enough of the laundry room and made a run for the door. The unexpected move yanked the leash from her hands and had her grip on the coat slipping. It was headed for the floor when Delacort appeared beside her and snatched it up before her brain even fully realized what was happening. He also had Lilith's leash, she noted as she turned to face him.

"Thank you," she said with relief.

"My pleasure." Delacort handed her the wet coat. "I shall take Lilith out while you tend to drying your coat."

"Oh, no! You don't have to do that. I can take her out," she said, reaching for the leash.

"Do you have another coat?" he asked, not releasing the leash she was trying to take from him.

"No. But I'm sure she'll be quick if I keep her away from the dig site and tell her to do her business."

Delacort had the good grace not to laugh in her face. "Your hair is still a little damp from your shower earlier, and you are wearing a T-shirt and jeans. You would catch your death out there."

"Oh, but—" her words died when his mouth suddenly swooped down to cover hers.

Six

Kissing Abril to silence her protests had seemed like a good idea when it struck Crispin. Actually, it had seemed like a good excuse to be able to kiss her, which he'd wanted to do since joining her at the window. But he'd meant it to be a quick kiss before he left to tend to Lilith. Unfortunately, he hadn't accounted for life mate attraction. Of course, like all immortals, he'd heard of life mate attraction; about how powerful it was. That it was all-consuming. Overwhelming even. But having never experienced it himself before this, he'd assumed the stories were exaggerated.

They were not. Crispin couldn't stop with a quick kiss. He did try to end it and raise his head, but the moment he did, Abril let out a breathy little sigh and he was lost. His mouth returned to hers at once, catching the tail end of her sigh in his mouth as he covered hers again. He did manage not to over-whelm her with his suddenly raging passion. He had just enough self-control to slow himself and give her a long, lingering, very deep kiss. But that control snapped when Abril moaned, slid her fingers into his hair to clasp his head, and arched her body into his invitingly.

Groaning, Crispin let Lilith's leash slip from his fingers so that he could slide his hands around Abril; the fingers of one spreading on her back, while the other grasped her bottom to urge her closer. Once he had her plastered against him, Crispin held her there with the hand on her ass, and brought the other around to find one breast through her clothes as he thrust his tongue into her mouth.

It felt amazing. Her body was hot and soft against his, her mouth eager and welcoming as she kissed him back with as much hunger as he was experiencing, and that was doubling by the minute as it bounced between them. But it wasn't enough. He wanted more. He wanted all of her. He wanted to rip her clothes off, kiss every inch of her, lift her onto the washing machine and—

The acrid smell of urine interrupted his thoughts and had Crispin freezing, his mouth breaking from hers as his brain struggled to think clearly enough to sort out an explanation for the unpleasant scent. Surely, she hadn't—

"Lilith!" Abril gasped with horror and was suddenly twisting out of his arms.

Releasing her, Crispin watched blankly as she ran to the dog, grabbed her leash and tried to pull the Labrador from where she was presently relieving herself . . . On Abril's muddy clothes.

Thoughts suddenly clearing, Crispin cursed himself

and crossed the room. Taking the leash from Abril, he hurried Lilith toward the door, saying apologetically, "This is my fault. I should have taken her outside right away as intended. Leave the mess. I will put your clothes in the wash when I get back."

He didn't wait for a response, but hurried Lilith through the house to the front door and outside.

"There you are. I was just coming in to talk to you."

Crispin paused on the steps at those words from his partner, and then followed Lilith down to the walkway. The Lab immediately tried to head to the left, toward the excavation site, but he reined her in and instead made her go to the right and the undisturbed grass waiting there.

"What were you coming to talk to me about?" Crispin asked as he walked Lilith toward that side of the house, as far away from the muddy hole as possible.

"They have finished with the preliminary report and pictures and have started on uncovering the skeletons," Roberts informed him. "While doing so, they've uncovered part of what might be a fourth skeleton if the hands are not from it and the first skull."

"So, there are either two skeletons that have been cut into pieces and strewn around, or four skeletons," Crispinus said solemnly. He considered that briefly and then said. "It will be four skeletons."

"Yes," Roberts agreed. "The bones are all five feet down. It's hard to imagine anyone digging several holes that deep just to bury hands here, skulls there, etc. We either have a mass murder here, or the victims of a serial killer."

Crispin nodded and glanced toward the excavation

site as someone climbed out carrying a medium-sized plastic drum he knew would contain the dirt and particulates from around the skeletons they were working on. "Do they think four will be the end number?"

"They do not yet know," Roberts admitted, glancing back as well.

"Do they have any idea how long the bodies have been down there?"

Roberts shook his head. "Not yet. Bill says he will not know until he gets them back to the lab."

"According to the sales contract, the house was built in the late nineties," Crispin told him.

"Then the bodies went in after that," Roberts decided. "They usually dig out wider than the foundation when building a house, and all the bones Lilith dug up were close to the wall."

Crispin grunted agreement.

"Where is Abril?" Roberts asked suddenly.

"Inside." Seeing the question in his partner's gaze, he explained, "Her coat was in the washer and needed to go in the dryer before she could wear it. She was going to bring out Lilith herself anyway, even without a coat, but I insisted on doing it rather than see her out here in the cold, coatless."

"Ah." Roberts hesitated, and then asked. "What are you going to do?"

"About what?" he asked warily.

"About her being your life mate."

Crispin gave a half laugh. "What do you think I am going to do? I am going to woo her."

"How?"

"How?" Crispin echoed with confusion, and then simply stared at his partner, because honestly, he had no answer to the question. He hadn't dated in centuries, millennia even. He had no idea how modern women liked to be wooed.

"I am not sure," he confessed finally, and then added, "Suggestions would be appreciated."

Alarm crossed his partner's face and then Alexander shook his head. "You are on your own here, my friend. I have not wooed a woman in more than two centuries and have no idea how to go about it myself in this modern era. I have no advice to give."

"Great," Crispin muttered, thinking that he was screwed then.

Abril stared at the empty doorway Detective Delacort had disappeared through and forced herself to take deep breaths. Her body was in complete chaos at the moment; tingling, wet, and wanting. And it was all Delacort's fault. The man was one hell of a kisser. In fact, she couldn't recall a single experience in her past where a simple kiss had affected her as much as the two or three minutes in Detective Delacort's arms had.

She frowned to herself at the thought. Detective Delacort? Dear God, she didn't even know the man's first name. Closing her eyes briefly as she squirmed inwardly with shame, Abril counted to ten to try to calm herself, and then counted to ten again before giving it up and picking up her coat. She had apparently dropped it while he was kissing her.

She tossed it into the dryer. A fabric softener sheet followed. She closed the door and turned the machine on, then surveyed the muddy clothes in the corner that Lilith had abused.

Part of her just wanted to throw the items out, but good sense made her open the washer door and cross the room to collect the pile of soiled clothes. Nose wrinkling with disgust at the acrid scent coming off the items, she straightened her arms to hold them as far away as she could, and picked up speed to get them in the washer and away from herself as quickly as possible.

Abril slammed the door closed and was just putting the laundry detergent into the dispenser drawer when the house phone began ringing. She quickly closed the drawer and turned on the washer before hurrying out of the laundry room and rushing up the hall to the living room to answer the phone there with a breathless, "Hello?"

"Oh, thank heavens! I was starting to worry. I tried your cell first, called twice and didn't get an answer, so tried the house phone. If you hadn't answered I was going to call the police for a wellness check."

"Gina," Abril breathed, dropping to sit on the couch. "Sorry. I was in the laundry room and my cell phone is in the kitchen. I didn't hear it ringing."

"The laundry room?"

She wasn't surprised at the query in her boss's voice. Gina had only left the morning before, and Abril had only stayed since the night before that. It *would* seem odd that she'd need to do laundry already, and what else would she be doing in the laundry room?

"Yeah," she said now. "I let Lilith loose to run around the yard while I was talking to you earlier and she decided to explore the excavated area. It had rained after the men left, the ground was muddy, she was digging and was filthy by the time I got off the phone and found her there. Then she . . . dug up a bone," she finally settled on. It was the truth, just not the whole truth, but would do for now. There was no sense upsetting Gina during her vacation, she told herself as she continued, "Lilith wouldn't come when I called and I fell in the mud while trying to get her. In the end, we were both chocolate brown all over, both needed a bath, and my coat and clothes needed washing. Hence why I was in the laundry room."

"Oh no! You poor thing," Gina said sympathetically. "Well, there's nothing urgent that needs taking care of today. You take the rest of the day off, make yourself a tea, put your feet up, and watch a movie cuddled up with Lilith on the couch."

Abril glanced at her watch to see that it was only 3:00. She usually worked until 6:00. Actually, she usually worked until well past 6:00, but the point was she'd already wasted two hours today with the police and whatnot—she blushed as she recalled the "whatnot" she'd enjoyed with Detective Delacort in the laundry room, and then pushed the memory aside and said, "Thank you, Gina, but that's not necessary. I still have a couple of things I wanted to get done today and—"

"And you can do them tomorrow," Gina said firmly. "I'm your boss. What I say goes, and I say you're taking the rest of the day off and relaxing."

"Okay. Thank you," Abril said solemnly, her gaze wandering to the large picture window at the front of the living room. It gave her a perfect view of Detective Delacort and his partner talking as they followed a leashed Lilith around the grass on this side of the yard. She watched them for a moment, worrying over what they might be talking about. Surely Delacort wouldn't tell Roberts about what had happened in the laundry room, would he? It had just been a kiss. One hell of an explosive, carnal kiss maybe, but still just a kiss. Besides she was single and he was single . . . Wasn't he? How the hell would she know? She didn't even know his name.

"Don't you think?" Gina asked.

Pulled back to her conversation with her boss, Abril frowned as she tried to catch up on what she'd missed while distracted by staring at Delacort. What had Gina been talking about?

"I mean, I gave him my number in case of *emergencies*. But Jackson deciding he wants to sit in on the casting for the commercial just doesn't seem like an emergency to me," Gina continued. "Especially when that won't be happening for another month at least. Honestly! People are such a pain in the ass at times. I don't have the patience for them. That's why I usually make you deal with them. I should have done the same with Jackson and given him your number instead of mine.

"Anyway," Gina continued, "I explained I'm out of the country, can't deal with him right now, and he should call the office. Of course, he knows the offices are in my house, so immediately asked who was at the house if I was out of the country in this *'Aha! I caught you!'* voice. He's such an ass," she said with disgust. "So, of course, I told him it was you. That you'd be there overseeing the renos the entire time I'm gone. Then he started asking all these questions. What was going on at the house? Why was there an excavator there and people coming and going, etcetera. I realized then that the real reason he called was to get the scoop on the renos, so cut him off, said my friends were waiting and I had to go and hung up.

"Annoying man," Gina muttered. "Honestly, remind me never to accept a job with anyone who lives on my street again. He's been nothing but a pain in the ass from the beginning, sticking his nose in everywhere and wanting to know everything I was having done at the house." Gina huffed out an irritated breath, and then said apologetically, "So, I thought I'd better call and give you a heads-up that Jackson will probably call, or maybe even show up at the door to grill you on what's going on since I didn't answer any questions."

"Thank you for the heads-up," Abril said with real appreciation. She couldn't stand Jackson either. There was just something about him that gave her the heebie-jeebies.

"Feel free to let his calls go to voice mail and not answer the door to him," Gina added. "At this point, I think I'd be fine with losing him as a client. I just wish I could lose him as a neighbor too."

Abril smiled faintly at the claim.

"Anyway, I should go. They're waiting on me to go to dinner."

Eyebrows rising, Abril glanced at her watch again. Italy was six hours ahead of London, Ontario. "Isn't it a little after 9:00 there? That's late for dinner."

"Not in Italy. Italians usually have dinner between 8:30 and 10:30. The restaurants that open before 7:00 are catering to tourists and we don't want tourist food, we want real Italian food."

"Ah," Abril said with understanding. "Well, have a nice dinner then."

"I will. Thanks. Call if there are any issues. Otherwise, I'll call again tomorrow to check in."

"Okay," she said, and responded to Gina's ciao with goodbye before hanging up.

Dropping back to lean against the couch, Abril considered everything for a moment. There were skeletal remains in the garden. Police vehicles were cluttering the driveway with a swarm of forensics people presently all over the house, or at least the side yard. A handsome detective who may or may not have a first name, and who may or may not be married had rocked her world with a simple kiss. And she might have to deal with the creepy and annoying neighbor, Jackson, who presently was also a client.

Great, she thought. It was all kind of a mixed bag of crap to her mind. Although, the kiss hadn't been crap. It was just that she knew so little about the man who had done the kissing that she was feeling vulnerable and even a bit embarrassed, but she still had to deal with him. Unless he too was embarrassed and uncomfortable and left his partner to deal with her from now on, she thought. For some reason, that possibility alarmed her.

Muttering under her breath about her own wishy-washy nature, Abril pushed herself to her feet and headed for the kitchen, only to change direction and head for the front door instead when the doorbell sounded. She'd expected it to be Detective Delacort returning with Lilith, so was surprised to open the door and find Officer Peters there.

"Your coffee cup. Thank you. It was delicious and helped warm me up," he said, holding out the empty cup.

"Oh, you're welcome," Abril said as she took the cold mug, and then feeling guilty, admitted, "Actually, I made the pot of coffee, but Detective Roberts was good enough to pour you a cup, and doctor it himself while I was busy getting info for them, so it's really him you should actually thank."

"He told me, and I did thank him," Peters said with a smile.

"Oh, okay." She paused briefly and then offered, "Would you like another cup?"

After a hesitation, he admitted, "I'd love another cup. But I'm afraid it would make me need to relieve myself and there won't be a porta potty here until tomorrow and—"

"What?" Abril interrupted with amazement. "A porta potty? And tomorrow? They won't be done today?"

"Oh." Peters blinked at her questions, glanced nervously toward where Detectives Delacort and Roberts were walking Lilith, and then turned back with resignation and said, "I guess they didn't tell you about the other skeleton."

"The other skeleton?" Abril echoed with confusion. "What other skeleton?"

"Apparently, while working on the first set of skeletal remains—the skull Lilith first revealed," he added to clarify for her, "while working on that, they uncovered evidence of at least one more victim near it. So, if the hands in the other corner don't belong to the bones in the first area, then there are four sets of skeletal remains that need to be uncovered, catalogued, photographed, and removed. It's a pretty lengthy process."

"How lengthy?" Abril asked, dread building in the pit of her stomach.

"Porta potty long," Peters said simply.

Taking that to mean the man had no idea exactly how long it would take, Abril cleared her throat and asked, "You can't even give me an estimate?"

Peters shook his head. "Sorry. There's only been one other case where a body had to be exhumed since I transferred here from Windsor. It took two, maybe three days to handle that one, but it was only one body. They're dealing with two to four here, and possibly more. I really can't say how long it will take."

Abril was fretting over that when he added reassuringly, "It'll get faster once the archeology students get here."

"Archaeology students?" Abril echoed with confusion.

"Yes. I guess an archaeology professor at the university is a friend of Bill's, the head of our forensics team, and the professor has agreed to bring his class out tomorrow to help out. They both think it will be a learning experience for them."

"A learning experience?" Abril tilted her head slightly as her mind raced. "Are they thinking this is an old gravesite for native Americans, after all?"

"No," he told her regretfully.

"Because the bones are too close to the house," she said for him.

"Yes," Peters agreed.

"Then how will it be a learning experience exactly?" she asked, not understanding that part.

"I gather that exhuming murder victims uses pretty much the same techniques as they use at archaeological digs. And this isn't the first time the professor has brought his students to watch the retrieval of skeletal remains, although it was only one skeleton at a time before this. So, of course, usually the students only get to watch, since all of them working around one body would be more disruptive than anything. But Bill apparently plans to put the students to work this time to speed up the dig. The professor's graduating class will help remove the skeletons and the dirt around them."

"I'm sorry, the dirt around them?" Abril asked with uncertainty.

Peters nodded. "As well as the dirt from directly on top of them." When she simply stared at him blankly, he realized more explanation was needed. "You see when skeletal remains are found and foul play is suspected, they take any dirt around the remains in case there is evidence in the soil that might help identify the victims, or explain how they died, or even help identify the murderer."

Abril considered his words, her mind slowly computing what she'd just learned. What it boiled down to was that it looked as if there were going to be police, forensics people, and archaeological students around for quite a while. For days, possibly weeks. Which meant the renovations would be delayed again . . . at least until the bodies were removed and the scene cleared for the construction crew to continue their work.

None of this was good news, but there was nothing that could be done about it. The only way that might've avoided all of this was if she had dug up and got rid of the bones herself rather than call the police. Which, of course, she would never have done even had she known the trouble the bones were going to cause. Well . . . probably she wouldn't have.

"Right," she said finally, running a hand through her

hair. Letting it drop to her side, she said, "You don't need to bring in a porta potty. They can use the bathroom here. You too, of course, and any other officers who have to be on site."

"Thank you, that's very kind of you. I'll let the others know."

When he then hesitated on the step, she asked, "Do you need it now? You mentioned not wanting more coffee because then you'd have to—"

"Yeah," Peters interrupted with a smile. "If you don't mind?"

"Not at all," she assured him and stepped back to let him enter, saying, "I'll make you that second coffee in the meantime."

She closed the door behind him once Peters was in. When he paused in the entry, she assumed he was going to take his shoes off. As she started into the kitchen, she pointed out, "There's a bench right there that you can sit on to take off your shoes."

"Yeah."

It was the concerned sound to his voice more than anything that made her pause to look at him. He was still standing, staring into the living room with a frown.

"What's wrong?" she asked, returning to his side and peering at the room now as well. The entry was actually almost part of the living room. The only thing delineating the two spaces being the flooring, marble in the entry area, carpet in the living room.

Her gaze sliding back to Peters, she realized that it was the floor he was staring at with an unhappy expression.

"You have cream-colored carpet here," he said finally.

"Yes," she agreed.

"Well, I don't think anybody working in the excavation should be coming in here and crossing the carpet. Even if they take their boots off they might carry in dirt on their clothes and track it through the house. Even I shouldn't be in here right now. I was down in the hole earlier. I don't wanna mess up the carpet."

"I think you're safe if you take your shoes off. I don't see any dirt on you," she said, glancing over his clothing. When he gave in and sat down on the bench to remove his shoes, she added, "But if you're concerned about the others who are actually doing the digging, there's a side door on the same side as the excavation, but closer to the back of the house. It enters into a short hall between the laundry room and another bathroom. The floor there is engineered hardwood. We can throw some plastic down, or use that heavy paper—dry sheathing I think they call it. The stuff they use to protect flooring during construction. There's still a roll of it here from when they were doing the interior renovations."

"That might be okay." Peters finished removing his shoes and stood. "Maybe show it to me before you go make that coffee, so I can see if it will work."

"Sure," she said lightly and started to lead him through the house.

Seven

"I wouldn't worry about it too much," Roberts said.

"Not worry about how to woo my life mate?" Crispin peered at his partner dubiously.

"I just mean stop panicking," Roberts said and when Crispin opened his mouth to deny he was, his partner added, "Do not even try to deny it. I can hear your thoughts, remember?"

Crispin let his mouth snap closed. He really hated being so easily read now. It was definitely a drawback to finding a life mate.

"Look," Roberts said, interrupting his inner grumbling, "you will have plenty of time to sort out how to woo Abril. This is not going to be a quick investigation. It will take days, maybe even weeks, to get the bodies out. You can use that as an excuse to hang around here and interact with her."

"True," Crispin agreed. They'd been brainstorming on ways to woo Abril for several minutes now, and not coming up with much. From what he had seen of modern society, there was more "hooking up" going on nowadays than actual dating. There was also a lot of phone play: texting back and forth, sexting, and sending nude photos seemed to be the order of the day. At least that was how it seemed from listening to their single, mortal coworkers talk.

Wooing in his day had been a completely different animal. But courting a woman had changed with the times. He knew that twenty or thirty years ago dinner and a movie had been the thing, and that would have made this all much easier. But apparently that was no longer the thing, and the phone was key.

Crispin was not someone who enjoyed texting, or the phone in general. It was his opinion that cell phones were one of the worst things to happen to mankind. He supposed it came in handy when your car broke down in a rural area, or when a sudden health issue struck a mortal, but otherwise it had become something of a pain in the ass. From what he had seen, cell phones had become addictive. Kids and adults in their early twenties and even older, appeared always to have to be on them. It made questioning them when on a case something of a challenge.

More importantly to him though, it meant you just couldn't escape people. When the telephone was first invented, he'd thought it was grand. It had made communication much swifter than using couriered messages and such, and if you didn't want to be disturbed, you simply did not answer. People would assume you were not home. Now, with cell phones, you couldn't do that. They had been made to carry with you. If you didn't answer, the caller knew you were avoiding their call. You were never unreachable with a cell phone.

He himself preferred to actually speak to people in person. At least that's what he told himself, but he supposed the truth was that he liked to avoid people as much as possible and preferred just to be left alone. With Abril, though, he knew it was going to be different. He wanted to see her face-to-face. He wanted to speak to her, and yes, he wanted to do all sorts of other things to her. He just needed to sort out how to woo her to the point of doing those things without overwhelming her so much that she ran for the hills.

"So . . ." Roberts said.

When he didn't continue, Crispin glanced at him in question. "So what?"

"You kissed her, and it was really hot."

"How the hell—" Crispin began furiously, and then stopped and simply scowled at his partner as he realized he had probably been shouting out the memory to Alexander since he'd joined him. Finally, he just said, "Yes."

Roberts smiled faintly and nodded, but then cautioned, "You might want to ease up on that."

Crispin peered at him sharply. "What do you mean?"

His partner hesitated and then said slowly, "Abril seems like a nice girl, but . . ."

He narrowed his eyes. "But what?"

"I just would not want you scaring her off with life mate passion before she gets to know you."

Crispin's eyebrows rose. "I thought people today were all about 'hookups' and such."

"Some maybe. I mean, that seems to be the case amongst the single cops we work with. But that does not mean everybody is like that and she may be some-one who is not. Besides, even if she is, the depth of life mate passion can apparently be overwhelming. It might scare her off if you move too quickly," he pointed out. "I just think you should take it slow. At least until I can get a better read of her and see how she is likely to react."

Crispin frowned. He wasn't sure he wanted his buddy to get a better read on Abril. He wasn't happy with Alexander reading him, but he definitely wouldn't be happy with him reading his mate. Especially when Crispin couldn't do that himself.

"Then just take it slow," Roberts said, obviously having heard his thoughts on the matter. "Let her take the lead."

Crispin nodded. That seemed a reasonable sug-gestion to him. Let her take the lead. He could do that. Maybe. It would help if he wasn't so attracted to the woman. He'd thought she was a cute, perky little thing on first seeing her, but now that he'd touched and kissed her, she was a goddamned god-dess. It would be hard to resist that attraction when she was stood in front of him, all soft and sexy. He would try though.

"In the meantime, we should go door to door and question the neighbors. We can take the car."

When Crispin glanced to him with surprise, Rob-erts shrugged and said, "I don't know about you, but I could use a blood break."

"Oh. Yes. Good idea," Crispin murmured. Now that Roberts had mentioned it, he was aware that he could use a bag of the red liquid himself and they had a cooler of it in the car. They could grab a quick bag as they drove to the first house on the block to start their interview with the neighbors.

Abril closed the file she'd been working on for the last couple of hours and glanced at the clock. It was almost 6:00. Close enough, she decided, her workday was done. Despite Gina's order, she hadn't curled up on the couch with Lilith and a tea for the rest of the afternoon. First, she had already spent several hours that day not working because of the skeletal remains that she had found. But more importantly, not putting in the time today on work that needed doing, would have just meant working longer hours the next day to do what hadn't got done. Actually, even with the work she'd done that afternoon, she'd probably be putting in overtime to finish what needed doing.

Deciding that wasn't something she wanted to think about just then, Abril turned off her computer. She then swiveled her desk chair around to get up, only to find Lilith's head immediately on her knees, her sad eyes looking up at her and tail slowly wagging.

"Wow, you're really good with the guilt there, girl," she said with amusement, but gave in and began to cuddle and pet her. Lilith's arrival in her office about five minutes after she'd sat down to work had told her that Delacort had returned her. A glance at the security monitor on her desk showed he hadn't come in with her and was still outside. He must've opened the door, let her in, and then gone back to work himself.

Installing the security system, all the cameras, and a magnetic vehicle driveway alarm that sounded anytime a vehicle drove up the driveway was the first thing Gina had done when she'd purchased the house. It had seemed a smart thing to Abril, considering Gina was a woman living alone. She was also often grateful for the cameras and the monitor in her office. Anytime the driveway alarm sounded in the kitchen, all she had to do was look at the monitor to see if it was something that she needed to address. Otherwise, she'd be having to jump up and run to the front of the house every time the alarm went off.

Sometimes, it was just someone pulling in to turn around on the road, or door-to-door salesmen she never bothered to answer the door to. Abril hadn't even realized there was such a thing as door-to-door sales anymore . . . until a guy trying to sell frozen meat delivery, and then someone selling solar panels or something had come to the door. The cameras and monitor had come in handy to help her avoid those salesmen, and were helping her at the moment by allowing her to see the activity presently taking place in the yard. The forensics team was still hard at work, but Roberts and Delacort were now nowhere to be seen. Their car was gone too, she noted. Officer Peters, however, was still there.

Abril decided then that it might be a good idea to take Lilith on another trip outside before she had to prepare dinner for them both. Not because she wanted to maybe chat with Peters to see if the two detectives were done for the night and might be back tomorrow. Certainly not! She was only thinking of Lilith's comfort.

The thought made Abril snort to herself. She so wanted to know if there was a chance that she'd see

Detective Delacort again. Shaking her head at herself, she caught Lilith's head in both hands, met her gaze and said, "Potty?"

Lilith immediately backed excitedly from her petting hands and hurried out of her office.

"I'd guess that's a yes," Abril said with amusement as she stood to follow her to the kitchen.

Unsure what had happened to the leash she'd put on the Lab when Delacort had taken her out, Abril fetched another one from the closet. She then glanced around for Lilith, unsurprised to see she was standing at the sliding doors, watching the activity outside as she waited. They usually let her out that door. It was just easier. Now, however, that wasn't an option.

"Come on, girl. Outside." Abril patted her leg and headed in the opposite direction. Lilith hesitated a moment, but then followed. She even sat patiently while Abril pulled on her shoes and her newly cleaned and dried coat. The Lab then stood, but remained still for Abril to clip the leash onto her collar.

Peters was leaning against his car over by the excavation site when Abril and Lilith stepped outside. Spotting her, he smiled and waved. She smiled and waved back, but then headed in the opposite direction, walking Lilith to the grass that stretched out to the right of the driveway. As expected, the Lab was ready for this outing and relieved herself pretty quickly. When Lilith then tried heading toward the other side of the house, Abril let her. But only until they'd reached Officer Peters. Reining her in then, Abril held her in check as she turned to ask him, "All by yourself now?"

"Yeah. Detectives Roberts and Delacort are out

questioning the neighbors. They'll be back though," he told her.

Abril just nodded, trying not to look like she cared. She peered toward the people working in the excavation. Officer Peters's car was much closer to it than it had been. But then she'd heard Roberts telling him earlier to move his car forward and sit in it to keep warm while he watched the site and waited for the forensics team. He'd moved it quite close. Standing at the front of the vehicle as they were, she could see right down into the large hole and the activity taking place. There were only two people now, kneeling around the first body that Lilith had dug up. It had only been a skull then; now the bones that made up the neck, the clavicles, the first couple of ribs, and the upper arms were on display. She could also see that what looked like the bones of the lower half of a foot had been uncovered next to the neck bones and above the left clavicle. Probably not the skull guy's foot, she thought with a frown and asked, "How late will they be working today?"

"I'm not sure," Peters admitted, and then grinned and added, "I'm just a lowly patrolman, no one tells me anything."

Abril smiled in return, but then glanced back to the skeleton and the workers in white overalls, booties, and gloves. "Well, they'll have to stop when the sun goes down. They won't be able to see what they're doing then."

"Yes," Peters agreed, and then added, "Unless they have work lights coming to light up the area."

"Work lights?" she asked with alarm, thinking that would be like a neon sign to the neighbors, rousing their curiosity and probably bringing them around en masse.

"But I don't think they do," he said quickly on noting her expression. "I think they only requested a tent. At least, that's all I heard Bill ask for when he called in."

"What do they need with a tent?" Abril asked at once. "They aren't sleeping here, are they?"

"They aren't, but I might be," Peters said dryly.

Abril raised her eyebrows. "Really?"

"Someone has to guard the site overnight to be sure it isn't messed with," he pointed out. "That might be me, at least until my shift ends. Or they might send somebody else out. I don't know yet."

Abril glanced back to the area in question. She didn't think they'd have to worry about human invaders messing with the site. Certainly, she wouldn't be going near it. However, there were a lot of dogs in the neighborhood, as well as coyotes and other animals in the woods behind the houses that might be interested in the bones. She supposed guarding it wasn't a bad idea. "But the tent isn't for you or whoever guards the site, is it? I mean you can hardly guard it if you're lounging around in a tent."

"No. The tent is to protect the site in case it rains again."

"Oh." She hadn't thought of that. "Sensible I guess."

Lilith was tugging pretty hard on the leash, eager to join the people working in the hole, digging up the treasure she'd discovered. Holding her back was starting to be a strain on her muscles, so she finally said, "I suppose I should take her inside, before she breaks loose and starts digging up more bodies or something."

"Yeah, Bill wouldn't like that. Digging is his job."

Abril chuckled at what was obviously a joke and gave him a little wave as she dragged Lilith away to take her inside.

She fed Lilith first, and then started her own supper. Sadly, it took much longer to make her meal than it had to heat up the homemade dog food Gina insisted on for her "baby." Lilith was done eating long before Abril was finished cooking fries and Bob's famous chili. Sadly, Lilith was ready to go outside again just as Abril deemed her meal ready and pulled out a plate to serve herself.

"Now?" She groaned, eyeing her unhappily. When Lilith whimpered, ran to the sliding door, and gave her the big sad eyes, Abril gave in with a sigh. "Fine. But I'm hungry. So, there will be no messing around. No sniffing half the yard before deciding on the perfect spot to poop. You will take care of business and come right back in. Understood?"

Abril wasn't surprised when Lilith didn't respond. Still, she muttered under her breath about how she'd got stuck watching the dog when she didn't have a dog herself as she set down her plate. Abril then turned the flames off under the chili, checked the fries in the oven, turned that off as well, and went to grab Lilith's leash.

A new vehicle had joined the others in the driveway when Abril stepped outside. It was a white van with the police logo on the side. She was eyeing it with interest when Officer Peters and another man appeared from the other side of the van, carrying items toward the excavation area. Abril was curious, but Lilith was tugging at her leash, forcing her back to what they were out there for.

Turning her attention to the Labrador, she followed her around the corner of the house. It was a spot Lilith always ended up going to whenever she needed to do number two. Abril supposed she felt more protected here. The main house was on one side, Abril in front, and the pool room jutted out from the back of the house behind Lilith. It left only one direction unprotected, and Lilith always faced that direction so she was covered on all sides.

"Yeah, I suppose I'd feel better pooping here too, girl," Abril murmured as Lilith began walking in a small circle with her nose to the ground.

"I would think you would prefer one of the indoor washrooms."

Abril jerked her head around to see Roberts and Delacort approaching. It was Detective Roberts who had made the teasing comment. Detective Delacort was actually scowling at him for it and when he said something to him under his breath, she was quite sure it was, "Do not embarrass her." At least, that's what it sounded like to her, and she thought it was sweet that he would be protective of her like that.

Roberts was less impressed. He rolled his eyes at his friend for his trouble.

Grinning at the interaction, Abril asked, "Done grilling the neighbors?"

"How did you know where we were?" Roberts asked, but it was Delacort who answered his question.

"No doubt Peters told her."

"Yes, he did," she admitted. "Find out anything new or interesting?"

The two men glanced at each other.

"You did!" Abril guessed with excitement. "Well,

you have to tell me. I mean I'm the one presently living here with a bunch of dead people in the garden." When they both hesitated, still looking at each other in question, she added bribery to the mix. "I'll give you some of Bob's world-famous chili and chips if you tell me."

"Chili and chips?" Delacort asked with what might have been interest.

"Mm-hmm." She nodded solemnly and assured him, "It's Bob's recipe and *really* good."

"Bob?" Delacort asked, a small frown pulling at his mouth.

"He was the cook in a restaurant he and his wife, Barb, owned and ran. I worked there for a while. His chili was kind of famous in the area for how good it was."

"Ah," Delacort relaxed and smiled faintly.

"Oh, go on," Roberts said lightly. "Take her inside and tell her what we learned over chili and chips while I see if the men need help with the tent."

"The tent is here?" Abril asked, but then thought that must have been what she'd seen Officer Peters and the new man carrying from the van.

"They were just starting to set it up when we pulled in," Delacort told her. "But we saw you outside with Lilith and decided we should first talk to you about our staying to guard the site."

"Now that we have, I should get over there and see what I can do to help." Roberts nodded at her, then turned to walk away.

Abril stared after him with amazement. His idea of talking about their staying to guard was apparently just mentioning it. Shaking her head, she watched as he disappeared around the corner of the house, and then smiled shyly at Delacort before turning to focus on Lilith.

It was ridiculous. She wasn't the shy sort as a rule, and certainly hadn't felt shy around him earlier. But now that they'd kissed it was different. Every time she looked at him, she felt a blush heating her cheeks. Mind you, that wasn't the only place she got warm when she looked at him. In fact, the heat that raced through her body when she was near him might very well be causing her blushes. It was rather embarrassing reacting to a near stranger like a bitch in heat. At least it was for Abril. Unfortunately, she didn't see an end to her response to him in the near future. Which meant she'd better get used to it, she supposed.

Lilith was quick about her business tonight. It was a great relief to Abril since she couldn't think of a thing to say to Delacort. He appeared to have the same problem so that they simply stood there in an uncomfortable silence until Lilith finished.

Eight

Abril could see the tent the moment they walked back around the corner to the front of the house. It was large and white. It also appeared to already be fully set up.

"It's big," she commented as they approached.

"It needed to cover the excavation site, and that's big," Detective Delacort pointed out.

"Yes, I guess." She eyed the tent walls as they undulated slightly under the influence of the light breeze that had started. It actually looked more like something that would be used at an outdoor wedding than a shelter for skeletons.

"They were pretty much done putting it up by the time I got over here," Roberts said, joining them.

Abril and Delacort both grunted in response and then she pointed out, "There are lights on inside the tent. Are they going to work all night or something?"

Roberts turned to peer at the tent where inner lights were making the walls appear to glow. "No," he said finally. "Actually, they're just using them to see by as they cover the half-buried skeletons inside with canvas. They are also setting up heaters in the hopes of drying the ground a bit so it will be easier for them to work with tomorrow. Then they will be heading out. I already sent Officer Peters away."

Abril glanced around, noticing only then that the officer's police car was missing. Despite Roberts's comment earlier about talking to her about their guarding the site, she said, "He thought he was going to be guarding the site tonight."

Roberts shook his head. "Delacort and I will be handling it."

"Is it normal for detectives to perform that task?" she asked with interest. "I would have thought it more something that patrolmen would handle."

"It normally is," Roberts agreed. "But this is turning into a bigger case than usually comes up, and we are concerned that someone living on the street may still be friends with whichever of the previous owners are responsible for the bodies here and mention our presence. They would no doubt realize what it's about, might worry they left some evidence behind with the bodies and come around to search the site, remove the bodies themselves, or otherwise disturb it. If so, we want to be here to prevent that. We might even catch the killer tonight."

Abril stared at him wide-eyed. "You think the killer will come *here*? Tonight?"

"It is possible," Detective Delacort said gently. "But if so, we will be here. That is, if you do not mind us sitting in our car in the driveway all night?"

"I don't mind," she assured him. "But you'd probably be more comfortable inside. In fact, if you lifted the tent flap on the kitchen side, you could actually watch the bones themselves from the house, and keep an eye on the whole yard through the monitor for the security cameras at the same time."

She was responding to Delacort, but looking at Roberts as she spoke, because she knew she just couldn't make the offer to Delacort without blushing wildly when she added, "You'd definitely be more comfortable inside where it's warm. You can make yourself coffee, or food if you like, and there are two guest rooms besides the one I'm using. You are welcome to use them. One of you can nap while the other keeps an eye out, then you could switch."

Much to her surprise Roberts beamed at her as if she had said something terribly clever. "Well, that sounds just fine. Why do you two not go inside and start on the chili and chips while I see to lifting the flap on the tent?"

He didn't wait for a response but left them and walked off toward the tent and the two men coming out of it.

"Shall we?" Delacort gestured back toward the front doors of the house.

"Yes," Abril whispered and headed that way at once, tugging lightly on the leash to get Lilith to walk with her. She didn't have to drag her this time. Apparently, out of sight was out of mind for Lilith. Now that the tent was up, blocking the bones from view, and possibly trapping any smell attached to them inside, the Labrador was no longer fighting to get to the excavation site.

That was something, anyway, she thought and

wondered what on earth she'd been thinking to invite two gorgeous men to stay overnight in a house she was house-sitting. One of whom she'd had a passionate exchange with earlier. Abril had thought it a good idea as she'd issued the invitation, but now she was second-guessing herself and feeling as nervous as a virgin on her wedding night.

The thought made Abril give herself a mental shake as she wondered when she had turned into such a ninny. Good lord! She had been dating since she was sixteen. Okay, so she hadn't had a ton of boyfriends, still she wasn't inexperienced. But now, one little kiss from the sexy beast walking beside her and she'd become a ball of anxiety.

Idiot. *Straighten up and fly right*, she told herself as she walked up the steps to the door. It was a phrase Bob had often used on her when she was doing something silly as a teenager. As it had then, it now made her stop slouching, stand taller, and lift her chin. She was a grown-up woman and could kiss who she wanted when she wanted. She had done nothing wrong.

Well, Abril tempered with a small frown, she had done nothing wrong if Detective Delacort was single. If he wasn't . . . That thought was too depressing to consider, so she pushed it away unfinished.

Abril wasn't surprised to find that both the chili and fries were now cold. She'd been outside much longer than she'd expected.

"Take a seat," she suggested to Delacort as she removed Lilith's leash and hung it back in the broom closet.

"Is there nothing I can do?" Delacort asked, standing by the chair he'd occupied earlier at the island, but hesitating to sit.

"Not really," she told him. "Everything was done earlier, now I just need to warm up the chili and put in a fresh batch of French fries." Even as she said that, Abril was pulling the now cold cookie sheet of dried out French fries from the oven. She set it on the island and then turned the oven back on to start it warming up again while she retrieved the frozen fries from the freezer.

Once she had the fries all set up and was just waiting for the oven to warm up, she asked, "Would you like a drink? I'd offer you a glass of wine or something, but I suppose you can't drink alcohol, being on the job and all. So, your options are ice water, orange juice, ginger ale, Coca-Cola, Sprite, and Cherry Coca-Cola," she listed off everything she knew was in the house that was nonalcoholic, and then added, "Of course, there is coffee or tea too."

Delacort hesitated, appearing uncertain for a moment and then simply said, "I shall have whatever you are having, please."

Abril's eyebrows rose slightly. "Are you sure? Because I'm having a Cherry Coca-Cola. It's my favorite at the moment."

"That sounds fine," he said. "Can I get the glasses for you?"

"No, I'm good," she assured him, retrieving the glasses herself from the cupboard beside the refrigerator. Abril used the ice cube dispenser on the fridge door to half fill one of the glasses, and then almost started to do the same with the second, but paused and glanced around to ask, "Ice or no ice?"

"Ice is good," he said agreeably, and then added under his breath, "I think." Abril heard him, but since she suspected he hadn't wanted her to hear that part, she pretended not to and simply turned to the refrigerator to fill the second glass half-full of ice as well. She then snatched two cans of the Cherry Coca-Cola out of the fridge, gathered up everything in her arms and carried it all over to the end of the island where Delacort was now sitting.

As he had earlier, he'd chosen the seat on the side that faced the view of the road, leaving her the end seat, kitty-corner to his own. He was actually sitting where she usually sat, while she would now be taking Gina's chair. She didn't mind really, but knew from earlier that it was going to feel a little weird taking her boss's place. Especially to eat. Shrugging inwardly, she quickly collected silverware and two place mats and returned to the island.

"I can do that," Delacort said, standing swiftly to take the items from her.

"Thank you." She almost gasped the words in response to his fingers brushing hers as he took the silverware from her hand. Knowing she was blushing again, Abril turned and hurried around the island to the range, and turned the burner on under the chili to start it warming. Once that was done, she didn't know what to do with herself and stood awkwardly watching the temperature display on the upper of the two built-in ovens, waiting to be able to put the fries in.

It took forever for the oven to heat up. A good ten minutes at least, during which she stood there twiddling her thumbs and racking her mind for some way to ease this awkwardness.

Abril was more than a little relieved when the oven dinged, announcing it had reached the needed temperature. She put the fries in the oven, then stood stirring the chili as it heated while she waited for the timer to announce it was time to turn the fries. The silence surrounding her and Delacort was uncomfortable enough that she almost turned on the television out of desperation. But Abril didn't in the end, so the minutes dragged on, passing like hours. She actually got excited when it was time to turn the fries. Mostly because it meant this torture was half over now.

She suspected she wasn't the only one relieved when the dinger sounded for the second time ten minutes later, announcing that the fries were done.

Abril pulled the fries out of the oven, piled a bunch of them on his plate, a lot less on her own, then used a large ladle to pour chili over top of each before sprinkling them with the cheddar cheese she'd shredded earlier.

Satisfied with her efforts, she picked up both plates, carried them to the island, and set one in front of Delacort. She then sat down and placed hers on her own place mat.

"There! I think we're all set," she said, purely for the sake of saying something and filling the silence. Then she pointed out, "The salt is right here." She turned the lazy Susan that was situated on the island so that the seasoning sat before both of them, and added, "And the pepper is too. If the chili isn't hot enough for you, I can grab some chili powder. Just let me know."

"I am sure it is perfect just the way it is," Delacort assured her, and then waited until she had picked up her fork, stabbed it through two French fries side by side with chili and cheese on them, and put it into her mouth. Only then did he emulate her and try the food.

Despite herself, Abril was on pins and needles as she waited for his reaction to the chili and chips. She told herself she wouldn't be offended if he didn't like it, but the truth was she would be crushed if he didn't care for the meal. It had been a staple in Bob and Barb's home, a couple who had become parental type figures to her after she'd fled her real parents in her teens. It had been several things for them, a comfort food, a tasty treat, and even something served on special occasions. So, she was more than a little relieved when he slid the first forkful of food into his mouth to chew and his eyes widened at the flavor.

"Is it all right?" she asked. His expression seemed to suggest it was, but she wanted to actually hear the words to be sure.

Much to her relief, he immediately began to nod. Once he'd swallowed that first bite, he assured her, "I think it is the best thing I have ever tasted. Certainly, the best food I have had in a very, very long time."

Smiling, Abril relaxed in her seat, then set more seriously to eating. Concentrating on her own food as she was, it wasn't until Delacort's fork clanked on his plate as he set it down that she glanced to him. The look of satisfaction on his face was almost orgasmic. Blushing at the thought, she quickly dropped her gaze to his plate instead. Her eyes immediately widened in amazement when she saw that it was empty. Abril wasn't even halfway through her own much smaller serving, yet his was completely gone, the plate scraped clean.

The man must have a Hoover for a stomach, she thought and asked, "Would you like more?"

She was getting to her feet and reaching for his plate even as she asked that, but Delacort snatched his plate out of her reach, and waved her back to her seat. "No. I am good. I am so full I shall make myself sick if I have one more bite. I should have stopped after the first half or even before that, but it was so delicious that I could not help myself," he admitted. Standing up then, he added, "You just sit down and finish your own food. I will take care of my plate."

Abril settled back in her seat and continued to eat as she watched him. She was a little surprised when he not only carried the plate to the sink, but rinsed it off, and then set it in the dishwasher. She was even more surprised when he then moved to the pot of chili on the stove and asked, "Should I cover this and put it in the refrigerator for you?"

"Uh . . . no, we should probably wait to see if Roberts—". The sound of the front door opening made her pause.

She was actually relieved when Delacort excused himself, saying, "That will be Roberts. I shall go see if there is any news."

Abril knew she would be self-conscious if the two men returned and she had to finish eating in front of them now that Delacort was done, so she began to shovel the food into her mouth, almost swallowing without chewing. She had just finished the last bite when Delacort came back into the room with Roberts on his heels.

"Are you ready for chili and chips now?" she asked Roberts as she carried her plate to the sink to rinse it. "I made extra fries in case you wanted some."

"Thank you, but no," Roberts said at once. "It smells

delicious and I have been told it is very good, but I have a delicate stomach. I am on a strict diet and so am afraid I have to decline."

Abril frowned slightly as she put the plate in the dishwasher, and when she straightened, asked, "Then what can I make for you? Soup? We have several varieties of soup that might be okay for your stomach. Or toast maybe? What can you eat?"

"I am good," Roberts assured her. "I packed my own meal before coming in to work today and ate it in my car just now before coming inside."

"Oh," Abril said with surprise. "Well, a coffee then?" she suggested, closing the dishwasher and walking around the island to the coffee pot.

"No," Roberts said with a light chuckle, as he strode across the room to stand at the sliding glass doors. Peering out the window, he said, "You are very kind, Abril. And thank you for the offer, but I am neither hungry nor thirsty."

Abril felt like a terrible host, but finally gave up on giving the man anything and turned to Detective Delacort in question. "Would you like coffee? I was going to make myself one."

"I shall have a coffee with you," the detective acquiesced. "Thank you."

A relieved smile curving her lips, Abril set to work making them both a cup of the dark brew. Knowing it would only be the two of them, she chose to use the Keurig single cup coffee maker rather than bother with a full pot of coffee. She set up the first cup, and was putting the chili in the fridge while she waited for the Keurig to do its magic when Roberts asked, "Is one of these switches to an outside light?"

Abril glanced over to see that the light that had glowed from the interior of the tent earlier was now off. It was pitch-black out there and the detective had his hands cupped on either side of his head, his face close to the window as he tried to peer outside. Thinking he was probably leaving marks on the window and she'd have to clean the door before Gina came home, Abril answered, "The third switch from the left controls the outside light there."

"Thanks. I shall clean the window later," Roberts said as if she'd spoken her concern aloud, and then reached over and flicked the third switch on the panel next to the door.

Light immediately burst to life outside, revealing that Roberts had lifted the flap facing the kitchen as she suggested. They had a clear view of the inside of the tent just outside the doors, and the hole it covered.

"Perfect," Detective Delacort said as he crossed the room to join his partner at the window.

"Yes," Roberts agreed. "This will make guarding the site much easier. We will not have to worry about anyone slipping in the back of the tent while we are watching the front as we would from the car."

"Well, then I'll leave you to it," Abril said, as she set the newly made coffee she'd prepared for Detective Delacort on the island.

Smiling at them both, she then slapped her leg to get Lilith to join her as she left. Abril really wanted to just stay in the kitchen with the two men, but knew she would just embarrass herself. She'd be unable to prevent herself from stealing glances at Delacort every chance she got. She'd also probably say something stupid and sound like a brainless twit. Which she apparently was, Abril decided when she realized she'd forgotten to make herself a coffee.

Abril paused in the entry, briefly debating returning to the kitchen to make herself that coffee, but then decided against it. She'd grab a soda from the little kitchenette at the back of the house instead. She couldn't make a fool of herself that way. Then she'd have to decide what to do next.

"What do you think?" she asked Lilith as she crossed the living room, headed for the hall that led to the kitchenette. "Shall we cuddle on the couch with a movie? Cuddle on the couch with a book? Or finish some more work?"

Despite mentioning the option of working, that wasn't really possible. She didn't have her laptop, and didn't want to walk past the men to get to her office and fetch it. She was feeling ridiculously self-conscious now and couldn't understand why one little kiss would cause that. She was so super aware of Detective Delacort, and of her own body's response to him that it was ridiculous.

The worst part was, she didn't know what to do about it or how to make herself comfortable with him again. If that was even possible. Sighing, Abril glanced down toward Lilith as she finished the question, only to pause with a small frown when she realized the Lab was no longer with her. Turning, she peered back the way she'd come and almost groaned when she saw that Lilith was standing in the foyer, sitting patiently by the front door. It was time for what Gina referred to as "the after-dinner walkies." The walk should have been taken after Lilith had eaten, but with her own dinner waiting, Abril had bypassed the walk and simply taken her out into the yard to do her business. She'd rather hoped to skip the after-dinner walk altogether tonight, but it was looking like Lilith wasn't down with that plan.

Resignation sliding through her, Abril gave up any hope of pop and the boob tube for now and retraced her steps to the closet across from the front door. She had only expected to retrieve her coat and shoes from it, but was pleased when she spotted the two leashes hanging from the peg shelf on the side wall of the closet. That was where the first two leashes had disappeared to. Delacort had assumed they belonged in the closet. Lucky her. It meant she didn't have to go back into the kitchen and face the men presently guarding the skeleton garden.

Abril donned her coat and shoes, snapped the leash to Lilith's collar, and headed outside with her. It was later than she usually walked Lilith and dark enough that she was now regretting not having done the chore directly after feeding her as she usually did. The lack of streetlights, combined with the houses being so far back from the road that their lights didn't reach it, meant it was nearly pitch-black on the road. Fortunately, her eyes adjusted somewhat as she walked up the driveway and she was able to see enough not to stumble over Lilith or her own feet for the walk. She couldn't see much more than that though. Everything more than a couple feet away was just dark black with only lights shining in the distant windows of the houses on either side of the street.

Hoping Lilith had better night vision, she wound the end of the leash around her wrist to ensure she didn't lose it and followed along behind her as they started up the road on the creepiest walk she'd ever taken. Abril had been raised in the country where streetlights were not a thing, but she hadn't been allowed out after dark as a child. She'd pretty much been a city dweller since then, and no street was dark in the city. So this was a new experience. One Abril didn't think she'd like to repeat as she glanced nervously around at every rustle of sound and there was a lot of rustling going on. Just rabbits and such, she told herself squinting hard to try to penetrate the darkness.

Damn, she would be sure she gave Lilith her nightly walk immediately after she ate from now on, Abril thought and then jerked to a halt with a squeak of alarm as a misshapen form appeared out of the darkness. Two forms, she corrected as they moved closer and she was able to see they weren't misshapen at all, but two people. It wasn't until the first person spoke that Abril realized that it was Gina's neighbor, Kim.

"Sorry. We didn't mean to startle you," the woman said as she came to a halt before Lilith and bent to pet her head briefly. Straightening, she added, "You're Abril right? Gina's assistant?"

"Yes." Managing a smile that she doubted the woman could see anyway, she glanced from Kim to the figure several steps behind her. Abril couldn't see the person that well, but suspected from what she could make out that it was a woman. Probably the dark-haired woman that had been with Kim earlier when she'd spotted them outside talking to the construction crew.

"I'm Kim Stone," Kim introduced herself. "I live in the blue house almost across the street from Gina's."

"Nice to meet you," Abril murmured, taking the

hand the other woman offered and shaking it briefly. Then she smiled faintly and added, "I guess I don't have to tell you who I am, you already know."

"Yes. Gina told me all about you at the neighborhood Christmas party."

Gina had told her about that but from what she'd said it hadn't really been a party in the traditional sense. The couple across the street from Gina had organized it. Everyone on the crescent had been invited. Appetizers and drinks had been on offer and everyone had stood around chatting. There had been no music or dancing. Really, it had been a gathering rather than a party, but Gina had enjoyed it and had most especially appreciated the chance to meet her neighbors.

"Gina also told me about the addition she planned to have built and the renovations she was going to have done," Kim said, moving a little closer, and her friend doing the same a couple feet behind Kim. "I gather they're going to pull out the indoor garden, fill it in and make it part of the living room?"

"Yes," Abril murmured and glanced down at Lilith when the Lab began tugging on the leash. She was surprised to see that the pup had moved behind her and was trying to pull her back the way they'd come.

"When do they plan to start on removing the indoor garden?"

Abril tore her eyes from Lilith to return her gaze to Kim's shadowy figure with a little confusion. There was no reason that she could think of for Kim to care about that.

"I just thought if Gina is going to get rid of the plants in the indoor garden, I'd love to take them off her hands," she explained, her voice an odd combination of friendly and wooden at the same time.

"Oh. Well—" Abril glanced down to Lilith with a scowl when the dog continued to pull, tightening the leash painfully around her wrist where she'd wrapped it. "Settle down, Lilith. We'll head home in a minute. You were the one who insisted on coming out here," she pointed out with a little exasperation.

When Lilith whined but sat down behind her and stopped pulling, Abril released a little breath of relief and shifted her attention to Kim again, blinking in surprise when she noted that the woman had stepped closer still. A lot closer. The invading-her-space kind of close.

The hair on the nape of her neck standing up, Abril started to take a step backward, but froze when Kim's hand shot out to clutch at her arm. Abril's gaze immediately moved to meet Kim's, but even as it did the other woman's eyes shifted a bit to the side and past her. In the next moment Kim had retracted her hand and started to back away.

"I should go. It's late. We'll talk again soon." In the next moment, the darkness almost seemed to swallow up Kim and her friend and Abril was alone again with Lilith.

"Well, that was weird, huh?" Abril muttered, and then was debating whether to continue this walk or return to the house when a scuff of sound behind her had her whirling around with alarm.

"Sorry. I didn't mean to startle you."

Abril couldn't at first see the speaker in the darkness in front of her, but she did recognize the voice as belonging to Gina's client and neighbor, Jackson. She also recognized from his tone that he wasn't sorry at all for scaring her. In fact, there was a smugness to his tone that made her think he had set out deliberately to do just that and was glad he'd succeeded.

Suspecting the man would pester her about being included for the casting of his commercial, which was business which should be dealt with during business hours, she opened her mouth to excuse herself, and then gasped in pain as bright light suddenly shone into her eyes. Abril raised her hand to try to block it, but still had to shut her eyes against the blazing beam. The damned thing was so bright it seemed to burn through her eyes and right into her brain after the darkness that had preceded it.

"Oh, sorry about that," he said now on a laugh. "Just wanted to make sure I knew who I was talking to. You can open your eyes now."

Abril risked squinting her eyes open the barest bit, relieved to find the light was now directed down at the tarmac. Lowering her hand, she let her eyes open fully and then started around the man's dark form, determined to return to the house. She'd had enough of Gina's neighbors and would be damned if she was going to get stuck out here talking shop to this one.

"Whoa, where are you going?" Jackson caught her arm as she tried to move past him, forcing her to a halt. "No need to rush off. It's actually lucky that I ran into you. I was going to stop by tomorrow to ask when Gina plans to start casting for the commercial. But why wait when we're here right now?"

Abril's mouth tightened. The man hadn't just

stopped her, he'd yanked her so close she could smell his disgusting breath. What the hell had he eaten? The only time she'd smelled anything so vile was when a mouse had died in the heating vent and the stench had permeated her office.

"My God, girl, you smell absolutely delicious," he complimented, dragging her closer so that he was practically grinding on her as he leaned down to press his face to her neck.

Abril immediately tried to pull away, but Jackson wasn't letting go. She actually thought she felt his lips and teeth scrape against her neck as he inhaled deeply and murmured, "Mmmm. Nice."

She was about to knee the man in the groin when Lilith suddenly jumped on him with a bark that was uncharacteristically vicious coming from the usually sweet Lab. Much to her relief, Jackson was startled enough that his hold on her slackened and she was able to pull herself free. Taking several steps backward until the darkness was all she could see again, and hopefully all he could see too, she said firmly, "Do not come by the house tomorrow. If you have a business question, call the office during business hours."

She didn't wait for him to respond but turned abruptly and hurried away tugging Lilith with her. Her heart was racing, adrenaline pouring through her body, and she was suddenly aware of the sounds in the night, including her own footsteps. Afraid that Jackson might follow the sound and harass her again, she moved onto the grass and then cut across Gina's huge yard, heading for the front doors, instead of walking back to the driveway and taking that up to the house.

Lilith ran along beside her, staying close rather than running ahead and tugging at the leash.

"Good girl," Abril murmured breathlessly as she drew her to a halt on the landing and reached for the door. "You deserve a reward for defending me from that pervert. How about a swim?"

Nine

"Maybe I should go out and make sure Abril and Lilith are okay," Crispin muttered, glaring out the front window. "I do not see them and they have been out there awhile."

"Abril and Lilith returned from their walk while you were putting the tent flap back up," Roberts said mildly.

Crispin blinked at this news. That had happened a good fifteen minutes ago. The tent flap Roberts had thrown over the roof of the tent so that they could watch from inside the house had slid back down. He'd made a run out to the car, found some clips in the trunk, and gone around to the side of the house to better secure the panel up and out of the way.

"Oh," he said finally, relieved she was okay, but wishing Roberts had said something earlier. He'd been fretting for some time now.

"You should go kiss her again."

Crispin's head jerked around with shock. "What?"

"You heard me," Roberts said calmly.

"I may have," Crispin agreed. "But I cannot have heard correctly. It sounded like you said I should go kiss Abril again . . . when you told me not an hour ago that I should avoid kissing her, lest I scare her off with life mate passion." He paused briefly, scowling at Roberts, and then asked irritably, "So which is it? Do I kiss her or not?"

Roberts turned from the sliding glass door he'd been staring through and said patiently, "I did tell you not to kiss her for fear of scaring her off, but now you are not doing *anything*. You are not even talking to her."

"Because I do not know what to say," Crispin said with frustration. "I have not had the occasion to speak to women who were not either relatives or work colleagues for ages. What do I say? How do I start a conversation? Should I begin by talking about the weather? Or by telling her that I think her eyes are as lovely as emeralds?"

"I am not sure," Roberts admitted apologetically. "But either is better than nothing. You two are not talking at all. You are barely even looking at each other, just stealing glances when the other one is not looking. You are both acting like a couple of awkward teenagers, all timid and bashful. Continue on this way and you will never win her to you. You need to make her love you so that she will overlook what we are and agree to be your life mate. But if you cannot talk to make that happen, then I guess you are going to have to try sexual persuasion."

"Sexual persuasion?" Crispin asked with interest, feeling himself harden at the very thought.

"Yes. I see that has caught your attention," Roberts said dryly, and then added, "Just do not try it in the pool. If you both pass out there, she will drown and all will be lost."

"Pool?" Crispin asked with confusion. He knew there was one here, but had no idea why Roberts was bringing it up as if he might drag Abril there to romance her. Chlorine and cold water did not seem a seductive scenario to him.

"The pool may not be where you would prefer to begin your seduction, but since that is where Abril is, I fear you have little choice," he said and pointed to the large screen of images from the security cameras that hung next to the television and said, "She apparently felt like taking a dip when she and Lilith got back from their walk."

Crispin peered at the monitor, quickly zeroing in on the section showing the interior of the pool room. Abril, in a rather attractive, sleek black one-piece swimsuit, was tossing a towel onto a wicker couch as she passed it on the way to the pool.

"Perhaps it is better if you do not find the pool conducive to seduction," Roberts said thoughtfully. "Maybe the cold water will clear your heads and the two of you will actually be able to hold a conversation."

Crispin was silent as he watched Abril walk down the steps into the pool. His gaze followed every curve of her body as it slowly disappeared into the cover of the water. When she then dove under, submerging her whole body, Crispin stood abruptly, only to immediately freeze as he realized—"I do not have a swimsuit."

"You could try au naturel," Roberts suggested.

Crispin's eyes widened. He felt himself harden even further at the suggestion and then he hurried from the kitchen. As he passed through the entry, he toed off one shoe and then the other. Leaving them there, he continued on past the indoor garden, removing his jacket and tie as he went. Both were lain over the end of the couch as he reached it. His shirt with all its buttons took a little longer to remove, but he did manage the task before reaching the end of the living room and the sliding doors that waited there. He tossed the shirt over the closest chair, and then opened the door and stepped out into the warm, sultry pool room.

That's when Crispin realized he still had his socks on. Bracing one hand against the wall, he quickly removed them, folded them over, and set them just inside the door.

Straightening, Crispin closed the door, and reached for his belt as he turned back to the pool room. It was L shaped, jutting out from where he stood with a table and chairs and then a hot tub straight ahead, before turning left and stretching out that way where the pool was.

Crispin unbuckled and removed his belt, then set it over one of the chairs at the table. His hands went to the snap of his pants then, but he suddenly stopped. Going au naturel as Roberts had suggested just seemed one step too far. He worried Abril would think it was presumptuous of him.

He debated the issue briefly, and decided not to take any chances. He left his pants on, walked past the table and chairs, and around the corner. Crispin now stood beside a wicker couch that he could imagine putting to good use. But for now, Abril was in the pool ahead of him. She hadn't noticed his presence yet. She was presently swimming away from him toward the opposite end of the pool. Crispin watched her for a minute, admiring her stroke, and then walked to the lip of the pool and dove in.

The water was surprisingly warm and silky as he moved through it. When Crispin surfaced, he found that Abril had stopped swimming and turned to face him in the water. He also saw the fear on her face just before recognition erased it and she relaxed in the water.

"Hi," she said weakly.

"Hi," he responded solemnly, and then added, "You should never swim alone. If you ran into difficulty there would be no one here to help you. You should always have a swim buddy."

"Lilith is here," she pointed out.

He glanced around, surprised to see the dog lying beside the pool watching them with interest.

"And she's actually been trained to pull people out of the water if they get into trouble."

Crispin didn't hide his surprise as he glanced back to her. "Really?"

She smiled faintly, but nodded. "Gina lives alone. She wanted to swim in her pool without having to worry about there being someone with her. So, she took Lilith to a dog trainer and had him teach Lilith what to do in case somebody was drowning. How best to hold on to them to get them to the pool steps, and then how to pull them up the steps until their head was out of the water, and so on."

Crispin shook his head with wonder as he eased a step closer to her in the water. "A dog as lifeguard. Amazing."

"Yes," she agreed. "But dogs are smart animals, they use them in war to track people, detect explosives, and patrol, as well as for search and rescue. Then there are guide dogs, diabetic alert dogs, mobility assistance dogs, seizure response and alert dogs, medical service dogs . . ." Her voice trailed off and she shrugged. "Dogs are amazing animals. It's no surprise they can act as lifeguards too."

Crispin just stared at her. He was listening to her, but wasn't really taking in what she was saying other than that she was giving a rousing speech about the awesomeness of dogs. Mostly, he was just watching her lips move and thinking he would like to kiss her.

Abril let her voice trail off as she became aware of the way he was staring at her. She managed to meet his intense gaze briefly, but then had to break the connection, and let her eyes drop to the water between them. She then blinked in surprise.

"Are you wearing your dress pants?" she asked with disbelief.

Crispin glanced down at himself, and then shrugged casually. "I do not have any swim trunks here."

"Oh. Right." Her gaze returned to his face again. It was only then that she realized he had moved a little closer. Ignoring that, she said, "What kind of material are they? They aren't wool or something I hope, or the chlorinated water might ruin them." And then her eyes widened. "You can't sit in wet pants all night."

"It will be fine," he assured her.

"No," she said at once, and decided, "We'll have to put them in the dryer when we're done swimming."

"Sounds like a plan," he agreed, seeming suddenly amused.

"It does, does it?" she asked, arching one eyebrow.

"It does," he confirmed, taking another step closer in the water.

Abril shrugged with feigned disinterest, and commented, "Well, if you don't mind sitting around buck naked with nothing but a towel on while your pants are drying, then I guess it's all good."

"Would you mind?" he asked, his voice softer . . . and deeper and a bit husky.

Abril swallowed, and found herself licking her lips. He was awfully close now. Just inches separated them in the water. They were so close that she had to tilt her head up to meet his gaze, her body naturally arching as she did.

"Would you?" he persisted.

Abril blinked in confusion. She had already forgotten his question and was, instead, thinking about the fact that, if he moved one inch closer, their bodies would be brushing against each other. She almost wanted to lean forward that one inch herself.

"Abril?" he whispered.

"Yes?" She was staring at his chest now. He looked like a marble sculpture, and she found her hand rising to flatten itself on his chest to be sure he was flesh and blood.

Abril thought she heard a small groan slip from Delacort at her touch, but she wasn't certain because she was busy struggling to suppress the moan she herself wanted to release at the rush of sensation that ran through her own body at that simple act. The man was beautiful. He wasn't huge or overmuscled. He was lean with well-defined muscles and had beautiful pectorals that she just couldn't resist brushing her hand over. Oddly enough, her body was just responding again when Delacort's hand closed over hers, stopping its movement. Her gaze shot up to his face.

He didn't look angry or upset in any way. In fact, judging by his heated gaze and hungry expression, anger was definitely not what she'd stirred in him. Even so, she offered, "I'm sorry. I shouldn't—"

Her words died abruptly when his mouth closed over hers.

As had happened when he'd kissed her earlier, passion exploded between them. When he released her hand to wrap his arms around her, Abril did the same, sliding her arms around his neck as she kissed him back. It wasn't until her legs began to drift a bit, rubbing against his, that she realized that she was no longer standing on her own feet. He'd raised her slightly out of the water to claim her mouth without having to bend his head too far.

Not wanting him to think that she was deliberately rubbing herself against him, Abril wrapped her legs around his hips and hooked her feet behind him, but that was even worse. She was no longer brushing back and forth against him under the water, instead her position left her groin perched firmly against his. For one moment, she considered letting her legs drop from around him again, then Delacort deepened the kiss, distracting her. She stayed where she was and responded to his hungry devouring.

Completely consumed by the heat and sensation

pouring through her body, Abril made a sound between a moan and a growl of protest when Delacort broke their kiss.

"We need to get out of the water," he muttered against her skin as he trailed his lips down her throat.

"Okay," Abril gasped, letting her hands wander over his back, feeling the hard muscles shifting as he began to caress her too. The hand he'd placed on her bottom to lift her slightly out of the water began to squeeze and knead the flesh while his other hand moved to her breast and began to do the same. The excitement those caresses sent charging through her body had her unconsciously arching and shifting her hips against him, grinding herself against the hardness she felt there. She then threw her head back on a cry at the surge of excitement it sent through her.

"Out," Delacort moaned against the skin of her throat as he buried his face there, his lips and tongue sending more tingles through her as he lathed and then suckled at her skin.

"Yes," Abril groaned, although it wasn't to the word he'd spoken so much as the way his body shifted against hers as he began to walk through the water. Wrapped around him as she was, every step was a caress across her entire body, his chest moving against her very erect and tender nipples, and his groin rubbing on her extremely excited core.

Mounting the steps, however, took it to another level. Perhaps it was because he'd tightened his hold on her, presumably to prevent dropping her, or perhaps so he could look over her shoulder and down her back to the steps he was ascending to avoid tripping. Whatever the case, the fine cord of tension that had been

tightening with each kiss and caress snapped on perhaps the second or third step. Abril wasn't sure which,
and didn't really care as her orgasm overtook her. She
didn't even really notice when Delacort stumbled and
started to fall forward with her, his own roar of release
filling her ears as he too came. She was so wrapped
up in the sensations charging over her, that she simply
tightened her arms around his shoulders and her legs
around his waist when he released her to reach out to
break their fall.

Ten

Crispin woke up on Abril, his head hanging over her shoulder, his forehead in the water up to his eyebrows. Lifting his head at once, he glanced in a panic at Abril's face. Much to his relief, he had managed to get her far enough up the stairs that while her head was lying in the water on the top step, it only covered her to her ears. Her face was above its surface.

Thank God for that, he thought, and then moved them both up the last two steps to rest on the concrete surrounding the pool so that only their legs from the knees down still hung over the lip into the water. Crispin then shifted to lie next to her and raised her to rest on top of him so that her head was tucked under his chin. He was quite sure that must be more comfortable than the cold, hard steps had been.

He was just letting his eyes drift closed again when Abril made him aware that she'd woken up by asking, "You aren't married, are you?"

Crispin froze, then lifted his head to look down at her, but her head was still lying sideways on his chest, her face turned away from him. It was how he'd settled her on his chest, but now he regretted that and reached out to put a finger under her chin to tilt her head upward. Once their gazes met, he said solemnly, "No. I would not kiss and touch you the way I have if I were married."

When Abril nodded, not hiding her relief before relaxing and closing her eyes again, he asked, "Are you?"

He assumed that Roberts would've told him if she was married, since the other man could read her mind, but still, it was best to know for sure and hear it from her own lips.

Much to his relief, she met his gaze with the same solemn expression he'd given her a moment ago, and assured him, "No. I too would not kiss and touch and allow you to kiss and touch me as we have been doing were I married."

Crispin nodded, and then let his head rest back on the cold concrete again, only to lift it once more when she asked, "What do I call you?"

He stared at her with confusion for a moment, before saying, "I do not understand. You can call me what you wish. You can use my name, or an endearment . . . sweetheart," he ended with a grin, using an endearment himself.

Abril smiled at his teasing, but said, "I don't know your name to use it."

"Of course, you do," Crispin said with a half laugh. "Officer Peters introduced us when we arrived today."

"Oh. Right," Abril said lightly. "So, your first name is Detective?"

Crispin blinked and then groaned to himself as he recalled that Peters had introduced them as Detectives Roberts and Delacort without including their first names. In truth, it was entirely possible that the man didn't even know their first names since he didn't ever recall giving them to the officer. He and Roberts tended to just use last names with each other as well as the other officers they worked with. A lot of members of the police force did.

"I apologize," he said finally with true regret. "My name is Crispinus Delacort."

Abril blinked. He'd pronounced his name as krees-pee-noos, sounding very Italian all of a sudden, which was why she asked, "Are you Italian?"

Crispin hesitated, and then said vaguely, "I lived there for a while."

Before she could respond, he'd lunged to his feet, taking her with him to stand at the side of the pool. Then he clasped her face in both hands, met her gaze, and said, "You may call me Crispin. Most of my family and friends do."

He followed that up by kissing her on the forehead before releasing her so abruptly you would have thought the brief caress had burned him. Actually, Abril could understand that reaction. While there was usually nothing sexual about a kiss on the forehead, it had still whipped up some excitement in her. Which was just damned weird, she decided as she followed him to the couch where she'd left her towel.

Shaking her head at herself, Abril commented, "We need to put your pants in the dryer."

The words had Crispin stopping to peer down at his slacks. They were soaking wet with water running off of the heavy material in rivulets.

"There are no men's clothes here," she added. "So, unless you have a gym bag or something in the trunk of your car with clothes in it, you'll have to make do with a pair of my joggers. Or a towel around your waist. It's up to you," she said, and then smiled naughtily and tagged on, "Although, I'd prefer the towel myself. I think it would look good on you."

Crispin's eyes widened slightly and then he grabbed her hand and dragged her to the sliding doors to the rest of the house.

Abril almost protested when they stepped onto the carpet, knowing they were both dripping all over it. Before she could, Crispin slammed the sliding door closed even as he whirled to press her up against the wall and planted his mouth on hers.

As it had been in the pool, his kiss was incredibly passionate, and her body immediately roared with excitement in response. Even so, when he tore his mouth from hers to begin kissing a trail down her neck, she gasped, "The carpet. Our clothes are wet."

"Right," he growled. "We should take them off."

"Oh, yes," Abril groaned as his hands closed over her breasts. He squeezed briefly through the cloth there, before removing one hand to tug the strap of her swimsuit down her shoulder, baring one breast. But then his words registered, her eyes blinked open in panic, and she dragged the strap back up, covering herself as she squeaked, "Cameras."

"I know. The cameras in the pool room are why

I brought you inside," Crispin said soothingly. And ran his tongue down her chest and along the curve of the top of her swimsuit to dip between her breasts.

"Yes, but—" Abril's words ended on a groan as he tugged her swimsuit aside to close his mouth over the nipple he'd again bared.

Forgetting what she'd been trying to tell him, Abril slid her hands into his hair to urge him on as he suckled on the suddenly aching nub.

"She is trying to tell you that there are cameras in the living room too, detective," Roberts's voice had them both jumping guiltily apart.

Feeling like a teenager caught indulging in some heavy petting by her parents, Abril moved away from Crispin and glanced wildly about, trying to find the other man.

"I am talking to you through the camera," Roberts said with amusement. "I apologize if I embarrassed you, Abril. But Crispin wasn't really giving you a chance to speak, and I thought I had best stop him before he got too far and embarrassed all of us."

Abril was about to say thank you, when Crispin stepped up beside her and quickly tugged the top of her swimsuit back into place, covering the breast that had been on display all this time. Definitely feeling that embarrassment Roberts had been trying to avoid, she muttered, "Towels are in that bathroom down that hall, Crispin."

She then rushed the half dozen steps to her bedroom and closed the door behind her with a snap. Leaning back against it, Abril closed her eyes and relived the past several moments with Crispin. From the pool to the living room, it had been hot, hot, hot. Some part of her brain did try to make her feel bad for once again letting the man do what he had. But then another part of her brain said, *Hey! At least this time you learned his name.*

Rolling her eyes at herself, Abril pushed away from the door and made her way across the bedroom to the attached bathroom. She needed to shower off the chlorine from the pool. It would be a cold shower, she decided firmly. Good lord! A couple of kisses and caresses from Crispin had more effect than an hour of the best foreplay she'd ever had in the past. She was aching with need and really just wanted to run back out, track down Crispin, and throw herself at him. The only thing keeping her from doing that was the fact that Roberts would no doubt see her chase after him on the cameras.

She'd embarrassed herself enough for one day, Abril decided, and closed the bathroom door firmly behind herself.

Half an hour later she was showered, dressed, and feeling much less frazzled. At least she was until she stepped out of her room and a sudden scratching sound from her right had her glancing that way. Her eyes nearly popped out of her head when she saw Lilith through the sliding glass doors to the pool room. They'd left the poor dog out there all this time!

Guilt assailing her at once, Abril rushed to the door and opened it to let the Labrador in. Cooing apologetically, she took the time to close the door and lock it again, then dropped to her knees to cuddle and pet the poor creature for abandoning her like that.

"We did not leave her in the pool room, did we?"

Abril glanced up to see Crispin approaching with

nothing but a towel around his waist. She could actually feel her blood heating and racing madly through her body to several points that included her face as she took him in. But when she felt a different liquid pooling low in her belly and running downward, she forced herself to tear her eyes off Crispin and look to Lilith instead.

She nodded, cleared her throat and said, "I'm afraid so. She's okay, though. Aren't you girl?"

Abril was very deliberately concentrating completely on Lilith to avoid gaping at Crispin. She had just been teasing when she'd mentioned the towel, but since she hadn't taken him any joggers, she supposed he hadn't had a choice.

Come to think of it, Abril thought as her eyes slid sideways for another quick peek at him, her joggers probably wouldn't have fit him anyway. They would've been like a second skin, emphasizing every lump and bump, and would've been about as decent as if she'd painted his naked flesh.

Distracted from her thoughts by Lilith constantly pawing at her arm, Abril peered at her in question. "What is it?"

Lilith responded to the question by turning and running through the living room to the front door. There she paused, and turned to look back at Abril.

"Right," she said with resignation as she straightened to follow the Lab. "Potty time."

"I shall take her," Crispin offered.

She didn't have to look over her shoulder to know he was following her. Abril could sense it.

"You don't have any clothes on, Crispin," she pointed

out. "And you are not standing out there in my boss's front yard in nothing but a towel."

"I have a suit jacket here I could wear with the towel. It is not wet. And it is wool. It would keep me warm."

"No," Abril said firmly as she headed into the kitchen to get Lilith's leash. She nodded at Roberts as she walked past where he sat at the island, and then glanced back to Crispin as she said, "You are not standing out in the front yard in your suit jacket and a towel either. The neighbors would go crazy, and Gina would kill me."

Crispin was definitely sounding disgruntled when he said, "Well, you shouldn't be out there by yourself with her. Someone has dropped who knows how many bodies in the garden here. And that someone could be out there even now trying to figure out if it is safe to approach the tent."

Abril swung around from collecting the leash from the closet to glare at Crispin. An expression that started to slip as her gaze slid over him in the towel. He had a beautiful chest. Giving her head a shake, she started walking toward him and then moved around him as she headed for the door muttering, "Thanks. Now I'm going to be a nervous wreck out there with Lilith."

"I can—" Roberts began, but Abril did not allow him to finish.

"Thank you, but no, Detective Roberts," she said firmly. "Lilith is my responsibility. We will be right out front. You'll be able to watch us on the camera." Pausing in the doorway between the kitchen and entry, she glanced back and asked a little anxiously, "You *will* be watching, yeah?"

"Yes," he assured her gently.

Nodding, Abril continued out of the room.

Gina kept a flashlight by the sliding doors in the kitchen for Lilith's nighttime potties. Sadly, Abril hadn't thought to grab that. But she also didn't want to go back into the kitchen and risk one of the men insisting on taking Lilith out for her. Roberts taking her out would've left Abril feeling guilty. Crispin taking her out would've left her horrified as she imagined all the foofaraw that would cause.

Sighing with resignation, Abril snapped the leash onto Lilith's collar, unlocked and opened the door, and led her outside.

For one minute after closing the door, at least until her eyes adjusted, Abril really couldn't see much. Lilith didn't appear to have the same problem and immediately dragged her down the steps and off onto the grass.

Not being able to see much didn't keep Abril from looking around a little worriedly. She could make out some darker shadows surrounding her in the inky night. But mostly it was just too ill lit to see much of anything. Except Lilith.

As pale in color as the Lab's fur was, Abril could actually see her lighter blur moving around. She wasn't sure, but suspected Lilith was sniffing out a spot to relieve herself, and simply let the pup lead her around as Abril continued to keep her eye open for any movement.

They said that animals could sense your mood and Lilith seemed to prove that true. She hardly looked around at all before settling on a spot, relieving herself, and then turning to lead the way quickly back toward the house.

Abril would never admit it to Roberts and Crispin, but she felt a distinct sense of relief when she closed the door behind them and locked it.

Praising Lilith for being a good girl and promising a treat, Abril unhooked the leash, set it on the table next to the doors, and then led the dog into the kitchen to get her the promised biscuit.

"Did you see anything out there?" Crispin asked as she gave the treat to Lilith.

"No," she responded, and then eyed him sharply. "Did you put your clothes in the dryer or the washer?"

"The washer," he said at once. "I hope you do not mind, but I thought—"

"No, it's good and of course I don't mind," she assured him. "I was asking because while your pants may already be ruined, they might not be. But if they aren't, it's better to wash them first to get the chlorine out before drying them."

A moment of silence passed, and then Roberts said, "You two should go play a game, or watch TV or something in the living room."

When Crispin turned to peer at him, his partner added, "I am taking the first shift guarding the tent. You might as well relax, Crispin. Besides, I am getting tired of looking at your hairy legs."

Of course, those words made Abril look at Crispin's legs. They didn't look overly hairy to her. While there was some hair, his legs were also shapely and muscular from what she could see. And she was presently seeing quite a bit. Crispin had reclaimed his seat at the island while she was outside, and his towel on this side had fallen away to hang down, leaving the one leg exposed very high up on his thigh.

Forcing herself to look away before she began to drool, Abril muttered, "I'll go check the laundry and see how long it will be until the washer is done."

She escaped the room without being stopped, and with only Lilith following her.

Eleven

"I noticed there is a sit-down arcade table for two in the living room," Roberts mentioned as soon as Abril was out of the kitchen.

Crispin glanced to him in question.

"You should go play games with her on it," he said. "You might both relax enough to actually talk."

"What can we talk about?" Crispin said with a little frustration. "I cannot tell her who and what I am."

"No, but you can tell her about some of the jobs we have had maybe, or talk about your family."

When Crispin glanced to him askance, Roberts said with exasperation, "I do not mean tell her about your family's origins. Just tell her you have brothers and sisters. And that your father has remarried and lives here in Canada, which is why you moved here seven years ago. To be closer to your father and his wife. Things like that," he suggested.

Crispin nodded slowly as he considered that. There *were* things he could talk to her about after all. And maybe if he told her about his family and such, she would be willing to tell him things about herself too. He'd really like to learn more about her.

"Go on," Roberts urged. "Catch her as she returns from the laundry room and convince her to play a game with you and talk."

Crispin eyed his partner with amusement and pointed out, "You know I am older than you?"

"Yes," Roberts agreed, and then said, "And?"

"And yet you are the one giving me instruction on how to woo my woman," he pointed out. "It is not as if you have any experience with life mates yourself. Do you?" he added, because for all he knew Roberts had found and lost a life mate before they'd ever met. The two of them were friends as well as work partners, and knew a lot about each other, but something like that might have been too painful to talk about.

"No. I have not yet had experience with a life mate," Roberts assured him. And then, a wicked grin curving his lips, he added, "But I am also not trying to think when my mind is stuck between Abril's thighs. So, my brain may be processing a little more clearly . . . and I am happy to help. But I expect the same in return when I find my life mate, if I am ever that lucky."

"You will find her," Crispin assured him as he stood up. "And I shall definitely return the favor."

After checking the wash, Abril led Lilith out of the laundry room and down the hall to the living room.

Once there, she told Alexa to set a timer for the time left on the washing machine.

Gina had an Alexa smart home hub, display, or speaker in nearly every room in the house. Abril had thought it excessive at first, but couldn't deny they came in handy. She waited for Alexa to tell her the timer was set, then turned, intending to head back to the kitchen. But she stopped abruptly when she saw Crispin coming around the corner toward her.

"Roberts mentioned there was an arcade table in here somewhere and suggested we play a game to pass the time," he announced, slowing as he drew near.

She half expected him to keep walking until he was almost on top of her and then kiss her again. That being the case, his words and the fact that he stopped a good three feet from her were both a surprise and maybe even a little disappointing. Not that she wanted him to ravish her, she told herself with sarcasm.

"How does that sound?" Crispin prompted. "Will you play with me?"

Abril's mind was definitely in the gutter, because the images that popped up in her head at those words had nothing to do with an arcade game. She had to physically shake her head to get the sexy, naughty images that had assailed her out of her mind. In a bid to avoid looking at him, Abril turned to look at the two-seater arcade table instead.

"I've never actually used it," she admitted as she walked around the couch and crossed the room toward the game. "I'm not even sure if Gina has. I think she bought it at one time because she used to enjoy playing games on an old one at a coffee shop near her university when she was in school. But it was way before my time."

"Then we will both be equally unskilled at it," Crispin said lightly as he followed her. "Come on. It will be fun. And we can talk while we play."

To Abril that almost sounded like a threat. Not that she would mind talking to him, but it seemed to be something they'd had trouble with up until now. The idea of scrambling to try to play a game she'd never played before, while trying to make conversation with a man she'd never yet been able to hold a conversation with was somewhat disconcerting. But when he turned on the machine and sat down in one of the seats, she gave in and took the opposite seat herself.

"There seem to be a lot of games on here," Crispin commented as they looked over the starting screen. "Which one do we try?"

Biting her lip, Abril looked over the list until she saw a name she recognized. "I've seen the movie *Pixels*, so how about we play Pac-Man?"

"What does a movie named *Pixels* have to do with Pac-Man?" Crispin asked with interest.

"Oh, well *Pixels* is about these older dudes who used to play arcade games when they were young and—" She stopped because, frankly, it would just take too long to explain and she admitted, "It would be easier just to show you the movie."

When he hesitated, she added, "I know Gina has *Pixels* in her Apple movie library. We could watch it first and then play the game," she suggested. "It might help us at least know what we're doing when we try to play."

When he nodded, almost reluctantly, Abril jumped

to her feet and started toward the other end of the living room and the entry. "We can watch it in the kitchen so Roberts can watch too."

"Roberts has to watch the tent," he pointed out with amusement. "That's what we are here for."

"He can watch the tent and the movie too," she said reassuringly. "Besides, it's probably only an hour and a half long. It'll be fun."

Much to Crispin's amazement, he actually enjoyed the movie. A surprise because he had never bothered much with movies before this. Especially since most of his life he'd done his best to avoid people as much as possible. All of his jobs previous to this one as homicide detective had been mostly solitary pursuits that left him unhampered by the thoughts, joys, sorrows, and madness of mankind. Both mortal and immortal.

In truth, this was the first job Crispin had taken in centuries that involved dealing with the public. He'd only taken on the job of homicide detective here in London at his father's request, to help out the rogue hunters in Southern Ontario. It seemed their numbers had been somewhat depleted of late by a good portion of the Enforcers finding their life mates. Finding a life mate tended to make immortals extremely undependable. A kiss goodbye in the morning could end up being a passionate encounter that left both life mates unconscious. It was hard to get to work on time when you were in an unconscious heap on your entry floor.

Crispin knew it wasn't just the need for hunters that had made his father call him about taking this job. He suspected Basil Argeneau was hoping his son would find a life mate, something he probably would never have done had he stayed home alone all the time. Crispin hadn't thought that finding a life mate was very likely at the time. Now he almost smiled as he could imagine his father's reaction when he told him about Abril.

"Surprisingly enough I actually enjoyed that," Roberts said as the credits began to roll.

Abril snorted at that claim. "You hardly watched it. You were staring out the window at the empty tent most of the time."

"It is what we are here for," he pointed out with a faint smile, and then insisted, "Besides, you are exaggerating. I saw far more movie than not, and am certain I did not miss any of the good parts. It was very entertaining. Thank you."

"Don't thank me. It's Gina's movie," Abril said, standing up and walking over to fetch herself a glass. Pausing, she turned to raise her eyebrows at the two men, "Does anybody else want some water? Or I can get you something else. Beer? Pop or a coffee maybe?" she added when neither man jumped at the offer of a beer. She hadn't really expected them to, but had made the offer anyway.

"I shall take some water, please. But I can fetch it for myself," Crispin said as he stood and moved down the kitchen toward her.

Ignoring that last part, Abril stuck one glass under the ice dispenser, let it fill halfway up, then turned and handed it to Crispin before setting the second glass under the dispenser while he carried his glass to the sink to add water to the ice cubes.

"I am not sure how a car being chased around by a big smiley face will translate in a two-seater arcade game, but it should be interesting," Crispin commented, handing her the glass he'd just filled with water and taking the glass of ice cubes from her when she stepped up to his side.

"I guess we'll find out," Abril said cheerfully.

"I guess so," he agreed.

As it turned out, the actual Pac-Man game was different than the Pac-Man they had seen in the movie. In the movie, the good guys had been called the ghosts, riding in cars being chased by a big yellow smiley face who was Pac-Man and also apparently the bad guy. In the game, they played the big yellow smiley faced Pac-Man, making him the good guy . . . maybe. Crispin wasn't sure who was good and who was bad, since as the yellow guy they occasionally went after the ghosts too. Although, the other guys, or ghosts, *always* seemed to be coming after them. Even so, he and Abril soon got the hang of it and it was actually fun.

Mind you, it was also terribly distracting and kept him from being able to start that conversation Roberts had suggested he have with Abril. At least at first. They had been playing for perhaps twenty minutes or so, when he finally got enough of a handle on the game to try to talk to her.

"Do you have any brothers or sisters?" It was Roberts suggesting he tell her about his own family that made him ask about hers. But her answer was a bit confusing.

"Not really."

Crispin took a chance and glanced up from the screen long enough to take in her expression. But he couldn't read anything from that and quickly looked back to the game. They were not actually playing the game together so much as playing against each other. One would play until they died, and then the other would play, and each would hope they got more points than their adversary in each round. Presently he was playing, but then that was the only reason he was asking questions. He would never ask her questions while she was playing. That would be unfair. He would be distracting her, and might cause her to die sooner than she otherwise would, losing on points.

After a moment to think about how he should respond to her answer, Crispin pointed out, "*Not really* is not usually an answer to that question. It is generally a yes or no question as a rule."

He glanced up again then to check her expression once more and was surprised to see a myriad of emotions cross her face. Sadness, regret, anger, and even grief were each briefly on display. Finally, she said, "It's a long story. I—look out!" she warned, and he shifted his attention quickly back to the game just in time to watch the red ghost get him.

"Damn," he muttered, letting go of the controls as the game screen shifted to face Abril.

Since he no longer felt he should distract Abril by asking questions, he prepared to sit back and simply watch her play. But she surprised him by asking questions herself now that she was the one playing.

"What about you?" she asked. "Do you have any siblings?"

"Several," Crispin admitted.

"How many is several?" Abril asked at once.

That's when Crispin hesitated. He didn't think answering twenty-two was likely to be taken well. In fact, he was almost certain she wouldn't believe him. In the end, he merely said, "It's complicated."

"The number of siblings you have is complicated?" she asked dubiously.

"Hey," he said as she gobbled up some strawberries and went after the ghosts to eat them. "You will not even tell me properly if you have any brothers or sisters, so have no right to complain about my answer."

"Fair enough," she said easily. "What about parents then? Do you have any of those?"

"Of course. I was not hatched," Crispin said with amusement.

"Are they both alive and still together?" she asked, her tone dry.

"Still alive," he answered slowly. "But they were never really together."

"They never married?" she queried, glancing quickly his way before returning her gaze to the game.

"Not to each other. Although my father got married some years back to someone else."

"So, you have a new stepmother," she teased. "Do you like her?"

"Yes," Crispin admitted. "They are perfect for each other. She makes him very happy."

"That's nice," Abril said. "I mean, you hear so many stories about the wicked stepmother, it's nice to hear about someone who likes theirs for a change."

When Crispin merely grunted in what might have been agreement, Abril asked another question. "What made you want to be a police officer?"

"I wanted to help people," Crispin said slowly, and knew that answer was kind of on the cusp of being honest. Because while it was true, he had wanted to help people, the people he had wanted to help were the rogue hunters who had been overwhelmed trying to keep up with depleted numbers. But he was quite sure that she would take it to mean he wanted to help the victims of crimes, and he did enjoy that aspect of his career, but that wasn't the reason he had joined the police force here in London. It was just that Mortimer had needed somebody on the police force to watch for cases that might include rogues and handle the mortals who stumbled into them. Which meant erasing their memories and taking care of these situations themselves. It was why both he and Roberts were here. They were the only immortals who lived in the actual city itself. Although there were others in nearby neighboring small towns like Port Henry.

"Do you like being a police officer?" she asked now, pulling him from his thoughts.

"Sometimes," he said, honestly, and then explained, "You are looking at a homicide detective who—sadly or perhaps happily—does not have a lot of homicides to investigate. Roberts and I spend most of our time chasing down punks, muggers, shoplifters, truants, or working other really not very important cases."

"The person who was mugged probably thinks their case is important," Abril commented distractedly as she tried to avoid getting eaten by ghosts in her game.

"Yes, of course, I apologize," Crispin said, and quickly assured her, "I did not mean to suggest that the victims of muggings do not deserve our help."

"It's okay, I understand. You don't have to apologize,

and I didn't mean it that way. I know you meant that you were trained for a job and now really don't get to do that, but do lesser jobs most of the time or jobs you consider less because it's not what you are trained for."

She paused, frowning slightly as if what she said wasn't quite what she meant, but was too distracted with her game to fix it. In the end, she gave her head a small shake as if pushing the issue aside and explained, "When I said the person who was mugged probably doesn't feel their case is unimportant, I just meant you should be proud of yourself. You help people. Even if not in the capacity you are trained for."

"Thank you," Crispin said softly because she was right. He may not have taken on the job of homicide detective expecting to be catching muggers instead of murderers. But he did help mortals and his real reason for having that job had nothing to do with homicide anyway.

Crispin wanted to ask her why she had become an executive assistant, but he didn't want to distract her while she was at bat, so to speak. It was one thing for her to ask questions of him because she could pick her moment. And she could ask the question and then simply listen to the answer while still concentrating on the game.

"So, I guess that means that you do like your job?" She glanced up, and seeing his expression, said, "Or maybe you don't like your job."

"I am not sure," he admitted. "I mean, some days my job is awesome."

"Days when you solve the homicide and catch a killer?" she suggested.

"I was thinking days more like today, when I encounter a beautiful woman who has me out of my pants within hours of meeting her."

Abril's jaw dropped and her eyes were wide as plates in her head as she gaped at him with a sort of horror. "I can't believe you just said that."

"Too much?" he asked lightly.

"Too much," she agreed with a wry twist to her lips. "Too much charm, too much leg on display, too gorgeous, too—"

"You think I am charming and gorgeous?" he asked with delight.

Abril snorted at the question, her concentration on the ghosts she was trying to outrun, and then muttered, "Oh please. You must know you are. You're nicely ripped, but not overly so. You have a handsome face, awesome smile, sexy bedroom eyes." She shrugged. "Gorgeous."

Crispin stared at her with wonder as she listed off his assets in a very distracted voice. He wasn't even sure she was really aware of what she was saying as she worked to avoid getting her Pac-Man killed, and he decided Roberts's idea had been a brilliant one. Crispin was quite sure she would never have admitted her attraction to him if she weren't so engrossed in the game. Not that finding him attractive was all that unusual. She was his life mate after all, which pretty much guaranteed sexual attraction. But it was still nice to hear anyway.

A groan from Abril drew his attention to the game screen to see that she had died. It was his turn to play. And his turn to ask questions.

"What made you decide to become an executive assistant?" he asked at once.

She took so long to answer that he began to wonder if she was going to deflect this question as well. But then she admitted, "I actually wanted to study to become a vet."

"Really? Why a vet?" he asked with interest. Crispin was a great animal lover himself and had toyed more than once with the idea of training to become a veterinarian for his next career when he was ready to move on from his present position.

"Because I like animals better than people," she said lightly and then chuckled when he glanced up with an expression of surprise tinged with concern.

"I guess that sounds bad. But it's only partially true. Maybe," she added under her breath, and then gave a little huff and said, "I suppose I should probably explain or you'll think I'm some kind of antisocial freak or something."

Crispin didn't comment and simply waited for her to say what she wanted to say. But he didn't think she was a freak. in fact, while she was mortal, she sounded much like every immortal he knew. Avoiding others for the sake of their own sanity. If that made her a freak, then so was every immortal on the planet.

"You see," she began, and then fell silent as a timer began to sound.

"Saved by the bell," she said lightly standing up. "I'll be back in a minute. Try not to get killed while I'm away."

Twelve

Abril was gone before Crispin could comment, heading up the hall off the living room with Lilith quickly rising to trail her.

Abril and her shadow, Crispin thought with amusement as he continued to play. The dog seemed to follow her everywhere, no matter who else was in the room with them when she left. He couldn't blame the Lab. He'd follow her around just as devotedly if it wouldn't make her think he was a weirdo creep.

He smiled faintly at the idea of trailing her everywhere, tongue hanging out and arse wagging. But then he moved on to pondering what Abril had been about to tell him. It was obviously going to be an explanation for why she liked animals better than people, but now he was wondering what that reason could be.

Mistreatment or betrayal by a person or people was the most likely answer, he decided. Perhaps a best friend, a family member, or even a lover. That last possibility made him scowl. He was no fool. She had no doubt had lovers by now in her life, but thinking about that made jealousy rear its ugly head inside him. Which was foolish. Others may have kissed, touched, and made love to her, but he already knew none of them would compare to him. Any pleasure she'd experienced in the past in these phantom lover's arms would be nothing next to what he and she enjoyed together. That wasn't because of any great skill on his part. It was just guaranteed because they were life mates.

Just thinking about the pleasure he'd already enjoyed with her and what was still to come made Crispin hard. Unfortunately, his cock growing and shifting was enough to dislodge his towel. While the left end of the towel lay across his lap, the right side didn't and dropped away leaving his outer leg and hip exposed. Crispin was quick to grab the fallen end and pull it back up. He then stood to rewrap it around himself more securely, wincing as the soundtrack from the game announced that the distraction had cost him a life. It was game over for him.

"C'est la vie," he murmured to himself and decided he should go check on his laundry. It should be done about now, he thought, and headed up the hall wondering where Abril had gone.

He got the answer to his question when he walked into the laundry room to find the washer door open, and her just turning on the dryer. She'd shifted his laundry over for him. He was just about to thank her for that when Abril suddenly jerked around in surprise, her hand actually going to her chest.

"Oh, you startled me," she breathed, letting her hand

drop away even as her gaze began to move down over his body in the towel. There was no mistaking that the first shock of fear he'd caused had passed and she was experiencing something altogether different in response to his presence. Crispin could hear that her heartbeat had sped up. Her breathing had also become short, shallow breaths, and he could smell her excitement in the air. It was as sweet as nectar, drawing him toward her as he said, "I did not mean to startle you."

A sound came from somewhere in the vicinity of the back of her throat that might have been a response. He wasn't sure. He was only sure of one thing. "I want to kiss you."

The words came out on a low growl as he continued forward. Although, he wasn't even aware that he'd moved until she took a step back and raised a hand as if to stop him.

Stopping at once, he waited, uncertainty plaguing him. He knew she wanted him, so why was she stopping him? They were life mates. Life mate attraction was irresistible.

"I'd like to kiss you too," Abril admitted softly and he started forward again, only to freeze when she took another quick step back and added, "But . . ."

She didn't complete the thought for a moment, as if waiting to be sure he wasn't suddenly going to jump on her, and then she swallowed and said, "But I don't want to have sex."

Crispin's eyes widened and horror slid through him at the words. Kissing would lead to sex. There was no doubt in his mind of that.

"Okay?" she asked her expression a combination of hope and pleading.

Crispin hesitated. He wanted to say that was fine, that he understood. And he wanted to promise that they wouldn't have sex. Unfortunately, he couldn't guarantee that. He very much feared he didn't have the self-control to be able to say with any confidence that kissing her would not lead to touching, and ultimately sex. No immortal would.

"I mean," Abril said when he remained silent as he tried to think what to do, "making out is one thing, but it just feels too soon for sex. Okay?"

Crispin hesitated again, but for a much shorter period this time before asking, "What is making out?"

That seemed to startle her. "You don't know what making out is?"

"I do not know what *you* consider to be making out," he corrected. She had eased his worries with the term *making out*. While it had been millennia since he'd bothered with such things, he did have younger siblings still interested and engaging in dating and such, so he was familiar with the term. But even amongst those siblings it meant different things. "For my youngest sister making out is just kissing and holding."

Raising his hand, he let one finger glide down her arm and felt her pleasure as it shimmied through her, through them both really. Moving the one step necessary so that no space separated them, and her nipples were brushing against his chest through her top, he added, "But for my youngest brother, her twin, it is kissing." He bent to place a kiss just below her ear and heard her sharp intake of breath as he felt a shaft of the excitement she experienced race through his own body.

"Licking," he said next, and licked then began to

suckle at her neck, just managing to keep himself from biting her too.

"Caressing." His voice was a hungry growl against her throat as he let his hand move to close over her breast and knead gently.

"Oh God," Abril breathed, arching into the caress.

Crispin had started this with the intention of going through a long list of the things he wanted to do with her. Everything up to, but not including, penetration, which was his brother's idea of making out. He should have known better than to think he could manage that though. Crispin was already struggling with wave after growing wave of passion as they poured over him. He was fighting desperately not to rip her clothes off and drag her to the floor with him.

Thinking of the floor made him realize they were in the laundry room which had a hard tile floor. If they fainted and fell here—

Pulling his mouth away from her neck, he released her breast to take her hand instead and turned to head out of the laundry room, pulling her with him.

"What's happening? Where are we going?" Abril asked with confusion as he tugged her up the hall toward the living room.

"What is happening is that we are going to make out in the comfort of your bedroom rather than on the cold floor of the laundry room," he growled.

Abril didn't protest his plan. She let him pull her through the living room into her bedroom and close the door before Lilith could follow. It was when he then turned to take her into his arms, that she put her hands up again and backed up. "No sex?"

"No penetration," he corrected. "Anything and everything you want, but no penetration."

Abril's eyes widened, and she swallowed thickly, then demanded, "Promise me you won't get caught up in this and end up taking it too far. I'm not on birth control. I do not want to get pregnant. Promise me."

"I promise," he growled and was on her before she'd even fully lowered her hands. Abril did not protest. When his mouth covered hers and urged it open, her lips parted at once and she welcomed his tongue with her own.

He kissed her so thoroughly they were both moaning within moments. As caught up as he was in the kiss, he wanted more, and Crispin quickly undid her jeans, then pushed them off over her hips. Abril gasped into his mouth as they dropped to pool around her ankles, then gasped again when he caught her by the waist to lift her out of them and carried her to the bed. He never stopped kissing her, but came down on her even as he lowered her to the bed. Abril kissed him back, her legs wrapping around his waist and that was when she froze, panic eradicating the passion that had been flowing between them just a second earlier.

Crispin didn't have to ask why. He'd lost his towel at some point between the door and the bed, and his uncovered erection was now pressing against her, knocking at the door so to speak.

Breaking their kiss, Crispin muttered, "Sorry," then untangled her legs from around him and shifted to the side so that his erection pressed against her much safer outer leg. When she lay still, uncertainty coming off her in waves, Crispin pushed her T-shirt and bra up and out of the way to have at her breasts. It was an attempt to distract her, and reassure her at the same time, and seemed to work. She began to gasp and moan again, her back arching, pushing her breasts upward in offering.

Crispin accepted the offer, his mouth closing over one nipple to lathe and suckle, then moving to the other to do the same. Abril was clutching at his shoulders, her head twisting, and legs shifting restlessly. But he wanted the wild passion they'd had in the pool. To accomplish that, he nearly slid his hand between her legs to touch and caress her, but then decided he wanted to taste the juices he made flow instead. Abril muttered a breathless protest when he gave off playing with her breasts, and then stilled as he slithered down her body until he could get off the bed and stand beside it. Catching her by the ankles then, he pulled her to the edge of the bed, then dropped to his knees on the carpet. Abril was completely silent and still. He didn't even think she was breathing as she watched him adjust her to his satisfaction. Once he had her right where he wanted her with her bottom half off the bed, her knees on either side of him, legs spread wide leaving her open to his attention, he bent his head to give her that attention. Abril cursed and bucked wildly, but he simply held her thighs open and in place as he devoured her.

Crispin would have liked to explore and lick every inch of skin on her body, but knew he wouldn't have got far before passion had overwhelmed them both. So, he'd hoped by going right to the glory, he'd at least get to explore her there thoroughly. Sadly, that was not to be, however. He was barely able to taste her before he felt the orgasm taunting him on the edges of his awareness. Helpless not to claim it, he plunged a finger into Abril even as he continued working her with his tongue, then cried out with her as passion overwhelmed both of them and pulled them into darkness.

Abril was still asleep when Crispin woke up. He'd shifted in his sleep so that he was now curled up on the floor at her feet rather than slumped with his head between her thighs. Probably a good thing, he decided. Otherwise, he might have just started in licking and kissing her nether regions once more and ended up unconscious again. While the thought was tempting, the idea of kissing and licking his way across every inch of her body before sinking himself into her and driving them both toward orgasm still had a hold of his mind. But there was only one way he could do that.

Getting silently to his feet, Crispin took a moment to gently shift Abril so that she lay properly in bed. He then fetched a throw from the living room, and settled it lightly over her before shutting off the bedroom light and leaving the room.

Lilith was nowhere to be seen. Guessing she was in the kitchen with Roberts, he glanced at the clock in the living room to see that they hadn't been out long. He still had time before he had to replace Roberts . . . and he intended to enjoy every minute of it. He just had to grab his pants from the dryer, and decide which guest room he was going to use.

Thirteen

Abril was in her office when Crispin found her. His intention when he started looking for her was to find her, kiss her, and seduce her. Her being on the phone when he entered the room, however, put paid to that plan.

For a moment, he simply stood there in the doorway looking her over. While she'd been wearing jeans earlier, in the dream she was now dressed for business in a blouse and skirt. She looked very professional . . . sexy professional to his mind. When she didn't hang up to greet him, Crispin realized that this wasn't going to be a quick phone call. He gave up his position by the door and walked over to sit on the couch across from her desk to wait. Abril didn't even seem to notice his presence. Her entire attention was on the phone call she was participating in. Crispin hadn't originally intended to listen in on the conversation. He was a big believer in privacy. However, the anxiety and stress and plain unhappiness in her voice soon caught his attention and had him listening closely.

"But I can help you," Abril said, sounding almost desperate. "You don't have to marry him. They can't make you. I can come get you and take you away. You can live with me."

A moment passed where Crispin could barely hear someone speaking on the other end of the phone, but not well enough to understand what they were saying, then Abril cried, "No! Please, Mary. I can help you. Let me help you. You are too smart to throw your life away like this. Please let me help you."

This time when Abril fell silent there was no faint speech coming from the other end. Instead, he could hear the loud buzz of the dial tone. Whoever she had been talking to had hung up.

Crispin waited several minutes, but when tears began to slide silently down Abril's cheeks, he stood, took the phone from her hand, and ended the call from her end as well. He then knelt beside her, took her hands in his, and asked, "What happened?"

For one moment, she simply shook her head, but then she gasped, "They want my little sister to marry Agustin and she's agreed. How can they do that? They know he'll beat her. He would've beaten me if I hadn't run away and they'd been able to force our marriage. Now they're just going to sacrifice Mary to him in my place. They don't care about the hell they're casting her into. I don't think they care about any of us. We're all just tools to use to get things they want."

"Who are 'they'?" Crispin asked with a frown.

Shame flashed fleetingly across her expression, and then she lowered her head.

"Who?" Crispin insisted, knowing it was important.

"Our parents," she whispered miserably.

Crispin stiffened, then straightened, scooping her up into his arms as he went. Carrying her back around her desk, he sat down on the couch and settled her sideways in his lap. For one moment, he wasn't sure what to say or how to start the conversation they needed to have, but finally he asked, "Are your parents the reason you wanted to be a vet? Are they the reason you prefer animals to people?"

A sigh sliding from her lips, she leaned her side against his chest and nodded. "They are both very religious." Her mouth tightened. "But not the good kind. According to the religion I was brought up in, women are less than men and should be submissive to them. Our only purpose is to produce more children, preferably boys. To that end, education is considered useless for a female. We shouldn't even think about going to college or university. In fact, females are not even allowed to finish high school. Most girls are dragged out of school at sixteen and forced to marry someone of their parents' choosing."

"Like Agustin?" Crispin suggested when she fell silent.

Abril's mouth tightened and her chin came up. "Agustin wanted me. I suspect mostly to be able to torture me," she said grimly. "We'd known each other all our lives and he was a bully all our lives. He came by it naturally. He was just like his father who beat his mother nearly to death several times that I know of, and took his fists to his children too including Agustin. Agustin grew up to be just like him. He managed to control himself at school after being suspended the first time he beat up somebody in the yard during recess, but then he just took to beating up kids on the way home. He was bad as a child, but just got worse as a teenager. While he still bullied the boys, he started harassing the girls too. Running up and groping them, acting like a pig."

"Including you?" Crispin asked stiffly.

Abril shook her head. "He couldn't bother me. At least not at school. I was always in the library, talking to Mrs. Thompson or reading the books she gave me." Smiling faintly, she told him, "Mrs. Thompson was the one who gave me a love for learning and encouraged me to get a higher education. She said my grades were good enough that I could get grants and scholarships to attend university or college and she planned to help me do it.

"Mrs. Thompson knew about my home life and the religion we belonged to. She knew most girls from our community left school at sixteen, the legal age where parents could take them out of school without getting into trouble with the government. Most of them were pulled out to get married. Others who didn't already have offers for marriage were pulled out to help on the farms and such at home. But Mrs. Thompson spent a lot of time with me, telling me that I didn't have to have that life. That I could get a degree and have a career and life outside of the community my family belong to."

"And it worked," Crispin said solemnly. "You are obviously educated, and you have a career."

"Not the career and education I wanted," she pointed out, but then said, "When my parents announced that Agustin's father had petitioned for me to marry Agustin,

I begged them not to agree. I told them I wanted to finish high school and go on to college or university and a career. I told them he would rape and beat me, probably to death, if they made me marry him.

"They didn't care. They said it wouldn't be rape, he would be my husband. They said any beatings he had to administer would be my own fault because I'm so rebellious, and they would no doubt even be needed to keep me in line. They scorned my getting an education, saying it was a waste for a female to bother with that nonsense. I didn't need an education to open my legs and make babies."

Crispin had to bite down hard on his tongue to hold back the words that wanted to explode out of him. The people she was describing, her own parents, were cold, heartless bastards. No doubt abusive too, although she hadn't mentioned them beating her. At the very least they were emotionally abusive. His heart ached that she had suffered this, and he wished he'd encountered her years ago and had been able to save her from it.

"So, you ran away," Crispin said softly, remembering what she had said at the start of this conversation. She'd run away and her parents were now making her sister Mary wed Agustin in her place.

This was a shared dream and he knew she was reliving something that had happened years ago; at least ten, possibly fifteen. She was no longer sixteen and he suspected this Agustin would not have waited this long to get himself a wife. So, in her dreams, her past and her present were colliding together. It made him wonder if their talk earlier was what had brought her past into her present. His asking about her family. He was sorry now that he had. He would do anything to take this pain away from her.

"Yes," she sighed the word. "I was desperate. I knew that if Agustin got his hands on me, I'd eventually end up dead. He hated me."

Crispin frowned at the words a little confused by them. "Why would he insist on marrying you if he hated you?"

"So he could rape me and beat me as often as he wished," she said unhappily. "To punish me for calling him a big ham-fisted oaf when he was picking on one of my younger brothers, and for rejecting him when he told me he was going to marry me one day and shut my sassy mouth."

"I see," Crispin said. "I presume Mrs. Thompson helped you run away?"

Abril shook her head. "I would never have risked involving her. She could've lost her job, or been harassed by the community if she had."

"Then how did you get away?" he asked.

She hesitated, and then explained, "They told me that I had to marry Agustin on my sixteenth birthday a month beforehand. It was so that I would have time to sew a dress for my wedding. That gave me a month to scrape together some money. Which I managed through doing chores and whatnot for anyone willing to pay me."

After a thoughtful pause, she said, "In truth, I suppose Mrs. Thompson did help me run away. She was the one who hired me for the most tasks, and convinced others to do it as well. She also paid me really well."

"Your parents let you do that?" Crispin asked dubiously.

"Oh, no," she said at once. "They had no idea. I started leaving early for school, and coming home about an hour or two after school ended. I told my parents I was spending that time using the sewing machine in the home ec class to make my wedding dress. That's the only reason they allowed it. Otherwise, I would have had to hand stitch it all, and I was rotten at sewing. Couldn't manage a straight seam to save my soul, and they knew that. Using a sewing machine was the only way I could have finished a dress in time."

"But while they thought you were making your dress, you were . . ." He let the sentence trail off because he had no idea what kind of chores she might have done.

"Helping Mrs. Thompson with tasks around her house, cleaning, gardening, and stuff." She paused briefly and added, "Pretty much the same stuff for the other teachers and friends of hers she convinced to hire me."

Crispin nodded.

"Of course, I couldn't take the money home. If my parents had found it that would've been the end of any opportunity to escape. So, I left the money with Mrs. Thompson. She promised to keep it safe for me. My birthday was on a Sunday. So, my last day of school was the Friday before. That afternoon, after school, I went to Mrs. Thompson's and she gave me all the money I had made that month. It was nearly three hundred dollars. I suspect Mrs. Thompson topped it up, because I was only expecting half that." Her mouth twisted with cynical amusement as she said, "I thought I was rich."

Sighing, Abril closed her eyes and said, "After giving

me the money, she gave me a file folder with copies of my school records in it. She said I'd need them to finish high school. I nearly burst into tears when she gave them to me. I hadn't even thought about school records, and I knew she wasn't supposed to do that. That she'd get in trouble if she got caught, but she took the risk for me anyway. I took the records with gratitude, but then she offered to drive me wherever I wanted to go. I knew she knew when my birthday was, knew what I was doing, and I knew she wanted to help. Mrs. Thompson probably would've taken me to the city if I'd asked. But I didn't want to get her into trouble. So, I said no thank you, left her home, and walked to the bus station."

"I knew my parents would come looking for me when I did not return home at the usual time. Once they realized I'd run away, they'd search. Agustin's father held a lot of power in our community. They would be desperate to keep him happy," Abril said grimly. After a pause, she shrugged and went on, "I knew the farther away I could get, the better it would be for me. My ultimate destination was Toronto. But that was several provinces and almost 1,700 miles away. My money wouldn't take me that far."

Crispin wondered where she was born and raised that was so far away, but before he could ask, she continued. "So, I kept twenty dollars back for food and bought a ticket for as far away in the direction of Toronto as I could get, then I hoped for the best." She paused and pursed her lips briefly before saying, "I don't even remember the name of the small town my ticket was supposed to take me to. I never got there whatever it was."

Crispin's eyes widened with alarm. "Your parents caught up to you?"

"No," she assured him. "I just got lucky. About ten hours later in the next province over, I had to switch buses. I grabbed my stuff and got off the one I'd arrived on, then looked around a bit. I had half an hour before the next bus I was supposed to take was leaving, and was pacing around when the girl at the counter told me there was a restaurant next door if I wanted to get something to eat or drink while I waited. I was hungry, so decided to go over and see if they had anything real cheap on the menu.

"As I approached the restaurant, though, I saw a big help wanted sign in the window. I sat down at a table, but found myself looking at that sign over and over. Finally, when a waitress came up to ask me what I'd like, I asked her about it. She said it was for a waitressing position and then asked me if I was interested. I said I might be. She got this shrewd look on her face as she looked me over and then she said, 'You aren't from around here.' I said, 'No, I just came in on the bus.' Then she asked me about my work experience. Of course, I only had the chores and tasks that I'd carried out for Mrs. Thompson and her friends to offer up. But she asked me where I was going, what my plans were. I told her I wanted to go to Toronto eventually, but needed to make money to get there. Then she asked me a couple more questions, more personal ones."

Abril shook her head. "Her name was Barb. And she should have been a psychologist. I don't know how she did it, but she got me to tell her all about my troubles. The community I'd grown up in. Their values. That I was running away from a forced marriage and only sixteen. It turned out that she and her husband were the owners of the little restaurant." She gave him a crooked smile and said, "Five minutes before my bus would've left, she said I could have the job."

Crispin smiled in return, but remained silent, allowing her to continue.

"It was a lucky day when I met her. Barb didn't just give me a job, she let me stay with her and her husband, Bob, until I made enough money to get my own little place. Bob was the main cook in the restaurant, but he was also a pilot who flew locally, crop dusting for farmers and such in the summer. They both became like parents to me, and insisted I didn't have to move out until I'd saved enough money to go to university. But I was determined not to be a burden to them.

"My apartment when I finally moved out was a little hole in the wall place in a dumpy area, but it was all mine," Abril said, sounding proud, and then she continued, "Barb also made sure I finished high school. She said if I didn't, she'd fire my ass, so I went to school during the day, and then waited tables after school until closing, went back to my little apartment to do my homework and fell exhausted into bed every night." She smiled faintly. "Then I worked double shifts on the weekends to save up money to get to Toronto. I think Barb did all that as much to keep me out of trouble as anything else. Between school and work I was too exhausted to date or get into trouble," she explained with faint amusement.

"She became like a surrogate mother, or a grumpy old grandma. She was family. I still call and write to her and Bob a lot.

"Anyway, I ended up staying long past when I'd made enough money to go to Toronto. I stayed until I graduated high school. As I mentioned, I wanted to be a vet, so I applied to every university that offered veterinary training. Getting into one is almost impossible. There are only three hundred spots open a year and they say that for every student who is accepted, there are seven hundred to a thousand who are rejected. It's one of the hardest programs to get into in Canada. I was determined that I would be one of the ones accepted, and I was," she said with a bright smile that quickly faded. "Only the grants, bursaries, and scholarships I managed to get wouldn't have covered even half of my tuition a year. I would have had to pay the rest myself with the cost of the dorm and food on top of that. I hadn't saved nearly enough for that.

"Fortunately, my guidance counselor helped me with the applications, and insisted I apply to other programs at other universities too in case I wasn't accepted into the veterinary programs. It annoyed me at the time, but in the end, she did me a favor. The grants and such I'd earned with my grades were enough to cover everything in other universities and different programs. So I changed direction and studied business."

She paused and then turned her face toward him to give him a self-deprecating smile. "Geez, poor guy. Ask me one question and I vomit my whole life story on you."

"It was more than one question," he said solemnly. "And I am honored you are sharing your past with me."

"You should be," she assured him. "I don't share it with many people."

Crispin smiled and then hesitated for a moment

about what to say next. Part of him wanted to carry out his plan to seduce and ravish her, right here on the couch. But another part needed to know—"Your sister was forced to marry Agustin in your place?"

"Yes, she . . ." Her voice died as she glanced toward the phone, and confusion covered her face. "That happened years ago. But I was just talking to her on the phone like it was happening today."

Her gaze slid around the large office with its cool gray walls, black desk, bookshelves, and couch. "This is the office I'm supposed to have when the addition is done. The one I use now was a bedroom. It's much smaller and the walls are lavender. I—" She sat up abruptly in his lap, and then turned to tell him, "I think this is a dream."

Crispin managed to suppress his amusement and nodded. "I believe you may be right."

"Wow. I never remember my dreams. I wonder if I always figure out I'm dreaming in the middle of them?"

Rather than address that Crispin merely said, "You will remember this dream."

"You think so?" she asked.

"I know so," he assured her and finally did what he'd wanted since entering her office and kissed her.

Fourteen

Kissing Abril in the dream was the polar opposite to kissing her in reality. They were not immediately overwhelmed with passion. Crispin wasn't experiencing her pleasure alongside his own and desperate to reach the end of the journey. He was experiencing only his own pleasure as he slid his fingers into her hair, tilted her head to the angle he wanted, and thrust his tongue into her mouth.

Abril sighed into his mouth and wrapped her arms around his shoulders as he made a meal of her mouth. When she then pressed instinctively closer and kissed him back, he almost smiled. This was what he wanted. With this slow burn, he could do so much more with her before their passion overwhelmed them and tossed them into unconsciousness. In fact, in their shared dream they wouldn't lose consciousness at the end, but could start again. With that in mind, he let the hand not presently wrapped in her hair begin to explore her body. He caressed her breasts through the blouse she was wearing, and then, since it was a dream, he wished the blouse away so that she sat in his lap in just a bra and her skirt.

"Yes," Abril breathed as he broke their kiss to shift his attention to her breasts. She watched him caress her through the lace of her bra and then moaned when he wished that away as well, and he was able to touch her without the impediment. When he found himself suddenly without his shirt on, Crispin supposed she must've wished it away. He hadn't even thought to do it himself, but he was glad she had when her hands began to move over his chest, even as he caressed her.

When he kissed her again, Abril responded with more demand, and then suddenly rose up to straddle him on the couch. He was still in his dress pants and she in her skirt, but he didn't feel the need to change that at the moment as she began to shift in his lap, rubbing herself against his hard cock through his slacks as they kissed each other almost desperately.

Crispin was a little surprised when she switched to the old-fashioned route and reached between them to undo his pants. But there was no denying the excitement it sparked when she slid the zipper down and then reached inside to grasp his erection. Crispin broke their kiss on a groan and let his head drop to rest on the back of the couch as she began to caress him. She was using the perfect grip and strength as she moved her hand slowly up and down his shaft. Distracted by the mounting pleasure he was experiencing he didn't notice when she began to shift off his lap until something warm and wet closed over his cock. Lifting his head abruptly, he opened his eyes to look down and saw that she had taken him into her mouth.

He knew this would speed things along and that he wouldn't be able to refrain from coming in her mouth. But he also knew it wouldn't matter. It was a dream. He could do that, and then immediately sink himself into her if he wished. Or he could return the favor and then sink himself into her, or he could—

The sensation of someone lightly slapping his arm made him glance around in surprise and open his eyes. He blinked in brief confusion when he found himself in the guest bedroom looking up at Roberts.

"Wake up, bud," Roberts said cheerfully. "Your turn on guard."

Groaning, Crispin let his eyes close and his head drop back, but only for a heartbeat. Then he tossed the sheets aside and sat up on the side of the bed before recalling the state his cock was in.

"Whoa, do not point that thing at me, Delacort. With the state it is in it might start shooting at me. I will make you a pot of coffee to help you wake up while you get dressed."

"Smart-ass," Crispin muttered, standing up and reaching for his dress pants. He'd donned them and was pulling on his shirt when a scream shattered the silence.

"Abril!" He was out of the room before he was finished shouting her name. He was just as swift making his way up the hall to the living room, and then to Abril's bedroom door. Crispin rushed in, taking in the situation at a glance. Abril was on the floor, crumpled up against the wall next to the bed and obviously unconscious, while a dark figure was escaping through her window. His gaze slid from one to the other, but it was Abril he went to.

Crispin was just scooping her up into his arms when movement behind him made him glance around in time to see Roberts was climbing out the window after the escaping intruder.

Mouth tightening, Crispin hesitated. His first thought had been to take Abril to his room, somewhere that hadn't been broken into and therefore seemed safer. He knew it probably wasn't truly safer, though—it had a window too. But he suspected Abril would feel safer there than here when she woke up. However, now that Roberts had chased the intruder outside, he was reluctant to leave the room until his partner returned and they could secure the window.

Crispin glanced down at Abril then, for the first time noticing that while she still wore the T-shirt she'd worn earlier, it and her bra were pushed up above her breasts. She also wasn't wearing anything else. He'd removed her jeans and underwear when they were making out earlier before the sex dream that had just been interrupted he recalled and frowned. He didn't want Roberts seeing her this way.

Crispin set Abril down on the bed, then made a quick search for something to put on her. He suspected getting jeans on to an unconscious woman would be a nightmare task, so was thinking to perhaps remove her bra and top and slip a nightgown on over her head. Then he came across joggers. After a hesitation, he snatched them up and returned to Abril. A nightgown would have undoubtedly been easier to put on her, but the joggers were loose enough that he managed the task with little trouble. Crispin then took the time to shift her bra and T-shirt back into place.

Once he had Abril dressed, Crispin scooped her up but then hesitated and glanced to the window, expecting to see his partner already climbing back inside. He wasn't, and Crispin frowned. He wouldn't have thought it would take this long for the man to return. Roberts should have had no trouble running the intruder to ground and capturing him. Immortals were stronger and faster than mortals. So much so that he wouldn't have worried even if it had been six mortal men out there that his partner was looking for, so he definitely wasn't going to fret over one. He was annoyed though. He wanted to get Abril to somewhere safe and examine her wound, but couldn't do that until he was sure his partner was safe. That annoyance began to turn to concern though as the minutes continued to pass without Roberts returning. So he was more than a little relieved when his partner finally appeared at the window and climbed back in. It was quickly followed by surprise, however, when he saw that his partner was alone.

"Where is the intruder?" he asked with confusion.

"He got away," Roberts admitted unhappily.

Crispin couldn't hide his shock. "What? How?"

"The intruder was immortal." The words were heavy and grim with meaning. And the two men stared at each other for a solid minute before either of them moved.

"Lock the window," Crispin ordered as he turned to pick up Abril again.

Even as he did, Roberts asked, "Do you want to call Mortimer or shall I?"

"I will," Crispin said firmly as he carried Abril out of the room.

He took her to his room, set her on the bed, but didn't immediately call Mortimer. Instead, he turned on the bedside light and quickly examined her head for the wound that had knocked her out. He found it on the side of her head, under the hair, and cursed as he felt the blood and the lump already forming there. Very aware that she was mortal, and therefore fragile, Crispin finally snatched his phone off the bedside table and punched in the number for the Enforcer headquarters.

Normally, he would have left the room to talk to Mortimer to be sure he wasn't overheard by Abril, but Crispin wasn't leaving her alone. Not when there was an immortal out there trying to get to her.

The very idea was a shocking one to him. Abril was mortal and as far as he could tell, had no connection to immortals. Why would one have troubled himself to attack her?

Fretting over that, and desperate to get help in sorting out what was happening here, he listened impatiently to the phone ring.

Fifteen

Abril woke up with a splitting headache and some confusion about where she was. It was the quick glimpse she had of what appeared to be a kitchen cupboard in front of her face before pain made her close her eyes again that had her bewildered. There had been no kitchen cupboards in her bedroom when she'd gone to sleep.

When had she gone to sleep? She wondered about that suddenly, and then wondered if she was dreaming. That thought had her recalling the dream she'd had, and she squirmed a little where she was lying as she remembered the sweet passion she'd enjoyed before Crispin had suddenly disappeared from her dream. His sudden absence had startled her awake only to be startled again as she saw a dark shape creeping across her room.

Abril had only managed one short scream before the intruder had turned toward her and—

"Abril? Are you awake?"

It was a woman's voice, one she didn't recognize, and Abril opened her eyes immediately, only to find herself meeting the concerned gaze of a striking blonde she'd never seen before.

"How do you feel?" the woman asked, some of the concern on her face easing as she saw that Abril was conscious and looking at her.

"Who are you?" Abril asked with a frown, and then glanced around and asked, "And why am I in the kitchen?" She looked down at what she was lying on. "Are these the cushions from the wicker couch in the pool room?" Her confused gaze returned to the woman then and she complained, "My head hurts."

"Let's take each point one at a time, shall we?" the blonde said with a faint smile. "I'm Dr. Dani Argeneau-Pimms. I am not sure where the cushions came from. You were already lying on them when I arrived. Apparently, Crispin didn't want to leave you on your own after the attack, and he had to be in here watching the monitor and the bones in the tent, so he made up this bed for you to keep you here with him and comfortable. And finally, on a scale of one to ten, how badly does your head hurt?"

"Twelve," Abril answered unhappily as she absorbed everything that the woman had said. A quick glance around showed she was lying on the floor between one side of the island and the adjacent counter. She couldn't see much of anything. "Where is Crispin?"

"Your dog needed to go outside so he took her," Dr. Dani Argeneau-Pimms answered absently as she began to dig through a black bag on the floor between them.

"She's not my dog. She's my boss's," Abril muttered, shifting to a sitting position. Doing so sent sharp pain stabbing through her head, but she simply ground her teeth together and continued until she was upright. Then she jerked her head around with a gasp of pain at a sharp sting in her arm. It felt like someone had stabbed her, and she saw that the good doctor *had* . . . with a needle she was just finishing pushing the plunger home on. Abril glared at her. "What—?"

"It will help with your headache," the doctor explained as she removed the needle.

Abril just continued to glare at her, mostly because she couldn't do anything else in that moment. Swinging her head around as she had done had sent even worse pain roaring through it, and she was fighting a sudden urge to vomit.

"Deep breaths in through your nose, and exhale slowly through the mouth," Dr. Dani instructed as she put away her weapons of torture. "It will help you fight the nausea."

Abril continued to scowl at her, but followed her directions, breathing in through her nose and then exhaling slowly through her mouth. Surprisingly enough, it actually worked, and the need to vomit slowly eased and then disappeared. Once she felt a little better, Abril asked, "Where is Roberts?"

"He's in the living room talking to Lucian and my husband, Decker," Dr. Dani told her, and then turned to meet her gaze again. For one moment, she seemed to be examining Abril's eyes.

Although she had no idea what the woman might be looking for, Abril held perfectly still and kept her eyes wide open for her anyway.

"You'll be good," Dr. Dani said finally, fully relaxing now. "Crispin took you in to the hospital to have your head x-rayed while they waited for me to get here. Fortunately, there was no damage done to your skull, which would've been bad."

"Definitely bad," Abril agreed dryly.

"So, we brought you back here to recover," Dr. Dani continued as if she hadn't spoken. "You'll need to get a lot of sleep for the next little while. A full eight hours a night at least, and then naps throughout the day. No physical activity beyond slow, short walks outside with your dog. No sex. No excitement of any kind, and I'll leave some pills here for your headache."

Abril blinked at the rapid-fire list of dos and don'ts, but was almost afraid to speak.

"I'll give Crispin and Roberts a list of symptoms to watch out for in case of a hematoma putting pressure on the brain. Those can end in brain damage or even death, so you should watch out for them yourself. They are slurred speech, weakness, numbness, decreased coordination, difficulty waking up, confusion, repeated vomiting, shaking, or twitching—things like that," she announced, and then added cheerfully, "But I'm sure you'll recover fine."

Abril just stared at her with disbelief, thinking the woman had a horrible bedside manner. She was shit with shots too.

"I don't normally give shots," Dr. Dani said apologetically. "Or talk much to patients really. I'm a gynecologist. Most people don't like to chat when you're giving them pap smears."

"You're a gyne—Why are you treating me then?" she squawked with dismay.

"Because Rachel wasn't available," Dr. Dani said as she picked up her bag and got to her feet. "She's much better with patients. Which is kind of weird when you think about it, because at least I work with living people. You'd think I'd be better with patients than her."

Abril just gaped at her, wondering what the hell that meant. *At least I work with living people?*

"Rachel works in the morgue," Dani said as if she'd asked the question out loud. "Anyway, your thoughts seem clear, so I really believe everything will be fine. It was nice meeting you, Abril."

She watched the blonde disappear from sight around the island, and then listened as her footsteps faded away. She was alone in the kitchen. For now, Abril thought. Crispin and Lilith should be back soon though.

That thought raised alarm in her. Not because Crispin would be back soon, but because Lilith would. She knew damned right well that if she was still on the floor when Lilith returned, the Lab would be all over her, licking her face, bumping against her . . . Abril could almost feel the pain all of that would cause her head. It was enough to have her shifting to her knees and grasping the edge of the counter to help her slowly stand up. As careful as Abril was, and as slowly as she moved, it didn't prevent her head from complaining by sending agonizing pain through her skull.

Leaning against the counter, Abril desperately began to suck air in through her nose and release it through her mouth as she wondered how long it would take for the shot Dr. Dani had given her to kick in. She hoped it was quick. She'd never experienced a headache as bad as this and would be happy not to experience it again.

The sound of the front door opening and closing was quickly followed by the tap of nails on hardwood as Lilith rushed into the kitchen, either in search of a treat, or looking for her, Abril supposed. She was actually surprised when Lilith came straight to her rather than sitting down in front of where the dog treat container resided on the counter on the other side of the island.

"Hi, baby girl," she said softly, reaching down to pet the Labrador's head. "Would you like a treat?"

"I'll get it," Crispin said quickly as he entered the room.

Knowing it would cause her pain, Abril fought the urge to turn her head quickly to look at him. Instead, she turned it very slowly. He was standing with his back to her and digging treats out of the container by the time she was able to see him. Abril wasn't sure if she was happy or not over the fact that he was dressed now. The last time she'd seen him, he'd been wearing nothing but a towel. Actually, no, she realized. He'd lost even that in her room when he'd . . . she killed that thought immediately since the memory of what they'd done wasn't just making her blush wildly, but was making her slightly hot and bothered.

Really, the last time she'd seen him had been in her dreams. He'd been wearing dress pants, she thought now in the hopes of driving the image of a naked Crispin out of her mind. But the memory of the wet dream she'd had about him did not ease her embarrassment or make her less hot and bothered. While their passion in the dream had been a little gentler and more of a slow burn, it had just been ratcheting up to volcanic levels when Crispin had suddenly disappeared from it.

The only saving grace was that he couldn't know what she'd dreamt of after he'd left her.

"How are you feeling?" Crispin asked as he turned to give the treats to Lilith. The Labrador had abandoned her the moment she heard him open the ceramic container and was now sitting pretty in front of him. *Tramp*, Abril thought.

"Abril?" Crispin queried, starting around the island now that Lilith was taken care of.

"I should feed Lilith," she murmured rather than answer his question. If she told him how she was really feeling she'd sound like a crybaby, because she felt pretty horrible just then.

"I already fed her," Crispin said solemnly. "Both breakfast and lunch."

"Wait. What? It was nighttime when last I . . ." She started to shake her head, and then caught herself. "Now it's not just the next morning, but after lunch of the next day already?" she asked with dismay. "Where is my phone? Gina usually calls after lunch. She'll freak if I don't answer."

"It is all right, sweetheart. Your phone is right over here on the island," Crispin said reassuringly and ushered her down the island to the seat she'd been using since the men's arrival. Abril suspected she should be offended that he did so by taking her arm like she was a little old lady he was helping across the road, but at the moment her brain was taken up with the fact that he had called her sweetheart.

"Here, see, she has not yet called. You did not miss anything. All is well."

Abril just stared at him. The man was talking to her like she was a wild horse he was trying to keep from bolting. Or a crazy person, she thought. But even that didn't overly distress her. He'd called her sweetheart.

"Stop looking at me like that," Crispin said suddenly, sounding almost alarmed.

"Like what?" Abril asked, her gaze moving over his lips as she recalled the pleasure they'd given her.

"Like you want me to kiss you and caress you and—"

"I do," Abril breathed, interrupting his list of all the things she liked best about him so far. A list that was making her hot and wet. A sensation that only increased when his head began to lower toward her. Knowing he was going to kiss her, she licked her lips and started to tilt her head slowly upward to meet him, then let her eyes close. A bare moment later, she opened them again because he hadn't given her the expected kiss.

"Dani said no sex," Crispin told her with regret.

"Maybe you could just kiss me," she suggested, suddenly almost desperate for him to do so.

"She also said no excitement," he announced. "And kissing you is one of the most exciting things I have ever experienced in my very long life. Hopefully, the same is true for you."

Abril stared at him wide-eyed, quite sure she never heard anything so sweet in her life.

"Are you hungry?" he asked suddenly.

She briefly considered saying yes in a suggestive manner, but then remembered she would soon no doubt have a phone call from Gina. The last thing she wanted to do was answer that call sounding all out of breath from messing about with Crispin, so she let the idea go.

For one minute, she didn't answer his question.

Instead, she concentrated on her body and any messages it might be sending her. But she wasn't feeling any hunger pangs. In fact, she was concerned about whether chewing might hurt her head right now too. That thought in mind, she decided waiting a little bit before she ate might be a good thing. Hopefully, once the shot Dr. Dani had given her kicked in, the pain would ease enough to allow her to try to eat.

Before she could say as much to Crispin, the soft drone of voices coming from the living room grew louder and then Roberts led two men into the room. Four men, she realized, when Roberts and the other two were followed a moment later by two additional strangers. No—she corrected as another man now entered—five. There were five new men she'd never seen before now in the kitchen with her besides Crispin and Roberts.

"It cannot be a coincidence," one of the newcomers insisted firmly. He was a tall man, with ice-blond hair and an air of authority about him. She eyed him with curiosity as he moved around Roberts to get to the coffee machine. Retrieving a cup from the cupboard as if he lived there, the man poured himself some coffee and added, "You know how I feel about coincidences." He shook his head and turned to lean against the counter, the freshly poured coffee in hand as he said, "First, there are bodies found in the garden and then an immortal breaks in?" He shook his head firmly. "They have to be connected."

"What is an immortal?" Abril asked, making her presence known.

Sixteen

Abril froze when the men who had just entered the kitchen turned as one to stare at her. She hadn't thought her question of what an immortal was would be a problem, but the silence and the expressions the men wore were suggesting the question was unwelcome. As she waited for one of them to respond, she found her gaze ranging over the group.

Like Roberts and Crispin, the five newcomers were all handsome. They were also all aged somewhere in the mid to late twenties. Each man was dressed in black, whether that was black jeans and T-shirt, or black leather pants and T-shirt. Three of them even had similar features to Crispin. In fact, the only way that any of them differed was that their hair color ranged from platinum blond to almost black and the length of their hair ranged from short to shoulder length.

They look like a bloody boy band, she thought. She could imagine teen girls throwing themselves at them, begging for autographs and squealing happily over being in their presence.

A short bark of laughter from one of the men caused a sudden shifting amongst all of them. Most of which consisted of them all turning away as if to hide their expressions. It was followed by choking sounds, and throat-clearing coughs, along with shaking shoulders that suggested they were laughing at her. Although she couldn't imagine why asking what an immortal was would cause such amusement.

Wondering if her head injury had made her misinterpret things, or perhaps her hair was standing up in all directions, Abril shifted her gaze to Crispin in question. But he seemed just as confused as she was, and merely stepped closer to her in support. The moment he did, she asked in almost a whisper, "Who are these men? Are they also homicide detectives?"

She suspected they couldn't be. At least, she found it hard to believe that London needed seven homicide detectives. Especially since Crispin had said that there were not enough homicides in London to keep him and Roberts busy.

"These are . . . coworkers," Crispin said, and Abril raised her eyebrows because she'd just decided they couldn't be homicide detectives, so what kind of coworkers were they? However, he misunderstood what her questioning look meant and quickly pointed to the ice blond saying, "Abril, this is Lucian Argeneau, the big boss."

Lucian was the one with the cup of coffee. He had similar features to Crispin and the same beautiful silver-blue eyes, but his hair was ice blond. Before Abril could ask if Lucian was related to him, and if when he said "the big boss" he meant this Lucian was the chief of police or something, he'd moved on. "The man next to him is Anders."

Anders was a handsome, dark-skinned man with a body a swimsuit model would kill for. He had slim hips, a narrow waist, and then a chest and shoulders that were twice as wide and muscular.

"This is Bricker," Crispin continued, waving toward a leaner dark-haired man with green eyes tinged with silver who didn't look anything like the other men.

"Decker," he said gesturing to a man with dark hair and who did have similar features to Crispin.

"And Cassius," Crispin finished, pointing to the last man who didn't just have similar features to Crispin, but could have been a twin except that his hair was blond rather than dark like Crispin's.

"They are brothers." The speaker was Lucian, the tall icy blond with the air of authority who appeared so arrogantly comfortable in Gina's kitchen. Before she could ponder long on the fact that his comment was almost like he'd read her thoughts, he added, "Decker is a cousin, and all three are my nephews."

Abril's eyes were widening at the nepotism of the local police force, when Lucian continued by asking, "Can you describe your attacker?"

Abril suspected he was arrogant in more than acting like he owned the place. She couldn't have said why she felt that way, this was only the second time he'd spoken, but she'd always been able to quickly peg people and know how to handle them. She suspected it had something to do with her childhood, where making a misstep could bring about grievous punishment.

"Your attacker?" Lucian repeated impatiently.

For a fraction of a second, her mouth thinned with irritation at his tone, but she quickly smoothed it out and considered the question. Her mind went back to her memories of the previous night and the intruder in her bedroom. She'd been in the middle of a rather spicy dream involving Crispin, the couch in her future office, and the ability she'd had in the dream to remove clothes with just a thought. Then Crispin had suddenly disappeared, surprising or perhaps disappointing her enough that she'd woken up.

Thinking about it now, she supposed that rather than Crispin's disappearing from the dream, it must've been some small sound made by the intruder that had woken her. Whatever the case, she'd opened her eyes and seen a dark figure creeping around the end of her bed. Abril hadn't even thought, she'd immediately opened her mouth and screamed. But it had been a short, sharp scream, cut off when the creeper had suddenly lunged at her.

She still wasn't sure what had happened. Whether she'd been hit or picked up and thrown, but Abril had got a glimpse of eyes glowing like a cat's in the dark, and then she'd suddenly found herself hurtling through the air. This was followed by pain exploding in her head and back as she'd slammed into the wall. She'd lost consciousness then, the image of her attacker's glowing eyes the last thing she'd seen before sinking into unconsciousness.

That thought made her frown, and Abril decided she must've still been half asleep and caught up in the strands of her dream to think his eyes had glowed. But putting the matter aside for a moment, she tried to concentrate on what she had seen of his face. Not much was the answer. She'd got an impression of short hair as black as the clothes he was wearing, but didn't even really have a vague impression of the face. Except that it been clean-shaven.

"What is it?" Crispin asked, and the question made her shift her attention to him, and then to the men facing them to see the disappointment on each of their faces.

"She does not remember anything but glowing eyes and short dark hair," Lucian announced.

His words made Abril stiffen a little. Had she spoken her memory aloud? She didn't recall doing so, but that was the only explanation for the blond knowing what she'd just been thinking. Perhaps the shot Dr. Dani had given her was kicking in and affecting her poor brain.

As soon as she had that thought, Lucian speared Crispin with a look and said, "You need to explain the situation to her."

"What?" Crispin asked, the word sharp and distressed sounding.

"You heard me. If an immortal is involved, and for some reason has targeted her, she is in a lot of danger. She needs to know the situation to protect herself properly."

When Crispin opened his mouth, she suspected to protest further, the man asked, "Are you sure she will remain in your presence, or that of one of the other men at all times, if she does not understand the danger she faces here?"

Uncertainty crossed Crispin's face as he turned to peer at her. And then her phone rang.

Abril scowled with irritation at the interruption;

Lucian's words were raising a lot of questions in her. What were immortals—which had now been mentioned twice—and why would they target her? And just exactly what danger did she face? These questions managed to get pushed aside when she saw *Boss Lady* on her phone's display. She immediately stood to leave the room and take the call. She didn't want Gina to hear the men and then have to explain why they were there. She was still hoping to avoid telling her boss about the discovery in her garden until after she returned. Hopefully the matter would be cleared up by then, and the contractors back to work. If she was lucky, and Gina extended the length of her vacation, the men might even be done a good portion of the addition before she came back. That might temper her upset on learning about the skeletons, the police presence, and all the gossip it all was no doubt causing in the neighborhood.

Abril waited until she was halfway down the hall to her temporary office before hitting Answer on her phone and greeting her boss.

Seventeen

"I rest my case."

Crispin turned from watching Abril's retreating back at those dry words from Lucian and met his grim gaze, his own expression unhappy. "Surely we can convince her of the seriousness of the situation and the necessity for her to stay close to one of us at all times without revealing what we are to her?"

He could hear the desperation in his own voice, and knew the others could too from the sympathy he saw on everyone's face but Lucian's. But desperate was how he was feeling. He had been counting on being able to make her like him, and seduce her with life mate sex, which was said to be addictive, before explaining who and what he was. He was sure that was the only chance he would have to claim her for his life mate.

Turning it around and telling her about immortals and that he was one before gaining her trust and hopefully binding her to him with sex, might make it impossible for him to woo her to his side. He was sure he needed both to soften the effect of the news Lucian was insisting he give her.

"Do you want her alive, but possibly not with you? Or do you want to have her dead?" Lucian asked simply.

"God, you are a cold bastard," Crispin snarled.

The accusation made Lucian's lips quirk upward in what could've been mistaken for a smile. "And your point is?"

When Crispin didn't respond, he pointed out, "She is alone, unguarded, and out of your sight this minute, Crispin." He paused briefly to let that sink in and then asked, "Do you think she would have walked away to take that phone call if she knew the peril she was in?"

Crispin didn't answer. He simply turned on his heel and strode down the hall to Abril's office.

Her office in reality was much different than the office they had been in during their shared dream last night. There was a desk, bookcase, couch, and even a filing cabinet, but the room was much smaller and the furniture all crammed much closer together. The walls were also a pale lavender rather than the pale gray from the dream.

He hesitated at the door, not wanting to intrude on her phone call, but when he heard her saying, "Yes, yes. Everything is fine here—" and then a pause before she said with sudden worry in her voice, "The work on the addition?"

While her voice was anxious, her expression was panic-stricken. Crispin finally gave up his position in the doorway and strode into the room. He moved quickly around her desk and bent to whisper in her free ear, "Rain."

Abril lifted her gaze to him as he straightened and echoed blankly, "Rain?"

"It's raining there?" came a distressed squawk from the phone.

Understanding then filled Abril's expression, and she offered him a smile of gratitude before saying into the phone, "I'm sure construction will not be delayed long. Everything will be fine, Gina. You just enjoy your vacation and do not worry about a thing. I've got this for you."

Crispin couldn't help but admire her for how she managed to not actually lie to her boss. She hadn't told her that it was raining. She hadn't even been speaking to her when she said the word *rain*. She simply hadn't corrected her. She also hadn't said that it was rain that was delaying construction, she'd simply said she was sure construction wouldn't be delayed long.

Abril was nodding as she now listened to the long tirade her boss was spewing down the phone line. But her gaze was on him the whole time and she was beaming at him with gratitude.

Smiling in return, Crispin settled on the couch to wait for the call to end. It took much longer than he expected. Gina apparently needed to vent about her frustration with the addition she was having built. She was speaking loud enough that he caught the better part of it. She was angry with the delays that had set back the starting date for months. She hadn't appreciated the further delays as the interior renovations had proceeded. The excavator breaking down had pissed her off, but now even Mother Nature appeared to be against her. Gina was sure that at this rate, she would never get to enjoy her new home in its completed state.

Abril listened patiently, making appropriate comments or sounds as needed. She reassured her boss as much as she could, and then managed to convince the woman to go back to enjoying her vacation and leave everything to her. The last thing Abril said before ending the call was a promise that she would take care of it all, and see everything was done as quickly as possible.

When she finally ended the call, Crispin commented, "It seems to me being an executive assistant is the equivalent of a fireman."

His words made her smile, and Abril nodded. "Pretty much. I spend the better part of my days putting out fires and trying to avoid future fires."

"Sounds stressful," Crispin commented.

Abril shrugged. "Maybe a bit. But at least it's never boring."

This time it was her words that made him smile, and then he sobered and asked, "How is your head?"

When she paused and tilted her head slightly, her eyes losing focus somewhat, he suspected she was checking on that situation herself.

"It doesn't hurt anymore," she said finally with surprise. Her gaze cleared and shifted to him. "I guess that shot Dr. Dani gave me is working."

"Good." Crispin got to his feet. "Dani said that avoiding bright light would help stave off headaches." His gaze slid to the open blinds on the large window in her office, and the sunshine pouring through it. He moved to close the blinds even as he asked, "Do you have any sunglasses around here?"

"Sunglasses?" Abril echoed with confusion.

"In case you had not noticed, this house is almost nothing but windows," he pointed out dryly.

"It is not," Abril protested.

"Every room has large plate glass windows, sliding doors, skylights, and any other type of window and door that would allow sunlight to flood the house. And most of them without any kind of window covering. It might be best to wear sunglasses to block the worst of it. That might help to keep the headaches at bay." Propping his hands on his hips then he raised his eyebrows. "So? Sunglasses?"

She blew out an exasperated breath, but opened one of her desk drawers and pulled out a pair of large-framed dark sunglasses. Putting them on, she asked in arid tones, "Happy?"

"Very," he assured her.

"Great," she said dryly. "But I'm going to feel ridiculous walking around inside with shades on."

"Well, you could go without and risk the headache," he pointed out. "Although I think those sunglasses look good on you. They make you look kind of mysterious and sexy."

Even through the dark lenses, Crispin could see the way her eyes widened at that statement. It made him want to pull her into his arms and kiss her. But very aware that Lucian and the others were just up the hall waiting for them, he resisted the temptation, and instead said, "You never answered my question earlier. Are you hungry?"

Abril considered the query seriously and then decided, "I think my appetite is returning. I could eat."

Positive that was a good sign, Crispin smiled as he

ushered her out of the office and back up the hall to the kitchen. He wasn't surprised to enter and find that the men had all taken up positions around the island, removing chairs from the counter-height table at the far end and dragging them over to do so. They were now deep in a discussion about the security measures that needed to be taken to prevent another attack, as well as how they might be able to find out what this was all about.

Crispin left them to it, grabbed another chair from the table, and carried it past where the others were sitting at the end of the island closest to the sliding doors, and down to the opposite end closest to the refrigerator. It was so that she could keep him company while he made her something to eat.

"All right," he said once he had her seated. He walked over to open the refrigerator. "What do you feel like eating?"

"I'm not sure what's available," she admitted, and before he could become concerned that her faulty memory was due to her head injury, she followed that up by saying, "Oh, right! There's the chili from last night. But other than that, there isn't much. Maybe some eggs and salad stuff. I was going to go shopping today."

"We beat you to it," Crispin announced. "Or Dani did. She made a quick stop to get groceries while I brought you home after the hospital," he explained.

"Oh?" Abril asked, sounding interested. "What did she get?"

"Let me see," Crispin murmured, his gaze sliding over the crammed shelves. "It looks like we have various deli meats, lettuce, tomatoes, onions, several types of cheese," he told her and then quickly listed off other items they might use, "Provolone, cheddar, mozzarella, Swiss. Any kind of cheese you'd want on a sandwich really. I know she got buns, too," he added, his eyes sliding to the cupboard where bread was stored before returning to the contents of the refrigerator. "There are sausages, steaks, bacon—"

"A sandwich would be fine," Abril interrupted, afraid she would expire from hunger before they got to the end of the list of things Dani had bought.

"All right," Crispin said, and then turned a raised eyebrow her way. "Hot or cold? I can make a three-cheese grilled cheese sandwich. I could cook up bacon for it too."

"Yeah right!" the man named Bricker said with amusement and told Abril, "Don't risk it. You'd end up eating little charcoal squares. He hasn't eaten since—"

"He cooks for our younger brothers and sisters all the time," Crispin's brother Cassius interrupted sharply, and told her, "Crispin used to be a chef."

"Really?" Abril asked with interest, her gaze moving from one brother to the other. Much to her amazement, Crispin looked uncomfortable and actually blushed.

"I do cook for my siblings. However, the chef business was a long time ago," he muttered, and then cleared his throat and said, "If you are not feeling like a grilled cheese, I can slice up tomatoes and onions, shred some lettuce and pull out all the fixings for Dagwood sandwiches." He paused briefly and then added, "My youngest brother, Cole, calls them that. They are sandwiches that have tons of meat and cheese and everything from pickles, tomatoes, and lettuce to Italian, ranch, or Greek dressing on them. It is a wonder that he can get his mouth around those sandwiches, but he seems to enjoy them."

"I wouldn't want to put you to all that effort," Abril protested. "Just something quick and easy would be good. Heck, I can make my own—" She had started to rise as she said this last part, but stopped both talking and getting up when a heavy hand landed on her shoulder.

"Sausages," Lucian announced as he forced her to sit down again. Moving around her to Crispin's side, he added, "Less bother."

He pulled a package of sausages out of the refrigerator, and then addressed the room at large. "I presume Dani picked up buns for the sausages?"

"I believe so," Roberts said moving to the cupboard where bread was kept and opening it to examine the contents. After a moment, he said, "Yes," and took out a package of buns.

Lucian nodded and turned to spear Abril with a look. "Where is the barbecue?"

Abril hesitated, a little annoyed at how high-handed he was being in deciding what everyone would eat. Nobody else seemed to mind, she acknowledged, or perhaps they were used to his entitled attitude. Her gaze moved to the sliding glass doors and the view beyond.

There used to be a large stone patio directly outside the sliding doors with the garden running along it. At least it had been like that when Gina had bought the place last year. Apparently, when the Bransons had bought the place there had been no patio. Just a large garden along the house with a stone pathway leading to the sliding glass doors. Of course, now both garden and patio were gone, and a tent blocked her view. She was surprised to see that it was filled with people, all working diligently on extracting the bones from the dirt. Her surprise wasn't because of what they were doing, but because she hadn't noticed that anyone was even out there before now.

Finally, she said, "It used to be on a stone patio just outside those doors, but the patio was removed to start digging out the foundation for the addition." She paused briefly to think, before admitting, "I'm not sure where they moved the barbecue to. Maybe around back on the patio outside the pool room."

"Find it, Bricker," Lucian ordered.

The man with dark hair and green eyes immediately nodded and headed out of the kitchen.

It was the sound of the front door opening and closing that had her suddenly thinking of Lilith and glancing around the kitchen for her.

"Where—" she began, only to pause when she heard the Lab's nails scrabbling on the hardwood. A sound Abril recognized as Lilith getting to her feet. It was followed by more clicking of her nails on the floor, and then Lilith came into view as she rushed toward the door of the kitchen, obviously intending to try to follow Bricker outside.

"No, Lilith," Abril said at once.

The Lab paused at once and then turned and came to sit at her side and nudge her hand, demanding attention. Abril gave in to the request and petted her absently, as Lucian began to bark orders, and the men began scrambling to fulfil them. Plates were pulled from the cupboard, silverware dragged from drawers, condiments were found and set on the island one after another. Meanwhile, Lucian, who had started all of this activity, was himself opening and closing cupboard doors in a search for something.

"What are you looking for?" she said finally. "Perhaps I can tell you where it is."

"Barbecue tongs," Lucian announced, switching his attention to drawers now.

"The drawer under the built-in ovens," Abril said helpfully.

Grunting what might've been a thank-you, Lucian tried that drawer next and found what he was looking for.

Feeling rather useless just sitting there, Abril stood cautiously. When she'd got up to leave the room to take Gina's call, her head had complained at the movement. Much to her relief, it didn't react this time so she headed for the cupboard where bread was kept, intending to see if there was another package of buns for the sausages. Eight wasn't going to feed them all.

"No, no, no!" Crispin caught her arm before she'd taken more than two steps and drew her to a halt. Turning her around, he urged her back into her chair, saying, "You are to take it easy for a while. Leave this to us."

Feeling a little disgruntled, Abril scowled at him briefly, but then told herself that it was a somewhat bitchy reaction, since he was only trying to take care of her. Resigned to sitting and doing nothing, she began to twiddle her thumbs in her lap, and simply watched the activity around her.

Abril wasn't used to sitting still. She was usually the one doing all the running and found she didn't like being catered to. That was probably not a normal response, she admitted to herself. But then she had never thought of herself as normal anyway. She'd always felt like the odd one out. Attending a public school where more than 90 percent of the students were "normal" and less than 10 percent came from the religious community on the outskirts of town where she had been raised hadn't helped. Being driven to run away two days before her sixteenth birthday to avoid being forced to marry an abusive man to please her family hadn't helped. And even now, as an adult, having no family and being completely alone in the world, set her apart from others as well. In truth, Abril had no idea what it felt like to be normal, a member of the pack.

She had always hoped that when she grew up, she would make friends, marry, and finally have a family she belonged to. But that didn't seem to be working out the way she'd expected. Perhaps it was due to her rejection as a child and desire to avoid inviting more of it, but whatever the case, she appeared to suck at dating. In university, she'd been too busy with her full course load, studying, and two part-time jobs to have much time to date, let alone make friends. Not that that had ever bothered her. It had quickly become obvious that most of the students at university seemed to want to just drink themselves to oblivion almost every night, which had never really interested her.

Once she had graduated and was out in the working world, the friend situation had not improved. Oh, she'd made acquaintance type friends at work in the various places she'd been employed before Gina, but no true friends. Eventually she'd resigned herself to being alone, and simply focused on her career. Not that she hadn't dated. For her, dating apps had been a lifesaver. She just wished they had an app for making friends. Not that any of the men she met on the dating apps had turned out to be husband material. Still, that didn't mean it wouldn't happen in the future.

For some reason thoughts of Crispin intruded just then. Not wanting to build her hopes up and place them squarely on the man, she quickly pushed those thoughts away though.

Sighing, Abril raised her head and then stilled when she saw that Lucian stood frozen, his gaze fastened on her. He wasn't the only one, almost every man in the room but Crispin appeared to be staring at her.

Feeling like a rabbit that had suddenly become aware of a nearby predator, Abril eyed them all warily until Cassius said, "You need to tell her, brother."

"He is right, cousin," Decker said solemnly. "I think she will take it better than you fear. She yearns for family. We can be that for her."

Abril blinked in confusion. How did he know she yearned for family? And what did he mean they could be that for her?

Maybe she'd misheard, Abril thought. That or her head wound had done some really serious damage and she was hallucinating or something.

"Gentlemen, I suggest you be more careful of what you say in front of her until things are explained," Lucian growled, and the words drew her attention to him again. She eyed him briefly, and then turned to Crispin in question. But when he avoided her gaze by turning away toward the refrigerator, she frowned and then slowly shifted her gaze back to Lucian. She didn't know why, but felt sure that if she wanted an answer to the questions now swimming around inside her head, he was the one most likely to give them to her.

Much to her disappointment, however, he slowly shook his head. "You will have to wait, little girl. I will give Crispin a chance to explain. But if he does not, I will myself."

There was no mistaking that those last words were a threat directed at Crispin. If she were to judge by the scowl on his face, Abril would have to say he wasn't happy to hear them either.

"I will speak to her after we eat." Crispin's voice was an irate growl.

Abril simply sat and stared at the men, watching them interact. A lot of what was going on was confusing to her. Lucian had called her *little girl* when she was guessing that she was maybe as much as five years older than him. And what were they talking about? Crispin had to explain things to her. What was there to explain or tell her? Add that to Decker saying she yearned for family and that he thought she would take something better than Crispin thought . . . What the hell did that mean? And what did it have to do with being family?

On top of that, who were these men, really, and why were they here? She had at first assumed they were all police officers, brought out because of the break-in. But if they were, that would mean that Crispin had family on the police force? Surely, he would've mentioned that to her when they were talking over the Pac-Man game if that were the case.

It was all very confusing to her, not to mention more than a little alarming. Abril was actually toying with the idea of saying she was taking Lilith outside, and then once she got her outside, sneaking the dog around to the garage and her car. The only problem then was where she should go? She supposed she could drive to the police station and find out exactly who these men were. If they were all officers and—Abril hadn't even finished the thought when it suddenly slipped away from her, along with the anxiety that had briefly claimed her. She was suddenly, inexplicably much more relaxed and now happy to simply sit there and wait for the men to feed her.

Somewhere in the back of her mind, the sudden calm did appear strange to Abril, but she didn't seem to be able to hold on to that thought either. In the end, she gave up, and waited for the sausages to be cooked so they could all sit down and eat.

Eighteen

"It is too soon for me to explain about immortals to Abril," Crispin protested pacing back and forth in front of Lucian on the driveway. He had brought Lilith out to relieve herself after they finished their meal. Roberts had taken her for a walk that morning as soon as they'd all returned from the hospital so that Crispin could stay to watch over Abril. The man had offered to do it again this time as well, but Crispin had wanted to stretch his legs and said he'd do it himself. He was now wishing he'd let Roberts take her, because it would have helped him avoid Lucian, who had followed to talk to him and insist Crispin explain the situation to Abril. "I have not had enough time to gain her trust and affection."

"She told you about her childhood, about her running away, and her history pretty much to date. She trusts you," Lucian said firmly.

"Maybe, but—"

"And I can see from your memories that she has experienced the shared passion with you more than once already," Lucian continued. "Your chances are fair that she will accept you and not need to have all memory of you erased."

"Fair is not good enough," Crispin snapped. "I have waited a long time to meet my life mate, Uncle. I am not going to lose her now."

"Her not knowing what she is dealing with here and taking the correct precautions could end with her dying," Lucian growled.

"I shall make sure that does not happen," Crispin insisted. "I will keep her safe."

Lucian rolled his eyes with exasperation and pointed out, "You are away from her side right now."

"The other men are with her," Crispin said defensively.

"Are you sure? Perhaps she has excused herself to go to her room to change clothes, go to the bathroom, or take a shower to wash the blood out of her hair."

When Crispin's eyes widened in dismay at the possibility, Lucian said, "You will do as you wish. And she is your life mate to lose. But do not come crying to me if she sneaks Lilith into her car and drives off as she considered doing earlier before I controlled her mind, veiled her memories of what was said, and made her relax enough to remain here."

Horror following the dismay, Crispin shoved Lilith's leash at Lucian and hurried back inside the house.

Until now he'd had no idea that Abril had considered running away. He supposed he shouldn't be surprised. It was how she'd handled her situation as a teenager. But then she'd had little choice in the matter. Her options had been to run away or be forced to marry a man—a boy really—she hadn't wanted to, and who, apparently, would have taken his fists to her with impunity. But Crispin hadn't even imagined she'd consider grabbing Lilith and fleeing *him*. He would never harm her. She was safer with him than anyone else on the planet. He needed to make that clear to her.

"He didn't!" Abril said with amusement, speaking loudly so that Cassius could hear her from where he waited in her bedroom. While she thought it a bit ridiculous that Crispin's brother insisted on standing guard while she tried to wash some of the blood out of her hair, the memory of her terror last night when she'd woken to the man in her bedroom had convinced her not to raise a fuss about it. She definitely felt safer knowing he was out there than she would have felt being alone. Abril didn't think she would be comfortable sleeping there after what happened, but then doubted she'd be comfortable in any of the bedrooms here now, even with all these men here. Unfortunately, she wasn't sure what to do about that yet.

"He did," Cassius assured her. "Crispin followed our youngest sister around on her dates for years before our father stepped in and made him stop. Although, frankly, I am not sure what danger he could have thought she would be in. She could have bench-pressed every one of the young men she dated."

Abril chuckled at this, imagining Cassius and Crispin's sister as some large Amazon. Her head now filled with an image of an Amazon bench-pressing a scrawny guy, she lowered the washcloth she'd been using and leaned closer to the bathroom mirror. She'd felt the crusty blood in her hair when she'd rested her head on her hand at the island. Feeling around then, she'd discovered that the dried blood seemed to be all over on that side of her head.

Much to her relief, she'd managed to remove most of the blood in the hair around the bandage. But she winced as she looked at the covered wound. All she could see was a bandage in the middle of her hair, but it was obvious they must've had to shave some of her hair away to stitch and cover it. That did not make her happy as she considered how bad it might look to have a bald spot once the injury got to the point where the bandage could be removed.

Straightening with a sigh, Abril decided to leave that worry for another day, tossed the washcloth in the laundry basket, and turned to walk out of the bathroom into the bedroom where Cassius sat on the end of her bed. She was just about to suggest they return to the others when Crispin appeared in the doorway, his gaze moving from her to his brother.

"Is Lilith done already?" she asked with surprise, her feet taking her to stand in front of him.

"Lucian has her," Crispin murmured, his hands reaching for her as if he could not resist. One brushed a tendril of hair away from her cheek, and the other glided along the skin of her arm.

Swallowing, Abril almost leaned into the touch, but

Cassius's voice reminded her of his presence as he said, "Do you need time alone to talk to her?"

"Yes," Crispin growled, but much to his surprise, instead of then leaving, Cassius merely narrowed his eyes on him. Crispin knew at once that he was reading his mind, and probably picking up on all the things he wanted to do to Abril to ease what he had to tell her. He was thinking that if he full on made love to her first, maybe she would not reject him right away when he told her what he was. But Cassius blew his plan all to hell, simply by reminding him, "Dani said she is not to have any excitement until she is recovered."

Shoulders slumping, Crispin let his hand drop away from her arm and nodded at his brother. He had forgotten that. He would not risk Abril's health by making love to her right now. Which meant he had to take the chance, and tell her without sex to help ease the way.

Crispin didn't like to think of himself as a coward, but in that moment, he certainly felt like one. Terrified of losing her, instead of leading her out of the room to somewhere where they could sit and talk seriously, he suddenly recalled something else Dr. Dani had said, and suggested to her, "Maybe you should take a nap. We can always talk later, and Dani did say you should be resting."

"Yes, she did say that, but I only woke up an hour or so go," Abril protested.

"It has been two hours and thirty-six minutes," Crispin said, glancing at his watch. "And it is already four o'clock. We will be starting supper in a couple of hours. If you take a nap now, you should be well rested for the meal and then we can talk after dinner. Maybe while we walk Lilith in the front yard."

Abril had started to frown at the suggestion at first, but that began to ease now. He'd apparently somehow made it sound reasonable to her. And perhaps it was. Frankly, he couldn't tell. He was just scrambling to find a way to woo her and keep her safe at the same time.

"All right," she said suddenly, and then she glanced briefly toward the window and added, "But maybe I'll just lie down on the couch in the living room."

Crispin didn't argue with her. He suspected she might be nervous of sleeping in here after the attack, so he merely nodded, and followed her out of the room. He had ushered her to the couch before he considered that she might want a pillow and blanket. Crispin immediately turned, intending to go back to fetch those off her bed, but paused when he saw Cassius coming out of the room with both items in hand. It seemed his brother had thought of what he hadn't. Giving him a grateful smile, Crispin took the items, placed the pillow on the couch, got Abril settled on it, and then covered her with the blanket.

"There," he said, offering a gentle smile. "You rest now. I shall wake you up in time for supper."

"Lucian will not be pleased that you have avoided talking to her," Cassius commented as they headed to the kitchen.

"Lucian can kiss my ass," Crispin muttered, with irritation. "It is not his life mate he is risking by insisting this conversation takes place now."

"True," Cassius said mildly. "Besides, at least this way you have gained yourself some time to figure out the best way to explain things to her."

"Yes," Crispin agreed, but wasn't sure there really was a best way.

"It is possible the bodies in the garden are the victims of the immortal who broke in last night," Decker was saying as Cassius and Crispin entered the kitchen.

"That is more than likely true," Lucian agreed. "It still does not explain why the immortal would attack Abril. The bodies in the garden have been discovered. Attacking her could not have been to prevent that. In fact, the attack is the only thing that suggested this was rogue related," he pointed out. "With the information we have at the moment, attacking her will gain them nothing."

The men were all nodding at that when Decker noticed their arrival and asked, "Has Abril said anything that might suggest she has any connection to immortals?"

Crispin shook his head and peered at his cousin with curiosity. He'd expected Decker to head back to Toronto with his wife, Dani, when she'd finished with Abril and left. However, he'd remained behind to help out. Which he did appreciate and hoped Decker knew that. Even as he thought it, Decker caught his gaze and nodded solemnly, obviously having read his thoughts. Before Crispin could again feel annoyance at the fact that he was so easily readable now, Lucian spoke, the irritation in his voice capturing everyone's attention again.

"So once again we have no idea what is going on."

"Well, at least we know who the target is this time,"

Anders pointed out. "We have had several cases in the past where we were not even certain of that."

"True," Lucian agreed as Crispin and Cassius reclaimed the seats they'd occupied during lunch.

When silence fell over the room then, Crispin found himself surveying the men all standing or sitting around the island. Lucian was the oldest having survived the fall of Atlantis. He himself was the second oldest having been born in 900 BC. Born in 600 BC, Cassius was next, then Anders who was six hundred and sixty some years old, while Decker was two hundred and seventy something and Bricker . . . Crispin knew Bricker was over a century old, but not by much. Most of the men here had found their life mates. They had claimed and turned them, so now knew the bliss immortals were said to experience once they were mated. It was only he and Cassius in the group who were not. Although, Crispin was on the verge of claiming his. He wished he could say he felt confident that he would be able to convince Abril to accept him as a partner in life, but he wasn't. The possibility was better than it would have been one hundred years ago though.

Sadly, ever since Dracula had reached the market, introducing "vampires" to society, it had caused nothing but trouble for his kind. While vampires were a fictional creation—well, really a bastardization of immortals—where vampires were dead and soulless and feeding off the blood of the living, in reality, immortals were neither dead nor soulless. They were as alive as any other human being. They simply needed to take in blood on a semiregular basis to survive. However, it didn't matter how you described it to mortals. As a rule, they simply decided immortals were vampires, and something to be feared.

Although, the movement over the last couple of decades in books, TV shows, and movies to present vampires as sympathetic, and even romantic figures, may have helped somewhat with their reputation. At least that was what he'd been told. That made him wonder if Abril happened to be a fan of one of the TV series, movies, or books that portrayed vampires that way. If so, it would greatly increase his chances of being able to claim her.

Unfortunately, Abril was a very sensible, practical woman. She didn't strike him as someone who would fantasize about vampire lovers and being one herself. In fact, she might be one who would be repulsed at the very idea, which was his greatest concern.

"How are we going to get to the bottom of this?" Lucian asked, his gaze flickering between Roberts and Crispin in question. "From what you have learned so far, the person behind the bodies in the garden has to either be a member or members of the family who lived here when Abril's boss purchased the house—"

"The Bransons," Crispin supplied.

Lucian continued as if he had never spoken, "—or the couple who built and lived here for three or four years before them."

"The Foleys," Roberts offered the second name they'd managed to learn while going door to door, questioning the neighbors.

"But you have not yet had the opportunity to talk to either couple?" Lucian finished in question.

"No," Crispin admitted. "We only found out the name of the original owners of this house from the last neighbors we spoke to. Most of the neighbors are newer, having moved onto the street in the last ten years or less. But the older couple who live in the first house on the street, the Jamisons, were one of the originals, who built their home at the same time as the Foleys. They knew the history of the house. Who had lived here, why and when they left, and so on."

"Which is?" Lucian questioned.

"The Foleys were a young couple with one child, a boy," Roberts explained. "They were hit by a drunk driver while driving home from a day out with their son. The young son was killed in the accident and the wife was paralyzed from the waist down and needed a wheelchair to get around. She and the husband remained here for about a year after the accident. The Jamisons said the wife had become a shut-in, and they thought the memories here were just too much for her to bear, so she and her husband sold and moved away. They had no idea where to though."

"We intended to do some research today, to find contact information for the Foleys and Bransons and to speak to them," Crispin added. "But then Abril was attacked, and our plans went to hell."

Lucian nodded. "Then perhaps someone should do that now."

"I can handle that," Roberts said, getting to his feet.

"Anders, go with him," Lucian ordered. "One of the couples is most likely responsible for the bodies and undoubtedly connected to an immortal. He should not go alone."

"I can go with him," Crispin protested as Anders got to his feet. "It is my job."

"Your job now is Abril," Lucian countered. "I suspect she would be terribly uncomfortable to wake up and find herself alone with five men she has only just met. Besides, the first thing you are going to do when she wakes up is have that talk with her."

Crispin's mouth tightened, but he didn't comment as Anders and Roberts left the kitchen. Once they were gone, he stood and moved to get a glass from the cupboard, then got himself some water. When he then turned and leaned against the counter to drink it, his attention moved to the sliding glass doors. He paused abruptly before the glass had reached his lips.

"What is happening?" he asked, his brow furrowing as he peered out at the empty tent outside. "Where did the forensics team go?"

"Their memories—along with Officer Peters's— were wiped and they were sent back to police head-quarters," Lucian told him.

"What?" Crispin asked with outrage.

"We are dealing with a rogue here," Lucian pointed out. "When dealing with rogues, we always make sure it is not on the mortal radar. This is no different."

"But what about the identities of the people buried here and the bones themselves?" Crispin asked sharply. "If the forensics team does not do the work, we will not be able to ID the skeletons. The victims and their families will never have closure."

"We shall gather the bones ourselves and take them back to Toronto where they will be put on a plane and flown to Bastian in New York. He can have his scientist do whatever tests are necessary; make a DNA match, and hopefully gain their identities. The mortals do not need to know about it for us to get the answers we desire."

Crispin wanted to protest further, but didn't really have a reason to. Lucian was right, mortal scientists weren't necessary to find out who the victims were. Immortals had the technology as well as the facilities to do that themselves. And it was better not to involve mortals in Enforcer business.

Still, it kind of chafed his ass that he and Roberts finally had a murder, even a multiple murder to solve, and would never get credit for it in their jobs among the mortals. He supposed he would just have to resign himself to the fact that his job was pretty much useless. Working on only four murders a year and spending the rest of the time on other, less important cases, just was not satisfying. He didn't feel like he was making much of a contribution.

"That is utter nonsense," Lucian said suddenly. "The reason we have immortals sprinkled among as many mortal police forces as we can is for situations just like this. To handle cases and situations where rogue activities have splashed over into the mortal world. The most important job Enforcers do is keep our existence off the radar. Certainly, we have a duty to make sure that our bad seeds do not hurt mortals, which we also do as Enforcers. But for our own people, keeping their presence on the planet a secret is very necessary for our preservation. And that is what you and Roberts have done in this situation. The two of you have definitely made a difference."

Crispin stared at him, a little surprised at the speech. From what he knew, Lucian Argeneau was not the type to give speeches and encouragement.

"Now stop whinging and show me how to work this Keurig thing since the pot on the proper coffee machine is empty," Lucian growled irritably, getting to his feet.

That was more like the Uncle Lucian he knew, Crispin thought with amusement and walked over to show him where the coffee pods were and how to work the Keurig.

Nineteen

Abril woke up to the smell of something delicious in the air. Nose twitching, she sat up on the couch, her gaze automatically going to the wall clock to see that it was 5:40. Covering her mouth as a yawn made it stretch open, she pushed aside the blanket Crispin had spread over her earlier and got to her feet.

It was almost time to feed Lilith. Actually, by the time she got the dog's meal ready it would be dinnertime for the Labrador, and then she'd need to take her outside for a potty break. A quick one though, because whatever was cooking smelled heavenly and was making her hungry.

Wondering who among the men was cooking, she headed for the kitchen, petting Lilith's head when the dog got up from where she'd been sleeping on the carpet beside the couch and walked at her side.

Abril expected to find at least a couple of the men in the kitchen, so was surprised when she entered to find it empty. Wondering where they'd got to, she moved immediately to the Keurig, sure that some caffeine would help her shake off the last of the sleepiness clinging to her. It was as she waited for the machine to spit out her chosen coffee that she happened to glance outside and saw that was where the men were. Well, at least five of them. Lucian, Bricker, Decker, Crispin, and Cassius were all out there working diligently away, digging up bones and placing them in large brown paper bags. They weren't doing it slowly and cautiously as the forensics team had worked. They were actually moving incredibly quickly. Almost unnaturally so, she thought with a small frown.

Biting her lip, she watched them for a moment, wondering where Roberts and the newcomer named Anders were, and then turned to doctor her coffee as the machine finished spitting it out. Once done, she carried it with her as she walked to the sliding glass doors.

"What's happening?" she asked after opening the door.

Her question had all five men pausing to peer her way.

After a brief silence, Lucian turned to spear Crispin with a look. Abril suspected it was a silent order to answer her question. It was unnecessary, Crispin was already straightening and heading toward the open door.

She thought he was just coming to speak to her through the opening. It had never occurred to her that he would come inside. The base of the hole they were all working in was more than five feet below the level of the door. It would have been impossible for her to get up and in through the entrance. However, he did so effortlessly, leaping up to step inside as if it was no more than a foot or so up.

Skittering back out of the way with surprise, Abril gaped at him as he closed the door.

"Wow," she breathed when he finished the task and turned to her. "That was hella impressive."

Crispin looked at first surprised, then chagrinned, and waved away her compliment as he muttered, "I used to do high jump in school."

"Oh. Right," Abril murmured and then her gaze slid to the men working in the tent and she asked, "What happened to the forensics team? Bill and those guys?"

"It was decided they were unnecessary. That it would save time if we collected the bones ourselves and sent them in for analysis and DNA testing. Hopefully we can identify them without forensics," he explained.

"But what about clues in the dirt and stuff? The forensics team was collecting the dirt around them in drums, in case there was something there to—"

"They got what was needed," he interrupted reassuringly.

Abril frowned. It didn't sound right to her, but then, what did she know? The only knowledge she had in this area was what she'd seen on TV shows. These guys were the police, so should know better what had to be done. Besides, the men would have the skeletons out in no time at the rate they were going. While the forensics people had used small soft brushes to sweep the dirt away and gather it in little increments, Crispin's coworkers were using large stiff bristle brooms to remove the dirt, then grabbing the bones and the tattered remains of their clothes as they were partially revealed and putting each set into a large paper bag. They appeared to be using one bag per body and were labeling them, although only with numbers. But then, what else could they label them with?

"Have they any idea yet how the victims died?" she asked as she noted that Cassius was writing a 4 or 9 on the bag he'd just finished filling and closed. Four, obviously, she told herself.

"How they died?" Crispin turned to peer out the window as if yearning to be out there with the men rather than inside answering her questions. But this was important to her, so she persisted.

"I mean, I know they're just bones, but I think I read somewhere that strangling someone crushes the hiatal or hyoid bone or something. Then too, broken bones would show if they were beaten, as would gouges or nicks in the bones that could be signs of stabbing or gunshot wounds," she pointed out.

By the time she finished, Crispin was staring at her with a faint smile, and said, "You are very intelligent."

Abril blushed at the compliment, and then waved it away. "No. I just watch a lot of crime shows on TV while doing paperwork at night."

"You take work home and do it on your own time?" Crispin's voice was heavy with disapproval.

"Now you sound like Barb," she said, smiling faintly as she thought of the restaurant owner who had pretty much adopted her after she'd run away from home at almost sixteen. Smile widening, she told him, "She's constantly giving me hell for working long hours past what I'm being paid for. She says I'm letting Gina take advantage of me."

"I agree with her," Crispin said firmly. "Everyone

needs time to themselves to relax. It is important for your health. Gina should not be taking advantage of you that way."

Abril clucked her tongue with irritation and shook her head. "Gina doesn't order me to work after hours. In fact, if anything she's constantly trying to send me home early to go chill when we aren't busy," she assured him, and then added, "But in return, when we are busy and I don't get everything that I need to get done during work hours, I do take work home and do it there. But it's my choice."

Crispin didn't look pleased, but didn't argue the matter further, and instead said, "We will be able to identify most of them. Several had wallets or purses nearby with IDs. Many who did not bore past injuries that might help give them names. One of the skeletons had an obviously broken, but healed, ankle. One had their arm broken in the past, but it too was healed. There are screws in the hip of one victim, which will definitely ID them, but there was not really anything on any of them to tell us how they died."

Abril's lips pursed with dissatisfaction. It would've been nice for them to have been able to tell how the people died, but she supposed that was a lot to hope for. Sighing, she pointed out, "So, they could have been shot or stabbed in spots that would damage organs, but not bones. Or they could have been suffocated instead of choked. Or they could have been poisoned or drowned . . ." She shook her head helplessly, her mind coming up blank on any other ways a person could be murdered without leaving signs on their bones. There were probably a ton of them, though.

Crispin nodded agreement, but his gaze was wandering to the sliding glass doors again, and she wasn't surprised when he said, "We should not need more than another twenty minutes or so to get the rest of the bodies out of the ground." Turning back, he offered her a smile and continued, "Supper should be ready by then. In the meantime, you just sit down, relax, and enjoy your coffee."

Before Abril could ask him what dinner was, he was pressing a quick kiss to her forehead and saying, "I should get back out there to help. We have bagged nine bodies so far, but every time we remove one, we seem to uncover another beneath it."

"Nine?" Abril asked with horror. It had been bad enough at three or four, but nine? That was the size of a bloody baseball team. Gina was not going to be happy when she found out about this. In fact, she might very well decide she wasn't living in a house where mass murder had taken place, and sell.

Abril almost groaned at the thought, because it would mean she would be the one getting the Realtor in, preparing the house for sale, going through tons of new houses to get a short list of ones Gina would like, then touring them herself, before Gina went out with her to see the best of the best and waiting forever for the woman to choose a house to move to. It had been a nightmare buying this place last summer. She was not happy at the prospect of having to go through it again.

The sound of the door closing caught her attention, and she glanced out to see Crispin crossing back to where he'd been when she'd first seen him out there.

And she hadn't got to ask what was for dinner, Abril thought with a cross between annoyance and amusement.

Deciding she'd find out for herself, she walked back to the built-in double ovens in the wall across from the far end of the island. She had felt the heat coming from them as she'd passed on the way to the coffee machine earlier, so knew that was where the smell was coming from.

The dials for both the upper and the lower ovens were on. She started with the lower oven, inhaling deeply of the lovely scents that immediately poured out at her along with the heat when she tugged the door open.

"Oh my," she murmured with pleasure as she peered in at the contents. Three nine- by thirteen-inch ceramic baking dishes were inside. Each of them was filled to the brim with lasagna, the cheese on top bubbling, and beginning to turn golden.

Smiling, Abril closed that oven and next opened the upper oven door. She'd expected foil-wrapped loaves of garlic bread to go with the lasagna, so her eyes widened incredulously when she found two more large baking dishes of lasagna there.

Good Lord, had they invited the entire neighborhood for dinner? Probably not, she acknowledged as she closed the door. But they must be expecting *some* company for dinner. There was no way they could imagine that seven men and one woman would eat five large lasagnas in one sitting. That was just crazy.

Shaking her head at the thought, Abril carried her coffee over to the island and sat down. She was debating turning on the TV to pass the time while she waited when her gaze fell on the digital clock that sat on the shelf below the TV. It was 5:50. Lilith's dinnertime was always six o'clock.

This thought had her glancing around for the dog.

She would've expected the Lab to be sitting, staring out the sliding doors at the men digging up her treasured bones. She had been lying on the living room floor next to her when she woke up from her nap. Abril knew the dog had started to follow her when she'd headed into the kitchen, but wasn't sure where she'd got to since then.

Deciding it would be a good idea to find that out, she stood and headed out of the kitchen to search for Lilith.

Abril took a sip of coffee, her eyes sliding to the remote control by her hand. She briefly considered turning the television on to fill the silence in the house, which made her glance at the clock to see what would be available on the idiot box. It was 5:58. So, mostly just news. Which they should really call bad news, she thought, because they never had anything good to say on the news shows. Other than that, there would only be reruns of old sitcoms. None of which interested her. Besides she would have to feed Lilith soon.

The thought made her glance around for the Lab, wondering where she had got to. She was pretty sure Lilith had come into the kitchen with her after her nap, but the dog was now nowhere to be seen. Afraid of what she might be chewing on or getting into on her own, Abril stood and headed out of the kitchen to search for her.

Twenty

"Have we got them all?"

Lucian's question had Crispin glancing up from closing the bag on the last body of bones they'd dug out of the ground. He followed his uncle's gaze to his cousin Jeanne Louise Argeneau-Jones, who was pushing what almost looked like a lawn mower across the dirt. Appearances aside, what she was pushing back and forth across the excavation site in rows was not a lawn mower. It was a four-wheeled radar surveyor, or at least that was what Jeanne Louise had called it. All he knew was that it had ground penetrating radar and had shown them where the last eight bodies had been.

Lucian had apparently had the forethought to tell Mortimer to check with the science guys at Argeneau Enterprises to see if there was an easier way to find any skeletons buried next to the house without digging up the whole damned area. They would have basically had to dig out the entire foundation for the fifty- by twenty-foot extension that was going in to be sure they got them all or at least ensure the construction crew wouldn't be finding more bodies.

Jeanne Louise had been the answer. One of their top scientists at the family company, she'd arrived shortly after Abril had lain down to nap. Within moments, the men had all moved out into the tent to watch Jeanne Louise push her radar machine around. At first, they'd merely marked each spot she said the surveyor indicated there were bones, but once she'd finished a row and started on the next, they began digging to remove the skeletons marked behind her.

It had all worked rather well, and quickly. They'd dug out the original four and eight more bodies in the last couple of hours to a count of twelve. Their serial killer had been prolific. Jeanne Louise had just finished marking where the last body was and had headed inside through the back door to use the bathroom when Abril had appeared at the sliding doors. Now that they had finished removing the skeletons she'd found, Jeanne Louise was just completing a last run with the radar machine to be sure they hadn't missed anything.

"That's it," Jeanne Louise said finally. Glancing to their uncle then, she added, "At least there are no more in the excavated area. Do you want me to check around outside the tent?"

Lucian was silent for a moment, his gaze moving to the back of the tent as if he could see through it to the undisturbed yard beyond. It hadn't been dug up yet, but Crispin knew the addition was supposed to run the length of the side of the house and twenty feet out.

"Yes, and another ten feet beyond that," Lucian

decided. "We will get the bone bags in the van and take down the tent while you do that. Hopefully there are no more, but if there are, it is better to find out and deal with them."

With five men on the job, it didn't take them long to stow the bags in the van and take down the tent. Jeanne Louise had only managed to check half the length of the house by then. Since she hadn't come up with anything in that time, Crispin suspected they were done and had found all the victims. Still, he knew she had to finish to be sure. The last thing they needed was for the construction crew to find a skeleton or two that they'd missed and cause a big stink that they'd have to clean up later.

"Decker, Cassius, and Crispin," his uncle said suddenly as they all stood watching Jeanne Louise, "The three of you go inside, clean up, check dinner, check on Abril, and set the table. We will eat as soon as Jeanne Louise finishes, if there are no more bodies," he announced, and then added, "Bricker, you are with me. We will remain with Jeanne Louise until she is done, just in case she does find something and we have to dig again."

There were sounds of agreement all around, and Crispin led his brother and cousin inside. Cassius immediately went to open the stove and check on the meal he'd made, while Decker moved to the sink to wash his hands. Crispin washed his hands as well, but he was glancing around the kitchen as he did.

Abril's coffee sat on the placemat in front of her usual seat at the island, but she was nowhere in sight.

That troubled him, mostly because it looked as if she'd hardly touched her coffee. If she'd had more than a sip of it, he'd be surprised.

"Maybe she went to her room to change or something," Cassius suggested, obviously picking up on his concern. "Why do you not go check?"

Crispin's gaze shot to his brother at the suggestion, but he bit back his irritation at being read. Mostly because Cassius's idea was a good one. Turning off the tap, he quickly dried his hands and said, "Yes. I will go see."

"Just knock on her door, brother," Cassius said in a warning tone. "Remember, Dani said no excitement."

Crispin mentally shot his brother the finger as he headed out of the kitchen, and almost smiled when Cassius burst out laughing.

He noticed Lilith sleeping on the carpet next to the couch in the living room, but paid the dog little attention as he hurried to Abril's room. In the end, he didn't knock. The door was open, as was the door to her bathroom and he could see it was dark. She obviously wasn't in either room.

Worry creeping up his back, Crispin turned to look at the couch in case she'd lain down again and he hadn't noticed, but she wasn't there either. His heartbeat starting to pick up with anxiety, Crispin headed down the hall to the laundry room, glancing through each open door on either side of the hall as he passed. There was no sign of her in any of the rooms. Spinning around, he hurried back the way he'd come, passing through the living room again as he rushed to and through the kitchen to the hall to the temporary offices.

"What is it?" Cassius asked as he raced past. "Did you find her?"

"No," Crispin's voice was short and worried as he quickly checked Abril's office, Gina's office, and the bathroom where he'd bathed Lilith. When he spun back around after finding each room empty, Cassius was coming up the hall toward him.

"She is not here?" Cassius asked with some of the concern Crispin was feeling.

"No," he growled, panic beginning to gnaw at him. Where could she be?

"Did you try the pool room? Maybe she went for a swim," Cassius suggested.

Crispin was moving before his brother even finished speaking. He was running by the time he hit the kitchen, and barely noticed Decker's startled glance as he flew past where the other man was setting the table.

"What has happened?" Decker asked.

Crispin heard his brother respond, "Abril is missing. Tell the others. Start a search."

Crispin didn't hear any more, he'd exited the kitchen, crossed the entry and was running through the living room by then. The door to the pool room was unlocked when he reached it. Thinking she always kept it locked, and its being unlocked meant she must be there he started to relax for a moment, only to tense up again as he saw that the pool room was empty.

"She is not here either."

Crispin turned to his brother at those surprised words. He hadn't realized Cassius had still been following him. For some reason he'd assumed he had stopped in the kitchen to talk to Decker. It seemed not, however. Cassius was standing there, appearing as perplexed as Crispin himself was feeling.

"Have you tried everywhere?" Cassius asked finally.

"Yes, every—" His voice died as he suddenly recalled the bathroom here in the pool room and hurried to that door. It was closed, but not locked and opened at once, only to reveal a dark and empty bath/change room.

Shoulders slumping, Crispin turned around and started back toward his brother, only to breathe, "Abril," with relief and change direction when he spotted her through the glass walls that surrounded the pool room. She was in the backyard, on the very edge of the property, staring into the woods with fascination.

"Thank God," Cassius said, turning to peer where he was looking, and then following when Crispin moved past him to the doors. The outer door was also unlocked. He slid it open, and stepped out, calling, "Abril?"

When she didn't move or even look around, he started forward, shouting, "Abril!"

"Abril!" Cassius added a little louder when she didn't react again.

The brothers exchanged a worried glance, then began to run.

Twenty-One

Abril thought she could hear shouting, but it seemed to be coming from a long way away. Frowning, she tried to push away the lethargy that had a hold of her, so that she could respond, but that seemed impossible.

"Abril! Abril!"

There was more than one voice calling her now, which immediately raised anxiety in Abril and guilt that she wasn't responding when she felt she should. But it felt like her mind was soaked in mud, the sticky slushy kind, clinging to her brain and making it slow and fuzzy. She was still struggling to get past that sensation when someone grabbed her arm and jerked her around on her feet. She found herself staring at a very wide chest, and then she raised her head and took in Crispin's concerned face.

"What are you doing out here? We were looking for you everywhere. We were shouting when we spotted you. Did you not hear us?"

She blinked at the barrage of questions and then glanced around, surprised to see that she was outside, standing on the edge of the yard with the woods at her back. She must've been looking into the trees before Crispin had turned her, but she didn't recall that. She couldn't remember why she'd come out here either.

"She has been controlled, Crispin," someone said, and her gaze slid to Cassius as he continued, "She is barefoot and not wearing a coat. We should get her inside and warm her up."

Abril didn't say a word. Frankly, she was still trying to sort out what had happened. When had she come outside? And why? And why on earth hadn't she at least put on shoes before coming out? Because Cassius was right, she was freezing. Had he said something about her being controlled? What the heck did that mean?

She was still fretting over this when Crispin scooped her up, crossed the yard, and carried her into the house. He took her to the kitchen without slowing or stopping.

Cassius was following them, and Lucian was in the kitchen when they entered. But the other men were coming from different areas of the house to join them as well.

"Where was she?" Lucian asked "What happened? Has she been hurt?"

"She was standing out at the back of the yard, staring into the woods behind," Crispin said, his voice tight.

"Parts of her memory are missing, including how she ended up standing in the backyard without her coat or shoes," Cassius added, his voice grim.

Abril was trying to ignore her aching head and

absorb what the man was saying when she felt Lucian's stare as if it were a physical touch. Shifting her attention to him, she scowled slightly. The man was staring at her with a concentration that was discomfiting.

Rude asshole, she thought with irritation, and then became aware of a shuffling sensation in her head that she'd never experienced before.

For one minute, she was afraid that this was all something to do with her head wound. Her confusion, her lack of memory, and whatever else they were talking about. At that moment, she couldn't even recall how she'd hurt her head. There was definitely something wrong with her, she thought unhappily.

"The injury to your head is from getting tossed around like a rag doll by someone who broke into the house through your bedroom window last night," Lucian said firmly.

The moment he spoke those words, Abril could recall the incident. Waking up to find a dark figure in her room. Screaming. The intruder almost seeming to fly around her bed to grab her. Their hand covering her mouth to silence her, and then they were cursing and tossing her aside like garbage when she bit their hand to make them remove it. That part of the memory was new. She was quite sure she hadn't recalled it before, but now she did. Abril even remembered her impact with the wall, but nothing after that until she had woken up with Dr. Dani leaning over her.

"Set her down, Crispin," Lucian ordered abruptly, his gaze on her becoming more natural and less intense.

Crispin hesitated, but then carried her to the island

and set her in the chair she had been using since the men's arrival. He then took the chair on her left and smiled soothingly when she turned her worried gaze to him.

"Everything is fine," he reassured her.

"Everything is not fine," Lucian growled, dragging one of the chairs over to her so that it faced her and then sitting in it before turning her chair to face his so that her back was to Crispin. "Tell me what you remember," he ordered.

When Abril hesitated, he said, "Tell me what you remember from when you woke up on the couch this afternoon until right now."

Abril swallowed and then cleared her throat and said, "I woke up, sat up on the couch, gave Lilith a pet, and then came into the kitchen and made myself a coffee. Then I went to the door, Crispin saw that I was up . . ." She glanced over her shoulder at him then and he gave her another reassuring smile. Her return smile was a little uncertain before she turned back to Lucian and continued.

"Crispin came inside. He told me that the forensics team had got what they needed, and you guys were taking over removing the bones. He said you'd probably be another twenty minutes, then you'd come inside and we'd have dinner."

"And then?" Lucian prompted when she hesitated.

"And then I went over and opened the oven and saw the lasagna, which smells really good by the way. My compliments to the chef." She smiled around at the room, because she wasn't sure which of the men had made it, and then continued, "I saw the lasagna and then looked at the time. It was 5:50.

I realized I had to feed Lilith soon, but she wasn't in the kitchen with me, so I thought I better look for her. I headed out of the kitchen to find her and sat down at the island with my coffee and took a sip. I thought about turning on the TV, saw the time was 5:58. I needed to feed Lilith, realized that she wasn't around, and thought I better go look for her, so I did, and then I heard Crispin shouting my name. He asked me why I was outside with no shoes on and brought me in here."

A moment of silence followed her explanation, and the men were all exchanging glances as if saying things she couldn't hear. She found it disturbing.

Abril immediately began to feel stressed out and confused. She wasn't sure what was happening and turned instinctively to peer at Crispin. He quickly offered her a reassuring smile and said, "Everything will be fine."

"Everything will not be fine," Lucian snapped. "And she definitely should worry as should you. She needs to be told what is happening here."

"She is not ready," Crispin insisted.

"When will she be ready, Crispin?" Lucian asked grimly. "When the rogue who attacked her in her room, and obviously controlled and forced her outside for some reason, finally kills her?"

Abril glanced over her shoulder to see the conflict taking place on Crispin's face. Meeting her gaze, he managed a smile and then said, "We will just guard her better. I should have stayed with her rather than go outside to work on the—"

"We were just outside the sliding glass door, Crispin," Lucian pointed out. "And yet this rogue was bold enough to break into the house and take her out anyway, even with a dog in the house."

Abril's mind latched on to the mention of a dog, and she suddenly realized she didn't know where Lilith was.

"Where is Lilith?" she asked with concern. The men immediately ended the glaring war they'd been holding and focused on her again as she continued, "It's past her dinnertime now, and I swear Lilith has an internal clock about food. She should be here bugging me for her supper."

"I saw her sleeping in front of the couch in the living room as I passed through on the way to the pool room," Crispin said reassuringly. "I am sure she is still there."

Bricker stood and headed for the kitchen door, saying, "I'll go wake her."

"Thank you," Abril called after him, and then stood to collect the dog bowl and carry it over to the refrigerator to retrieve Lilith's homemade dog food. She had just set the food and bowl on the island, and was about to go get a large spoon to start dishing it out when Bricker called from the other room, "Something's wrong! I can't wake her up!"

Concern rushing through her, Abril hurried out of the room, aware that the men were following. Bricker was kneeling next to where Lilith slept in front of the couch, shaking the dog and getting no response.

"She's breathing but won't wake up," he said with a frown when Abril knelt next to him to look at Lilith herself. "I think she's been drugged."

Abril ran a hand down the Labrador's back. She could feel that she was warm, and when she leaned down and rested her cheek against Lilith's side, she could hear that she was breathing as Bricker had said. She straightened and sat back on her heels though when Lucian knelt on Lilith's other side and lifted her eyelids to reveal her eyes. Abril had no idea what he was looking for, but whatever it was, he appeared to find it. Releasing the lid and allowing it to close again, he glanced to Decker, who had remained out of the way by the indoor garden, and said, "Call Anders's wife. I think Bricker is right and she has been drugged, but better to be safe than sorry. I want Valorie to check her out."

"Anders's wife, Valorie, is a vet," Crispin explained reassuringly as he knelt on her other side.

"Did someone forget to clean up and track dirt in here from the excavation site?" Cassius asked suddenly.

Abril glanced around to see that he was standing on the other side of the couch, peering down at the floor with an annoyed frown.

"There's dirt here on the carpet," he added when no one responded.

Abril made a mental note to have the carpet cleaned before Gina returned, but other than that didn't really care and turned her attention back to Lilith.

The pup looked so sweet and peaceful. She really was a good dog, Abril thought and listened as Decker began murmuring somewhere behind her. He was telling someone that Lilith appeared to be asleep but wasn't waking up and Lucian wanted her checked out. She heard him give Lilith's breed and say he wasn't sure of her age. Realizing he must be talking to this vet, Valorie, Abril said, "She's two years old."

She listened to him relay the information, and then instinctively glanced to Lucian to ask, "Will she be all right?"

"We shall have to wait and see," he said grimly rather than offer a platitude.

It was Decker who said, "Valorie will see to her. She said she will head down right away."

She turned to offer him a grateful smile, but he wasn't looking her way. He was putting his phone away and frowning slightly as he toed at the ceramic tile around the indoor garden. "There is some dirt here too."

Lucian straightened. His expression was grim. "Is the dirt in the garden disturbed?"

Decker raised an eyebrow and then bent to move aside a large frond of one of the umbrella plants behind the Naked-man orchids. "Yeah. There is a footprint here and some obvious digging. It looks like somebody either started to dig and stopped, or dug and filled it back in."

"Get a shovel and start digging," Lucian ordered.

Cassius moved over to examine the garden, and then glanced to Abril and asked, "Will digging up the indoor garden be a problem?"

Abril shook her head. "The gardens are going to be removed anyway, and the hole filled in with gravel then concrete. It's going to be carpeted and made part of the living room," she told them solemnly. "Do what you need to."

She didn't really care if they dug up the garden. She just had no idea why they would. But then she had no idea what was going on right now. Why had she been outside? Why couldn't she remember getting there? Why had Lilith been drugged? If she had been. And why were the men suddenly so on edge and acting weird? She had all these questions and no answers. Worse yet, though, was that she still felt a little fuzzy. Her memory was hazy with some holes in it, and she just didn't feel right.

"Where would I find a shovel?" Decker asked, straightening from the garden.

"There are some in the garden shed," Abril answered quietly.

"You will not go to the shed to get shovels," Lucian said at once. "I do not want whoever is watching the house to know we have discovered what they are looking for if they didn't manage to dig it up."

"You think it was something in the garden and not Abril they were after?" Bricker asked with interest.

"Why else dig in it?" Lucian said dryly.

Bricker grunted with a nod, and then pointed out, "They could have found what they were looking for already."

"I do not think so," Lucian said thoughtfully as he walked over to join Decker by the indoor garden. "I suspect between Lilith and Abril interrupting them they did not have the time."

"The holes in her memory," Cassius said with understanding. "She left the kitchen, then was abruptly in the kitchen and leaving again."

Lucian nodded, and then announced, "You will not go to the shed to get shovels. Dustpans and other items from inside the house will have to do."

"There's a snow shovel in the garage still," Abril announced, running her hand down Lilith's smooth fur again. "I was going to move it to the garden shed, and then we had snow again just a couple weeks ago, so it never got moved. It's leaning against the far wall in the garage."

"Is there a way to get into the garage without having to go out and be seen returning with the shovel?" Lucian asked.

"Yes. Down that hallway," she said, pointing to the hall to the laundry room. "There's a door that opens into the back of the garage."

"I'll get it," Bricker offered, hurrying from the room.

"What do you think is in the garden?" Crispin asked with curiosity.

"Probably another body," Cassius suggested when Lucian did not respond.

"Well, why would they try to get that out? I mean it was a big risk to break into the house and try to dig out the garden. If that was what they were doing," he pointed out. "And we've already discovered the bodies outside. What would it matter if there's one more here?"

Lucian shook his head slowly. "Who can say? But there is obviously something there they want badly enough that they would take the risk of entering the house when it was not empty. Abril must have interrupted them repeatedly and prevented them getting very far," he said. "They must have wiped her mind and sent her back to the kitchen the first time, or perhaps several times for all we know, then took her outside the last time."

Bricker returned then with the shovel. It was large, at least two feet wide. It was made for shoveling lots of snow and would be awkward to use in the garden. But it was the best they had at the moment. It was better than using a dustpan, or a spatula, Abril supposed.

"Gently," Lucian ordered when Bricker stepped into the garden. When he tried to move the fronds of the umbrella plant aside with one foot, Decker joined him and simply pulled it out. He then pulled out a couple more before getting out of his way.

"Thanks," Bricker said and then set to work.

"Perhaps we should take Lilith into the kitchen and let her rest where we can watch her," Crispin said suddenly.

"No," Abril said at once. She knew he was just trying to get her out of the living room and shook her head in refusal. "I want to see what's in the garden too."

In the end, they did have to resort to dustpans and anything else in the house they could find that would be useful as a tool to help. It was mostly due to impatience on the part of the other men. They couldn't stand the wait when Bricker was working alone, so joined him. They dug and dug, deeper and deeper with no results.

"How deep is this damn garden?" Bricker asked with irritation.

Abril shrugged and stood. Leaving Lilith where she was, she moved closer to the garden. "I have no idea. This house is slab on grade. No basement. For all I know there is no bottom and they just left an open hole in this part of the house for the garden to be a real garden."

"Unlikely," Lucian announced. "It is more likely it goes down as far as the foundation."

"I think we are already past the foundation point," Decker said dryly, shifting some of the dirt away from the edge so it would not fall back into the hole. They had to be at least four feet down already.

Lucian shook his head solemnly. "Even for slab on grade, they dig a foundation until they reach firm ground. If there is peat moss or something else in the area—"

"There is," Abril interrupted to say. "The contractor said they would have to dig ten feet down to get past the peat, then backfill with gravel before pouring the concrete for the slab on top of that." She smiled crookedly at the memory and said what she'd thought at the time. "It just seems silly really. According to him that's how the original contractor poured the foundation for the main house too. It means there is a basement under here that's full of gravel. I always figured it would be easier just to have an actual basement."

"Found something!" Bricker said suddenly.

Twenty-Two

Abril joined Lucian at the edge of the hole and Crispin followed, stepping up on her other side as they watched Cassius, Decker, and Bricker all now begin to work with smaller tools on their find.

"It looks like it is just another skeleton," Decker said with confusion, his movements slowing.

"Well, dig it out," Lucian growled impatiently. "We cannot leave that skeleton here any more than we could the ones outside. Besides, I suspect it is *not* like the other skeletons at all."

"What makes you think that?" Bricker asked as he continued to drag dirt away from the skeleton with his hands.

"Because if it were like the others, the rogue would not have risked coming in here to dig this one up," Crispin said solemnly, and then turned to Abril and took her arm. "I really think we should go wait in the kitchen and let them deal with this. We can set the table and prepare for dinner."

"The table is already set," she pointed out. "I am fine here."

Crispin opened his mouth on what she knew would be another attempt to lure her away from the garden, but just then there was a curse from Bricker.

"Goddamn, Lucian. You were right." His tone was grim.

Curious, Abril tugged her arm free of Crispin's grip and knelt to get a better look. It was only the skull that was revealed so far, and nothing she hadn't already seen from the garden outside. She had no idea why Crispin had been so eager to keep her from seeing it.

"*Is* it the same as the others though?" Lucian asked softly next to her.

Abril glanced up at the man standing on her right, and then turned back to again examine the skull that had been revealed. This time she looked more closely and noticed that something was off about it around the jaw area. What—? Her eyes widened as she noted that this human skull had canines like a dog. Long, pointy canines or . . . fangs?

"Shit," Cassius breathed. All three of the men in the hole had paused and sat back on their haunches as if to distance themselves from their find.

Abril's gaze snapped from the fangs to Cassius, then to Lucian, and finally Crispin. They all looked grim and tight-lipped. "Those aren't fangs, are they? I mean, they're joke fangs or something. Right?"

When silence met her question, Abril was sure the answer was no, though the very possibility seemed ridiculous to her. They had to be fake. Didn't they? But why would anyone bury a skeleton and put fake fangs in their mouth?

"I believe it is time you had that talk with Abril, Nephew," Lucian said firmly.

She turned to Crispin in question to see that he was avoiding meeting her gaze.

"What do you have to tell me?" Abril asked finally.

When Crispin hesitated, Lucian snapped, "No more delays, Nephew! Now! Or I shall do it myself."

Mouth tightening, Crispin took her hand and led her into the kitchen. Abril expected him to stop there, but instead, he continued on through the kitchen, up the hall, and into her office. There he closed the door and urged her to sit on the couch. He then dropped to his haunches in front of her and took her hands in his. "What I have to tell you is—Well, it might be scary," he admitted apologetically. "Which is why I have hesitated to tell you this before now. But also because I was not sure how to do it. I do not want to distress you."

"You're distressing me right now with this buildup to it," she told him with a small frown. "Just tell me."

"Right," he muttered, and then glanced down at their entwined hands and paused for another uncomfortable moment or two, before finally saying, "First off, I do not want you to be scared. We would never hurt you. And I hope you believe that."

"Okay," Abril said, beginning to get a little weirded out.

"In fact, I could never hurt you. I care about you a great deal. You are very important to me," he said.

Abril's eyebrows rose slightly. She wasn't used to men speaking so freely about their emotions, but aside from that, they had only known each other a very short while. As attracted as they were to each other, it was still a bit early for her to be "very important" to him. But she let that go for now and simply waited for him to continue . . . and waited . . . and waited.

Just as she was about to suggest that perhaps they could discuss whatever he was having trouble saying to her later, he opened his mouth and blurted, "I come from a family of scientists."

She blinked at that announcement. It was so anticlimactic. Abril had expected some earth-shaking revelation, not that he had science geeks in his family. She also didn't see what this had to do with the skeleton in the garden, and the fangs that may or may not be fake. Deciding he would hopefully get to that later, she cleared her throat, and then said, "Your parents are both scientists?"

"No. Actually, my parents are . . . well, both of them have had many different careers, but presently my father is a lawyer and my mother"—he hesitated—"I guess you would call her an entrepreneur." Shrugging, he continued, "When I say I come from a family of scientists, I mean, other family members. Like my cousins, grandparents . . . and some ancestors."

"Okay," Abril said, and then again waited. She didn't have to wait as long this time.

"Well, they—some scientists, not necessarily my ancestors—were looking into different ways to cure diseases like cancer and such. Ways that would avoid needing dangerous and invasive surgeries."

When he paused as if waiting for her to respond, she said the only thing she could think to say at that point. "Oh."

Apparently, it was enough because he continued, "And they actually came up with a brilliant idea. It was nanos. Bioengineered nanos that would cure illnesses, even injuries." He paused briefly and then said, "The nanos were bioengineered."

"You mentioned that already," she pointed out gently.

"Right," he said uncomfortably. "So, these nanos use blood to do their work and to propel themselves. Do not ask me how," he added quickly. "I do not know the specifics. But somehow the nanos, once injected into the host would go to any site in the body where there is an injury or illness and heal it."

When she just stared at him silently, absorbing his words, he rushed on, "You see the scientists programmed the nanos with a map of both a male and female body at their peak condition. Which is basically twenty-five to thirty years old," he informed her. "They then programmed the nanos to return their host to that condition. Unfortunately," he added with a grimace, "the scientists who came up with that assumed that they could be injected into the human body, and they would—Well, I mean, imagine somebody got shot," he tried. "The nanos were supposed to go to the site of the injury, recognize that the bullet did not belong, force it out of the body, and repair the wound without ever having to have somebody cut them open to dig out the bullet, or sew anything up. It is all taken care of by the nanos."

He paused briefly, looking pleased with himself for the explanation, but Abril was staring at him with confusion. She still had no idea what this had to do with the fangs in the jaw of the skeleton in the indoor garden.

Pushing that concern aside for now, she clarified, "So, these nanos would go and repair wounds, and—what? Surround and kill cancer cells, illness, and anything that didn't belong?"

"Yes. Basically," he said with obvious relief and then sat back.

Abril simply stared at him, waiting. Not sure that the conversation was over yet. Finally, she raised her eyebrows and asked, "Is that all you wanted to tell me? I mean it *is* a lot," she assured him. "It sounds like a brilliant invention. If they ever get it working properly, or get it approved by Canada Health, or the FDA or whatever, then that would be amazing. A real boon to mankind. You should be very proud of your family."

Crispin began to frown at her words and opened his mouth to speak, but before he could there was a thump on the office door that made them both jump. It was followed by Lucian Argeneau's voice through the door, barking, "Dear God, Nephew! You are worse at communication than your father. Do you need me to come in there and explain things to her? Or are you going to finish this properly?"

"I can do it!" Crispin snapped. "Just get away from the door and stop eavesdropping."

They waited in silence, but when no other sound followed, Crispin apparently decided Lucian had left and turned back to her with a very long and weary sounding sigh. Offering a weak smile then, he said, "I apologize. What I just told you was only part of the story."

"Have they done human trials with these nanos yet?" Abril asked.

"Much more than just trials," Crispin admitted. "A

dozen or so patients were treated with them when they were first developed."

Abril's eyebrows flew up at that. Not because she didn't believe him, but because she couldn't believe that it hadn't made the news that these nanos existed and were being used. Finally, she said, "I guess they didn't work."

Crispin gave a start, obviously surprised by the comment. "What would make you think that?"

She shrugged and then said reasonably, "Well, I haven't heard anything in the news about bioengineered or miracle nanos, so I assume they did not work well."

"Actually, they worked very well," he assured her, and then hesitated and reluctantly admitted, "Not exactly as they expected though."

"How so?" Abril asked with interest.

"Well, they intended for the nanos to do their chore, cure whatever illness or injury their host had, and be done. They were programmed to self-destruct once they finished restoring their host to peak condition. Then they would be flushed out of the body just as any other waste leaves."

"But that didn't happen," she suggested, and when he looked surprised, she pointed out, "You did just say it didn't work as expected. So, I presume if they expected them to do their job and then disintegrate . . ." She shrugged.

"Right," he said and then nodded. "And yes, you are correct that the nanos did not self-destruct and disintegrate on completing the repairs to injuries or healing illnesses that they were injected into the patient to deal with. It was not the fault of the scientists," he said quickly, apparently concerned that she might think less of his relatives for the perceived failure. But then he frowned and admitted, "Although . . . I mean, I suppose, ultimately, it was their fault for not considering that the human body is constantly in need of repair in one way or another."

Abril's eyebrows rose. "How so?"

Crispin frowned and then said, "Cells are constantly dying because of age and environmental factors, etcetera. I guess the scientists did not consider that the nanos would see those issues as something they needed to repair as well before self-destructing. But they do, so that they just never self-destruct and leave the body." Seeing her expression, he explained, "Sunlight damages the skin and the nanos take care of it. The simple passage of time causes cells to die and the nanos take care of that. Pollution does damage to the lungs and skin microbiome and—"

"And the nanos take care of that," Abril said for him.

"Yes," he said and added, "Ultimately, there is always something to repair or fix, so the nanos just never self-destruct and leave the body."

Abril merely nodded, but didn't really see a problem with that. It sounded pretty good to have nanos in your body ready to heal should you have an accident or get stabbed or something. You wouldn't even have to wait for an ambulance to arrive and the paramedics to inject the nanos, she thought and then Crispin spoke again.

"And that is how we came to be immortals," he finished with a gusty sigh, and then straightened from kneeling in front of her, and moved to sit on the couch beside her instead.

Abril automatically started to nod, and then stopped and shifted sideways on the couch to face him. "Wait. What? Immortals? What are you talking about? I thought these nanos healed wounds and stuff?"

Crispin's satisfaction drained away like runoff water. Frowning, he shifted to sit sideways to face her as well and thought for a moment before saying, "Well, you see because the nanos do not die and leave the body, they remain."

"Of course," she said dryly. "But what was that about how you became *immortal*?"

"Not me," he said quickly, and then frowned and said, "Well, yes I am too, but I didn't become immortal. I was born immortal." He paused briefly and then explained, "My mother was an immortal, so I was born with the nanos from her and the nanos make anyone they reside in young, healthy, and immortal."

Abril stared at him blankly for a moment, and then said, "Young? You didn't mention anything about them making their host young."

"They were programmed with the anatomy of both a human male and female at their peak condition, which is twenty-five to thirty," he reminded her. "The nanos thought they were supposed to . . ."

"Make their host young?" she suggested.

He nodded slowly, something about her tone making his eyes turn wary. "Basically, yes."

Abril considered what he'd said, and then asked, "So if an elderly person—someone in their eighties, for instance—if they had cancer and were given the nanos to try to cure them, the nanos would not just cure the cancer, but make the older person young too?"

"Well, yes and no. They would still be eighty years

old, but their body would be healthy and at its peak condition."

"Which is twenty-five to thirty," she pointed out. "Much younger than eighty."

Crispin nodded.

Abril sat back slightly, her expression showing her awe. "Your family has discovered the fountain of youth."

He relaxed a little. "Some people have called it that."

Abril sat up abruptly. "Why is this not known everywhere? This should be on the news. It's a miracle cure. We should be calling CNN right now."

"Unfortunately, it would not be considered good news," he assured her.

"What? That's crazy! Why isn't it good news?" Abril asked, finding it hard to believe it wouldn't be welcomed as the great miracle cure it was. Then her eyes widened, and she breathed, "Oh. Right. I get it. We already have a population problem and are doing untold damage to the earth because of it. Clear-cutting forests, causing pollution, causing the extinction of different species . . ." She sighed. "If everybody knew about this and demanded access, that would be the end of death. There wouldn't be a square foot left on the planet where a person wasn't standing."

"Yes, that is an issue," he agreed. "But there is another problem."

"What's that?" she asked with surprise. She would have thought the one she'd just mentioned was really the only one.

Crispin hesitated, and then said, "I did mention that the nanos are bioengineered. They use blood to both propel themselves, as well as to make more of their kind in the body. They often even use blood to perform their repairs and healing." He paused briefly and then admitted, "But often, they use more blood than the human body can produce."

Abril considered that briefly, and then said, "So, what do they do?" she asked, and before he could answer did it herself saying, "I guess they get blood transfusions to make up for that or something."

"That is exactly what they did," he said, sounding relieved.

Abril was more than a little relieved herself. The image of the skeleton in the garden with its fangs had flashed briefly through her mind as she'd considered what he'd said. She'd actually thought for a moment that maybe the fangs had been the answer to the issue of needing blood, and what they were talking about was that the patients had essentially turned into vampires to get the blood they needed. She was more than relieved to learn that wasn't the case and the patients with these nanos were given transfusions to deal with the necessity for blood.

Smiling crookedly, she told him, "Honestly it doesn't sound like a bad trade-off. I mean, I hate needles. But putting up with a transfusion every once in a while, in exchange for looking young and being healthy for the rest of your days doesn't seem like a bad deal." She paused briefly as she considered what she'd just said, and then asked, "So, by immortal you just mean long-lived, right? You guys don't live forever. No one lives forever."

Crispin hesitated and then told her, "Barring being set on fire, or having their head cut off and kept away from the body long enough that it cannot reattach, immortals can live indefinitely."

Abril's mind was in sudden chaos. "Indefinitely?"

Crispin nodded, his expression solemn.

"How long is indefinitely?"

He was silent for a moment, and then said reluctantly, "Lucian was born in Atlantis several millennia ago."

Abril stiffened, her gaze fixed on him as she said with disbelief, "Atlantis?"

"That is where the nanos were developed," he explained.

"Atlantis," she repeated, her brain having trouble accepting what he was telling her. A short, disbelieving laugh slipped from her lips, and she said, "You want me to believe that scientists thousands of years ago in the mythical land of Atlantis, developed bioengineered nanos that are the fountain of youth and that Lucian, your uncle Lucian, who is presently sitting out there in Gina's kitchen, was born way back then and way over there—wherever there is?"

"Was," he corrected, and when her gaze went blank with confusion, explained, "My uncle was born way back then, and way over there where Atlantis *was*. Atlantis fell. It no longer exists."

She stared at him silently, amazed that he was continuing with this line. It was so ridiculous. "From my understanding, Crispin, toilet paper was invented in New York in the 1850s. Before that, they were using leaves, sticks, moss, shells, corn husks, and water to clean themselves after taking a shit. But you want me to believe that thousands of years before that, your ancestors came up with bioengineered nanos that—"

"Atlantis was more developed than the rest of the planet at that time," he interrupted her to say. "They were far in advance of the rest of the world. But they kept those advancements to themselves."

"How?" she asked at once and didn't hide her disbelief. In her experience, it was almost impossible to keep secrets in this world. How could the Atlanteans have kept such advancements from their neighbors on the planet?

"Atlantis was separated from the rest of humanity by mountains and the ocean. And while they had the equipment and ability to cross the mountains, or take ships around to their neighbors and the rest of humanity, they were very insular and uninterested in that. They—Well, actually they were kind of snobs, I guess," he admitted with a grimace. "They did not feel the rest of humanity had anything to offer them, so they never shared their knowledge."

"They never looked outside their own little island or whatever it was?" she asked.

"It was a peninsula, not an island," he corrected. "And they did on occasion check on their neighbors. Every once in a while teams of scientists would go out and explore the rest of the world. They often returned with new plants never encountered before, or minerals and metals not readily available in Atlantis. The information they brought back was apparently put into our history books." He shrugged. "But that was all they went for: historical and scientific purposes. There were no tourists traveling out and about. The rest of the world was, of course, not very advanced in comparison to our people, so there was really no reason for anyone but scientists or explorers to be interested in leaving Atlantis with all its advances."

"Right," she murmured thoughtfully, not sure if she believed him or not. Although, if he was lying, she did have to wonder why he would bother.

"Besides, Atlanteans did hold the belief that they should not have undue influence over other tribes," he explained. "I mean, just imagine discovering a primitive tribe without any previous contact with the modern world. We with our cell phones, planes, and weapons would seem like gods to them. It would be terribly unfair and affect their natural development."

"Right," she breathed, and then said slowly, "So, they had these nanos that were basically miraculous. But they didn't share them with others, and instead kept them for themselves." She tilted her head and peered at him in question. "So how did they come to the rest of the world in the end? The Atlanteans with their nanos I mean. Like Lucian who you say was born there." She arched her eyebrows. "I know Atlantis disappeared ages ago. Is that when they supposedly joined the rest of society? Because they were forced to?"

"Basically, yes. Atlantis fell. A series of earthquakes and a volcanic eruption separated the peninsula from the rest of the continent, and Atlantis sank into the ocean. Most of the population was lost. The only people to survive were those who had been given the nanos. Like Lucian. They crawled out of the wreckage and were forced to join the rest of the world."

Abril stared at him for a moment, her mind ticking over the information he was giving. She still wasn't sure she believed him, but decided to go with it for now. "I don't suppose any of the survivors thought to stop to grab the equipment needed for blood transfusions on their way out of the sinking Atlantis?"

"No," he acknowledged. "I suspect they were all too focused on surviving the collapsing world around them to think of that."

"So, no more transfusions," she guessed, "and the nanos gave their hosts fangs to get the blood they needed to do the work they were programmed to perform."

He looked almost relieved that she had been the one to say that as he nodded. "Exactly. They also made us stronger, faster, and gave us the ability to see in the dark."

"She does not believe you, Nephew. She is just humoring you," Lucian bellowed from the kitchen. "Show her your fangs."

Eyebrows rising, Abril turned expectantly to Crispin, but he hesitated, and as he did, she began to wonder how Lucian had known she didn't believe Crispin. She wondered, too, how the hell he knew what they were talking about. Her office was up a long hall, and the door was closed. Surely, he couldn't hear them? And even if he could, he couldn't possibly condone this nonsense his nephew was spewing.

"It is not nonsense," Lucian called out.

He *could* hear them. How the hell could he hear them from the kitchen? Wait! She hadn't said that out loud. She'd merely thought it. How the hell did he know what she was thinking? She would have asked except that Crispin chose that moment to open his mouth wide. At first, there wasn't much to see, just his tongue and two rows of perfectly normal human, aka non-vampire, teeth. She was about to say as much when movement drew her gaze to his right canine as it began to shift and dropped down, suddenly becoming a very pointy fang. One that exactly matched the one on the other side of his jaw where his human canine had been a moment ago.

Twenty-Three

Abril stared at the fangs protruding from Crispin's jaw for one horrified moment and then closed her eyes briefly. When she opened them again, the fangs were gone. They'd disappeared somewhere. His teeth looked normal again as he closed his mouth.

"Abril?" he asked softly when she just stared at him. Alarm entered his expression as if he could sense her emotional withdrawal.

"Stay with me," he whispered, reaching for her.

The words weren't really registering with her, but his touch did as his fingers found her. One set traced a path down her outer arm, while the other slid around her neck to cup her nape. Both sent shivers of awareness through her despite the fangs she'd just seen in his mouth. When the fingers on her arm trailed up again, and the ones at her neck shifted to glide into her hair, Abril closed her eyes and bit her tongue to hold back the moan that tried to escape her.

The moment her eyes were shut, her brain started shooting several scenes at her one after the other; the skull Lilith had unearthed in the garden, Crispin the first time she'd met him, a damp and newly washed Lilith on a mud-free floor after Roberts and Crispin had cleaned them both, Crispin taking the dog out for her, complimenting her on her chili, the kiss in the laundry room, their passionate moments in the pool; her, Crispin, and Roberts laughing and enjoying the movie *Pixels*, her and Crispin talking as they played Pac-Man, the bliss he'd given her in her bedroom, their talk in her office, the sex dream, the fanged skeleton in the garden. Finally, the images stopped and her eyes opened so that she was left staring at him. Crispin. Detective Delacort. Crispinus Delacort . . . with nanos.

"Okay," Abril breathed. After a moment she spent trying to calm her thoughts and body, she cleared her throat. "Wow. So that's how vampires were really made. Not some ancient curse, just science."

"We are not vampires!" Lucian bellowed, his voice reaching her all the way up the hall from the kitchen where he no doubt still sat at the island.

Abril blinked, feeling as if that ridiculous shout from the kitchen had snapped her out of some kind of fog. Lucian was ridiculous. A grumpy, bossy asshole, and if there was one thing she'd learned in her life, it was how to deal with assholes. As for Crispin, he was . . . Crispin. He was a man who had kissed and caressed her to heights of passion she'd never before experienced. Cared for her when she was wounded. Comforted her when she'd been upset about her sister marrying Agustin . . . Although, that had been a dream, she supposed. But it hadn't felt like one, and she wondered if he had somehow entered her dreams. Was that even possible? She supposed the only way to find out was to ask, so did just that.

"My dream . . . I was on the phone with my sister, and you came into my office. Did you—"

"We had a shared dream," he said gently, interrupting her. "I was there with you. I experienced it all with you."

"Oh," she said faintly, recalling the conversation they'd had after Mary had hung up on her. She'd told him about her childhood and running away. She didn't usually tell people about that so quickly, if at all. Barb and Crispin were the exceptions, and Barb had ended up being a surrogate mother of sorts. Better than the mother she'd been born with, certainly. She had obviously instinctively trusted Crispin just as she had Barb on first meeting. Perhaps she could trust her instincts here as well. Maybe Crispin was a good vampire.

"Explain to her that we are not vampires, Crispin!" Lucian shouted.

Crispin rolled his eyes with irritation at the man inserting himself into the conversation. He wished he could take Abril outside for a walk to finish this talk in peace, but knew that was not a good idea, so offered her a smile and said, "We are immortals, not vampires."

Abril seemed to consider that and then asked, "What's the difference?"

"Vampires are mythical creatures who are dead and soulless. We, immortals, are neither dead nor soulless. We are humans who have been given a scientific advancement that allows us to remain healthy and live longer."

Abril nodded slowly, but asked, "How did your people originally get fangs if they didn't come with the nanos?"

"They did come with the nanos, just not right away," he said quietly. "They were not a programmed part of the nanos, but when Atlantis fell . . . Well, the nanos *were* programmed to keep their host at their peak. They needed blood to do that. But when the fall happened, the surviving Atlanteans spread out into the world. None of them were scientists who had worked with the nanos, and as you guessed, no one had managed to bring out any of the items needed for transfusions.

"On top of all that, most of those survivors were apparently injured during their escape, some grievously so. They all needed blood, but with no transfusions to aid with that, they were quickly starving for it and in unbearable pain. Some set themselves on fire to escape the pain. Others did it out of fear that the terrible pain would make them desperate enough to attack their new neighbors. That they would become mad and vicious animals who slaughtered mortals to get the blood they needed and even drink it, which of course they had never done before when transfusions were available," he pointed out. "The very idea of drinking human blood was horrifying to a lot of them."

Abril nodded with understanding and he supposed she would naturally be horrified at the idea too.

Offering her a smile, he continued, "Fortunately, for those who remained, the nanos did what they had to do to ensure their survival. They brought on fangs and other things in their hosts to help them get the blood the nanos needed to continue to do their work."

Abril's head came up slightly. "What other things?"

"They made them stronger, faster, gave them night vision . . ."

"Abilities that would make them better predators," she realized.

Crispin nodded, his expression almost apologetic. "Yes. Predators. But only because there were no more blood transfusions and the nanos needed the blood."

Abril grunted, her expression troubled.

"We are not the vampires of fiction," he said firmly. "We are not dead and soulless, and we have laws. We do not just go around preying on people. In fact, we do not bite people anymore at all. And even when we did, we were not allowed to feed to the point of death. We could only take so much, and had to erase their memories of our presence, and replace them with pleasurable experiences so that no one knew we existed.

"We understood that anyone finding out about us and our nanos would be a problem that could end in our being hunted down as a people and killed. Or, if they did not outright kill us, they would want to be like us. And even back at the beginning, directly after the fall, the immortals knew that would be a bad thing for the population at large."

Abril nodded in understanding but couldn't help thinking that others knowing would also have reduced the population they could feed off as well.

"We have a lot of laws to protect both ourselves and mortals," he assured her. "As I said we are not allowed to feed unto death, but the truth is, now that there are blood banks, it is against our laws to feed off of humans at all, unless it is an emergency."

"An emergency?" she asked, her gaze narrowing.

He hesitated and then said, "If an immortal is terribly injured and has lost a lot of blood somewhere away from blood banks or the ability to get bagged blood, it is safer to feed off of a mortal or two than to risk being overwhelmed by blood lust and attacking and killing anyone."

She nodded slowly at that, and then said, "Tell me about your laws."

"We are allowed to turn only one mortal in our lifetime. We are allowed to only have one child every century. We are never to do anything that would reveal our existence to mortals. And, as I said, here in North America we are never to feed off mortals unless it is an emergency."

"Here in North America?" Abril asked at once.

Crispin shifted uncomfortably before admitting, "Different areas have different councils and so different laws. North America has the North American council with its laws, Europe has its own set of laws, and South America has its own council and laws as well and so on."

Abril almost asked if feeding off a mortal was legal or not in these other areas, but suspected she really wouldn't like the answer, so set it aside for now, and instead asked, "And how do they ensure these laws are followed?"

"We have immortal police not dissimilar to human police. They are called Enforcers. That is their official title. We usually call them hunters, because that is their main task, hunting down rogue immortals who are harming mortals."

"Is that what you are?" she asked. "An Enforcer masquerading as a homicide detective?"

"Not really," he answered slowly, and then grimaced and added, "I mean, I would be included in the hunt if there was one in the area—"

"As there appears to be," she pointed out.

Crispin nodded. "Yes, that is why Roberts and I are on the police force here in London. So that we will be the first to become aware if there is a rogue in the area that is harming, turning, or killing mortals. They have at least one immortal on each of the police forces in every city, and a couple in each of the provincial police forces, and the RCMP as well. Our jobs are to keep our eyes open for rogue activity, and if we spot any, report to Garrett Mortimer, the head of the Immortal Enforcers. He then sends out other Enforcers to take care of the situation. Of course, the reporting immortals—in this case, Roberts and I—would help the Enforcers get control of the situation."

"Roberts is a vampire too?" she asked with surprise.

"We are not vampires," he reminded her gently.

"Aren't you? You have fangs and—"

"We are immortals," he insisted. "Vampires are something that was made up based on a loose description of immortals, but have nothing to do with us. We are not predators so much as—Think of us as hemophiliacs," he interrupted himself to say. "We occasionally need to take in extra blood to survive because of a sudden loss of blood in our bodies. The only difference is that we are not bleeding out. The nanos are taking and using it."

"Other than the nanos, I'm pretty sure that's true

of vampires too," she argued gently and pointed out, "They need blood to survive too."

"But vampires are dead and soulless," he repeated insistently. "We are not dead and we do have souls. Also, garlic does not affect us. Nor do crosses—our skin does not burn if we touch them. We do not sleep in coffins. We do not run with wolves or turn into a cloud of bats. We cannot crawl up walls or across ceilings. We *can* walk into churches and not burst into flames. We can go out in the sun without bursting into flames, too." He paused and then acknowledged, "Though we do tend to avoid going out in the sun without protection to avoid using up more blood than absolutely necessary." He shook his head. "We are not vampires."

Abril didn't argue the point, mostly because she couldn't. Vampires *were* dead and soulless, and from what he had described his people were not. "Okay, so you prefer the name *immortals*." She raised her eyebrows. "But you aren't really immortal, are you? You said fire and decapitation will kill your kind."

Crispin gave a slight nod and told her, "Fire is the more efficient method to kill us. For some reason the nanos make us highly flammable. We go up like a roman candle."

"Yeah, but it's messy and probably stinky," she pointed out. "I would think that would make decapitation more efficient."

"But decapitation only works if the head is kept away from the body long enough."

"You don't sound too sure," she noted.

"Mostly because I am not," he admitted. "I have heard that cutting off the head and keeping it away from the body can kill us, but I also know that if you reattach the head within a certain timeframe, the nanos will heal it all the way around and reattach whatever needs reattaching and the victim will survive."

"No way!" she said, her eyes growing wide.

"It is true," he assured her.

"Well, how the hell do you know it's true? Did someone lose their head and then . . ." She paused because she couldn't even imagine what might have happened next. It was hard to believe anyone would then place the head up against the neck to see if it would reattach. She supposed they might have put the body and head together for burial, only to then have the healing happen as a complete surprise. Or maybe the whole head reattaching itself was an urban myth for immortals.

"It is not an urban myth," Lucian barked from the kitchen and Crispin's mouth tightened at his interference and then smiled at her sympathetically.

"I used to think it might be just a story made up from the past, but recently it was proven true when a scientist started doing things like that to our people in an effort to see what they could survive," Crispin said, his voice tight. "He was cutting off the head and trying to see how far away you could have it from the body before the nanos would not be able to fix it, or for how long it could be held away from the body before the nanos shut down and could no longer reattach and repair it. He was also performing other rather horrible experiments on immortals; cutting off limbs, cutting them in half, etcetera."

"He sounds like a fun guy," Abril said dryly. "Hopefully, he was stopped?"

"Yes." It was one word, heavy and grim.

"So, if I cut off your head and bury it in a box away from your body, you would eventually die. But not right away," she said slowly.

"Yes," he admitted, eyeing her a little leerily.

"Alternately, I could douse you in gasoline and set you on fire and that would kill you."

He nodded slowly, his gaze now narrowed on her. She seemed awfully interested in how to kill him.

"So, the only ways for your kind to die are both horrible," she said, "I mean, burning alive has to be excruciatingly painful physically. But having your head cut off . . . If you don't die right away, you must be aware that your head has been removed from your body and—Good Lord! How long does it take for the brain to die after decapitation? How long would you be just alive, but not attached to your body and aware of everything including that you were indeed dying?"

"I have no idea," Crispin admitted. "I am sure the scientist found out, and that someone else knows from his notes, but I am not that someone."

"Hmm," Abril muttered with dissatisfaction, then gave her head a small shake, and said, "Okay, so your ancestors were Atlanteans who developed an incredible cure using bioengineered nanos that basically make you stronger, faster, able to see in the dark, and almost indestructible."

Crispin gave a slow nod, but his expression was dissatisfied, and he reluctantly said, "They also gave us the ability to read the minds of mortals and any immortals younger than us, as well as to control the minds of mortals and any immortal younger than us. But it is believed that was purely to make it easier for us to feed without everybody knowing about us," he rushed out.

"You can read my mind and control me?" she asked her voice rising with each word.

"No," he quickly assured her.

"You just said—"

"I should have explained," Crispin interrupted. "Lucian, Bricker, Decker, Cassius, Roberts, and Anders can all read your mind, know what you are thinking, and can control you if they wish," he admitted and then added swiftly, "But I would never allow them do that. At least not if I realized they were doing it."

"But you supposedly can't?" she asked with obvious disbelief.

"That is the truth," he said firmly. "I cannot read or control you."

She considered him briefly, wanting to believe him, and then asked, "Just me? Or do you simply not have those two skills for some reason?"

"Just you," he admitted.

"Why?"

Crispin hesitated and then said slowly, "There are three different reasons for why an immortal cannot read a mortal. First, there have been cases where mortals with brain tumors were unreadable to immortals. That is not always the case though. I gather if the tumor is lodged in a certain area, it can block an immortal from reading them, but in other areas of the brain it will have no effect on that skill at all."

Abril supposed that made sense.

"Another reason is insanity. Immortals sometimes cannot read the mind of an insane person. I do not know if it is because their thoughts are too disorganized and chaotic, or their brain is diseased, but they can be impossible to read."

"Well, as far as I know I don't have a brain tumor, nor am I insane. I don't think," she added with uncertainty, and then smiled crookedly and pointed out, "I mean, insane people don't usually think they're insane, do they?"

"You are not insane, and you do not have a brain tumor," he assured her. "The others can read you, so the first two reasons are not why I am unable to read you."

"Which brings us to reason number three," she said, and when he didn't respond right away, she tilted her head and said, "Three must be really bad if you don't want to tell me what it is. Am I dying of something horrible like mad cow disease, or—"

"No," he interrupted with dismay. "The last reason is not bad at all. At least, I hope you will not see it as bad. I hope you will be as happy as I am to hear it."

Abril's eyebrows rose slightly, and she pointed out, "The only way we'll know is if you tell me."

Crispin nodded, took a deep breath and then said, "The third reason for an immortal to be unable to read a mortal is if they are a possible life mate."

"Life mate?" she echoed with relief. Honestly, that didn't sound bad at all compared to mad cow, late-stage syphilis, or any of the other diseases that could damage the brain. "What is a life mate?"

Twenty-Four

Abril's question echoed in Crispin's head. "What is a life mate?"

This was where the conversation was going to get tricky. The answer to this question and how she would take the news was the important bit. It made Crispin almost wish he could call out to his uncle and have Lucian explain about life mates. Problem was, his uncle was an ass, and would employ neither tact nor concern in explaining and that probably wouldn't help his odds in convincing Abril to be his life mate.

"Crispin?" Abril said finally when he had been silent too long. "What is a life mate?"

"A life mate is . . ." Crispin began and searched his mind desperately for the perfect way to explain this to her. Finally, he said, "Because immortals can read mortals and any immortals who are younger than them, as well as be read by any immortals older than themselves, it is difficult for us to spend a lot of time in social environments."

"Social as in bars, dance clubs, etcetera? Or social like people at all?" she asked for clarification.

"Pretty much people at all," he admitted.

"Huh. That can't be good for their mental health," she commented.

"No. Not very," he acknowledged. "Centuries alone can make an immortal . . ."

"Go cuckoo for Cocoa Puffs?" she suggested when he hesitated again. When he then blinked at her in confusion, she tried, "Cray, cray?"

His eyebrows drew together in bewilderment.

Abril rolled her eyes and then reeled off a list of words. "Bonkers? Crackers? Barmy? Gaga? Bananas? Batty? Unhinged? Crazed? Daft? Stark raving—"

"Yes," he interrupted finally, amusement pulling at his lips as he got the drift of what she was asking. But he did pause to wonder when insanity had become synonymous with the names of various foodstuffs like bananas and crackers? Never mind the rest of the words she'd used. What even was *cray, cray*?

"So being alone a lot makes rogues insane, and . . . ?" she prompted when he didn't immediately continue.

"And when immortals go mad, they usually go rogue," he said simply, and when she stared at him, he said, "The truth is they are probably suicidal, wishing to end their very long existence, but have not the courage to end their own life and so act out to ensure someone else does it for them."

"So, rogues are basically committing suicide by Enforcer," she said. "I get it. But what does any of that have to do with what a life mate is?"

Before he could answer, she asked, "Is a life mate like a girlfriend, or wife, or something?"

Crispin was almost relieved by the question. It made it easier for him to explain. At least, he'd been a little at a loss as to how to explain the significance of a life mate until that moment. Now he said, "It is similar to a girlfriend or wife, but much, much more for several reasons. One reason is because, as I told you, a life mate is someone the immortal cannot read. This allows the immortal to be in their presence without the fear of them knowing his or her thoughts. It makes them a perfect partner, partially because they have someone they can spend time with comfortably and not have to constantly be alone."

"But what makes them unreadable?" she asked, and then added, "And I understand that not being able to read them would make them someone you would be more comfortable being around. I mean, we all have stray thoughts that may be unkind, but is that the only reason that they are good life mates?"

"No," he said firmly. "Life mates are not life mates just because they cannot read each other. That is a large part of it, but there is much more to it than that."

"Like what?" she asked at once.

"Well, life mates always have much in common. Their tastes are very similar. They get along very well. They have a great deal of passion for each other." He paused, obviously struggling, and finally just said, "They are just perfect for each other."

"But why can't they read each other?" She asked what she'd started out asking and he'd neglected to answer.

Crispin frowned, and then said slowly, "We think the nanos recognize some kind of energy signal in the person that matches their host and makes sure they cannot read each other."

"And you think that's the case with me?" Abril asked with interest. "That the nanos recognized a similar energy between the two of us?"

Crispin shrugged slightly. "That is the conclusion everyone is coming to. Mostly because of what my aunt Marguerite and the young woman who is married to the winged man said about how they recognize life mates. They say that life mates have a similar aura or energy to each other, and they recognize that and realize they would be good together."

"I'm sorry," Abril said, shaking her head. "Back that up. The young woman who is married to the winged man?"

"I think her name is Stephanie," Crispin said, trying to recall for sure, but he'd never met the girl so was just going by tales he'd been told. He thought though that Stephanie was her name. Leaving that worry for now, he added, "Marguerite and this girl are both conciliari." When Abril opened her mouth, he quickly answered what he thought her question was going to be and said, "A conciliare is kind of like a matchmaker for immortals. They are good at recognizing life mates and pairing them up."

"Crispin," Abril said solemnly, "That is all really interesting and I'm sure I'll have questions about concilly whatevers later, but right now I'm more interested in the *winged man*."

"Oh." Crispin stared at her blankly for a minute, trying to think what to say. He really didn't feel like stopping to explain about that business when he was trying to tell her about life mates, and that she was one for him, and how much she meant to him. But he supposed there was nothing else for it, so quickly said, "All right, well you remember that scientist I mentioned who was performing those experiments on immortals?"

"Yes."

"Well, he was also performing other experiments, including genetic splicing of human and animal DNA. One of the results is a birdman."

"What?" Abril gasped. "Oh, my God! What—"

"You are getting off topic, children!" Lucian bellowed from the kitchen. "Crispin, finish telling her what life mates are and that she is one for you and get it over with. I am hungry and the lasagna is getting cold."

Crispin scowled toward the door, silently telling his uncle to go to hell. He knew the man could hear his thoughts and would no doubt get the message, but wasn't surprised when he got no response.

"I'm normally pretty easygoing and even-tempered," Abril said, drawing his attention back to her. "But your uncle really gets under my skin."

"Do not feel bad, he has that effect on everyone," Crispin growled.

For some reason that made her grin. He smiled in return and then said, "Okay, so basically, the nanos recognize life mates and the immortal—or immortals because life mates are not always one mortal and one immortal, sometimes it is two immortals," he explained. "Anyway, we think the nanos are then responsible for all of the symptoms and attributes of life mates. We are not certain, of course, but that is the present supposition. All we know for sure is that it works, and that if we find someone we cannot read, they are most likely our life mate."

"What are these symptoms and attributes?" Abril asked. "Besides not being able to read them, I mean."

"We become interested in food and sex again," he stated.

"Again?" she asked, eyebrows flying up.

"Well, as we age immortals tend to grow tired of food and sex . . . and pretty much everything else, really."

"Which is what leads to the suicide by Enforcer thing," she said, sounding almost resentful at the thought of someone putting the Enforcers through that. Or perhaps she was more disgusted that completely innocent mortals were hurt or killed to get the Enforcers to end the rogue's life.

Crispin shrugged. "Well, I imagine it would take a lot of fortitude to set yourself on fire, and I'm not even sure it is possible to decapitate yourself. Suicide by Enforcer is probably the easiest route," he pointed out. It was something he had thought about a great deal. He was very old himself and had considered ending his life more than once, so had some sympathy for the rogues. Who was to say he might not have gone rogue himself eventually if he had not encountered Abril? Or wouldn't still if he was unable to claim her?

"Anyway," he said abruptly, "we are getting off topic again. The point is as we age, we grow tired of food and sex and other things we enjoyed earlier in our lives. However, the arrival of a life mate in our life can reawaken those desires in us. We suddenly find ourselves enjoying food again, among other pleasures."

"Were you tired of food and sex?" she asked, finding that hard to believe. The man had been a sexual dynamo during each of their encounters.

"I have not had sex since 766 BC and have not eaten since 751 BC," he said simply, and then added, "Until meeting you."

Abril could feel the blood leaching from her face as she took in his words. "I'm sorry? When was the last time you ate or had sex?"

"766 BC for sex, and 751 BC for food," Crispin repeated.

"Are you telling me that you were born—BC means before Christ, right?"

"Yes," he said, sounding almost apologetic.

"So, you were born in—"

When she paused to do the math, he saved her the trouble. "I was born in 900 BC."

Abril just stared at him, her mind having difficulty absorbing what he was telling her. If what he said was true, Crispin was well over 2900 years old. That was old. Crazy old. That just seemed like madness to her. It couldn't be true.

"You appear upset," he said unhappily.

Abril started to shake her head, but then stopped because, frankly, she wasn't sure what she was. She wanted to say she wasn't upset, but she couldn't think of how to describe what she was feeling in that moment. Dismay. Shock. A certainty that this had to all be some kind of weird dream she was having. The only thing she really wasn't feeling was horror, which rather surprised her.

Deciding to push aside her feelings on the subject, and the fact that she'd been making out with and was still lusting after a man who was older than America, Europe, and pretty much anything else she could think of, she focused on a more manageable fact, and returned to the original subject. "All right, so finding a life mate reinvigorates your interest in food and sex. What else?"

Crispin had opened his mouth to answer, when another question struck her and she stalled him by saying, "Oh, wait! Are the nanos why kissing and making out with you is so hot?"

He nodded. "Life mates experience each other's pleasure along with their own. It grows in mounting waves, overwhelming them at the end so that they both lose consciousness. We believe that is because of the nanos."

"Damn," Abril breathed. She'd avoided thinking about the fact that she'd fainted after each passionate encounter with Crispin. The first time in the pool because she'd woken up lying on the man and had immediately been more concerned with other things. Like that she was lying on the man. Her head had been nestled on his chest, her groin cuddled against his, and her body had been instantly aware and eager to go another round with him.

She hadn't thought about it after the time in her bedroom because she'd woken up to the intruder and been knocked out. It had basically slipped her mind by the time she woke up with a pounding headache and Dr. Dani leaning over her.

"Back to your question," Crispin said, regaining her attention. "Shared dreams are another symptom, which we also had."

"Yes," she acknowledged solemnly. "So, you think I'm a life mate to you."

He nodded.

"Which means what?" she asked.

"Which means you are the one person that I could spend my life with happily."

"One out of how many?" she asked. "How many other life mates are out there for you? I mean, they say there's more than one fish in the sea. Is there more than one life mate for an immortal too?"

Crispin hesitated, and then said, "You may be the only one ever. Some immortals have been fortunate enough to find a second life mate after losing the first. But that is not guaranteed. You may be the only possible life mate I ever meet."

"Why do you say a *possible* life mate? Am I or am I not your life mate?"

"I only say possible because you can refuse to be my life mate," he explained gently. "As far as I am concerned, you *are* my life mate. There is no question. However, I cannot force you to agree to become my life mate, so, you are a possible life mate. I very much hope that you would be willing to be my life mate."

"I see," she murmured.

While she was still considering what he'd said, Crispin quickly assured her, "I realize this is all new to you, Abril. And this is a lot to take in, I know. I will not rush you. I am not asking you for a decision on if you agree to be my life mate or not. I am just asking you to keep an open mind and allow me to court you."

Abril peered at him with surprise. *Court you* was such an old-fashioned term.

"But we can set this aside for now, and simply deal with the issues at hand."

"Issues?" Abril asked with uncertainty. Which ones, she wondered. There seemed to be so many of them to her. There were skeletons in the garden outside, one in the indoor garden, and seven vampires—or immortals as they preferred to be called—wandering around inside her boss's house, one of whom she had the serious hots for.

"The issue of the rogue attacking you," he explained gently.

"Oh. Right," she said and could feel herself blushing. It was a little embarrassing to admit, even only to herself, but she'd quite forgotten about that nonsense what with everything else she'd learned.

Crispen eyed her with worry. "Are you okay? I know this was a lot of information to take in in a very short time. It is perfectly understandable if you—"

"I'm not freaking out, if that's what you're asking. At least I don't think I am," she added with a weak smile. "I mean, this *is* a lot, but I think I'm okay. I'm handling it."

Crispin nodded, looked away, and then back to say, "As I said, I will not push you on the matter of us. I know this is early days and far too soon to expect—"

"Crispin," she interrupted quietly.

When he paused and peered at her in question, she said, "This *is* a lot. And I would appreciate some time to think about everything. But honestly, I'm not looking at you like a monster or something if that's what you're worried about. I'm not suddenly seeing you as some blood-hungry fiend. You've explained it all pretty clearly. It sounds like a medical issue. You have nanos which help you stay strong and healthy. But they also cause a need for blood. Not unlike how it is for hemophiliacs . . . only with the nanos." She rolled her eyes at herself and then added, "Anyway, the point is, we can just hang out and see—" She paused and frowned there. "I was going to say we could just hang around and see if we like each other, but I actually do like you already. Although," she countered, "I don't really know much about you, so maybe it's actually just lusting after you. But I mean if the nanos choose life mates—Are you sure the nanos are right when they choose life mates? They never make mistakes?" she asked, knowing that she sounded terribly disorganized in her thinking right then, but her brain was kind of still bouncing around with the information it was trying to organize and file away.

Expression serious, Crispin clasped her arms, making sure to touch her only where her skin was covered by the cloth of her sleeves, and said, "I know many life mate couples, and all of them are happy and in wonderful relationships. Even one couple who have been together since Atlantis."

"What?" she asked with surprise.

Crispin nodded firmly. "Nicodemus and Marzzia Notte. They were life mates in Atlantis before the fall, and they are still passionately in love and happy together all these years later. There are others like them who have been together centuries or millennia, and are happy and content together still. In fact, I have never heard of a life mate couple who were not happy and passionately in love."

They were both silent for a moment, and then Crispen peered at her seriously and said, "Lucian said you were considering running away. Putting Lilith in the car and just leaving."

Abril paused briefly, surprised at the fact that Lucian had read that from her mind. But supposed she shouldn't be, not after everything she'd learned. Finally, she admitted, "I did consider doing that at one point."

"And now?" he asked.

"And now I don't feel like doing that," she said simply and then admitted, "I was confused then, and distressed at everything that was happening around me. I felt like there was something going on that I didn't understand. Which was true. But now that you've explained the situation to me, that feeling has receded."

There was no mistaking the relief on Crispin's face at her words. Now he offered her a smile. "I am glad to hear it. And I hope that in the future rather than simply leaving or running away, you would feel comfortable enough to come to me and talk to me about whatever is distressing you."

"I think I could do that," she said slowly. "You appear to have been honest with me, so I suppose I can be honest with you too."

"Good." He smiled at her widely and then stood and said, "Unless you have any more questions, I suppose we should join the others and find out what Anders and Roberts learned."

Abril's gaze widened slightly. "Are Anders and Roberts back?"

"Yes. They returned shortly after we came into your office."

"How do you know?" she asked in surprise. "Can you guys send mental communication to each other, or something?"

Crispin smiled faintly. "Since they can all read my mind right now—"

"Wait, so you're saying everyone in the kitchen is older than you?" she squawked with disbelief. While they all looked around the same age, it was hard to believe there were beings around who were born in 900 BC, let alone earlier.

"No. Well, Lucian is, but the others are younger."

"Then how can they all read you? You said immortals could only read the minds of other immortals younger than themselves."

"Ah, yes, I suppose I should explain that," he said with a slight grimace. He then took a moment before saying, "While it is true we cannot usually read immortals older than ourselves, finding a life mate tends to temporarily change that. Even the oldest immortal is easily read by all other immortals, no matter their age, once they encounter their life mate. At least temporarily," he added. "That usually goes away after a year or so. As does the fainting."

"Why?" Abril asked at once.

Crispin shrugged helplessly. "No one knows for sure. It is presumed though that the fainting at the culmination of sex is because it is all so overwhelming at first and that once the couple adjusts to the extremes in passion they are better able to handle it and remain conscious. As for being suddenly readable by everyone . . ." He hesitated and then said, "I suspect that has to do with our minds struggling to accept everything happening. Busy processing all the new feelings both emotional and physical suddenly assaulting us, I believe our minds might just be dropping the ball on blocking others from reading us. But that too ends after a year or so."

Abril nodded slowly, and then returned to her earlier question. "Okay, so how do you know Anders and Roberts are back? Can you or can you not communicate mentally?"

Crispin paused briefly before saying, "I suppose I could send them messages in my thoughts since they can read me right now. But I don't think they can send them to me. The truth is, I just heard them return and can hear their voices in the kitchen even now as they speak."

Eyebrows rising slightly, she said, "I suppose that has something to do with your nanos. You did say they made you faster and stronger. Did they give you better hearing too?"

Crispin nodded. "And better sight as well."

They were both silent for a moment, and then he asked, "Any more questions? I am happy to answer anything else you want to know."

Abril shook her head and stood up. "Let's go find out what Roberts and Anders have learned. I will be very interested to find out whether it was the Bransons or the Foleys who are responsible for the bodies in the garden and why."

"Me too," Crispin admitted as he opened her office door for her.

Twenty-Five

The men were all in the kitchen when Crispin and Abril entered. Every one of them was bustling around. Three large bowls of salad that someone had made were already on the island. Steaming ceramic dishes of lasagna were even now being set on the island too, but with hot pads to protect the granite. Butter, bread, and Parmesan cheese quickly followed before Crispin could even usher Abril to her seat.

"What would you like to drink?" he asked as he got her settled.

"Oh," Abril said with surprise and started to stand. "Water, but I can get it. I—"

"Sit," he insisted, pressing lightly on her shoulder. "Allow me to fetch for you for a change."

Abril sat back down, but was obviously uncomfortable doing so. It was plain to see that she was used to doing things for others, and not having others do for her. That was something he would have to change, he decided as he got them both a glass of ice water. He had never met anyone who was so determined to do everything for those around her. She deserved to have things done for her for a change.

Crispin suspected it would be a struggle convincing her of that though, as he carried the glasses back to the island and settled beside her even as the others claimed their own chairs.

"Start your report, boys," Lucian said, not even bothering to glance at Anders and Roberts as he gave the order.

Crispin glanced around with surprise at the words. Mostly he was surprised that Lucian had waited for him and Abril to be present to hear the report from the men. But then he realized his uncle had probably already read the news from Roberts or Anders's minds himself. So, his uncle ordering them to give the report was really only for Abril's benefit. And possibly for Bricker's and Decker's too, he thought, since they were the only two immortals here that were younger than Roberts and Anders and couldn't read them.

"We had no problem finding the Bransons," Roberts announced, and then smiled at Abril and told her, "They moved to Port Glasgow by the way, and seem very happy there. They are not responsible for the bodies in the garden."

"You are sure?" Lucian asked solemnly as Abril smiled with relief.

Roberts nodded. "Positive. They had no knowledge in their minds of the skeletons in or outside of the house. I think it must have been the couple before them, the Foleys," he said firmly, and then frowned and added, "I suspect the Foleys must have stayed in the area for a while after the Bransons bought their house. Or at least they stayed in contact with them, because we learned that Mr. Branson had wanted to put a patio around the side and back of the house when they moved in. In fact, that had been his intention when they bought the house. They had even already hired a contractor to do the job before actually moving in. It was all arranged to start a couple weeks after they got possession.

"However," he said now, his expression solemn, "shortly after moving into the house, Mr. Branson suddenly canceled everything. He said digging up the garden to remove the plants and put in footers seemed a lot of work and expense for a deck, so he decided to leave most of the garden, and simply lay stones to make a smaller patio, just big enough for a barbecue, a table, and a couple of chairs." Roberts paused a moment, and then added, "However, there is no memory in his mind of why he suddenly decided against the deck. The decision was just suddenly there in his memory. It was not something he pondered or considered."

"You suspect the Foleys decided on that for him and put it in his mind," Lucian said solemnly.

Roberts nodded.

Lucian accepted that and then asked, "And the Foleys?"

Roberts grimaced apologetically, and admitted, "We were unable to find them. We spoke to their Realtor, but while they did use him to sell their house, they did not use him to buy the next one, and we could find no reference to them anywhere. At least not the right Foleys. There were Foleys in the directories, but not the couple we were looking for. That is why we were gone so long," he added. "We had to go and interview every Foley listed in the directories."

"They have changed their name then," Lucian said thoughtfully.

"That or they are squatting somewhere, or living with mortals they are controlling or something," Roberts said. "Whatever the case, the Foleys must be responsible for the bodies in the garden, because the Bransons are not."

Lucian and the other men grunted with agreement. While Cassius and Roberts weren't eating, the rest of the men were busy shoveling food into their mouths while Crispin and Abril were still both just serving themselves their own lasagna.

"So, how do we find them?" Crispin asked as he set the serving spoon back in the lasagna dish.

Lucian was silent for a minute, apparently considering the matter, and then he announced, "Obviously, we cannot find them. Therefore, we must hope that they try to break in again to dig up the indoor garden."

Crispin was frowning over that when Lucian speared Abril with a look and said, "You are not to leave the house until they are caught. And stay away from the windows. I do not want them reading your mind and learning that we have already found what they are looking for. They could then just give up their attempt to get in, and disappear. Unfortunately, their trying to break in again and getting caught is the only way to capture them at this point. If they've changed their name and so on, it would be almost impossible to find them. All they have to do is pick up stakes and move again."

Abril nodded in agreement, but said, "I wonder why

they killed the immortal in the indoor garden? I mean, from what you said, Crispin, it sounded like rogues usually go after us mere mortals."

Crispin didn't answer right away, but considered her question as he chewed the lasagna in his mouth.

Just as he was doing so though, Bricker said, "Maybe they didn't. Maybe it was the mortal victim buried with them in the indoor garden that killed the immortal."

Crispin nearly choked on the lasagna he was swallowing at Bricker's words. When he coughed and sputtered, Abril quickly began to pound him on the back, but her gaze was on Lucian as she asked, "There was a mortal body under the immortal in the indoor garden?"

"More like beside it," Decker said.

Crispin had picked up his water and gulped some down to finish clearing his airways. Now he set the glass back, and snapped, "And you did not think to tell us this?" His gaze shot to Lucian. "Uncle?"

Lucian gave him a supercilious look, and announced dryly, "Crispin there was a mortal buried in the indoor garden with the immortal."

"Thank you," he said with disgust and shook his head.

"Oh, right," Bricker said with realization. "You were in having your talk with Abril by the time we came across the second skeleton."

"The immortal was female by the way," Lucian announced. "And the mortal male."

"Are you sure?" Abril asked with interest.

"There were high heels strapped to the immortal's— what used to be her feet, and she was wearing the remains of what at one time had been a short black dress," Lucian informed her. "The mortal skeleton was wearing jeans, a T-shirt, and men's boots."

"Oh." Abril nodded and agreed, "Probably a woman immortal and male mortal then."

"Probably?" Lucian echoed with disbelief.

"What?" she asked with a grin. "You've never heard of cross-dressing?"

Lucian opened his mouth. Closed it. Then muttered something under his breath that even Crispin with his immortal hearing didn't catch before turning back to his food. He picked up a forkful of lasagna, paused, and then scowled at Abril and said reluctantly, "As for your first question on why the rogue would kill an immortal, I suspect the rogue was mortal either directly before or during the killing of the immortal."

That caught everyone's attention. Every man, including Crispin himself, was now staring at his uncle with surprise. Abril was the only one unsurprised. Nodding as she scooped some lasagna up on her own fork, she simply said, "Makes sense."

"It does?" Bricker asked with interest.

"Well, sure," Abril said, seeming surprised that everyone couldn't see that. "The story was that their son died, and Mrs. Foley was paralyzed in a car accident," she pointed out. "But a car accident wouldn't kill or paralyze you guys. So, they couldn't have been immortal at the time of the accident."

A smile was creeping over Crispin's face at the fact that he had himself a brilliant life mate, when she impressed him some more as she continued to speak.

"And, I don't know how much blood you guys go through on the daily, but I'm guessing it's not a crazy amount. I mean, I haven't even seen any of you taking it in since arriving."

"We have been *taking it in*, as you put it," Lucian assured her. "We just have done it in our vehicles which are outfitted with special coolers to keep the blood from going bad. We thought it best not to bring the blood inside and risk you seeing it and becoming alarmed."

"Ah, that was sweet," she said with appreciation, although Crispin suspected it was as much because she wanted to fluster his uncle as that she truly thought it was sweet. And it appeared to work. Lucian looked a bit taken aback for a moment, but then regained his usual scowl.

Cassius was the one who explained, "How much blood an immortal needs to consume daily varies depending on their age, their size, and whether they have done anything that might make the nanos work harder. But the average immortal probably consumes no more than one bag a day. Hunters usually live more strenuous lives that include more exposure to sunlight and injury and such, necessitating their taking in anywhere from one to four bags a day. Older, and exceptional immortals can get away with a bag every other day if they are not going out in sunlight or doing anything else to set the nanos to work. However, newly turned immortals need much more blood for the first little while after they are turned."

"Right," Abril nodded. "Well, a human body holds eight to ten pints of blood, and those bags you say you consume are usually around a pint if they're from a blood bank. So, with the twelve mortal bodies outside, and the one inside that would add up to somewhere between one hundred and four to one hundred and thirty pints. That's a lot of blood to consume in just a week or so, even for two people."

Every man there stared at her with surprise until Crispin asked, "A week or so?"

"Hmm." She grabbed a piece of bread and started to butter it. "They held a street party out here last year at the end of August. I think it was mostly a welcome to the neighborhood barbecue for Gina really. Anyway, Gina didn't want to go alone and asked me to come with. So, I did. I accompanied her, met this neighbor and that, ate, and so on. But, at one point, I was chatting with a lovely older lady, probably that Mrs. Jamison you mentioned, although she told me her name was Lois and didn't mention her last name."

"Mrs. Jamison's name is Lois," Crispin told her.

Abril nodded. "Well, she told me the history of Gina's house. Sort of. What she told me about was the people. The Bransons were nice. Mrs. Branson loved to garden. Their children were so polite. That kind of thing."

She waited just long enough for the men to nod, and then continued, "What she told me about the family that lived here before the Bransons was that it was a tragic tale. They'd lost their child and the wife had been paralyzed. She too loved her garden and used to work on it daily in the summer and Lois used to stop and chat with her on occasion on her morning constitutional. But after the accident the wife obviously couldn't work in the garden anymore. Still, she could be found outside every morning, sitting in her wheelchair either supervising the people her husband had hired to tend to the garden in her stead, or just enjoying it. And they were usually both sitting outside, enjoying a coffee together when Lois and her husband went for their after-dinner walk around the crescent.

"However, just about a year after the accident, the wife stopped appearing in the garden in the mornings. There were still lights and movement in the house at night when Lois and her husband took their after-dinner walk, but the couple no longer sat out having coffee in the garden. Lois suspected the husband had left his poor wife. Especially since the husband's truck was no longer seen leaving or returning, but other vehicles and people began to show up. Sometimes it was couples, sometimes a man or a woman, and once even a couple with children. Lois decided they must have been family helping the wife pack up, because a week after those 'comings and goings' started, a moving truck was in the driveway and a for sale sign was in the front yard."

"So," Crispin said slowly as everything he'd learned began to coalesce in his head. "An immortal somehow showed up in their life a week before the house sale, and . . ." He paused briefly, considering everything again, and then guessed, "Something happened that ended with the immortal and the husband being killed and the wife getting turned."

"What?" Bricker asked with surprise. "You think the husband is the mortal inside?"

"They were the only ones buried there," he pointed out. "They must have been buried at the same time if they were close enough to each other in the indoor garden for you to find the mortal while digging up the immortal."

"Yeah, they were pretty close. One of his legs was over hers," Bricker admitted, and then said, "And the immortal's head was actually down by her feet."

Crispin winced, his mind immediately going to the conversation he'd had with Abril. He wondered now how long the poor immortal's head had survived knowing she had been decapitated and was dying. Had she watched her grave being dug? Had she hoped the woman would place her head near the neck when she tossed her in, so her body could heal itself? Only to lose that hope when she found herself thrown down by her feet? Was she aware when the dirt started to cover her?

"That doesn't guarantee they were not buried a day apart or something though," Bricker argued. "I mean the immortal could have died first, and then a mortal was lured to the house for feeding and the garden dug up again to put him in it."

Crispin shook his head with certainty. "Human corpses start to stink pretty quickly. I think it only takes something like a day or two if they are not refrigerated, so I doubt the immortal was buried and then the garden was dug up again to bury someone else. The smell would have been unbearable, especially for a newly turned immortal unused to the increase in their olfactory senses." He paused briefly, but then added judicially, "Although, the mortal in there could have arrived with the immortal and may not be the husband."

"Or," Bricker said now, "maybe two immortals came to the house for some reason. Something happened to kill the female immortal that was in the indoor garden, and possibly the husband, and the other immortal took control of Mrs. Foley for some reason, or turned her because she was a possible life mate."

Lucian shook his head. "I suspect Crispin is right and it was a lone female immortal here, and that she and the husband died while the wife was turned."

"I think so too," Abril agreed. "But my decision is based mostly on a hunch. I suspect you don't do hunches, Lucian, so what makes *you* think that?"

When Lucian merely scowled at Abril, Crispin answered for him. "Because one hundred and four to one hundred and thirty pints of blood in a week for one immortal, even a newly turned immortal, is excessive. It can cause terrible pain and sickness. If an immortal had been present after the mortal was turned, they would have known that and prevented the new immortal from consuming so much. That immortal would also know better than to feed off mortals and risk being labeled rogue and suffering the punishment. While a newly turned immortal with no one to train them would have no idea of our laws and the punishment for them."

When Lucian grunted an agreement, Abril glanced to Crispin and asked, "So if it is Mrs. Foley and she had no idea of your laws—"

"As with the mortal legal system here in Canada," Lucian said, interrupting her, "ignorance of the law is not an excuse for committing an offense."

"It could still be just an immortal who lost his mind, went rogue and is now on an endless blood orgy," Bricker argued.

Abril looked at him with interest. "So, you've had a lot of mortals going missing or other signs of rogue activity in the area over the last twenty years and are only now doing something about it?"

"No," Crispin said quickly, scowling at Bricker for saying anything that might make Abril think they'd allow something like that to happen without doing anything about it. Turning to Abril he assured her, "It has been pretty quiet here. In fact, this is the only sign of rogue activity we have had since I joined the London police force seven years ago."

"There was that business with Armand and Eshe some time back," Bricker pointed out. "I think it was before you and Roberts started in London though."

"That was not in London," Lucian snapped. "It was in a small town farther out, and that rogue was dealt with."

"Abril brings up a good point though," Crispin said. "Whoever killed the people here could not have been active in the area since or we would have a very high number of missing people on the books. Either they have moved elsewhere, which makes it doubtful that they would have heard that the house had sold and renovations were being made that would include digging up the bodies. Or they learned how to feed without killing their meals."

There were grunts of agreement around the island, and then slowly everyone began to eat again.

Twenty-Six

"How long am I going to be restricted to the house and away from the windows?"

Crispin glanced over at that question from Abril. She'd spoken in a near whisper, probably in the hopes that Lucian wouldn't hear. He wasn't surprised it failed and his uncle answered.

"Until our rogue is found. Or until we are certain the rogue has left the area and will not return here."

Abril did not look pleased at this news. Crispin couldn't blame her. He didn't much care for that answer himself. It would be hard to woo her while she was confined to the house, and not even the entire house, but rooms that did not have windows.

The thought made him frown and wonder how many rooms there were in the house like that. The only one he could think of was the laundry room. That thought made him glance toward the kitchen windows facing the front yard and driveway. His eyes widened when he saw that the blinds were closed.

"While you were in the office with Abril, I had the men close all the blinds there are in the house," Lucian announced. "That includes her bedroom. Although I suspect she will not wish to sleep in there after her earlier experience."

"Crispin closed the blinds in my office earlier, and the couch in there is a pullout bed," Abril announced. "I can just sleep in there tonight. One of the men can have my room."

His uncle grunted what might have been an acknowledgement, and then said, "Crispin will remain with you to ensure your safety."

Crispin glanced quickly to Abril to see irritation flash across her face. Lucian had not suggested, he had announced it as if she had no choice in the matter. He wasn't at all surprised that she was annoyed by that. It seemed obvious to him that the only person she generally took orders from was her boss. Otherwise, Abril was used to making her own decisions and depending on her own counsel on issues. It had no doubt been that way since she was sixteen and had run away. Although, he was sure that the Barb and her husband Abril had mentioned to him might have been wise counsel on occasion, the ultimate decisions had always only ever been Abril's in the end since leaving her family.

Much to his surprise, despite her obvious irritation, Abril didn't protest Lucian's order, but simply finished rinsing off her plate, and carried it over to put it in the dishwasher.

"Crispin, go fetch your woman's things from the guest room she was using, and take them to her office," Lucian ordered.

"I can fetch my own things," Abril protested.

"You would need to go through the living room to get to your room," Crispin pointed out solemnly. "There are no blinds on any of the windows in there."

Abril clucked with irritation. "The Foleys must've been idiots. I swear most of the windows in this house don't have any kind of covering. What were they? Exhibitionists?"

Crispin smiled faintly and said, "To be fair, the house is so far back from the road and surrounded by trees that it is doubtful window coverings are needed as a rule."

"Yeah, well they sure would come in handy now," she muttered with irritation, and then sighed and met his gaze. "Thank you in advance for getting my things. My suitcase is in the closet. Just throw everything in and bring it around. No need to pack it nice." Turning away then, she started walking toward the end of the island, saying, "I'll be in the office."

Crispin was watching Abril's derriere as she walked around the island to the hallway. She had just headed up it and disappeared from his sight, when Lucian said, "You should also go to the room you chose for yourself and were napping in when the intruder struck. Roberts stopped at your place and picked up your go bag for you. He put it in there."

Crispin's eyebrows rose slightly at this news, but he knew he shouldn't be surprised. He and Roberts both kept go bags in case of something exactly like this happening. They also had keys to each other's homes for the same reason.

"Thanks, Alex," he murmured, nodding at Roberts.

"Happy to help," Roberts assured him. "Speaking of which, want any help packing Abril's things?"

Crispin almost said yes, and then realized that Abril's things would include intimates like panties and bras and shook his head. "No, thank you. I can manage."

Abril dropped into her desk chair and turned on her computer, her mind on the fact that Crispin had been tasked with the chore of packing up her clothes. In truth, she didn't really mind when it came to her jeans, dress slacks, T-shirts, tops, and dresses, etcetera. However, she was a little less blasé about his sorting through her underwear. Oddly enough, she didn't mind the idea of his seeing her pretty brassieres and panties. It was the granny panties and sports bras she was less thrilled about.

Sighing, she quickly typed in the password to unlock the screen, opened her web browser, and clicked on the Netflix icon. Abril stopped there though. She couldn't watch a movie at her desk if Crispin was going to be in the room too. The couch was in front of her desk. He wouldn't be able to see it and it would be rude. Aside from that, honestly her desk chair really wasn't comfortable enough to be sitting in for an hour and a half to two hours.

Standing, she turned the desktop computer so that it faced the sofa, and then walked around and quickly removed the cushions from the couch. Those went onto the top shelf of the closet after she removed the blanket and pillows she kept stored there and set them on the corner of her desk.

Closing the door then, she quickly pulled out the sofa bed. It already had sheets on it from the last time she'd used it. All she had to do was spread the blanket over it, put the pillows on, and voila! She had a bed. Well, she and Crispin had a bed. Because with the bed pulled out, the only space left in the room was a four-foot square area between her desk and the closet door. There really wasn't room for Crispin to even spread out on the floor, let alone to bring in a single mattress from one of the guest rooms and lay it out. The man was going to be sleeping with her.

"Oh, yeah, you can stop thinking about that right now," she told herself firmly. The very thought had raised her temperature and made her mouth go dry, which made her think she should fetch a drink and maybe snacks for the movie she intended to put on.

Nodding to herself, she headed out of her office.

Lucian was alone in the kitchen, seated where he'd been when she'd left. His gaze was scanning the various images showing on the monitor and then sliding to the windows where the blinds were now open to check the front and side yard.

Abril ignored him as she went into the pantry to consider the snacks she'd purchased and stored there. White cheddar popcorn, barbecue corn chips, extra flavor sour cream and onion chips. Which would Crispin like?

She considered that briefly, and then shrugged and grabbed all three. She had no idea what he liked, so it was better to be safe than sorry. Abril carried them out of the pantry, pushed the door closed with one foot, hurried to her office and dumped everything on her desk before heading back out to the kitchen.

"You are not supposed to be in rooms with uncovered windows," Lucian said, glowering at her as she walked over to the refrigerator and opened it.

"Then you shouldn't have opened the blinds," Abril said with irritation. "I need a drink."

"And apparently more food despite the fact that we just finished eating," he said testily. She guessed he only said it to point out that this was not her first foray into the kitchen and he hadn't said anything the first time. To be fair, she suspected that had been him showing great restraint. She assumed it was also why he'd been peering out the windows so hard, to be sure there was no one outside staring in to see her.

Grabbing several different cans of pop, she let the refrigerator door close and had started toward where Lucian sat at the island near the hall entrance when he suddenly growled, "Stop."

Abril stopped, but asked, "Why am I stopping?"

"Someone is walking past the house."

She hesitated, then set the pops on the island. She then moved to the window over the sink and tugged aside the blinds that were still closed there, but just enough to see out. Abril immediately relaxed when she saw the lone woman walking the golden retriever.

"That's Kim," she told Lucian, releasing the blinds. "She is a Realtor. Her house is that blue one across the street and a little to the left."

"And can you tell if she is a mortal, or immortal, and a threat or not?" Lucian asked dryly.

"No," she admitted. "But I bet you can. Is she immortal,

Lucian? Or can I grab a couple glasses and some ice for the pops so I can go back to the office now?"

"Crispin can get the ice," Lucian said sounding irritable again. "Speaking of which, Crispin, stop talking to your brother, collect Abril's luggage, and get it to her office."

He hadn't raised his voice above a normal speaking tone and Abril was staring at him, thinking that Crispin would never hear him from the bedroom, when he entered the kitchen at a rather shocking speed.

Abril gaped at him as he shot past her and disappeared down the hall, reeling under the realization that he had actually heard Lucian. The knowledge made her now worry about what exactly Roberts had heard while she and Crispin had had their passionate encounter in the laundry room. She had already known that he had heard or at least witnessed part of what had taken place in the living room after they came in from the pool, but she had put that down to the cameras. There were no cameras in the laundry room. But if his hearing was as good as Lucian's, Roberts had probably heard every moan, sigh, and gasp as she and Crispin had made out in the laundry room. If so, he'd known exactly what they were doing.

That was rather embarrassing, she decided.

"Abril is not in the office!"

Crispin's panicked voice reached the kitchen a heartbeat before he did. That panic was also on his face, until Lucian pointed her way and he spotted her still in the corner between the window and the refrigerator.

"What are you doing out here?" he asked with surprise, hurrying over to catch her arm and usher her toward the hall, making sure to position himself between her and the windows. "You should not be out here now that the blinds are open."

"I know," she said with a little exasperation. "But I was thirsty. I also got us some snacks. I thought we could eat them while we watch a movie," she told him and when he glanced at her empty hands, she said, "I already took the snacks into the office, but the drinks are on the island and I didn't get glasses or ice cubes."

"Oh. Okay. Well, I put your suitcase and overnight bag in the bathroom across the hall from your office so that you can change and do whatever women do before bed in there when you are ready. But in the meantime, a movie sounds good."

"Actually, I think I'll take a quick shower and put on some pj's now to be comfy while we watch the movie," she announced, breaking off from him to enter the bathroom as they reached it. "That way if I fall asleep during the movie I won't have to wake up enough to do it then."

"Sounds like a plan," Crispin said with amusement. "I will go back and get the drinks while you do that then."

"Okay," she said lightly, and smiled at him before easing the bathroom door closed. She waited until she heard his footsteps moving away up the hall, and then turned to peer at the items he'd set beside the sink counter.

As he'd said, Crispin had brought both her suitcase and her overnight bag, and both were full. He hadn't just packed her clothes, which were very neatly folded by the way, he'd also gathered all her items from the bathroom, from her toothbrush and Waterpik, to her face soap and lotions. She didn't think he'd missed a thing. Not only was the man fast, but he appeared to be as detail oriented as she was, Abril thought to herself as she turned on the shower.

Abril wasn't someone to relax and take her time over her bedtime ritual. She was usually exhausted by the time she started it, and rushed through everything to get it done and get to bed. It was no different tonight. Not because she was exhausted, but because she knew Crispin was probably waiting for her. All told, she probably only took fifteen minutes in the bathroom, and that included her shower. She then closed up her suitcases and set them in the hall just so the bathroom wouldn't be so cramped when he wanted to use it.

Pulling the bathroom door closed, Abril then hesitated outside the closed door to her office, suddenly shy about entering.

"Stop dillydallying and get in your office," Lucian suddenly barked from the kitchen.

"Oh my God!" Abril snapped as she reached for the door handle. "Is it possible to have any privacy at all around you people?"

"No," Lucian said promptly.

Glaring at the back of his head where he sat at the island, she opened her office door and entered.

"Lucian can be difficult," Crispin told her with sympathy, letting the blinds slide back into place from where he'd tugged them aside to look out at the side yard where the excavations were taking place.

Abril pushed the door closed and shrugged. "He's not as scary as he thinks he is."

Crispin's eyebrows rose slightly and amusement pulled at his lips. "He will be crushed to hear that, I am sure. I am also sure most people would not agree with you."

"Most people didn't grow up with my father, Agustin, and Agustin's father," she said dryly as she crossed to the bed and then stood there uncertainly.

"I like your pajamas. They are quite nice," he said after watching her get settled. He was still hovering by the blinds that covered the sliding doors, looking like he didn't know what to do with himself she noted, but smiled faintly at the compliment.

She was wearing pajamas she'd got from Costco that consisted of long pajama bottoms in a pretty pale green and pink floral design, a sleeveless top with a green and white lattice pattern on it, and a housecoat that matched the pajama bottoms. She thought it was attractive, but it was also comfortable. It was something she wouldn't be self-conscious about wearing around the house, despite the men presently filling it. That was part of the reason she'd chosen it. But she'd also chosen it over the sexier, slinkier nightgowns she'd brought with her because Lucian had ordered Crispin to remain with her tonight. She hadn't wanted him to think she was intending to jump him or something.

Not that she was opposed to them making out again. In fact, the very idea sent tingles through her body. But she didn't want to seem too forward or fast. Besides, now that she knew Lucian would no doubt hear every sound that came from her office, she was thinking that making out might not be a good idea.

Apparently taking the fact that she hadn't yet got into bed as a sign that she was uncomfortable, he offered, "I can spend the night in your office chair if it would make you more comfortable."

"No," Abril said at once. "My desk chair isn't very

comfortable at all. I think Gina bought it with the thought that the discomfort would keep me from falling asleep on the job."

When Crispin chuckled at the claim, she asked, "You aren't expected to stay up all night watching the side yard, are you?"

"No. Cassius is in Gina's office doing that," Crispin told her.

Abril's eyes widened and shot to the wall behind her desk. It was the wall between her temporary office and Gina's. There was definitely going to be no making out tonight.

"Well, then," she said, her voice a little squeaky. "There's no reason for you to sit up all night in my torturous desk chair. Besides, I wouldn't be able to sleep with you sitting up, staring at me anyway, I'd feel too guilty. We can share the bed."

Crispin nodded, and then glanced from the office door to the blinds covering the large window on the outer wall, before saying, "I am not sure which side of the bed you prefer, but I think it would be better if I sleep on the side closest to the window just in case the intruder does try to break in through this room."

Abril nodded, and then removed the robe covering her pajama set, and quickly tugged the sheet and blanket aside and climbed into bed on the side closest to the office door. She settled on that side with her pillow stacked behind her back so that she could watch Netflix on her computer and then realized she couldn't turn the movie on from where she was. Tossing the sheet and blanket aside, she shifted to her knees and crawled to the end of the bed to grab her mouse off her desktop. She then crawled quickly back to her original position and pulled the sheet and blanket back over her before glancing to Crispin.

He had sat down on the end of the bed and was removing his shoes and socks. He then stood, turned toward the bed, and hesitated.

"You aren't going to sleep in your clothes, are you?" she asked. "Didn't Lucian say something about Roberts bringing your go bag? Doesn't it have pajamas in it?"

"No pajamas," he said apologetically as he shrugged out of his suit jacket.

Abril considered him, but when he then started to climb onto the end of the bed, she said, "You are not going to be comfortable enough to sleep in your shirt and pants. You'll also wrinkle them terribly." She hesitated, and then finally said, "You could just sleep in your boxers. I trust you."

Crispin raised one eyebrow. "And how would you know that I wear—" He paused for the briefest moment and then smiled wryly. "Right, you changed my laundry from the washer to the dryer after the pool incident."

Abril nodded with a grin. "I thought they were adorable."

She wasn't surprised when Crispin blushed. His boxers had cartoon ducks on them and the words *butt quack* on the back down the middle.

"My sister will appreciate that. They were a gift from her last Christmas. She has an interesting sense of humor and would feel injured if I did not wear them."

Abril chuckled at the claim, but felt a tinge of melancholy that she didn't have a relationship like that with her own sister. Or any of her siblings for that matter. She was kind of jealous actually.

Turning toward her desktop monitor, she fiddled with the mouse briefly to give him privacy as he stripped off his shirt and pants, and commented, "It sounds like you have a good relationship with your siblings. You humor your sister, and seem to get along with Cassius too."

"I am close with all my siblings," Crispin admitted, sounding distracted, and she could hear the rustle of clothing as he undressed. She didn't dare glance at him until the bed depressed as he climbed into it. She sensed rather than saw when he then pulled the sheet and blanket over to cover himself.

When she finally looked over, he was adjusting his own pillow behind his back. Her gaze swam over his beautiful naked chest, and then she quickly forced her gaze back to the monitor to avoid the possibility of drooling like a dog over a biscuit. The thought brought Lilith to her mind though, and concern immediately licked at her. Turning to him, she asked, "How much longer until this Valorie person gets here?"

"I am not sure," Crispin admitted solemnly. "But I am sure she will be here as quickly as she can. I am also sure that Lilith will be all right. I stopped to check on her while I was gathering our items and her breathing seems fine. She appears to simply be sleeping."

Abril gave him a grateful smile, her eyes traveling downward of their own volition to caress his chest. Damn, it was fine! It was just as beautiful dry as it had been in the pool. Mouthwateringly so. Giving her head a shake, she forced herself to look at the monitor again and asked, "What kind of movies do you like?"

Crispin finally finished arranging his pillow to his

liking, and then glanced toward the monitor. "I am not sure. I have not spent a lot of time watching movies and such. Only occasionally when my younger sister stayed with me."

"What kind of movies do you watch with your sister?" she asked with curiosity.

"Cartoons when she was a child. Horror when she was a teenager. But lately she appears to be into what she calls tragic romances."

"Tragic romances, huh?" Abril asked, trying not to wince.

Crispin nodded. "Although, I will never understand why she likes to watch things that make her cry."

Abril smiled faintly. "Yeah, I've never understood why people would want to watch those myself. Life is sad enough without adding something else to cry about."

He grunted an agreement and then offered, "I did enjoy *Pixels* when we watched it though."

Abril kept that in mind as she glanced through the movies available on Netflix until her gaze landed on *Mr. Right*. Clicking on it, she said, "You might like this. I do. I guess we'll see if you do."

Twenty-Seven

Abril found herself spending more time watching Crispin's face as he watched the movie, *Mr. Right*, than she did actually watching it herself. Much to her relief he seemed to enjoy it. She was glad. It was a favorite of hers, one she'd seen three times already, and Abril normally didn't watch any movie more than once.

Halfway through the movie, she paused it to ask if he was hungry or thirsty.

Crispin only hesitated a moment, before saying, "In fact I am." Climbing off the bed he added, "Wait here and I will fetch us some snacks and drinks."

He was out the door before her gaze landed on the collection of items on the corner of her desk. The popcorn and chips that she had collected earlier, and a selection of sodas that he had obviously brought in while she was changing. She considered calling out to him and reminding him of the items in the office, but the sodas had been sitting on her desk for a while now, and would no doubt be warm, so she didn't say anything, and simply waited for him to return.

Crispin hadn't closed the door all the way. Abril realized that when she heard Lucian say with disgust, "Butt quack?"

She had to bite her lip to keep a laugh from escaping her when she heard that. She was glad she had, otherwise she wouldn't have heard Crispin's response when he asked mildly, "Are you looking at my ass, Uncle?"

Abril was still smiling at that when Crispin returned to the room five or six minutes later with two Dagwood type sandwiches and glasses full of ice cubes on a tray, as well as a bag of chips dangling from his mouth.

She immediately scrambled off the bed to help him, taking the chips and then closing the door behind him.

"Thank you," Crispin said as he walked around the bed to climb onto it from his side. He waited for her to get back in beside him and then set the tray down a little in front and between them. "I was not sure what kind of sandwiches you like, but I hope these will do."

"Do?" Abril asked with amusement. "It looks like you have everything from the refrigerator on those sandwiches. How did you make them so quickly?"

"Immortal skills," he said with a grin, and then confessed, "Actually, Bricker was out there making sandwiches and had everything out on the island. I just had to throw them together, and get the drinks." He paused briefly and then confessed, "I also took the chips he had out for himself. It sped things along."

Abril chuckled at this news as she reached for the nearer sandwich.

"How is it?" he asked the moment she took a bite. "My brother and sister like these, but I am not sure how they taste so was not sure you would like it."

Abril glanced at him with curiosity. "You've never had a Dagwood sandwich before?"

When he looked surprised at her question, she grimaced and said, "Oh. Right. You haven't eaten since 751 BC." Her eyes widened with realization. "Man! You haven't eaten for centuries."

"More like millennia," he corrected. "Close to three in fact."

"Three millennia," she murmured.

"Only a little over two centuries short of three millennia," he pointed out.

"Because you were born in 900 BC," she remembered and felt her earlier horror on learning this returning. She'd had so much to deal with at the time, she'd kind of pushed this information aside to concentrate on the other stuff. Now, however, even the Dagwood wasn't distracting her from the fact that she was presently in bed with a man older than dirt.

"Yes, 900 BC," Crispin agreed, concern beginning to pluck at his expression as he peered at her. "I realize that must be something of a shock to you."

"A shock? Oh no," she assured him. "All my dates have been born before Christ. It's just the type of guy I like. Thousands of years old." And then she closed her eyes, shook her head, and muttered, "Wow, and Barb thought a seven-year age difference was a red flag when it came to men."

"Abril," he said gently. "This should just tell you how important you are to me. I have waited millennia to find you."

For some reason that made a short laugh slip from her lips. "And Barb accused me of being choosy because I'm thirty-two and haven't settled down with anyone yet." Raising her head, she glanced to him, and explained, "She wants grandbabies."

When his eyebrows rose at that, she explained, "Barb and Bob were unable to have children of their own. I think that's why they pretty much adopted me. So, they are counting on me to present them with the grandchildren they yearn for."

"Ah." Crispin was still eyeing her with concern.

"I mean, I knew you guys could live a long time, and you did tell me your age and everything earlier, but there was so much information coming at me at the time that I didn't really consider the fact that you're so old," she admitted, and then frowned and added, "Sorry, I know that may be a rude thing to say. No one likes to hear they're old. I'm just a little surprised and unsure how to feel about this. You look so young, and I was hoping that you were older than twenty-five or thirty or at least closer to thirty than twenty-five. In fact, I was counting on that, I just wasn't expecting—"

Crispin ended her rambling by kissing her.

For Abril it was actually a relief that he shut her up. She had really just been rabbiting mindlessly on, and wasn't sure she even knew what she'd been saying. Mostly it was panic talk. But she stopped worrying about it as his kisses roused the usual passion inside of her. Those kisses of his were like a drug that she couldn't get enough of, and Abril threw herself into them with the eagerness his passion inspired. In fact, she did not just respond, she basically didn't just kiss him back, but climbed right into his lap. When she heard the jangle of plates and glasses clanking together, she recalled the tray Crispin had set on the bed. Abril stopped kissing long enough to glance over her shoulder.

Fortunately, the tray hadn't upended, and nothing on it had been disturbed to the point of spilling. As she watched, Crispin used one foot to push the tray farther away from them, toward the end of the bed where it would be out of danger, and then she turned back to peer down at his face.

She was on her knees, with his legs straight out on the bed between hers which put her head higher than his so that he was looking up at her, his head tipped back. Abril peered solemnly at his beautiful face, noting that his silver-blue eyes were more silver than blue right now, and then she lowered her head and kissed him. She kissed him eagerly and with demand, and for some reason, her aggressiveness drew a sound like a growl from Crispin's throat. And then his hands were all over her. Touching her through the cloth of her pajamas. Finding and caressing her breasts. Squeezing and kneading them briefly before he suddenly began to tug her pajama top upward.

Abril broke their kiss so that he could remove the top. He pulled it up over her head and tossed it aside, then immediately set to work on her bra.

Recalling how well the immortals could hear, Abril left him to it and reached for the mouse. She clicked on the movie to make it start up again, filling the room with the loud sound of gunfire, and then dropped the mouse just as her bra slipped away and Crispin's mouth closed over one nipple. Abril moaned then, unconcerned that she would be heard over the movie playing, and let her fingers glide into his hair to cup his head as he suckled and nipped at the erect nub.

The moment she did, Crispin let his hands drop down to her behind and began to squeeze and knead her flesh through the soft material of her pajama bottoms. He used those caresses to pull her lower body tighter against him so that she was leaning back somewhat, arching into the attention he was giving her one nipple with his teeth, tongue, and lips.

Abril gasped at the excitement charging through her. And then Crispin murmured, "I want to make love to you," before his mouth closed over her nipple.

The only response Abril could give was a moaned, "Oh God."

She wanted to say sex was off the table as she had in the laundry room. She really didn't want to have a child at this point in her life. Crispin could talk about life mates all he wished, but they had just met and her mortal morals couldn't accept that they were meant to be together forever so quickly. But when his one hand released her ass to slide around between her legs and rub her there, she forgot all about her concerns, and threw her head back on a cry as the excitement she'd been experiencing was increased a hundredfold.

The sensation he was causing in her was so strong, she hardly noticed when he began to pull her pajama bottoms down. Abril was too caught up in the waves of excitement building and pounding through her. It wasn't until he had to remove his hand to get it out of the way so that he could finish tugging her pajama bottoms off her hips that she noticed, and then it was only because she didn't want him to stop touching her.

Much to her relief, Crispin didn't stop for long. He barely tugged her bottoms halfway down her thighs before returning to caressing her, but now without the cloth of the pajamas between them.

"Oh yes," Abril groaned, and began to ride that hand as much as she could without pulling her nipple from his suckling lips. She was on the edge of finding her release when Crispin eased his caresses, and moved away from the center of her excitement.

Letting her nipple slip from his mouth, he licked a path to her other breast and growled again, "I want to make love to you."

The moment the last word left his lips, he closed them over her second nipple and began to suckle and tease that one.

Caught up in everything she was experiencing, Abril went willingly when he suddenly urged her backward until she lay flat on her back. He then began to tug her pajama bottoms the rest of the way down her legs from where they rested halfway down her thighs. He watched her face as he did. Abril knew he was giving her the chance to say no. That this was when she should make it clear that they shouldn't risk pregnancy, but her body was aching for him. She wanted to feel him inside of her, filling her body with his.

So, instead of saying no, she licked her lips and began to run her own hands over his body. One caressed what she could reach of his chest, smoothing over hard muscle and skin, while the other searched for and found his erection. The moment she did, Abril closed her hand around him like a glove, and slid it his length.

Crispin immediately stilled, a choked sound slipping from his mouth, but Abril too had paused, because her caressing him sent an incredible thrust of excitement through her own body. It startled her, and they both remained frozen for half a moment before the excitement began to wane, and then Abril ran her hand along his length again and another sharp shaft of pleasure raced through her.

The shared pleasure he had mentioned, she realized. A symptom of life mates. She was actually experiencing his pleasure alongside her own . . . and it was amazing, she acknowledged. Awesome.

"Shared pleasure could be addictive," she breathed with wonder as she began to caress him again.

"Yes," Crispin growled, catching her hand before she could bring them both to orgasm. "It is and once an immortal is mated, they are never unfaithful. No one can compare with their life mate when it comes to pleasure."

He had caught her other hand too as he spoke, and now pressed both to the mattress on either side of her head as he shifted to lower himself onto her.

Using his knee, he urged hers to open so that he could rest between her thighs, and then shifted to enter her. When Abril had had her hand around him, he hadn't seemed extremely long, but he had a great deal of girth so she wasn't surprised when his first thrust stopped with him only halfway in, and he had to withdraw and press forward another time to complete the act.

She didn't mind. There was no pain. But she again felt his pleasure as her tightness closed around him, and was amazed to know that this was what men experienced when they entered a woman. Because the pleasure was almost excruciating. Bending his head to kiss her, Crispin slowly withdrew and then eased back in again.

Abril returned his kiss almost wildly, and then wanting more than the slow, gentle thrusts he was using, drew her feet up so that her knees were raised, and lifted her hips into his movement, urging him to go harder and faster.

Growling, Crispin gave her what she wanted, and began to thrust more quickly, but only for a handful of times before the passion that had been growing and rushing over them in mounting waves suddenly exploded. Abril cried out into his mouth as she began to shudder and convulse.

The pleasure she was experiencing was so overwhelming, Abril was hardly aware of it when Crispin broke their kiss to shout out with his own pleasure as he poured himself into her. She was already sinking into the gentle darkness waiting for her.

"So, can immortals make mortals pregnant?"

Crispin had woken up pretty much crushing Abril into the mattress, so had swiftly shifted them so that they were lying properly on the sofa bed and she was resting on his chest. He had also been running his hand lightly up and down her back as she slept, but now stopped and glanced down at her.

Unfortunately, he had again set her down with the side of her face on his chest. He couldn't see her expression.

"I—yes," he said finally, guilt assaulting him as he recalled her saying in the laundry room that she didn't wish to get pregnant.

"Well, I guess it's Plan B for me," she said, a resigned tone to her voice.

Crispin frowned. He did know what Plan B was. The pill women took after unprotected sex. And he felt terribly guilty that she felt she needed to take it.

"I am sorry," he said solemnly.

Abril sighed and rolled off him to lie on her back, then sat up and scooted backward so she was reclining against the couch again. Running her hands through her hair, she said, "There's nothing to apologize for, I wasn't exactly screaming at you not to do it. I wasn't even whispering it."

"But you did say earlier in the laundry room that—"

She silenced him with a hand over his mouth, and peered at him solemnly. "This immortal sex is some pretty powerful stuff, Crispin. I don't blame either of us for getting carried away. Although I'd think I'd be used to it by now maybe. I mean this may have been the first time we actually had sex, but we've messed around three times now."

"It is not the immortal sex, it is life mate sex," he said gently. "The shared pleasure is only something experienced by life mates, and is famously overwhelming for both parties. It is why we both lose consciousness at the end."

She stilled at those words, and asked, "You fainted too?"

Crispin nodded with a grimace that suggested he was uncomfortable admitting to something as weak as fainting.

"Wow, sex so good you faint." She shook her head. "I guess that's kind of special."

"It is definitely something special," he told her solemnly. "Aside from ensuring fidelity, I suspect it also allows for quick bonding between mates."

"Quick bonding, huh?" Abril smiled faintly and then paused and seemed to consider that, before saying, "Yeah maybe. I mean, I would definitely say it's addictive. My body is already humming and wanting more."

Crispin was immediately seated upright beside her, hope on his face. "Does that mean you would like for me to make love to you again?" he asked, careful not to touch her anywhere, in an effort not to sway her decision. Which he knew he should've done the first time, but he hadn't intended to make love to her then. He had merely kissed her to stop her anxious rambling and had intended on then talking to her and soothing her worries about his age. He should've known better. He had heard about the ferocity of the passion between life mates. He had also already experienced it in the laundry room and the pool and the living room. He definitely should've known better.

Abril distracted him from his fretting by shifting to straddle him.

The second time Abril woke up, she was on her back and Crispin was lying on his side next to her, toying with the nipple closest to him. She didn't know how long he had been doing that, but her nipple was already hard and her body was writhing with mounting excitement.

She immediately reached for his head, pulling him down to kiss her. As their tongues began to tangle, Abril reached for his cock and began to caress him. When Crispin caught her hand and tried to pull it away, she resisted and used his distraction to push him over onto his back, then slid down his body to take him into her mouth.

Abril had never been overly fond of giving blow jobs. It wasn't that she minded, but it gave her no pleasure, so it was purely an act meant to give pleasure to her partner. But with Crispin, it was an entirely different experience. She felt every surge of pleasure that ran through him as if it was her own, and aside from enjoying them, they were somewhat educational. She quickly realized which pressures, speeds, and moves gave him the most sensual gratification, because it did the same for her.

Sadly, rather than use that to prolong the experience, she found herself doing exactly what felt best . . . which led to a very quick, explosive end.

The next time Abril woke up it was to find Crispin's face buried between her thighs, returning the favor. She knew he must be experiencing the same excitement she had while performing fellatio on him, because he was far too good at it not to be getting cues from their shared pleasure. Unfortunately, that again led to a very fast ending. On the bright side, it was mind-blowing.

Crispin was still asleep when Abril next woke up. That was a first, usually he woke up before her. Now she briefly considered how she should wake him. Another blow job? A hand job? Climb on top of him and take him inside of herself? It was while she was debating the matter, that she realized that she was extremely thirsty.

Easing away from him, she slid to the end of the bed and the corner nearest to her desk. She wasn't sure when, but Crispin had obviously moved the tray to the desk at some point while she was unconscious. Probably after the first time he'd made love to her, Abril thought. She didn't remember seeing it after that.

Now she eyed the glasses on the tray and grimaced. The ice cubes had melted, and she knew the pops would be warm. She considered opening one of the pops and sipping from it anyway, but her nose wrinkled at the very idea. Giving in to the inevitable, she got out of bed.

Her pajamas were lying in a pool on the floor. She quickly donned them, pulled on her robe, and tied it up as she opened her office door. Abril then immediately froze as she saw the figure moving past her door. It wasn't one of the Enforcers. In fact, it wasn't even a man, but a tall, well-built woman dressed all in black.

For one moment, terror had Abril completely unmoving to the point that she wasn't even breathing for fear of drawing the woman's attention. But it didn't matter, something made the intruder turn her head toward her. Knowing the woman could take control of her, Abril instinctively screamed and slammed the door closed between them.

Twenty-Eight

"**W**hat is it? What happened?" Crispin was awake at once, and sitting up even as she scrambled over the bed to put it between herself and the door she'd just slammed shut.

Seeing her panic, his head swiveled toward the door and he was immediately out of bed. Honestly, the speed with which he moved was more than a little shocking. One moment he was sitting up in the bed, and the next he was at the door, pulling it open.

What followed was mass confusion and chaos. At first, Abril thought the intruder had tackled Crispin and was rushing him toward the bed. But when the back of his legs hit the bedside and he tumbled onto the mattress, it wasn't just the intruder who crashed down on top of him, but the intruder, Cassius, Decker, and Bricker. The five of them ended up in a pile on the bed, with Crispin at the bottom.

Abril stared wide-eyed as the quintet began to tussle, and then movement drew her gaze to the doorway. Lucian and Anders were standing there, simply watching with interested expressions. Roberts stood behind them, but at least he looked concerned.

The battle being four to one, it was a short scuffle before the men had subdued the woman and dragged her off Crispin on the bed.

"Take her to the kitchen," Lucian ordered. "We will question her there."

He then waited for the woman to be escorted out of the room by her captors, before glancing to Crispin and ordering, "Put on some pants before you come out to the kitchen. I have no interest in staring at your butt quack."

Crispin was left gaping when the door closed. For one moment, Abril wasn't sure why he appeared so shocked, but then he turned to her and said, "I do believe Uncle Lucian just made a joke."

Abril simply offered a weak smile. She suspected that was something unusual when it came to his uncle, but was more concerned with the intruder and any explanations she had to give. With that thought in mind, she quickly bent to pick up his slacks and shirt from the floor and walked around the bed to hand them to him before slipping out of the room and leaving him to dress. It seemed like the smarter move. If she'd stayed around his naked body much longer, they might not have left the room at all.

The men had the intruder seated on one of the island chairs when Abril came out. Much to her surprise, the woman wasn't tied up or anything. But then she supposed it wasn't necessary. Decker and Bricker stood on either side of her, and Lucian was seated with his own chair facing hers. The other men were ranged around the room on all sides. There was really no chance she would escape.

Abril had barely had that thought when she became aware that the room was utterly silent. A curious glance around showed her that the men were presently giving the attractive female intruder that strange, concentrated stare that they had used on her so often. The one she absolutely detested and now knew was probably the men reading her—and now the intruder's—mind.

Abril didn't comment, but looked the woman over. She'd only got a quick glimpse of her before slamming the door closed and scrambling across the bed to get as far away from it as she could. Now she peered at her, a small frown forming on her face as she took in her dark hair pulled tightly back into a bun, and her sharp, yet beautiful features. It was hard to believe she'd mistaken her for a man the night she'd been attacked in her bedroom, but then it had been dark, and the woman had been all in black. She was also rather tall and strong for a woman. She'd obviously had her hair pulled back then too, which she'd thought was just short hair. Abril supposed she could be forgiven the mistake.

Like the men, the intruder looked no more than twenty-five or so, possibly thirty. But this house had been built about twenty-five years ago and this woman, if she was Mrs. Foley, had been a married woman with a child then. She had to be at least forty-five now. Probably more like fifty years old. Maybe even more. Those nanos were something else, she thought, and then her eyes narrowed.

"You were with Kim," she said slowly as she recognized her. "I saw the two of you outside talking to the construction crew the day the excavator broke down. I went out intending to talk to you both, but you were already at the end of the driveway by the time I grabbed my coat and got outside." Abril thought the woman had also been the figure she'd seen with Kim on her night walk with Lilith, but couldn't be positive, and now asked uncertainly, "Are you and Kim friends?"

The woman merely snorted at the suggestion.

"She is a friend to no one," Lucian assured Abril solemnly as he sat back in his seat, the concentrated expression leaving his face.

"The control thing?" Abril guessed and when he nodded, she felt anger well up in her at the thought of this woman controlling Kim. She hadn't had much interaction with her herself, but Gina had said she'd met the wife and mother at the street party and that she was very nice.

"Your neighbor Kim has been under her control since the morning you saw them together here," Lucian told her. "As has the rest of Kim's family. She has been living in their home to keep an eye on this house."

Abril's eyes widened in alarm. "Are they all okay?"

She knew she wasn't going to like the answer when Lucian hesitated before giving it. She suspected he did not often hesitate about anything.

Finally, he said, "They are presently tied up in the basement of their home. She has been keeping them as cattle for blood until she got her husband's body back. Her intention then was to finish them off, place them in their beds, and set the house on fire to hide how they really died."

Abril's mouth opened slightly on a gasp of horror and she turned to stare at the monster before her before bursting out, "What the hell is wrong with you? Killing your husband, an immortal, and the twelve other victims in the garden wasn't enough? You had to add to their number?"

"There have been far more victims over the years than the ones we found here," Lucian told her solemnly while the woman just stared through Abril coldly. "Fortunately, not as many as there could have been. But only because she learned that overfeeding just causes pain, and so reduced the amount of blood she took in. She also started keeping her prey chained up in her basement like Kim's family is now. She kept several at a time that she could feed off of as needed. They eventually died due to her not feeding or caring for them properly, but then she just replaced them with someone new. Usually someone from Toronto or other nearby cities that she visited to be sure there were not too many missing persons cases here."

Abril was still reeling over what he'd just said when Lucian ordered, "Roberts, Decker, go to the neighbor's house and take care of Kim and her family."

The two men nodded and immediately headed out of the kitchen.

Lucian then turned to gaze over the remaining men before saying, "Anders and Bricker, I need you to go to the rogue's house to see to the victims chained up in her basement there."

"She has victims there too?" Abril asked with surprise. She'd have thought one houseful at a time would be sufficient.

"Yes," Lucian said solemnly. "Including someone

named William who is apparently somehow connected to you?"

"William?" Abril's eyes widened. "Not me. Gina. He's her boyfriend. Or was until he left one day for milk and never came ba—Oh my God, you bitch!" she snapped at the woman. "You took William? Gina thought he left her. She was crushed! Why the hell would you do that?"

"She saw the construction company trucks here during the interior work and wanted to know what renos were taking place. She could have simply read his mind or that of one of the construction crew, but found William attractive and wanted to play with him . . . whether he wanted to play or not."

"Oh my God," Abril breathed unhappily. She'd been cursing poor William for the last two weeks since he'd disappeared so abruptly. She'd even told Gina that he wasn't smart enough for her along with other insults to the man's character and intelligence in an effort to ease the blow of what she'd thought was his rejection of her boss. Meanwhile, the whole time he'd been kidnapped and held against his will to be this woman's . . . What? Was she feeding on him? Torturing him? What? Sighing, she asked, "Is he okay?"

Lucian was silent for a moment, and then said carefully, "He was alive the last she saw him."

He raised his hand in front of Abril's face when she started to speak and despite herself, she obediently went silent. The moment she did, Lucian finished addressing the two men. "You know where her house is? You read it from her mind?"

Anders nodded. "It is the first one when you turn left

off this crescent. The big white one with the woods surrounding it."

Lucian grunted an acknowledgment. "You will need to call Dani or Rachel in to help the people chained up there. Possibly both. It would be a good idea if one of them checked over this Kim and her family as well."

When Anders and Bricker immediately left the kitchen, Cassius asked, "What do you want me to do?"

"You and Crispin are going to guard this creature while I call Mortimer, and then we shall wait until backup arrives to take her away," Lucian announced and pulled out his phone as he stood up.

Abril sensed movement behind her and glanced over her shoulder to see Crispin stepping out of the mouth of the hallway now wearing his dress slacks and shirt. He'd left the tie and suit jacket behind. Their gazes met as he approached, and he offered a crooked smile and a soft touch on her arm that she suspected was meant to reassure her. But then he was past her and taking up position where Bricker had been on one side of the intruder. Obviously, he'd heard everything and knew he was to guard her. Now he was doing the concentrated look thing on the dark-haired woman.

Her gaze shifted from him to Cassius, who had already moved to take Decker's spot.

The woman now had a guard on either side of her again, but Lucian was no longer in front of her. Instead, Abril stood there, her hand resting on the back of the chair Lucian had been occupying. Feeling uncomfortable, she took in the woman's gaze, noting that a cruel smile had begun to pull at her lips as she peered back.

Suspecting she was trying to freak her out, Abril raised her chin and said calmly, "Damn, those nanos do good work." She let her gaze scrape with distaste over the other woman's young and healthy appearance. "It's just a shame the scientists didn't upload the meaning and value of morality to the nanos alongside those maps of the female and male body at their peak. They could have programmed them to destroy monsters like you if you became their host."

Abril saw the confusion that crossed the woman's face in response to her words, and her eyebrows rose slightly. "You have no idea what I'm talking about when I say nanos, do you?"

The woman glanced sharply at her, and then away, her expression angry.

"Not feeling like talking?" Abril asked.

"Just get your stakes and crosses and get it over with," she growled, vibrating with fury.

"Wow, you really don't have a clue," Abril said with amazement, and then told her, "Crosses won't do a thing to you, Mrs. Foley."

The woman glanced at her sharply. "How do you know my name? You are human. You couldn't possibly read my thoughts like they can."

"I don't know your name," Abril said with a shrug. "At least not all of it. What is your first name?"

Her mouth tightened, and she remained silent. It was Lucian who said, "Diane Elizabeth Foley," as he returned to join them, having apparently finished his phone call.

Abril removed her hand from his chair as he settled in it again, her gaze returning to Diane Foley as she wondered what the woman thought she was if she had no idea about nanos.

"She thinks she is a vampire, of course," Lucian said, answering her unspoken question.

Abril glanced at him with a start. "But she was out in daylight with Kim the other day. Surely she must realize—"

"She does not," Lucian assured her, not even bothering to let her finish the thought. "She found out sunlight would not kill her when one of her victims escaped and ran outside. Mrs. Foley instinctively gave chase. It was only once she had recaptured her victim and was dragging her back to the house that she realized she was outside in full sunlight and not bursting into flames. The only explanation she could come up with for it was that she was a young vampire. She thought perhaps only the ancient ones burst into flames in daylight and she would be safe for a while. Still, she was cautious every time she went outside during the daytime and avoided it as much as possible. However, there are times when she cannot avoid it, like when she accompanied your neighbor Kim over here so that she could put a halt to the excavation taking place."

Abril turned on him sharply. "The excavator—?"

"Is not broken," he finished, interrupting her. "She simply controlled the operator of the excavator to make him turn it off and believe it was broken, and then controlled the site supervisor to make him think they would have to halt work for the rest of the day and bring a repairman in the next morning. She intended to remove the skeletons both inside and out that night. She knew the deaths would be traced back to herself and her husband if the bodies were found and wanted to protect both of their families from the scandal that would erupt with the discovery."

"Of course, Lilith put paid to her plans by digging up those bones in the afternoon, and you calling the police. Once they showed up, her plan changed. She would not bother with the immortal's remains and was only interested in removing her husband. She knew she could no longer save their families from the scandal, but she wanted her husband with her."

Abril had noted the brief confusion that flickered on Diane's face when Lucian said the word immortal, and supposed she shouldn't be surprised the woman had no idea what she was. There had been no one to tell her. Or train her. It was almost enough to make her feel sorry for the woman, except that Diane had apparently killed a butt load of people over the years, and hadn't stopped even when she'd figured out she didn't need to drink her victims dry, and that taking in that amount of blood was bad for her. She'd apparently simply kept them as cows for her to milk of blood as she wished. But she hadn't had the basic decency of a farmer who kept their cows healthy and well. Instead, she'd kept them chained in her basement, probably terrified, underfed if fed at all, and miserable.

"Tell her the rest, Crispin. I cannot be bothered," Lucian said, sounding as disgusted as she felt.

Twenty-Nine

Crispin turned to focus his concentration on Diane Elizabeth Foley. Her mind was an open book, easily read. He almost wished that wasn't the case as he sorted through her memories. Her being easily read meant she wasn't insane. She was just a coldhearted nasty bitch if he were to judge by her memories and feelings. She hadn't always been. Prior to the tragic accident that had taken her son's life and left her body broken, she had been a kind and loving wife and mother. But her losses had twisted her up inside. Not mentally, but emotionally. She was bitter and angry and had decided the world owed her. To her mind, she should be able to do whatever the hell she wanted, no matter who it hurt or killed, and didn't even feel a twinge of conscience about it. Her son had been taken from her, she had been paralyzed, and then had lost her husband too and she wanted to burn the world down for it.

Mouth setting, he sorted through the house of horrors that was her memory and began to speak. "As Lois Jamison said, Diane and her husband were in a car accident. They were hit by a drunk driver. Her husband got away with mere scrapes and bruises, but their five-year-old son died and Diane was paralyzed. She also took a lot of internal damage. Not only could she not walk, but she would never be able to have another child and could not even indulge in sexual activity with her husband. Shortly after the accident, he started going out and having one-night stands to—"

"It wasn't shortly after!" Diane snapped. "It was a full year later. A year during which I repeatedly begged him to go satisfy the needs I couldn't take care of anymore." Her mouth compressed, but then she added, "John was my husband. I loved him. I didn't want him to have to go outside our marriage, but I couldn't satisfy him that way and I wanted him happy. I was actually relieved when he finally started going out to bars and picking up women. Relieved!" she insisted furiously after the briefest pause, and then a short, bitter laugh huffed out of her. "I did it to keep from losing him and lost him anyway."

She glowered at them all. "My husband loved me and was a good man. A truly good man. That's why it took so long to convince him to go out and have flings. Any other man would have jumped at the chance to bang barmaids with his wife's permission. But not my John. I even had to blackmail him into it."

"Blackmail?" Abril echoed with surprise and the other woman nodded.

"I threatened to kill myself so that he would be free to have a true wife if he wouldn't go out and find women to take care of his needs," Diane said cooly and at Abril's shocked expression, her lips twisted slightly. "I would not have done it, but he didn't know that."

"But why make him do something he didn't want to do?" Abril asked, sounding truly mystified.

"Because I am not a fool," Diane said as if she thought Abril was. "He did love me, but no man can do without sex for long. And this way I could control it. Had I not convinced him to go out and have one-night stands, he eventually would have ended up having an affair with someone, someone he might come to love and leave me for. I wasn't going to lose my husband too. He was all I had left."

Scowling, she shrugged her emotions away and continued. "So, he finally agreed to do it. But there were rules we both agreed on. He was to go out and pick up women from bars on the weekend only. The weeknights were ours. And there was to be no emotional attachment. He was to sleep only once with any of the women he encountered."

When she paused again, Crispin explained, "Picking up women at the bars is how John came across the immortal presently buried in the indoor garden. She frequented the same bar he did. He'd noticed her and found her attractive, but suspected she was out of his league so had not approached her. One night, though, he was engaging in intimate activity in his car with one of the string of women that he used for sex and saw her come out—"

"In his car?" Abril interrupted with a grimace. "He could have at least brought her here or taken her to a cheap motel or something. Sex in cars is uncomfortable and—"

"Of course, in the car," Diane growled. "John had too much respect for me to bring any of these tramps to our home, and certainly wouldn't have wasted our money on a motel. He either went to their home, or—if they didn't live alone—made do with the car in the bar parking lot."

She glared at Abril for daring to sound critical of her husband for this choice, and then fell silent.

Crispin met Abril's gaze and went on, "One night he and a woman were engaged in intimate activity in his car in the bar parking lot when he saw the immortal come out with a man following her. John apparently thought they were together and going to indulge in the same thing he and his companion were doing. But she was not with the man. He had followed her out with the intent to attack her. When he did so as she was unlocking her vehicle, she revealed her immortal strength in her effort to defend herself. She left her attacker unconscious and bleeding on the ground when she drove off, but she had also captured John's interest.

"After that, he began to watch for her anytime he went to the bars. He noticed that she had a routine. She'd enter, look around, seem to settle on a man—usually one who was on his own—take his hand and lead him to the washrooms. Curious, John followed one time. She led the man she'd chosen into the men's room. They were in one of the stalls by the time he got into the room, and he watched them through the crack between the stall door and wall. He quickly realized she did not want these men for sex when he saw her bring out her fangs, bite her 'date,' and take in his blood. John slipped away before he was noticed—"

"—Only to rush to the bar," Diane interrupted defensively. "He was going to have the bartender call the police or send the bouncers in to save the guy, but then realized he couldn't start squawking about vampires or they'd just think he was either crazy or drunk. He was trying to decide what story to use to get help when the couple came back out of the bathroom. The man seemed perfectly fine. He was even smiling and the woman kissed him, then settled him at the bar where she'd found him and left."

"Wait," Abril said suddenly, her questioning gaze shifting to the men in the room. "That means this immortal was a rogue too?"

"It would seem so," Lucian said. "She was not killing her 'dates,' but should not have been biting them either. Had we discovered her, she would have been punished."

"Punished how?" Abril asked, but Lucian ignored her and turned his attention back to Diane.

"Continue," he ordered.

For a moment, Crispin didn't think Diane would. It was obvious from her expression that she resented his bossing her about like that, but then she apparently decided she wanted to tell her story more than she wanted to defy Lucian and said, "John came home that night and told me everything. At first, I had no idea why he was telling me what I thought at the time was a ridiculous story. I didn't believe him, of course. I mean . . . vampires?" Her eyebrows lifted with obvious incredulity. "I thought he must be drunk and just mistook what he'd seen. In fact, I was getting pretty annoyed with him and telling him to take himself to bed when he said that perhaps if we got the vampire to turn me into one, I'd be able to walk again. Maybe everything would be fixed and he could make love to me too instead of having to pick up strange women in bars."

She lowered her head briefly and then raised it again, her expression carefully empty. Giving a shrug, she admitted, "That actually gave me pause. I still didn't believe he'd seen what he thought he'd seen, but the idea of being able to both walk and be with my husband again caught my imagination and I began to daydream after that . . . about being a vampire and whole again."

Her mouth thinned. "I remember wishing it was true. I hated being paralyzed. Hated that my husband had to look elsewhere for sexual pleasure because I could no longer provide it. And I hated that we'd lost our son and I could never provide him with another. I hated everything, and I didn't deserve it," she told them grimly. "I was a good, dutiful daughter, and then I was a good faithful and caring wife and mother. I always did what was expected of me. Never slutted around, never broke the law, never even went above the speed limit and what was my reward?" she asked bitterly. "To lose everything because of some drunken asshole they never even caught so didn't punish for what he did to me."

"Never caught?" Abril asked with surprise.

"The driver apparently wasn't hurt, or at least he was well enough to jump out of the car and leave before the police got on scene, and then the owner of the vehicle claimed it had been stolen."

Crispin noted the way Abril frowned at this news so

wasn't surprised when she asked, "Then how did they know the driver was drunk?"

"There were several empty beer cans and one half-full liquor bottle in the car," Crispin said quietly when Diane just glared at her for interrupting. When the woman continued to hold the expression without speaking, he added, "John knew Diane didn't fully believe his story, but he was determined to find the vampire and somehow bring her back to turn his wife. He tried to research vampires to find something to help him subdue her and get her back here, but in the end, he went for brute force. He purchased and wore several necklaces and rings with crosses on them and bought a bat. Then he started frequenting the bar almost nightly until she returned. He never told Diane what happened, but one night he came home with a beautiful woman unconscious in his arms and—"

"He didn't have to tell me what had happened," Diane interrupted impatiently. "He'd started taking a bat out with him when he left for the bar and the back of her head was caved in. I had a pretty good idea what had taken place without his having to explain."

Resentment plain in her expression, she added, "And yes, she was pretty, but other than that, she just looked like any other woman. John kept insisting, though, that she was a vampire."

Before the woman could continue, Abril turned to Crispin in confusion. "The way you describe immortals I assumed you couldn't really be hurt, that you'd heal quickly from any injury other than having your head cut off or being set on fire. But you *can* be hurt? And if you can, why wouldn't he just drug her or something?"

"I presume either because he did not think of it, could not get any, or was not sure what would work. If it was the latter, he was right, normal drugs do not usually work on us," Crispin said, answering her last question first. "The nanos clear them out too quickly." When Abril merely nodded that she understood, he added, "But of course we can be hurt. Bullets and knives will pierce our bodies, our bones can break and our skulls can be crushed and caved in. The only difference is they will not kill us and we heal very quickly. But an injury as grievous as Mrs. Foley described would incapacitate us for some time."

"Oh," Abril nodded, her expression solemn.

"As I was saying," Diane went on heavily, obviously annoyed at the interruption to her tale, "John insisted she was a vampire and begged me to cooperate. He loved me and wanted our life back. Even if I might never be able to have a child again as a vampire, I'd be able to walk. We could dance, travel, and so on, but most important, he could make love to me and stop feeling like a cheating asshole. Of course I wanted all that too, so I finally agreed to let him use her to turn me."

She paused briefly, her expression unhappy and then continued, her voice low and solemn. "He said he'd researched it and while vampires usually bit their victim before turning them, he didn't think that was actually necessary. He suspected ingesting the vampire's blood was enough to do the trick. So he cut her wrist," she said, and then released a short, sharp laugh. "Actually, he very nearly severed her hand from her wrist he cut so deep, then he pressed the gushing wound to my mouth. I drank as much blood as I could stomach from the wound and was just trying to push her arm away when the vampire woke up."

Diane paused and shook her head with a sort of awe. "The next thing I knew I was yanked from my wheelchair and flying through the air. I hit something, probably the wall," she guessed and shrugged. "I'm not sure what I hit, but the pain in my head and upper back was blinding and that's the last thing I remember so I guess I must have lost consciousness.

"I don't know how long I was out, but when I woke up . . ." She shook her head, her face blanching with the memory that was returning to her and then she suddenly straightened, all emotion leaving her face. Her voice was much stronger and colder when she said, "When I woke up the vampire was lying a few feet away with her head missing and John was sitting on the floor with me, cradling me in his arms. I was confused, in terrible pain, and unbearably hungry and he . . . I remember thinking that he smelled sooo good."

Abril seemed confused that would be the woman's thought at such a moment, so Crispin explained, "By good, she means John smelled absolutely delicious to her." When those words didn't clear Abril's expression, he added, "Like a steak on legs."

Abril's eyes were wide with incredulity now and Crispin nodded solemnly. "She was mid turn. From her memories of the scene at that point, it does not appear that her husband had even realized she would need blood, let alone arranged to get any for her turn. Sadly, this led to Diane attacking her own husband

while she was out of her head with the turn and drain-
ing him dry before passing out again."

"Liar!" Diane roared with fury, trying to rise up off
her chair. Both men immediately caught her shoulders
and forced her to remain seated. She glared at Crispin
and growled, "I would never hurt my husband! The
vampire must have injured him horribly before he was
able to cut off her head, and then he bled out before I
woke up."

Crispin shook his head. "In your memories of that
night, when you woke up the second time you were lying between the headless woman and your cold, dead
husband. There was a bloody machete lying near the
immortal's body, but other than that there was very
little blood anywhere else. So, while your memory of
him shows him so pale he appeared to be drained of
every drop of blood in his body, he did not bleed out
naturally."

Diane Foley shook her head in denial, but her expression was stark now as she struggled with the guilt
of what she'd really known all this time, but had done
her best to deny. Leaving her to her inner battle, he told
Abril, "The second time she woke up, she was no longer in pain and could walk. Better than that, she was
strong. She buried the immortal, her head, and John
in the indoor garden, cleaned up the mess, including
showering and changing her clothes. By that time, her
stomach was beginning to cramp with the need for
blood, and—" Noting Abril's confusion, he paused
to explain, "She was not done turning. That takes a
while as a rule, but with the injuries she'd taken in the
car accident there was even more to repair than would
normally be the case. She needed a lot of blood, and

probably a week or two for the turn to reach the stage where she would remain conscious and seem normal despite the little repairs continuing under the surface."

When she nodded, he continued, "Anyway, when the pain became unbearable, she passed out on the couch. She was still there when she was awoken the next afternoon by knocking at the door. Half asleep, she stumbled to open it and found a couple of Jehovah's witnesses on her stoop, eager to press pamphlets into her hand and talk to her about the Lord. Diane invited them in."

Sighing, he met Abril's gaze and said, "They were the first bodies in the outdoor garden. She buried them in the dark of night and drove their car out into the country, dumped it there, and walked back."

Abril grimaced, but then gave him an encouraging smile and he continued, "Unfortunately, Jehovah's witnesses did not come around every day at dinnertime. But the next day her sister did come. Along with her husband and teenage daughters. With everything that had been happening, Diane had forgotten she'd made plans the week before and invited them to dinner. They were the next four in the outdoor garden and then she had to get rid of *their* car too."

Abril's jaw dropped. Eyes shifting to Diane, she gasped, "Your own sister? And your nieces?"

Diane scowled at her. "My sister was a know-it-all bitch who always got everything she wanted, and my nieces were spoiled brats. As for my brother-in-law . . . don't even get me started. I always loathed the pompous ass."

When Abril just gaped at the woman, Crispin carried on with the tale, now eager to get it done. "After that, she invited different friends to dinner who also ended in her garden."

"Really?" Abril glared at the woman with disgust.

"They deserved it," Diane snapped. "They all pretty much abandoned me after I was paralyzed. Hell, my best friend even tried to hit on my husband." She scowled, and then added, "Besides, I didn't kill all my friends, just the fair-weather ones. After that I started going out to get my meals."

When she fell silent, Crispin continued. "She did start going out to 'get her meals.' She went to bars, brought home men, drained them, and buried them in the garden. She had gone through the twelve victims we found outside before she accidentally discovered that she could control the minds of her victims. More importantly, she had a better idea of how much blood she could take without it killing them while still satisfying her need. A need that had finally begun to wane now that the worst of the turn was over with," he added.

"After that, the people she feasted off survived their ordeal. At least for a while . . . more's the pity," he added dryly and explained, "Because while she could control them, she did not at first know that she could wipe their memories. So, she kept them rather than risk their blabbing about her. She was chaining them up in one of the guest bedrooms, but was sure it would be safer to keep her victims in a basement, away from prying eyes. Besides, she could not risk the neighbors noting that she was walking again or that her husband was missing, which would lead to questions. So, she decided she needed to move. She went out to the bars, found a man who lived alone in a house with a basement, and went home with him.

"After feeding on him, and tying him up in his basement, she came back here to collect her other victims—the still living ones and took them there. The next day she contacted a Realtor to sell this house. Everything was fine at first. Her husband's company built the house, but they'd put the deed in her name to protect it from his company's creditors. It wasn't until she went to sign the sales contract for the house that there were any issues, and that was because her Realtor mentioned that Mr. Branson planned to dig up the gardens and build a deck that would run along the side and back of the house. Diane could not have that, of course, and went straight to the Bransons. She took control of Mr. Branson to make him drop the idea of the deck, cancel the contractor, and then had him arrange for a small patio instead. One that wouldn't need the garden being dug up."

Meeting Abril's gaze he said, "She had no desire to dig up rotting bodies. Just taking control of Mr. Branson and ensuring he did not have the garden dug up for any reason seemed the best bet, but she was not sure how long her control would last. She felt her only option was to move close by and keep tabs on the Bransons.

"Diane checked out houses in the area. She decided the house around the corner was good. It had lots of property—forty acres," he told her, and then added, "Most of those acres were woods too, where she felt she could bury any future bodies in peace. She visited and controlled the couple who owned that property so that they would give her a tour of the inside, and found the house itself was large and lovely with a basement. It was perfect. But it was not for sale . . . until she controlled the minds of the couple so that they would sell her the house quickly and for much less than it was worth. She then moved herself and her victims in there.

"Things went along fine for quite a while. Eventually, she learned she could wipe the memories of her victims, but by then she enjoyed their tears and terror when she chained them to the walls of her basement, so she continued to keep what she considered her cattle."

"They *were* my cattle," Diane growled with irritation. "And it wasn't that I enjoyed their tears and terror, but their blood tasted better after a scare than it did if I just took control of them and snacked without upsetting them." Glowering at Abril's horrified expression, she snapped, "Are you going to try to tell me you don't prefer tasty meals to bland ones?"

"My meals aren't people," Abril snapped back and then turned to Crispin and said, "I'm guessing everything was fine until Gina started to dig up the garden? How did she even know about that? Surely, she wasn't still watching the house all these years later?"

"She was," Crispin responded. "But as the years continued to pass without issue, she began to check on them less and less often until it was only about once a year. Every spring," he said meaningfully.

"Ah," Abril breathed with understanding.

"Yes," Crispin said, nodding. "She was doing her yearly drive-by check a few weeks ago, and saw the construction company trucks in the driveway. She was concerned, but did not know the Bransons had moved, and the men were all obviously working inside not outside. She was debating going in to find out what was happening, when a delivery truck pulled up. She read the driver's mind to see that he was delivering kitchen appliances. She thought the Bransons must be doing a kitchen renovation. That was not a problem, so she left but decided she would keep a closer eye and come around weekly for a while. The next time she came around, they had started the excavation for the foundation of the addition."

"I was already past the driveway when I spotted the excavator. I pulled into a driveway, intending just to use it to turn around and come back here, but Kim came out of the house before I could back out. I read her mind, found out that the Bransons had sold the house, and then learned what she knew about the renovations taking place. Then I took her over to control the workmen to stop the digging for the day." She shifted in her seat, her expression irritated. "I thought I'd just get them to pack up for the day and then come for the bodies both inside and outside that night and everything would be fine. I wouldn't even have to keep an eye on the house anymore."

"But Lilith put paid to your plan," Abril murmured, echoing Lucian's words from earlier. She then said, "I'm surprised you didn't just come over as soon as the men left and set to work digging out the bodies. You could have taken control of me, and if you'd stayed low no one would have seen you in the hole."

"I had things to do," Diane said with irritation. "I thought it was all sorted. I'd stopped the digging before they'd uncovered the bodies and could come back once night fell to take care of the rest. So, I wiped Kim's memory and went to the grocery store as I planned. By the time I came back that afternoon to check on things, the place was crawling with police and I realized the bodies outside had been found. At that point, all I could do was remove my husband and the immortal from inside."

"Okay," Abril said. "So why didn't you just come over and control us after forensics and Officer Peters left? You could have even made us dig up the bodies for you. Instead, you tried to sneak in and then attacked me when I woke up and caught you coming in through my bedroom window."

"I already knew I couldn't control them and wasn't sure about you," Diane snarled unhappily.

"How—?" Abril began but Diane interrupted her impatiently.

"Because I was at Kim's when they were doing their door-to-door interviews. I controlled Kim so she wouldn't answer the door when they knocked, but it was like they knew someone was there. They just kept knocking. It was fucking irritating. So, I tried to take control of them and send them away, but I couldn't. I tried reading him"—she gestured toward Roberts—"and couldn't. I was going to try this one"—she nodded to Crispin now—"but they gave up and left before I could. It bothered me that I couldn't read or control them. Besides, I was getting a weird buzz off of them. I decided to follow and try to work out what was up."

"And she witnessed Crispin and Roberts drinking bagged blood," Lucian said with obvious displeasure.

"We were parked on the side of the road at the end of the crescent where the woods are," Crispin said quickly. "There was no one around to see."

"Except for her," Lucian snapped.

"How could we know she would run through the

woods following us and then lurk in the trees and watch us feed?" Crispin said impatiently, and pointed out, "A mortal would not have been able to keep up with us on foot, and we had no idea this was immortal related at that point."

"Why didn't you just take off when you realized immortals were investigating? They'd already discovered the bodies outside, what were two more?" Abril asked Diane.

Crispin suspected she was trying to break the tension in the room as he and Lucian glared at each other. When Diane didn't deign to respond to her question, he reluctantly broke the glaring contest with his uncle and said what the woman wouldn't. "That was the last thing she wanted to do once she realized that we were what she thought were vampires. The realization made her more determined to get the bodies out of the indoor garden. Not just her husband any longer, who she wanted to give a proper burial to, but now she wanted—needed—to remove the body of the immortal as well. She wasn't afraid of the police catching up to her, but she was terrified that if we discovered the decapitated body of one of our own, we would hunt and punish their killer mercilessly. That scared the hell out of her."

"Why?" Abril asked at once, her gaze sliding to Diane and back. "It's not like you guys are bloodhounds or something. You wouldn't have been able to sniff her out. Would you?" she added with uncertainty.

"No," he assured her and then pointed out, "But she did not know that. She had no guidebook for the skills of vampires except for fictional novels and such and some of those claimed that older vampires had all sorts of weird abilities. She feared one of us *might* be able to find her somehow using . . ." He hesitated as he tried to understand the thoughts in her head. "Paranormal woo-woo?" he said uncertainly, and then gave his head a shake when Abril grinned and nodded. Apparently *woo-woo* was a word now, he thought, and continued, "Diane was sure she would be found, and then killed for the immortal's murder."

"But her husband killed the vampire—er . . . immortal," Abril pointed out.

"Yes, but she had been an accessory after the fact, and she had willingly consumed her blood."

Abril nodded in understanding, and thought being an accessory to a crime was punishable in human law too.

"Mortal law," Lucian growled irritably. "We are human too. And while immortals have our own set of laws, and you mortals have yours, still, we are all human."

"Okay, mortal laws," she said with exasperation, and then pointed out, "You know, if you didn't go around reading people's minds, you'd be less likely to hear things that piss you off."

When Lucian glowered at her, Crispin spoke up distracting him.

"Anyway, worried about retribution if the 'vampire' was found, she broke in to try to get the bones out and injured you when you woke up and started to scream."

"Hey!" Abril turned on Diane. "You didn't *have* to hurt me. Why the hell didn't you just take control of me?"

"She did not know she could," Crispin said when Diane just sneered at her. "She assumed you were one of us too."

Abril nodded in understanding and then said, "I'm guessing when that first attempt didn't work out for her, she tried again when she saw you guys out digging up the bones in the tent and that's why my memory is all buggered up during the time you guys were outside and why Lilith is—" Pausing, she turned accusingly on the woman. "What did you do to Lilith?"

"I sprinkled some animal tranquilizer on raw meat and gave it to her when she heard me and came to investigate," Diane said abruptly, and assured her, "I would never hurt a dog. I'm not a monster."

Abril looked briefly relieved and then eyed the woman with a sort of bewildered and horrified expression. Crispin supposed she was wondering over the fact that the woman thought that killing and torturing humans but not dogs meant she wasn't a monster.

He himself had seen too much in his three thousand years to be surprised by anything people, mortal or immortal, said or did.

"Why was I outside when the men came back in?" Abril asked finally. "What happened that ended up with me standing witless on the edge of Gina's property barefoot and without a coat?"

"You kept coming out of the kitchen," Diane complained. "I wiped your memory and sent you back the first two times, but the men came in before I could do it the last time. I had to take control of you and cart you out of the house to the woods at the back of the property to get the couple of minutes I needed to do it again."

Crispin swallowed the rage he was feeling toward the woman, speared his uncle with a look and said, "Someone else will have to take over from here, because—What the hell happened?" he snapped with sudden frustration. "I can see from her mind that Diane saw you all take off in the van leaving Abril and me here alone. She decided there would be no better time for it, and approached the house. She stopped outside the sliding glass doors of Abril's office, which was the only room in the house where there was a light on. When she heard the movie playing . . ." Abril bit her lip at this news, worrying that Diane might have heard more than the movie playing, and wouldn't that be embarrassing if it was true? But before she could get too distressed at the thought, Crispin continued, "So, she decided it would be safe to get in, get the skeletons out of the indoor garden, and get out."

He paused briefly, raising his eyebrows at first Cassius and then Lucian and asked, "Where did you go? And why the hell would you not tell me you were leaving us here alone so that I could be on alert?"

"We only drove around to the end of the crescent, and we did not warn you because it was a last-minute plan type of thing," Cassius said soothingly, and explained, "Lucian had sent me to Gina's office to watch the side yard, but when I got there, I noticed that the lock on her sliding glass door had been tampered with and would no longer engage. I reported that to Lucian. He suspected that was due to the intruder of course, and she probably planned to enter that way. But he also worried that with so many of us here, she might hesitate. He thought that our leaving would embolden her. So, we all piled into the van, making a lot of racket in the driveway as we did in the hopes that she would notice, then we drove around the curve to the end of the crescent, parked on the grassy verge, and came back on foot through the woods behind the houses.

"She was entering Gina's office through the sliding glass door when we reached the tree line at the back of the yard. Lucian wanted to let her get to the indoor garden before we tackled her. It is a wide-open area that we could surround her in, and he thought that would make it harder for her to escape. He sent me and Decker to follow her through Gina's door so she could not flee back that way if she sensed anything was afoot, while he and Roberts, Bricker, and Anders were to enter through various doors around the house, so that we were coming from all directions and she would have no avenue of escape."

"That might have worked," Crispin acknowledged reluctantly.

"Yes, except it did not," Cassius pointed out. "Decker and I had just entered Gina's office when we heard Abril scream and the slam of a door closing. We rushed out into the hall. Diane saw us and turned to run toward the kitchen to escape us, but Bricker was coming that way, and then you opened Abril's door. She lunged toward you, and we jumped her, and . . ." He shrugged. "Here we are."

Silence fell over the room and Abril turned to look at Diane Foley again. The woman had been pretty much expressionless throughout the telling of her life and misdeeds, although anger had flashed out once or twice. There had not been even a hint of guilt or regret shown.

Some part of Abril felt bad for the woman. Diane had suffered a terrible tragedy in the loss of her son, and on top of that had been paralyzed herself. Then she had lost her husband too in a plan he'd instigated and that they'd hoped would give them back at least part of the life they'd enjoyed before that accident. That was worthy of pity.

But the feeling was immediately erased in the face of everything that had followed. The woman had killed twelve mortals in the first week after she'd been turned. No. Actually, she'd killed thirteen that first week if you included the husband. And while she hadn't killed the unknown immortal, she'd been a party to it. Diane certainly would have known from the start that the "vampire" would have to be killed. While it had probably been self-defense in the end, Abril suspected the plan all along had been to murder the woman once they'd used her to change Diane. Surely, they hadn't thought they'd be able to let the vampire live after using her like that? They must have known that the immortal wouldn't have taken that lying down, and that the vampire would have killed them both for it if they didn't kill her first.

No, Abril thought. She had to have realized it would end in the immortal's death. On top of that there were all the deaths that had happened since at the hands of this woman; she couldn't even guess how many the woman had killed over the last twenty years. Not kind, merciful deaths either. Diane *was* a monster. She probably would have killed Abril too during that first break-in if the men hadn't come running. Abril supposed she should be grateful that Diane had only knocked her out during that encounter, and taken control of her afterward when she had interrupted her digging in the garden.

She did find it odd though that Diane had no problem killing people, yet had merely drugged Lilith. She could have easily snapped the Labrador's neck or something.

Letting her breath out on a small puff of air, she glanced to Lucian and asked, "What happens now?"

Lucian opened his mouth, and then paused as the driveway alarm sounded. Standing, he walked over and peered out the window, a satisfied smile flashing briefly across his face before he said, "Our backup has arrived."

Thirty

Abril glanced up from her computer monitor to her office door when a soft knock sounded.

"Come in," she called and waited to see who it would be. So far she'd had visits from Crispin's aunt Eshe, who was married to his uncle Armand Argeneau, his cousin Nick's wife, Jo, and a brief one with his aunt Basha . . . or was Basha a cousin too? Abril couldn't remember. It was hard to keep everything straight when you suddenly had your boyfriend's family unexpectedly thrust at you.

Did I just call Crispin my boyfriend? she thought with alarm. They hadn't agreed to be boyfriend/girlfriend. Maybe she shouldn't presume—

"Oh, hi!" She smiled enthusiastically when Crispin slipped into her office.

"Hi," he greeted her with a grin as he walked around her desk, only to pause and bend to pet Lilith when the

pup got to her feet and demanded at
by nuzzling his knees.

Abril chuckled at the dog's eager antics.
happy to see her up and about and acting like her old
self after that drugging business courtesy of Diane
Foley. The vet Lucian had sent for had driven down,
arriving just minutes after the backup that had flown
in had arrived in the SUVs they'd rented on landing.
Valorie Moyer-Andronnikov was her name, and she
was Anders's wife. She'd been kind and soothing as
she'd examined Lilith, and then had assured Abril that
the pup would be fine. She *had* been drugged and just
needed to sleep it off.

Abril had been grateful to hear it, but had also actually felt bad that the woman had driven all the way
down here in the end, since by that time they'd already
known Diane had drugged the pup from the men reading her mind. Still, it had made her feel better to hear
the drug wouldn't harm the Labrador.

Watching Crispin giving the dog some lovin', she
smiled crookedly and asked, "Is it bad that I feel jealous that she's getting all the affection right now?"

Crispin glanced up with surprise and then amusement curving his lips, he straightened. "I do not think
so. But maybe that is just because I have been jealous
all day that Lilith got to stay in here with you while
I was stuck in the kitchen with Cassius, guarding
Bloody Mary out there."

"Bloody Mary?" Eyebrows rising, she stood and
walked around her desk to greet him properly.

"Bitey Betty?" he suggested.

"Oh, that's awful," Abril assured him as she urged

...close enough to wrap

...ing his arms around her ...ne is not a name that goes ...urder to mind."

...efly and then shook her head. ...come up with is Diane the Death... ...h! Dracula Diane." She frowned slightly and ...d, "For some reason that reminds me of a song I heard once." Shrugging, she lifted her face to his and asked, "Were you planning on kissing me? Or am I out of luck?"

"Sadly, you are out of luck," he said solemnly, "Because while there is nothing else in the world that I would rather do than kiss you right now, that would lead to us doing other amazing and delightful things that leave us in a sweaty, naked heap on your office floor."

"I'd be all right with that," Abril said a little breathlessly, her body already responding to his nearness.

"I would too," he assured her. "However, Lucian would not, since he actually sent me in here to get you. He and the boys are leaving, and he wants to talk to you first."

Abril couldn't hide her surprise. "They're leaving already?"

"Just he, Decker, Bricker, and Anders. They're taking Diane back to Toronto to stand before council."

"That leaves Cassius, your uncle Armand and his wife, Eshe, your cousin Nick and his wife, Jo, and . . ."

"Basha and Marcus," he finished for her when she hesitated, not wanting to get it wrong and call her an aunt if she was a cousin, or vice versa. Of course,

Crispin didn't know that, she acknowledged as he told her, "They will still be around for a couple days. Your neighbor Kim and her family are all set and taken care of, but there were apparently ten people chained up in Diane's basement and more than half are in very bad shape, physically as well as mentally. It is going to take a little time to sort them out." He paused briefly and then added, "Unfortunately, your boss's boyfriend, William, is one of them."

Abril nodded. She felt bad for the victims in Diane's basement and could only imagine what they'd been through, but asked, "How were Kim and her family taken care of exactly?"

"Their minds were wiped and new, more pleasant memories of a couple of days of family time were put in their place," he explained reassuringly. "They have only been under Diane's influence since the excavator supposedly broke down. She did not have the time to torment them like she did the victims in her basement. She was too busy watching the goings on over here and trying to break in, so less effort was needed with them. They are all good now."

Abril nodded and then asked, "And William and the others? How bad off are they?"

Crispin hesitated and then admitted, "They are in much worse shape. Although," he added quickly when her shoulders slumped, "there is some hope that they will all survive. Or at least most of them will."

Her mouth tightened at this news. Diane Foley was responsible for a hell of a lot of misery and death. But there was nothing to be done about that now except pick up the pieces. Swallowing, she asked, "And then what? I assume you erase their memories as well.

Does that mean William won't recall where he was, or why he's been missing for two weeks? How do you explain things to them? And what about their families and friends? Can you put thoughts in their mind? What—?"

"All of them will be given new memories that will cover for where they have been since they went missing from their lives."

"What kind of story can possibly cover William disappearing for two weeks? You aren't going to erase Gina from his memory, are you?" She frowned at the very thought. Gina really cared for William and was suffering from what they'd all thought was his sudden abandonment of her.

"No. Of course not," Crispin said reassuringly. "As for how to explain his absence, they will probably move his car to a parking lot, take him to one of the hospitals in the city, and put the memory in his and the hospital staff's minds that he was hit by a car while walking from his vehicle to the store to buy lottery tickets or something. That he's been unconscious, had no ID, so the hospital staff had no way of contacting family or anyone until he woke up to tell them who he was and who to call." He shrugged. "Something like that."

Abril let her breath out slowly and then murmured, "Milk."

Crispin blinked in confusion. "Milk?"

"That's what he left to get the day he disappeared," she explained. "He was running out to get almond milk for his coffee. He's allergic to dairy and Gina had run out of the almond milk."

"Right. Good to know. I'll tell Lucian that so he can pass it on to whoever does the hospital transfer."

Abril nodded, but briefly wondered how Gina would handle his sudden reappearance. She'd no doubt be happy as hell, but then probably be determined to put the equivalent of a dog tag on him so that something like this couldn't happen again. A gold dog tag, of course, engraved with his name, and her number to call in case of an emergency.

"Come on," Crispin said abruptly, urging her toward the door. "Lucian is not the most patient of men."

"Really?" she asked with dry amusement, but dragged her feet. "What does he want to talk to me about?"

"I presume he just wants to say goodbye and thank you for your hospitality while he and the boys were—"

Abril's lips widened with amusement when he stopped. "You can't even speak the lie, can you?"

"No," he admitted on a sigh. "I have no idea what he wants. I cannot read him. But he will probably be a pain in the ass and rude."

"Something to look forward to then," Abril said sarcastically as she opened the office door.

Lucian was seated at the island when Abril and Crispin entered the kitchen. But Diane was no longer in the seat she'd been in since they'd captured her the night before. Roberts now sat there, and Diane now stood between Bricker and Decker who each had her by an arm. She looked as salty as could be and actually glared at her when she entered, as if the situation she found herself in was somehow Abril's fault.

Frankly, Abril didn't care what the woman thought

or felt. She would just be relieved to see the back of her. She hadn't managed to sleep a wink last night knowing the woman was here in the house, guarded or not. She was just so damned cold and evil. So, Abril ignored Diane and focused on Lucian instead.

"I hear you and the boys are leaving," she commented.

"Yes. We have to take Mrs. Foley before the council for judgment. It is best to deal with it quickly."

"What will happen to her?" she asked with curiosity.

"As I said, she will go before the council," he repeated, and when she scowled at him impatiently, he rolled his eyes and added, "Then she will no doubt be staked and baked."

"Staked and baked?" Abril asked incredulously. She had no idea what that meant, but suspected it was not good.

"She will be executed," Crispin said solemnly, not bothering to explain the actual way it would happen, or what staked and baked meant exactly.

Abril suspected she didn't want to know. It was enough that the woman would be eliminated. She had never been a big advocate of death sentences, but then this was the first time she'd encountered someone who was so evil and had killed so many people over the last twenty years.

Biting her tongue, she stepped out of the way when a gesture from Lucian had Decker and Bricker escorting Diane from the kitchen.

"Now," Lucian said as soon as the trio had left the kitchen. Turning to Abril he raised one eyebrow. "Are you going to agree to be Crispin's life mate? Or do we have to erase your memory and remove you from his presence?"

"Uncle," Crispin growled in warning.

"It is better to know now and get it over with than to waste time on hope," Lucian told him firmly, and then looked at Abril again and asked, "Well? Which will it be?"

Abril turned to Crispin to ask with disbelief, "Agree to be your life mate or they erase my memories and remove me from your presence? Seriously? Whatever happened to dating and stuff?"

Crispin opened his mouth to say something, but before a single word could leave his lips, Lucian said, "I am the one asking questions, little girl. And I expect an answer."

Scowling, she rounded on the man. "You are a bossy prick, sticking his nose in where it doesn't belong and I'm getting really tired of your high-handed bullshit. I mean, who the hell died and made you the lord and master?"

"Most of Atlantis," he snapped back.

"Bricker is going to be seriously upset that he missed this," Roberts murmured, sounding amused.

She thought Cassius might have cracked the briefest smile, but it was quickly gone and he merely grunted in agreement.

"Abril, sweetheart," Crispin said soothingly, "Lucian is—"

"Lucian is tired, bored, and ready to go home to his beautiful life mate and children," Lucian interjected, getting to his feet. "So, I shall save us all some time and tell you, Crispin, that she has already decided to be your life mate. I just wanted you to hear her say it. But since she has decided to be pissy . . ."

"*I've* decided to be pissy?" Abril asked with disbelief.

"Yes," he said simply, and then turned to head out of the kitchen, barking, "Make sure we have everything we brought with us, boys, and let's get moving. If we are quick, we can make it home before dawn." Pausing at the doorway, he swung back to spear Cassius with a look. "I presume you are staying to help Detective Roberts out until Crispin gets the worst of this new life mate business out of his system?"

"Yes," Cassius said at once. "I already discussed it with Alexander and he is fine with that."

"Good," Lucian said abruptly and then glanced from Abril to Crispin and announced, "I expect an invitation to the wedding."

He was out of the room before Abril could grab something to throw at him. The man was just—

"We shall be in Abril's room," Crispin announced, catching her hand and tugging her in the same direction Lucian and the others had just gone. Obviously by room, he meant the guest bedroom she'd been using and not her office, she thought wryly.

"That's fine," Cassius called after them. "We will take care of getting the contractors back here to resume the work on the addition."

"And we'll handle Lilith too until you surface," Roberts added reassuringly. "You two go on. You have a lot to talk about."

Abril highly doubted it was talking Crispin was interested in. She fully expected him to have her naked on the bed before the door had finished closing behind them. So, she was a little surprised when instead, he urged her into the room, pushed her toward the top of the bed, closed the bedroom door and then simply leaned back against it, as far as he could get away from her while still in the same room.

Confused, she tilted her head and eyed him in question. "Is there something wron—?"

"Have you really decided to be my life mate?" he asked solemnly.

Abril hesitated.

"Was Lucian wrong?" he asked sounding amazed at the possibility.

"He wasn't wrong," she said and when he started forward, said quickly, "But he wasn't right either."

Crispin stopped abruptly, just steps away. His eyes narrowed. "I do not understand."

Abril heaved out a sigh and then said with some exasperation, "Well, neither do I. I mean what is a life mate? I want to agree to be yours, but how can I when I don't know what that entails?"

Crispin was frowning now. "Abril, I explained that a life mate is someone we cannot read or control, who cannot read or control us. Someone we can—"

"Live in peace with yada yada yada," Abril said impatiently. "So basically, a human tranquilizer."

Crispin arched one eyebrow, his lips twitching. "If you feel like a human tranquilizer for me, then I have been doing something wrong in the bedroom . . . and the pool room . . . and your office . . . and—"

"Crispin," she interrupted with exasperation, "What does being a life mate *mean*? What would be expected of me? Is it like a wife? Would we marry? Or would I be a walking blood bag for you to feed off of when you felt hungry? What?"

He relaxed suddenly, a gentle smile pulling at his

lips and then closed the distance between them. Taking her hands gently in his, he said, "A life mate is very much like a wife, but it is an unbreakable bond."

She frowned slightly. "Unbreakable? Like no divorce?"

"Unbreakable like the bond will never break and the passion will never die," he explained. "I, of course, would be very pleased to marry you with a proper wedding, but whether we marry or not, we will always be life mates, no matter where we are." He fell silent for a minute to let that sink in and then said, "And you will never be a walking blood bag to me. Immortals sometimes will bite their mortal lovers if both parties agree, but once both parties are immortal that just cannot happen. It is too dangerous. The nanos will not mix and blend. The original nanos see the new nanos as an invading force they must remove and a battle will take place in the body that can kill the host."

"Really?" she asked with surprise.

"Yes," he assured her.

Abril was silent for a minute, and then cleared her throat and said, "You said *once both parties are immortal.* Does that mean . . . ?"

When she couldn't give voice to what she really wanted to know, he said solemnly, "It is customary for an immortal to use their one turn for their life mate so that they may live out their long lives together. I would wish to turn you."

Abril winced at the very idea and admitted, "I really don't like needles and I'm not a big fan of pain either. In fact, I'm kind of a wuss about stuff like that. I don't know if I could—" She shook her head, and then said, "And it's such a big commitment to make when we've only known each other for a matter of days. What if—"

Crispin silenced her with a kiss. Abril thought it was terribly unfair of him to do that, for all of ten seconds and then she was kissing him back, all her worries and fears pushed out of her head by the passion he stirred to life in her.

Breaking their kiss a moment later, Crispin pulled back and began to undo the blouse she'd donned when she'd given up trying to sleep this morning as he said, "I will not rush you. We can take our time. I wish to woo you anyway, and we will do nothing until you are comfortable."

Giving up on her buttons, he reached down to slip his hand under the skirt she'd put on that morning, purely because it was so convenient for moments like this. Though, she wouldn't have admitted it to anyone.

When his hand began to glide up her thigh, pushing her skirt before it, Abril gasped and shifted, widening her legs as his fingers found her panties and tugged the cloth aside. She groaned when he then began to caress her where she really needed his touch.

"Crispin, I can't think when you—I need to ask—"

He eased his caresses at once so that both of their minds cleared a little and leaned his forehead on hers as he whispered, "What do you need to ask, love?"

Panting a little still, she opened suddenly anxious eyes and asked, "Lucian won't wipe you from my memory if I don't agree right away?"

He smiled faintly at the worry in her expression. "No. The truth is he has read your mind. He thinks you are willing, so part of you must be. He will give us the time it takes until you are completely ready."

"Oh," she breathed and smiled crookedly. "That's good, because I really, really lust for you, and I like you a lot so far, and would hate to lose you."

"You will never lose me, Abril," he assured her solemnly, and began to caress her again as he eased her back onto the bed. "I have waited three thousand years for you. Now that I have found you, you are stuck with me."

"I can handle that," she groaned, arching into his caress. "Now shut up and love me."

"Always," he breathed and kissed her hungrily as he gave up caressing her to quickly unzip his pants. A moment later, his erection had pushed its way out of his boxers and slacks, he'd tugged her panties aside again, and was sliding into her. It felt like finally finding home.

Explore more from the Argeneau Series

A Quick Bite

Love Bites

Single White Vampire

Tall, Dark & Hungry

A Bite to Remember

Bite Me If You Can

The Accidental Vampire

Vampires Are Forever

Vampire, Interrupted

The Rogue Hunter

The Immortal Hunter

The Renegade Hunter

Born to Bite

Hungry For You

The Reluctant Vampire

Under a Vampire Moon

The Lady Is a Vamp

Immortal Ever After

One Lucky Vampire

Vampire Most Wanted

The Immortal Who Loved Me

About a Vampire

Runaway Vampire

Immortal Nights

Immortal Unchained

Immortally Yours

Twice Bitten

Vampires Like It Hot

The Trouble with Vampires

Immortal Born

Immortal Angel

Meant to Be Immortal

Mile High with a Vampire

Immortal Rising

After the Bite

Bad Luck Vampire

Discover Lynsay Sands's
Highland Brides Series